Praise for the novels of Allyson James

"Sweet, funny, and deliciously erotic."
—*Romance Reviews Today*

"Enchanting . . . Unique . . . Hot and steamy . . . [Ms. James] is a talented author who has written just the kind of story I love to read." —*Coffee Time Romance*

"Masterful . . . The characters and their story captured both my imagination and my heart." —*Fallen Angel Reviews*

"Extremely satisfying . . . Ms. James has created a masterpiece." —*Just Erotic Romance Reviews*

"Very carnal . . . Intense." —*The Romance Studio*

"Funny and lighthearted . . . thoughtful, serious, sexy . . . it has everything! One of my all-time favorites."
—*Cupid's Library Reviews*

THE
BLACK
DRAGON

Allyson James

BERKLEY SENSATION, NEW YORK

THE BERKLEY PUBLISHING GROUP
Published by the Penguin Group
Penguin Group (USA) Inc.
375 Hudson Street, New York, New York 10014, USA
Penguin Group (Canada), 90 Eglinton Avenue East, Suite 700, Toronto, Ontario M4P 2Y3, Canada
(a division of Pearson Penguin Canada Inc.)
Penguin Books Ltd., 80 Strand, London WC2R 0RL, England
Penguin Group Ireland, 25 St. Stephen's Green, Dublin 2, Ireland (a division of Penguin Books Ltd.)
Penguin Group (Australia), 250 Camberwell Road, Camberwell, Victoria 3124, Australia
(a division of Pearson Australia Group Pty. Ltd.)
Penguin Books India Pvt. Ltd., 11 Community Centre, Panchsheel Park, New Delhi—110 017, India
Penguin Group (NZ), 67 Apollo Drive, Rosedale, North Shore 0632, New Zealand
(a division of Pearson New Zealand Ltd.)
Penguin Books (South Africa) (Pty.) Ltd., 24 Sturdee Avenue, Rosebank, Johannesburg 2196,
South Africa

Penguin Books Ltd., Registered Offices: 80 Strand, London WC2R 0RL, England

This is a work of fiction. Names, characters, places, and incidents either are the product of the author's imagination or are used fictitiously, and any resemblance to actual persons, living or dead, business establishments, events, or locales is entirely coincidental. The publisher does not have any control over and does not assume any responsibility for author or third-party websites or their content.

THE BLACK DRAGON

A Berkley Sensation Book / published by arrangement with the author

PRINTING HISTORY
Berkley Sensation mass-market edition / November 2007

Copyright © 2007 by Jennifer Ashley.
Cover art by Aleta Rafton.
Cover design by George Long.
Hand lettering by Ron Zinn.
Interior text design by Laura K. Corless.

ISBN: 978-0-425-21844-0

BERKLEY® SENSATION
Berkley Sensation Books are published by The Berkley Publishing Group,
a division of Penguin Group (USA) Inc.,
375 Hudson Street, New York, New York 10014.
BERKLEY SENSATION and the "B" design are trademarks belonging to Penguin Group (USA) Inc.

PRINTED IN THE UNITED STATES OF AMERICA

10 9 8 7 6 5 4 3 2 1

ACKNOWLEDGMENTS

Thanks go to Kate Seaver, my terrific editor; to Allison Brandau, editorial assistant; and to all those at Berkley who make books possible. Special thanks to Kendra Egert for her excellent graphics and videos that bring the dragon books to life (www.myspace.com/allysonjamesauthor). Thanks also to all the readers who love dragons!

1

When Saba Watanabe was four years old, she woke screaming from a nightmare. In it black smoke pursued her, thick inky tendrils that threatened to devour her at every step. She ran and ran, her small legs pumping, her straight bangs flopping into her eyes and blinding her.

She was in a cavern, a huge place cut of solid rock that glittered and glowed with gems and veins of pure gold. A beautiful place but for the nightmare that pursued her.

She dashed down a corridor pocked with round niches that seemed to contain interesting things like fat old books and scrolls of paper. She didn't have time to stop and examine this wonder, because the black curls of smoke would catch her at any moment. She knew it would wrap tendrils around her ankles and pull her down, and then the smoke would flow over her and smother her.

Panting, she raced around another corner, somehow knowing that a way out was near but unable to find it. She ran and ran, and suddenly the corridor ended in a blank wall. Sobbing, she beat on the wall with her small fists, crying in gasps.

She turned and faced the evil pursuing her, trying to
summon the strange feelings deep inside her that she could
sometimes use to prevent bad things from happening to
her. She brought her shaking hands up, palms out, and said
to the darkness, "Stop."

The inky black tendrils reared up, as though surprised,
then she heard laughter. Gathering itself into something that
looked like a mouth, it launched itself at Saba's small form.

Saba screamed, then she gasped and sat straight up in
bed. She shook all over and her hands sweated, but it had
been a dream. *Only a dream*, her father would say. *It can't
hurt you, Saba-chan. It's not real.*

Usually she would take comfort in papa-san's words,
pull the covers over her head and go back to sleep, but tonight the darkness of her bedroom seemed to stalk her. The
comforting yellow glow of her night-light had gone out,
and the darkness was absolute. Her heart raced as she saw
the blackness from her dreams gathering on the floor, thick
like oily smoke.

"It's not real," she whispered. "It's only a dream."

But the dream raised its head, chuckling, blackness
ready to consume her. She started to scream, but the sound
cut off as the darkness rose to form a canopy over her bed.

Slowly, slowly it began to settle toward her. When it
reached her bed, she would die; she knew this better than
she'd known anything in her short life. She watched it
come, unable to speak, unable to breathe, hands clenching
the bed covers until they ached.

She seemed to hear the voice of her Japanese grandfather whisper in her mind. Old *Ojii-san* had a small, wrin-
kled face and a gold tooth that showed in his frequent
smiles. He'd taught Saba Japanese words and told her fairy
stories, some funny, others frightening, but they always
contained a beautiful maiden and a happy ending.

Ojii-san had told her one particular story about nightmares, and the memory of it flooded her now. Unclenching
the blanket, she clapped her stiff hands three times and
shouted, "Baku, Baku! Come and eat this dream!"

She had no idea if the Baku, a Japanese god, would come all the way from Japan to California to save her, but she clapped and shouted again, liking the strength of her words against the darkness.

There was a hiss and a blinding flash, and then a creature more bizarre than any she'd ever seen appeared beside the bed. It had a lion's head, a row of hideously pointed teeth, a horse's body, a tiger's legs, batlike wings, and a long, hairy tail. He was horrible, but Saba felt no fear, even though he was more than six feet high and nearly over-whelmed her small bedroom.

The Baku snarled and lunged at the darkness. He snuf-fled and snorted as he gobbled up the darkness, pursuing the inky blackness around the room as it tried to disperse and flee. Saba watched, round-eyed, as the Baku chased the darkness in its almost comical attempt to escape.

The Baku cornered the remainder of the black smoke against the closet door, opened its mouth, and sucked the blackness in past its gleaming teeth. Saba heard a keening wail, and suddenly the darkness was gone. The night-light came back on, and the room felt right again.

The Baku raised itself up on its strange tiger's legs, pat-ted its stomach, and gave a loud belch. Saba laughed.

The Baku padded to the bed, lowered its head and snuf-fled Saba's cheek, tickling her. She laughed again and pat-ted its nose, and the Baku gave her a loud, smacking kiss.

It moved away a few steps, waved its paw, then went into a tumbling back flip and disappeared with another flash of light. Saba clapped in delight.

Not a moment later, her bedroom door flew open and the worried faces of her mother and father peered in. Saba's mother was American, very beautiful with brown hair and lovely eyes. Her father was Japanese and had been born in Japan. He was the same height as her mother and had wise brown eyes like *Ojii-san*.

"What is it, sweetheart?" her mother asked. She sat on the edge of the bed and gathered Saba to her. "Were you dreaming?"

Saba pushed away, too excited for the embrace. "Mama-chan, I saw the Baku! I called for him and he came, just like *Ojii-san* said he would."

Her mother's smile turned indulgent. "That's nice, sweetheart. Do you feel better now?"

"He ate the nightmare and kissed me good night."

"I'm pleased, darling." Her mother stroked fingers through Saba's fine black hair.

Her father peered over her mother's shoulder, eyes warm with excitement. "You saw the Baku?"

"Yes, papa-chan. He came and ate the nightmare."

Her father beamed with pride, his smile wide. "It is not everyone who can see the Baku, Saba-chan." He patted her head. "You will grow up to be a very wise woman, a very wise woman, indeed."

Twenty-four years later

As the Bay Area Rapid Transit train descended into the tunnel beneath the bay, the few inhabitants of the car drifted into the next compartment, leaving Saba alone. That was fine with her, she thought, blowing her bangs from her forehead, trying to find coolness in the stuffy car. Her eyes were sandy after the all-day seminar she'd attended in Oakland, the drab dinner she'd been taken to at a generic hotel, then the late ride back to San Francisco on a train with the heat cranked too high.

All this after a night of magic performed under the full moon in the park across from her apartment house on Octavia Street. She'd drawn down the moon and consecrated some new stones and enhanced the protection around her apartment house, because she'd become uneasy of late. Too much darkness in the shadows, too many feelings of being watched when no one was there.

Working strong magics always tired her and getting up early on top of it made her more than ready for her soft bed and a good night's sleep. Cool linen against her skin, warm

blankets to keep out the chill, pillows scented with laven-
der. Malcolm's energy lingered in that bed, no matter how
many times she changed the sheets, his dragon magic imprinted there, notwithstanding he was permanently out of
her life.

The energy he'd left behind manifested in her dreams
sometimes, and she'd see Malcolm, a tall man of honed,
naked muscle, intense eyes darkening as he pinned her
with strong hands and laid his body over hers.

Mmm. Her tired mind turned to sexual fantasy as the
train swayed in darkness under the waters of the bay. Malcolm had known how to touch her with skill, how to bring
her to climax with his fingertips until she was screaming
with it. Even now the memory triggered heat between her
thighs.

She willed herself to stop thinking about him. Malcolm
was gone, returned to Dragonspace without regret eight
months ago, and Saba needed to get on in her life without
him.

Easier said than done. The dragon turned man haunted
her dreams and her daydreams and wouldn't let her be. She
even still carried, in a silk pouch in her pocket, the
diamond-hard crystals he'd given her—*dragon's tears,*
he'd called them. They would summon him to her if she
was in dire need, or so he'd said. She'd never been bold
enough to use them and find out.

"Blessed Be," said a deep male voice.

Saba jumped and opened her eyes. She hadn't heard
anyone come into the car, and few strangers used the greeting of the Goddess. Saba wore a long raincoat against the
January rain, which covered the Wicca tattoo on her arm,
and she'd left off her pentacle jewelry today for the seminar.

She only signaled she was a witch to people she
trusted, and she'd never seen this man before. He sat opposite her, clad in the mundane garb of jeans and raincoat
and gloves. His white fall of hair, gathered at the base of
his neck, was a pale smudge in the dim light of the car, but

he was not an old man. His eyes shone pure emerald green, and his sensual mouth was red, his body strong and taut with muscle.

Saba sensed power inside him, a volatile, immense strength just contained by the outline of his body. She didn't need to give more than one glance to his square face and intense green eyes to know what he was.

"Dragon," she breathed.

"Witch," he countered, showing white teeth in a smile. "I have need of you, Saba Watanabe."

"What for?"

And what was he doing here? Dragons could not cross over from Dragonspace and become human unless a witch gave them strong magics to do so. Saba had reason to know that the spell to create a door to Dragonspace was difficult and draining; she'd attempted it herself once upon a time for Malcolm—and the magic had nearly undone her. The spell had failed, too.

The dragon looked annoyed at her lack of awe. One thing she'd learned about dragons was that they possessed astounding arrogance, even the good ones like Caleb.

"I have need of you," he repeated, voice hard. "I heard that a witch called Saba Watanabe knows of dragons. That she was once a minion of a dragon."

"And who told you all this?"

"A friend. One we both know."

Saba fingered a black stone in her pocket and let the back of her mind form a spell of warding while she tried to assess the dragon. True she had been under Malcolm's thrall, true he'd put his dragon mark upon her. She'd been under Malcolm's complete power, had helped him and healed him and stuck by him, understanding why he did what he did when others did not.

Malcolm had released her when he'd returned to Dragon-space, and that release had turned her heart inside out. She could not forget her pain when he'd turned away, eyes glittering with joy that his eight-hundred-year exile was over at last. He'd dived through the doorway to Dragonspace, putting everything human, including Saba, behind him, making it clear he never meant to return.

That had been eight long months ago. It could be that he had sent this dragon, a friend, to Saba because the dragon needed help.

Wait. *Malcolm, friend, help.* No, those words did not go together. Malcolm was a black dragon, creatures notorious for their coldness, vast intelligence, love of solitude, and disdain for all other life forms, including other dragons. The probability that Malcolm had a friend and had sent him to Saba was slim.

"What kind of dragon are you?" she asked cautiously.

"A powerful one," he said. "And I need your help, Saba."

"What for?" she repeated.

Another flicker of arrogance moved through his eyes. "Were you this rebellious as a minion?"

"I was. And I'm not fond of the term *minion.*"

"Then I will have to do this differently."

He did not move, but Saba felt a slight push on her mind, white and silver threads trying to twine her thoughts, ready to entangle and ensnare her. He was sending a dragon mark meant to bind and enslave her to his will, just as Malcolm had done.

Saba clutched her stone and said three words of power. A sparkling shield rose between her mind and the dragon's, and the white thought threads clicked against it like wires on glass.

"You have power, witch," the dragon growled.

"Self-defense." Saba grabbed her umbrella and stood up, ready to find a more crowded car. "The first spell I learned after Malcolm left was to resist a dragon mark."

The white-haired dragon surged to his feet, and her heart beat faster. Dragons were powerful creatures, merely testy on their best days, out-and-out dangerous on others. The best course of action was to assume the worst and leave them well alone.

"You should not resist me," he said.

"I beg to differ," Saba answered and lunged for the door.

The dragon caught her before she'd gone two steps. Powerful hands seized her and dragged her to the far end of the car. This was the last car, with none behind it, no one to see him grip her throat and slam her hard against the glass. Blinding pain rocketed through her head and white danced on the edges of her vision.

"You should be pleased and proud to be my slave." He pinned her to the glass with his large body, his breath like stale apples on her cheek. "I need a witch to do magic for me, and you will obey and do it."

She gritted her teeth against pain. "I won't. I don't even care what you want me for."

His eyes were hot and green, sharp like emeralds. "It would be much easier if you let me put my mark on you." His body pressed hers, the ridge of his hardness flat against her abdomen. "Believe me, it will be much, much easier on you."

Trying to ignore fear and pain, Saba began to form words of magic, calming her mind to build up energy inside her. In fury the dragon thrust his fingers into her mouth, twisting her tongue.

"You only do spells for me, witch. If you don't, I'll hurt you in ways you can't even imagine. You will learn what I'll do to you if you disobey."

Saba glared at him, wrenching away from his hand. "Bite me."

He snarled in rage and threw her across the car. Saba hit a pole with bone-rattling pain before she slammed to the floor. Her umbrella flew out of her hands to slide out of reach under a seat.

Before she could climb to her feet, the dragon was on her, his hands again locked around her throat. He knocked her head to the floor, slamming it until she tasted blood. Fear rocked through her. He could kill her, he was strong enough, and no one could reach her in time. The train was eerily quiet.

He pressed her legs open with one knee and wrenched her skirt upward, exposing her thigh-high stockings. "I always wondered what the black dragon saw in you. Now that I am human, I think I understand."

Saba screamed. She kicked, but the dragon pinned her legs and slapped her across the face. She fought with all the strength she had, twisting and writhing so he had to spend all his time keeping ahold of her.

She had to get away. Run to the next car, scream for help, find *someone*. The train seemed impossibly empty, and she couldn't understand why, unless the dragon had used his manipulative magic to keep others away. And, chilling thought, if he'd marked other people in the train, they'd help him, not her.

Saba forced the clamor in her mind to still. Witch magic was best when the witch had time to ground and center herself, to cast a circle, to light candles and raise energy in quiet solitude. She knew protection spells she could call when she was frightened, but right now her spinning mind couldn't form the words or the images she needed.

All she had were the perfect crystalline spheres in the little silk pouch in her pocket. She was never certain why she'd not buried them in a drawer after Malcolm had gone, why she kept them on her nightstand and tucked them into her pocket each day. She kept telling herself that once she put away the dragon's tears she could make a clean break, but something would not let her lose track of them.

She had no idea how to make them work or if they'd work at all. She used all her strength to roll away from the dragon, grunting as he backhanded her across the mouth. She thrust her hand into her pocket and fumbled for the pouch.

The dragon grabbed her wrist, crushing it to the bone. "No you don't. What have you got in there? Mace?"

He wrenched her hand from her pocket. She balled her fist around the pouch, nails tearing at the Chinese silk, a gift from her friend Lisa. As the dragon tried to rip the pouch from her grasp, Saba's thumb caught in the rip, and she felt the crystalline coolness of the stones roll to her palm.

"Malcolm!" she screamed.

The white-haired dragon reared back, his eyes burning points of green. "Bitch." He slapped her.

There was a sharp tearing sound and the crystals leapt from Saba's hand. The train car filled with harsh, pounding magic that seared through every molecule until Saba thought her head would burst. A spear of light shot from the dragon's tears, blasting through the car and lighting up the tunnel rushing past, earth and snaking pipes and cement.

The white dragon shouted in rage. Saba clapped her hands over her ears, trying to shut out the high-pitched whine of the magic, but it grew until she felt herself being crushed to a fine point. She dragged in her breath, scrambled away from the white dragon, and hauled herself onto a seat.

A man stepped through the brilliant shaft of light. He was taller than the average male, somewhere between six and a half and seven feet, his naked body a honed perfection of muscle. Long black hair swirled around his shoulders as though he'd been walking in a windstorm.

His arms were thick and corded with muscle, a tattoo of a dragon on his strong bicep. Black hair dusted his chest and brushed downward toward his pelvis, picking up again in a fine line below his navel. His large, thick stem pointed straight downward, suggesting how immense he would be when erect. The man's face was square and hard, his expression cold as frost on a January day, and his eyes spoke of power.

Those eyes took in Saba in a quick glance, and she self-consciously put her hand to the trickle of blood on the side of her mouth where her lip had split.

Anger rolled from the man like a devastating wave. He turned that anger on the white-haired dragon who'd gotten to his feet, glaring at the newcomer in apprehension and fury.

Malcolm attacked him. The white dragon drew a dagger, its shaft glittering in the magic light, but Malcolm knocked it aside and slammed the white dragon's body over a seat.

Saba scrambled to her feet and snatched up the fallen knife. Every spell she tried to think of slipped from her mind as fast as it formed, and she clutched the knife, ready to plunge it into the white dragon if she got the chance.

They fought hard, Malcolm's muscles bunching and flowing as he hauled the other dragon toward the opening the dragon's tears had formed. The white dragon resisted with all his strength, but Malcolm pulled him inexorably toward the slit, face set and grim.

They struggled on the brink, the white dragon growling, Malcolm fighting silently and fiercely. When the white dragon slipped, Malcolm hauled him up and hurled him through the opening.

The dragon disappeared in a flash of white. A strong wind blew through the portal, clear and clean, sending Saba's hair dancing.

Malcolm slowly lowered his arms. Saba remained frozen in place, unable to move or speak.

He walked slowly toward her, every step deliberate. His eyes flickered as his gaze roved her, taking her in from the top of her wind-tossed hair to the tips of her black ankle boots. She remained motionless, unable to even draw breath to say his name.

Malcolm's muscles rippled as he lifted his hand, the tattoo moving on his biceps. He touched the bruised side of her mouth, and under his fingers, the pain lessened, the wound tingling as the skin tugged itself together.

His touch moved to her lower lip, his fingertip running the length of the cut, closing it tight. A tiny drop of blood lingered on his fingertip, and he licked it away before he feathered a kiss across her lips.

Saba was too dazed to do anything but accept the kiss. She stared up at him as he straightened and traced her cheek once more.

"Malcolm," she whispered.

He continued to stroke her cheek, his head moving a little to one side as though studying her. He said nothing, not to ask who the white dragon was or why he'd attacked her, why she was on the train, not even, *So how have you been in the last eight months?*

His silence so mesmerized her that she couldn't blurt out any questions. She could only stand and feel him and wish she didn't love the contact of his fingers on her skin.

The door behind her rattled, and Malcolm flicked his gaze to it. The normal sounds of the train came rushing back, the clicking of wheels, the hiss of the speaker as the conductor prepared to announce the next station, a person innocently moving into the car in search of an empty seat. The white dragon's strange hold over the train had gone.

Malcolm gave Saba a final caress then turned swiftly, stretched out his arms, and dove through the slit. Just before the opening snicked shut, she saw a black speck of dragon in the distance spread his wings and take flight.

The slit vanished, the light died, and the train heaved itself upward to Embarcadero Station. A passenger walked calmly into the car and plopped down on the far seat, not noticing a thing. Saba retrieved her umbrella, smoothed her hair with shaking fingers and sat down.

Just before the train slid to a halt, she reached down and picked up the dragon's tears from the floor. Their crystalline structure had shattered, and they lay in scorched black shards in her hand.

2

Black dragons had the power of healing, Saba remembered as she examined her face in the bathroom at home. The side of her mouth bore only faint bruising where the white dragon had hit her, and her lip had closed completely.

The remainder of the journey home had been mundane and uneventful, thank the Goddess. She'd left the train at Civic Center and boarded a bus for the rest of the journey. Hopped off near Lafayette Park and walked to the big square mansard-roofed house on Octavia that housed four apartments. Saba herself owned the house and rented out the other three apartments, courtesy of Malcolm the black dragon. The day after Malcolm had departed last summer she'd gotten a phone call from the broker explaining that she needed to come in and sign some forms because Malcolm had deeded the house to her.

Malcolm had told Saba he would give her the house when he left, so the phone call hadn't been a complete surprise. But seeing the forms in black and white had been something of a shock. She hadn't turned down the offer because she'd been renting in a run-down building in

SoMa that hadn't been the safest place to live alone. In addition Malcolm had obtained employment for her at Technobabble, a prominent database software company whose owner happened to be one of Malcolm's minions. She hadn't had the guts to turn that down either. In the last eight months, she'd worked her way up to senior programmer—*that* she'd done on her own.

The veneer of protection Malcolm had left over the house, which Saba had reinforced with witch wards, remained undisturbed tonight. If the white dragon or any other intruder had come while she'd been away, she'd have instantly known. But everything was in place in the hundred-year-old house, same as always.

A traumatic situation that could have ended far worse than it had deserved a long soak in a hot bath and a good cry. She succeeded with the bath, a quick scrub under the shower followed by lowering herself into the Japanese-style soaking tub Malcolm had installed. But the tears wouldn't come. Every time she thought the flood would burst from her, her eyes remained stubbornly dry.

Shock, she thought. The event had been too bizarre, too unexpected, *too* traumatic. The waterworks would likely happen two or three days from now when she least expected it and could least deal with it.

But she was a witch, and she'd learned ways to combat evil and fear. After the bath she gathered silver candles, salt, amethysts, incense, a bowl of water, and her wand from the special sandalwood cabinet she had purchased to house them and carried everything into one of the apartment's two spare bedrooms.

This room contained her altar to the Goddess and God, the walls hung with art that reminded her of the mystical along with her personal culture. Several Japanese silk panels, each depicting a single iris and a line of calligraphy, hung next to paintings of the goddess Diana and the horned God. Saba liked the aesthetic art from her Japanese heritage, simple, plain paintings that spoke volumes. She'd hung Japanese paintings in the living room as well, one of them depicting a black dragon.

The altar table stood on the north wall, always adorned with seasonal flowers. Saba rolled up the bamboo floor matting she used instead of a rug, revealing the sketched outline of her circle which encompassed most of the room. She set the altar in the center of the circle, then placed the incense, water, one candle, and the salt in the four corners: north, south, east, and west. She walked three times around the circle, her wand pointed downward in her shaking hand, watching the silver nimbus rise from the line to close over her head like a large bubble.

Safety. After saying her calls to the elements, she stood at the altar and invoked the Goddess and God to enter the circle with her. Her tears almost released when she felt the calming presence of the deities but stopped before she could do more than sniffle.

She knelt in the middle of the circle and placed the broken dragon's tears on the altar. They'd cut into her hand when she called Malcolm's name, though now her palm bore only a faint scratch. She remembered the great pounding magic when the portal between the human world and Dragonspace opened and wondered if her blood touching the stones had made the summons stronger. A detached part of her mind told her she ought to research that.

Tonight Malcolm's human features had been the same as when she'd first seen him, when she'd awakened, tied spread-eagled across her bed in the SoMa apartment, to find him sitting across the room leafing through her personal Book of Shadows. Had she, the summoning witch, stuffed him into the form with which she was most familiar? Or was this the projection of his true self, and would he look that way no matter who summoned him?

Wouldn't it be nice if her emotions let her treat this as a scientific experiment? Then she could view tonight's events with dispassion instead of this nerve-wracking turmoil.

But her mind flooded with fantasies about a gorgeous, black-haired male dragon in human form she'd likely never see again. The magic of the dragon's tears had allowed her to call him when things were dire, but the crystals were useless now.

Sighing, she ended her meditation, took down the circle, put her things away, and went to bed.

She dreamed of Malcolm. She remembered the first time he'd invaded her life, back in her tiny studio apartment. He'd appeared out of nowhere, a powerful dragon-man, weaving his mark around her to make her do his bidding. She'd helped him against her better judgment, but she'd been compelled to by the black and silver thought strands that wound through her mind and his strange powerful eyes.

Malcolm had pleasured her in return, deep, bone-jarring pleasure that she'd never felt before or since. What he'd done with fingers and lips and tongue had brought her to incredible orgasm again and again, but he'd never had full sex with her and never let her pleasure him in return. She'd wanted to lie with him, to touch his body and share the joy, but he'd always held himself away from her.

The night she'd tried to explain that his holding back hurt her, he hadn't understood. How could he? He was alien, a dragon from another world who was human only in shape.

But oh, what shape. She saw him in her dreams, tall and firm of body, his shoulders broad and replete with muscle, his waist narrowing to taut hips, and the erection between his legs long and tight, lifting from wiry curls at its base. His biceps tightened as he leaned over her, his breath smelling of spice and male, his musk filling her.

His voice rumbled low in his throat as he said her name, and the silver black bands of his thoughts slid down to twine hers. A beautiful man who'd enslaved her and made her his own. She'd eventually helped him because she believed in him, but at first she'd been bound, *his*.

When he'd severed the bond and returned to Dragonspace, it had taken her weeks to get over it. No, that was not true. She'd *never* gotten over it. Here she was eight months later, still dreaming of the way he'd touched her, his fingers warm, his caress as erotic as ever.

"Malcolm," she whispered.

"My witch." His voice was a dark, velvet rumble.

He climbed over her on the bed in her dream, his knees on either side of her hips. He lifted her hands and slid his fingers over her wrists, softly pinning her to the bed. She felt his lips touch hers, and she kissed him back, loving the dark way he made her feel.

She dreamed he wound silk cords around her wrists. He attached the other ends of the cords to the headboard, stretching out her arms, then he eased the sheet from her body and bound her ankles in the same way.

There she lay spread before him in nothing but her skin, her body warming in delight as his gaze roved her. "As beautiful as ever, my witch."

She tried to answer. She wanted to shamelessly beg him to touch her, but her lips were heavy and she couldn't say a word.

He bent over her, not to kiss her, but to study her more closely, as a dragon would new booty he had found for his hoard. "You always sleep so soundly," he murmured.

"Only when I dream of you," she tried to say, but again, her mouth would not move.

A skilled witch could control her dreams and dream what she wished. Saba had begun to master the art, but whenever Malcolm appeared in the dream world, her control shattered. She would dream of him tying her up and gazing at her, but she could never make him pleasure her, could never make him have sex with her and ease the deep ache he'd caused long ago.

Even now wakefulness came at her, not allowing her to enjoy vicarious fulfillment. She struggled, wanting to escape the frustration of the visions, yet at the same time wanting to prolong them. Malcolm laughed softly and withdrew, fading into the darkness of the night.

With a gasp, Saba came awake.

The light across the room was on, though she remembered snapping it off before climbing into bed. She was lying spread-eagled, her hands and feet bound to the bedposts with her own silk cords she used for witchcraft. She lifted her head.

Malcolm sat, dressed, in front of her computer, his long legs stretched out in black leather pants and squared-toed boots. His eyes flickered as he read the screen in front of him, but when he heard her stir, he glanced up, black hair sliding against leather-clad shoulders, eyes piercing the gloom.

"You sleep soundly, my witch," he said.

Saba stared at him in shock for a full minute, then dropped her head back to her pillows.

"Goddess," she groaned. "Not again."

Malcolm fingered the leather jacket he'd found still hanging in the wardrobe, the leather cool. "You kept my clothes," he observed.

When he'd entered the dark apartment, he'd easily found his way to the bedroom, his mathematical brain remembering precisely where everything in the house lay. Saba hadn't moved the furniture much, and his dragon sight let him avoid the pieces she'd dragged into different positions.

She'd been fast asleep on the wide bed that used to be his, bare limbs tangled in sheets. She'd left the mica-shaded lamp on beside the bed, which touched her limbs and curve of cheek with soft, dark light. She liked to sleep naked, and he'd spent a long time looking down at her before he'd touched her. So easy it had been to ease her body open for him, so easy to press light kisses to her lips. She dreamed, and never woke.

He gazed now at her slim, tight body, the rounds of her breasts tipped with dark nipples, the twist of black hair between her thighs. He hadn't been able to resist fastening her to the headboard and footboard as he had the summer night he'd first met her. The bonds were loose, not meant to be cruel, meant to be a joke between them, but her glare told him she saw nothing funny.

Back then Saba had struggled to break the cords and had to wait for Malcolm to free her. Now Saba severed her bonds with a fierce bite of magic that smelled of burning wire. She sat up and dragged the sheet over her, which made her even more delectable. Her tousled hair fell over her oval face, her dark eyes regarding him in unconcealed fury.

"I forgot all about your clothes," she said, the shift of her eyes betraying her. "I pushed them to the back of the closet to make room for mine."

The fact that she hadn't forgotten at all and lied about it made his heart beat faster. She hadn't wanted to erase him completely from her life but didn't want to admit it.

"I didn't need them," he said. "Caleb lent me clothes."

"Caleb?" she asked, confused. "How did you get here? I summoned you with the dragon's tears, but then they were spent. It takes a witch to let a dragon into the human world."

"Lisa let me through." Lisa was not a witch but a silver dragon, a being of immense-power, and if she wanted to create a doorway to let dragons out of Dragonspace, there was nothing to stop her.

"Oh," Saba said. "I see I'll need to have a talk with Lisa."

Malcolm looked back at the computer to hide his amusement, but he could not keep his gaze from her for long. He wanted to feast his eyes on her. Beautiful, strong, fiery, fierce Saba. Being a black dragon, he could have compartmentalized the memory of her and tucked it away while he concerned himself with higher problems of physics and theoretical mathematics, but for some reason, he'd never been able to banish the picture of her entirely.

Not even the pleasure of calculating probabilities to the *nth* decimal point could make him forget almond-shaped eyes that grew dusky with desire, wisps of black-brown hair like silk under his fingertips. He couldn't forget her impatient glare, the growl of irritation when she said, "*Mal*colm!" Her laugh of triumph when she completed a spell that healed him from a sword wound. He'd taken her in his arms and kissed her on the littered floor of her apartment after that, nearly ripping her clothing from her body in his frenzy.

"What exactly do you want?" Saba demanded. "You were adamant about leaving this world behind and getting back to Dragonspace, now you've gone to Lisa and asked to be let in again. Why?"

"Several reasons." He leaned back in the chair, trying to let his logical mind take over, but the nearness of her, the memories of her scent and taste distracted him. "First, I wished to learn who the white dragon was and why he attacked you."

"You don't know?" she asked, eyes wide.

"I do not know every dragon in Dragonspace. I was hoping you could tell me."

She blinked. "I haven't the faintest idea. I was minding my own business on the train, and there he was, pinning me to the floor and assaulting me."

"Why were you on that train at all?" he asked, watching her reaction to his questions. "You still work at Technobabble in the Financial District and leave your office at five-ten every afternoon, stopping at Sylvia's delicatessen for a salad and chocolate chip cookie. Today you were instead traveling on the seven twenty-four train from Oakland to San Francisco. Since your family lives in Berkeley, you could not be returning from a visit with them, as you would have boarded the train at a different station. Therefore, today you deviated from your usual routine, which might have some bearing on what the white dragon wanted."

She stared at him. "How do you know all that, Sherlock? Don't tell me you've been spying on me from Dragonspace."

Malcolm tapped a few keys of the computer keyboard. "I am a black dragon. Compiling and comparing information is what we are best at."

"But how did you know all that? Is there a spyhole in here or something?" Her face went pink, her dark eyes outraged as she contemplated what he might have seen through a peephole.

"Not exactly," he said calmly, touching the slips of paper he'd laid out on the desk. "As you said, only a witch can open a way for a dragon, and so there are no holes through which to spy on you. But while you slept, I made a few simple deductions. You are listed on the Technobabble website as a senior database programmer, and that list was updated only last week. Your parents' home is listed at the public records office, giving its exact address in Berkeley. In your raincoat pocket I found a canceled ticked for the BART which was stamped with the name of the station where you purchased it and the date and time." He lifted the ticket from the table.

He went on. "I also found receipts from Sylvia's delicatessen, where you have purchased a baby-greens salad, a chocolate chip cookie, and a double latte four times in the last week. Each purchase was made between five twenty and five twenty-five in the evening, and it is approximately a ten-minute walk between the delicatessen and the building that houses Technobabble. The slight difference in times can be put down to how long you had to wait in line."

Saba gaped in disbelief at the receipts he now held in his hands. "You figured all that out by going through my pockets?"

"That today you deviated from routine? Yes."

He saw Saba make an effort to close her mouth and try to behave nonchalantly. "I see I'll have to clean out my pockets more often."

"So why did you change your routine?" he asked again. "What did you do today?"

Saba blew out her breath and scrubbed her hand through her short hair, a remembered gesture that tugged at his heart. "I went to the Greater Bay Area Database Programmers semiannual seminar. The latest in platforms and real-world applications. I can't see how a dragon would be interested in that."

"Databases appeal to dragons," Malcolm replied. "Our

minds work in much the same way. Black dragons' minds, anyway."

"Well, the white dragon didn't mention databases. He said he needed a witch who knew about dragons. That would be me." She proceeded to tell him how the white dragon had greeted her on the train, tried to mark her, and then physically attacked her when she would not cooperate.

Malcolm pressed his fingertips together to conceal his fury as Saba told of the assault that had almost turned to rape. Somewhere inside him the dispassionate black dragon who assessed problems mathematically listened, but his very human body felt a rush of adrenaline and rage and the need to avenge her.

"You'd never seen him before?" he asked sharply. "Yet he knew your name."

"He knew about you, too," Saba countered. "Knew I'd once been a black dragon's slave."

"Not slave," he began.

"That's what *you* say. Your mark on me made me do anything you wanted."

He gave her a long look, even through his anger enjoying the challenge in her dark eyes. "I tried to put my mark on you again tonight. I couldn't. You have grown strong."

He had looked forward to weaving his strands of thoughts through hers, touching again the music that was Saba, like strings of oriental bells or running water. But he'd found himself turned away. Even in her sleep he hadn't been able to penetrate her mind.

She gave a short laugh. "The first thing I learned after you left was how to resist a dragon mark. I didn't want *that* to happen again."

Though he'd been frustrated at not being able to mark her, her answer gave him pleasure. "I knew you would be a powerful witch, and you have become so. That will be an asset."

"For what?" she asked, suspicious.

"I will tell you, in time. Right now, I am more interested

in this white dragon. Why did he come to this world, and who allowed him to?"

"I doubt Lisa would have done it." Saba's eyes glinted like onyx. "Then again, she let *you* through."

He lifted his shoulders in a smooth shrug. "I was very persuasive."

"Caleb didn't try to stop you?"

Malcolm thought of Caleb, the golden dragon who had convinced Lisa Singleton to be his mate. Caleb had been there tonight in his human warrior's body with long golden hair and large blue eyes. He'd not opposed Lisa, but he'd glared at Malcolm and growled all kinds of dire warnings about what Malcolm had better not do while he was in the world.

Malcolm couldn't blame Caleb for not trusting him—Malcolm had nearly gotten Lisa killed the last time he was here. Malcolm had needed Lisa and her magic, and she'd been hurt by his actions, though he hadn't meant her to be. Caleb was understandably wary.

He'd promised that his intentions this time were benevolent, and Lisa had seemed pleased with him. Malcolm hadn't mentioned Saba or the white dragon or his destination, wanting to find out more before he brought them into the matter, but Lisa had pulled him aside before he'd left the house and whispered, "Tell Saba hello for me."

"Lisa says hello," he said now.

"I saw her the other day, her and Caleb," Saba said. "In Chinatown."

"Ah. And how is the good Ming Ue?"

Ming Ue was a magical woman, a mage, who served the best dim sum in San Francisco. Ming Ue had known Malcolm for what he was the moment he'd entered her restaurant, and she had shown him reverence rather than fear.

"The good Ming Ue is fine," Saba answered impatiently. "I still want to know what you are doing here."

"And I've told you. To find out what you know about the white dragon."

"Nothing. End of story. You threw him back to Dragon-space. Didn't you chase him around there?"

"I tried to locate him, but I could not. He may or may not have made his way back to San Francisco—I returned because I did not like the idea of him roaming your world at will."

The way Saba's face paled, she didn't much like the idea, either.

"Will you help me hunt him?" he asked.

Side by side they could track down the white dragon, find out what he wanted, and rid the world of him, kill him if necessary.

"Do I have a choice?"

He looked her over again, the soft light of the lamp glowing on her wisps of black hair, her fine skin, the dark eyes that regarded him with intelligence and suspicion. Was she, somewhere inside her, happy to see him? Malcolm had never been self-deceptive and he wondered if he only imagined the interested spark in her eyes.

"My mark is not on you." He rose from his chair and approached the bed, no longer able to keep the distance of the room between them. "So you do have a choice."

She watched him warily, not moving the sheet, not shifting aside and welcoming him into the bed. He reached down and traced her cheek, loving the feel of the softness under his fingers. Her skin grew pink at his touch, and her eyes darkened.

"You can do as you like now," he said. "My witch."

He let his fingertip skim her lower lip, which had been bloody and cut when he'd seen her in the train. The lip was whole again, healed by his touch. Her blush deepened, and he saw a flicker of desire in her eyes, unmistakable this time. Her tongue moved across her lips the slightest bit, catching his fingertip.

Sudden heat shot through his body, fiery tendrils flaring from his finger through his torso down to his groin, where his erection lifted and extended. *Want you,* he thought. *I missed you.*

She moved her head, and his finger slid away from her mouth, the moment ending.

"I'll help you," she said in a hard voice. "I want to know what the white dragon is up to myself. But right now I need to sleep. I have to work in the morning."

His gaze wandered to the silhouette of her under the sheets, the enticing way the cloth draped her limbs.

Saba pulled the sheet higher and glared at him over it. "I meant sleep alone. There's another bedroom down the hall, if you remember."

He seated himself on the edge of the bed and smoothed his hand over her hip. "You used to like to sleep with me."

She reddened. "Yes, after we'd been fighting something or running from something or one of us had nearly been killed."

"We both fought this day," he reminded her.

"Well, I don't need it to become a habit."

Malcolm stroked her hip with his thumb, irritation stirring. He wanted her, had wanted her all the long months he'd been in Dragonspace without her. She wanted him, too, but by the hardness in her eyes, he could see she would not open her arms and invite him into the bed. She'd rejected him once before, when he'd offered pleasure and she'd said no for complex human reasons he didn't understand. She'd been very, very angry at him.

"When I was in Dragonspace," he said, "I read many books. There is much written about pleasure between a man and a woman. I learned many things."

He felt her pulse quicken, saw her pupils widen, but her mouth became a firm line. "No, you don't," she said, raising her forefinger in his direction. "No seduction. Not this time."

He continued to caress her, saying nothing. He knew she remembered when he'd leaned her up against the front door of this very apartment and unzipped her pants and dipped his tongue inside her. She'd been angry at him just before that, trying to leave him, but her resolve had crumbled at his touch.

The look in her eyes told him that she remembered, that she knew he'd try seduction again, and that she was prepared to fight him. The fact that she braced herself to fight told him more than words that she wanted him. If she hadn't wanted him, she'd not fear his tactics. Knowing that was enough for now.

"Rest then," he said softly. "I will continue to research."

She looked startled as though she expected him to continue to argue, and he felt a trickle of mirth. He would take it slowly. They had many problems to solve, and they would solve them, and after that he would have time. She would give him back his life, and he would spend it making her see why she should not resist him.

He moved his hand to the curve of her waist and leaned to brush a kiss to her lips. Her mouth moved beneath his, but she stopped it and turned her head, her breath coming fast.

Malcolm sat up again and straightened the sheet over her. "Sleep well."

He felt her gaze on him as he moved back to the computer, but he pretended not to notice. He also pretended not to notice that though she laid down again and arranged herself in a sleeping position, her breath remained quick and shallow, and never moved into the deeper pulses of sleep.

In the morning, she glared at him again when he insisted on accompanying her on her commute to work. They rode busses downtown, transferring where needed, and Malcolm stuck close beside her, his eye out for the white dragon or anyone who might bear his mark.

He felt a warmth of pride in his Saba as she parted from him in the Financial District, despite her exasperated look. Malcolm had honored her wishes and not climbed into bed with her last night, even when she'd finally slid into sleep. He'd finished his research on the computer, shut it down, and gone to the kitchen for the one human food he'd missed: coffee.

He'd listened to Saba sleeping fitfully in the other room while he read the newspaper and turned on the television to catch up with what had been happening in the human world in the last year. By the looks of it, same old, same old.

By the time he'd finished, showered and put on fresh clothes, Saba had risen and donned a bathrobe, giving him an evil look as he handed her a cup of fragrant coffee.

"I did not come to enslave you, Saba," he repeated.

She looked delectable in the oversized robe, her hair mussed from the pillow, her eyelids drooping from lack of sleep, slim hands cupping the coffee mug.

"I'm just remembering the last time you burst into my life," she answered. "I did spells I wasn't ready for, almost got myself killed, went up against a megapowerful witch and a horde of demons, and was nearly wrecked in a barge. I can't help wondering what kind of crap you'll drag me into this time."

She was beautiful when enraged, her dark eyes flashing, her cheeks pink, wisps of hair falling over her face. She was right that he had caused her much trouble, but he'd also taught her about the power she had buried deep inside her. He'd touched a part of her no man had ever touched, drawing from her the truth of herself.

"The circumstances you outline were unforeseen," he said. "I regret any hurt you suffered. But the power we shared was incredible. You haven't forgotten the power?"

Raw, copper-tasting power, a combination of her earth-connected witch magic and the fire magic of dragonkind. It had been heady and mind-bending.

"No." She slammed her coffee cup to the counter. "I haven't forgotten." She turned her back and walked out of the kitchen, her backside swaying enticingly.

Malcolm watched her sway again under her raincoat as she walked away from him down the street toward the building that housed Technobabble. He knew that under the coat she wore a tight black skirt that molded to her form and set off her legs to perfection. Saba was not a tall woman, but her legs still seemed to go on for miles. In lacy

black stockings, they made him remember what it was like
to lower his head to her, to lick . . .

He indulged himself in that vision for a few moments.
Soon he'd be able to share with her the true purpose of his
visit here. He would ask for her help, and he would explain
exactly why he needed her and only her.

First, though, he had a few things to take care of. The
scent of danger had been high when he'd fought the white
dragon. He wasn't sure what the danger was, or if the white
dragon had anything to do with Malcolm's present dilemma.
He also wouldn't rest easy until he knew exactly who had allowed the white dragon through from Dragonspace, and why
he'd been so eager to find Saba.

He watched Saba move away from him awhile longer,
appreciating the tilt of her head as she looked for traffic before tripping across the street in her high-heeled ankle
boots. Beautiful witch. He craved the taste of her, the feel
of her body under his hands. It wouldn't be long before he
could have all of her and make her understand her part in
this. Until then he'd have to content himself with looking.

He remained on the street corner, watching until Saba
dove through the doors into the high-rise that housed her
office. Only then did he turn away and head back up Sacramento Street toward Chinatown and his destination.

Lumi's bicycle shop, in a Chinatown alley off Sacramento Street, was dim and dusty, but the tall, lanky young Chinese man had plenty of bicycles stacked in the back for repair and a number of "sold" tags on high-priced bikes in the front. The shop was doing well.

Malcolm sensed a web of dragon magic over the lintel as he ducked inside the store. Caleb's and Lisa's and a faint lingering whiff of Malcolm's own—lucky magic, Lumi's grandmother Ming Ue would call it. She considered dragons very lucky.

Lumi Juan, who looked up from tightening something with a wrench, obviously thought not all dragons were lucky. When he saw Malcolm he closed his eyes and groaned loudly.

"Just when I thought my life was back together," he said, "you walk in. Lisa promised me you went back to Dragonspace."

"I did."

Lumi straightened up, a rawboned, slender man in his twenties with black hair, a handsome Asian face and eyes that had once seen pain and darkness. Lumi had been invaluable to Malcolm during his last visit, but Lumi had also spent most of that time terrified.

"How is Grizelda?" Malcolm asked politely, naming the young and naive witch who had taken up with Lumi when she'd sensed he was another innocent caught up in the mess. He felt Lumi's affection for her even now.

Lumi held his wrench nervously. "Grizelda is fine. No offense, but why didn't you stay in Dragonspace?"

Malcolm found the remnants of the black dragon threads he'd woven around Lumi's mind eight months ago and gave them a brief tug. "I need your help, my friend."

He groaned again. "Why me? What's so special about me?"

"You know so many people." Malcolm leaned negligently on the counter, easing his touch on Lumi's mind. The winding threads remained, but he had no reason to pull them.

"I *used* to know people," Lumi corrected him. "I am clean and straight and don't hang with bad people anymore, not even for you. And don't think it's the threat of prison keeping me clean, it's not. It's having to face my grandmother." He shuddered. "No, thank you."

Malcolm suppressed his amusement. The diminutive Ming Ue ruled her family, all far taller than she, with an iron fist. "I am pleased to hear Ming Ue is doing well."

Lumi gave him a dark look. "If you're around again, she'll want to see you. She has a thing for dragons, especially black dragons."

"In China, the black dragon is the emperor's dragon, distinguished by having five claws." Malcolm held up his hand and spread his five digits. "I'm sure your grandmother will be pleased to know you are helping me again."

Lumi growled something under his breath. "What happened to your own contacts? You had quite a following."

Malcolm shrugged. "I still have them, but many were minions who did my bidding because I rewarded them, and I didn't reward them to think. What I need now is information from someone smart enough and courageous enough to help me. You must know someone who is trustworthy, who has brains, who has integrity."

Lumi looked glum. "I do."

Malcolm glanced around at the bicycles carefully arranged, the tools kept lovingly on the bench, the neatness despite the cramped and dark space.

"I will visit Ming Ue," he announced, "and return later today. You will have a contact for me by then."

"You're serious about this?"

"I am serious about everything. I am trying to prevent something bad from happening, and most of all, to keep Saba safe. You want that, too, don't you?"

Lumi didn't flinch under his gaze. "Of course. Saba is a friend."

"Good. Then you will find someone for me."

Lumi heaved a heavy sigh. "Yes, you know I will. Leave it to me."

Malcolm smiled faintly. He brushed his fingers over the counter, strengthening his black dragon magic and twining it with the gold and silver magic already there. Lumi would be well protected and prosperous, whether he liked it or not.

The good thing about database programming, Saba thought as her fingers roved her keyboard, was that it claimed a person's entire attention. Trying to hunt down the bug in a subroutine kept her from thinking about Malcolm and the strong sexual dreams she'd had about him, knowing he wandered her apartment while she slept.

That is, programming kept the thoughts out of the front of her mind. Every time she took a break, even to run to the bathroom, the image of Malcolm naked in the train thrust itself in front of her. She'd shiver, her body warming, at the same time her better senses tried frantically to steer her back to mundane problems in her subroutine.

Last night he'd offered to pleasure her, and she'd been

hard-pressed to tell him no. She had determined to resist him if she ever saw him again, but she realized now it had been easier to decide that when he was out of sight. When she'd thought him gone forever, it had been simple to believe she could do without his hot breath on her skin, the skillful way he massaged her through the blankets, the darkening in his eyes that told her he wanted her.

She leaned her forehead against her computer monitor and half-moaned. She had to put him out of her mind. He'd left her; why was she so anxious to relive every touch and kiss? Why did she visualize him doing it all again?

Subroutines, she thought hastily. *Subroutines. The cure for an overactive libido.*

But subroutines couldn't erase Malcolm from her mind, and she spent the morning going warm then cold, hot liquid pooling between her thighs, her nipples pearling every time she thought of him.

She half expected Malcolm to wait for her at lunch, lurking near the front door as she exited the building. When she did not see him, she made herself suppress feelings of disappointment and hurry half a block to Sylvia's delicatessen. Thank Goddess it was cold and windy, which helped cool her scalding face.

She placed her order and found a seat in the crowded sandwich shop, nodding greetings to the people she saw there day in and day out.

"Saba, how *are* you?" A blond, crop-haired girl named Mamie slid into the seat beside her and plopped down her paper-wrapped sandwich. "You look distracted." She smiled knowingly. "So, what's his name?"

Malcolm, Saba almost said, then she shook her head, wishing the heat between her legs would go away. "It's no one," she said quickly. "I had a long day yesterday and no sleep last night."

Mamie, twenty-six and man crazy, wasn't satisfied. She lay a well-manicured hand next to Saba's. "What does he look like?"

Saba sighed, giving up the pretense. "Dark hair, beautiful eyes."

"Built?"

"Stacked," Saba said miserably. "With a tattoo."

"Oh, honey." Mamie grinned in delight, then she looked wary. "He's not gay is he? That's the trouble with man-hunting in San Francisco, not only are all the women out hunting with you, but half the men are, too."

"He isn't gay."

Mamie brightened. "Well, aren't you the lucky one? What's his name, have you slept together yet, can I meet him?"

Saba burst into laughter at her friend's eagerness. Mamie was as fierce a matchmaker for other women as she was for herself, often telling Saba, *Honey, I might as well get it right for someone else if not for me.*

The laughter was a release and a relief, though the tightness inside Saba didn't go away. "He was in my life before, and it didn't work out. I don't expect it to work out now."

"He came back for a reason, right?" Mamie peered at Saba closely. "Or is he no good?"

"It's hard to tell." Saba chewed her sandwich, trying to think. "He wants something, but I'm not sure what."

"Well, I'm going to interpret that as a good sign. He's got you under his skin, and he can't get you out of his mind. He's back to try again."

"You sound like a country-western song," Saba observed.

Mamie picked all the sprouts off her sandwich and ate them with her fingers. "That's because they're so true, aren't they? I have to meet this guy."

"He might pick me up after work. He rode the bus down with me this morning. He's a bit—protective."

"Aw, that's sweet. My last boyfriend couldn't care less if I made it home alive. He lived to lie on my couch and eat my food and watch ESPN, which was fine as long as the sex was great. Then he didn't even want to do that." Mamie shook her head. "So I kicked him out. I want my next guy to think sex is the only sport on the planet." She sighed. "But he'll probably be gay."

At least talking to Mamie lightened Saba's heart a little. But only a little. She walked back to work, checking around her not only for Malcolm but keeping a sharp eye out for the white dragon. Malcolm's arrival had somewhat mitigated the terror she'd felt when the white dragon assaulted her, but not entirely.

She recognized that his healing magic had not only made her skin whole again, but also helped heal her mind from the trauma of the attack. But the shock of seeing Malcolm again and the disturbing eroticism of him on top of a lack of sleep was taking its toll. She was surprised she could still walk and speak coherently.

She got back to her glassed-walled cubicle a bit early, so she threw her purse into her drawer and made a phone call.

"Saba!" a deep voice roared on the other end. Saba held the phone a few inches from her ear and hoped the entire building couldn't hear him. "How is our favorite witch, today? Lisa is resting. The baby is moving much."

Pride burst from Caleb's voice at the fact that his wife was eight months pregnant, muted only by a note of worry. Saba knew that his first son had been cruelly murdered long ago and that Caleb couldn't quite hide his fear of losing something so precious again.

"That's all right, don't disturb her," Saba said quickly. "I called to talk to you. I need to ask you something."

"Shoot," Caleb answered. "Malcolm isn't being a bastard, is he? I'll kick him in his dragon balls if he is."

"So far, he's fine," Saba answered, crossing her fingers. "I wanted to ask you about white dragons."

Caleb didn't answer right away. Saba pictured his handsome face: the usually messy golden mane of hair, the large blue eyes contemplating the view of the Presidio from his and Lisa's apartment window.

"Why?" he asked finally, the usual good-humored note

gone. "White dragons are evil, Saba. Stay away from them."

"I met one on the train, yesterday. He knew my name."
Quickly she outlined the incident, including using the
dragon's tears to bring Malcolm to her rescue. Then, she
added, "Malcolm is worried about what he wants, but he
didn't explain much to me. Tell me about white dragons."

"Frost dragons," Caleb rumbled. "Creatures of ice who
inhabit the northern climes of Dragonspace, a place like the
Arctic of your world, but even colder. They are great dragons, like the golden and black, very magical, but cold-
blooded. Nasty, vile creatures. Stay away from them."

His description lowered the temperature in Saba's cubicle a few degrees. "Why do you think one would come
here? If they like ice, San Francisco should be too warm
for them."

"Whatever the reason is, it's sinister. I'll tell Lisa, and
we'll pour some extra magic around you to keep you protected."

"You're sweet, Caleb."

He snorted. "How many times do I have to tell you
golden dragons are not *sweet*? I'm a warrior, a badass. I
kick ass. *Sweet*." He trailed off into mumbling, but Saba
heard the note of amusement behind his growling tone.

She felt a pang of envy that she tried to subdue. Caleb
and Lisa were happy together, with the kind of quiet happiness that meant hand-in-hand walks in the park, sharing ice
cream cones, and best of all, making deep satisfying love
in the dark of the night. The two together performed some
of the most powerful magic Saba had ever beheld, and yet
the small glances between them spoke of happiness that
had no fanfare but could not be shaken.

Caleb and Lisa's relationship reassured her that there
could be true love in the world, but also reminded her that
quiet and *Malcolm* didn't go together. Her prior relationship with Malcolm had been turbulent and maddening, and
his sudden appearance in her apartment last night had been
just as nerve-wracking.

"Malcolm is looking into the frost dragon problem," Saba said. "That's why he came back." She sensed other reasons, but she wasn't ready to talk about what she sensed.

Caleb muttered more dragon words under his breath. "If a black dragon is worried, it's bad. I'll talk to Lisa," he promised again, then they said good-bye.

Saba hung up and brought her computer out of hibernation. Picturing facing another four hours of horny madness, she reminded herself to focus entirely on work. *Subroutines. Not Malcolm.*

A few tears swam in her eyes and the lines of code in her pop-up windows blurred. Her treacherous imagination again pictured his upright body as he stepped through the white light on the train, how every limb and muscle had been in perfect, beautiful proportion.

Drawing a ragged breath she shook her head and made herself click open her e-mail. At least a dozen people had sent messages while she'd been at lunch, with subject lines varying from details of their last meeting to who was collecting for the receptionist's birthday lunch.

Good. Inane e-mails were like a cold slap in the face. She clicked open a message without a subject and froze.

One line in capital letters faced her on the screen. She instantly knew damn well who had written the words, even though the address showed nothing but a string of cryptic numbers.

The e-mail read: "IT WAS NICE MEETING YOU ON THE TRAIN, WITCH. I LOOK FORWARD TO TASTING YOU AGAIN."

Malcolm's visit to Ming Ue in her unprepossessing dim sum restaurant in a Chinatown alley went much as he predicted. Ming Ue, an elderly Chinese woman with vibrant black eyes, bowed low to Malcolm, then shouted at her long-suffering nephew to bring out the best food and tea for the honored black dragon.

As at Lumi's bicycle shop, the dim sum restaurant was

overlaid with golden dragon magic and Lisa's silver magic, bringing luck and prosperity to all within. Last summer, Malcolm had paid for repairs and upgrades to Ming Ue's restaurant after a band of demons had trashed it. He'd woven his own magic into the foundations before he'd departed for Dragonspace, making the place stronger than ever.

Despite the upgrades to the building, the interior of the restaurant looked much the same. As he took his seat, Malcolm glanced at the recently painted white walls hung with black paper cuttings in approval.

"You did not overmodernize," he said.

Ming Ue scrunched her lips. "My customers don't want an upscale chichi restaurant. They want good dim sum. Chichi is for yuppies."

Ming Ue's nephew, Shaiming, brought out a pot of fragrant tea and a platter heaped with dim sum, smiling shyly as he dispensed the treats. Ming Ue poured tea for him, and Malcolm waited politely, knowing that Ming Ue thought it an honor to serve him.

Malcolm lifted the warm teacup to his lips and drank, mouth and nose bathed in steam. He swallowed, closing his eyes briefly. "An excellent tea. You are wise, Ming Ue."

"I know that," she said, black eyes snapping. "I also know you would not have come here without purpose, black dragon. Black dragons are powerful and vastly intelligent creatures, easily bored by a back street dim sum and tea shop."

"On the contrary." Malcolm lowered the teacup and looked interestedly at the spread of food brought for him. "Black dragons can spend much time contemplating the flavor and aroma of every different kind of tea grown in your world, past and present. We can spend days on this pursuit, comparing, sorting, classifying. And then we can start with the dim sum."

"I've always known black dragons were true gentlemen," Ming Ue said, heaping *sui mai* and *ha gow* dumplings on his clean white plate. "But even so you did not come here to compare my pot stickers with Auntie Mim's on Bush

Street. Mine are much better, anyway. She caters to tourists."

"I did come to seek out your wisdom," Malcolm replied. "And to taste your most excellent food."

"Flatterer." Ming Ue gave him a dark look, but he could tell she was pleased. "What can I, a powerless old woman, do?"

Ming Ue was a long way from being a powerless old woman, and they both knew it. Malcolm acknowledged her modesty with a nod.

"I may need your help before all this is out," he explained. He outlined the story of the white dragon, and Ming Ue shook her head. "White dragons, they are trouble. I will heed your warning and be on the lookout for him. Lumi . . ."

"Is under my protection and is already helping me. Saba was vulnerable on that train under the bay, and she has learned to resist my mark. You will help me in protecting her?"

Ming Ue smiled. She liked Saba. "Of course. The Japanese girl is a friend to dragons, and she will become a great mage." She leaned over the table and peered at him. "But who protects you, black dragon?"

He felt faint surprise, but realized he shouldn't have. Ming Ue was a wise woman, and she no doubt sensed what Malcolm had, that he was weakening. "I am still quite powerful," he said.

"But not so much as you once were, am I right?"

"Yes, you are right," he replied, quietly holding the small teacup in his great hands. "And I do not know why. It troubles me most that I do not know why."

"You need her." Her dark eyes twinkled. "You need Saba."

"Yes," he repeated. "Convincing her will not be easy. It is this for which I need your help."

"Ah." Ming Ue pondered, her face alight with enjoyment. "There I might have an idea. Saba likes folk stories— her grandfather told her many tales of ancient Japan and of the Japanese gods, and she likes to hear my stories of

China and the palaces of the emperor. Perhaps if we make you into a fairy tale, she will like that."

Malcolm couldn't resist the chuckle, even though his thoughts remained troubled. "You are a devious woman, Ming Ue."

"I have learned to be. I will help you if you do something in return for me."

"Name your price," Malcolm said.

She smiled, her face a mass of wrinkles. "A wise black dragon would not promise so fast, but my price is not high. It is Chinese New Year in a few weeks. We will be part of the festivities in Chinatown, and I want you there, to help carry the dragon. Imagine what luck New Year's will bring with a black dragon to see it in."

Malcolm bowed his head once and gave his word. Then Ming Ue lowered her voice so her customers would not overhear and leaned to him over the table, outlining exactly what he should do in order to recruit Saba to help him.

Malcolm listened, half-amused, imagining Saba's outrage if she learned what ruthless matchmaking Ming Ue was performing behind her back. But it would be necessary to save his life.

Malcolm finished the tea and all of the dumplings Shaiming had brought for him, then rose to leave, he and Ming Ue exchanging formal phrases of departure. He made his way back to Sacramento street and the bicycle shop, reflecting with surprise how much he'd missed tea and dim sum.

Lumi seemed more resigned to see him this time, accepting his role again as one of Malcolm's minions, though he did not look entirely happy about it. Malcolm waited in the back room while Lumi talked to a customer who wanted a bicycle for his daughter. After Lumi made the sale and unlocked the bicycle for the man, he pulled down the shade on the door and flipped his cardboard sign around to read "Closed."

"I have a friend who agreed to meet us at a bar nearby,"

he told Malcolm. "It's not exactly in a good neighborhood, so be careful. My friend, he's kind of an expert at any strange shit that goes on in San Francisco. I mean *really* strange shit. It happens; he knows about it."

"I assume he's dangerous," Malcolm said.

"Well, yeah," Lumi said, then locked up his shop and led him away.

They walked through Chinatown, Lumi greeting friends and fellow shop owners, then they crossed Bush Street and headed several blocks west and south into the Tenderloin. They moved down unmarked alleys, dark and dismal, not the tourist San Francisco by any stretch of the imagination. Tourists finding themselves back here would swallow hard and charge back to the main streets, desperately seeking the happy clang of cable cars.

Malcolm followed Lumi without worry, his black dragon magic encircling them like a net to keep any predators out. The bar was housed in an unprepossessing building with a long old-fashioned glass and wooden front door. The paint on the wooden frame was peeling and a dispirited-looking homeless man with a dirty face sat with his back against the bricks a few feet down.

Inside it was nothing special, just a long room with an ordinary-looking bar on one side, a few chairs and tables on the other, and three pool tables in the back. It was early afternoon in the city and the only occupants were the bartender, two bikers playing pool, and a heavily muscled Japanese man sitting at the bar.

Lumi led Malcolm to the Japanese man. He wore a black leather coat that creaked as he lifted his beer bottle to his lips and had black hair that he'd gathered in a short ponytail. He looked to be in his thirties, his face unlined but hard as though he'd seen much. His almond-shaped brown eyes flicked over Lumi and Malcolm without much interest, but he indicated with his bottle that the two should join him.

Malcolm took a seat on the man's left, and Lumi hoisted

himself on a barstool on his right. Malcolm ordered himself a beer and told the bartender to bring another for the man between them. Lumi stuck with soda water.

The man acknowledged Malcolm's generosity with a dip of his head when the bartender brought the drinks.

"Thanks for meeting me," Lumi said to him, watching bubbles dance in his glass. He cast a nervous glance at the bikers, who were leaning on cues, watching them.

The Japanese man smiled, showing a mouthful of unusually pointed teeth. "It's my pleasure. Don't worry about them, my friend. No will bother us. No one ever bothers me, they know better."

Yakuza, perhaps, Malcolm thought, thinking of the organization of Japanese gangsters, then the next moment realized, *No. Not Yakuza.*

"You are not human at all," Malcolm said once the bartender had moved off. "You smell wrong."

"Nice to meet you, too," the man said, still wearing the pointed-toothed smile. "Call me . . . an imp. I'd show you my true form, but I'd scare the piss out of everyone, including you."

"I doubt it," Malcolm said smoothly. He took a sip of beer, liking the cold bite on his throat. "I'm a dragon."

The imp's eyes widened. "Swear to the gods?" He looked Malcolm up and down. "True, you don't smell human either. Poor Lumi, stuck with a pair of stinky paranormals."

"You can call me Malcolm," Malcolm said, ignoring his joke.

"My name's Axel." The man thrust out a hand and caught Malcolm's in a rock-firm grip. "It isn't really, but that's what everyone calls me, and it's good enough. Lumi says you're looking for something. If it's supernatural and in San Francisco, I know about it. It's not always safe knowledge, if you know what I mean, but I can be pretty ferocious." He winked.

The man was about six feet tall, below Malcolm's

height and not as bulky as Malcolm, but he did have a quiet menace that would keep any but the most determined away from him. Unfortunately, a white dragon would be determined.

"I'm looking for a witch," Malcolm said.

Axel grinned again. "Hey, you want a psychic reading or a love spell, you can look that up in the phone book."

"A specific witch," Malcolm explained. "I don't know who she is, but she'd have been working some particularly powerful magic lately, as large as creating a door to another world and bringing a creature through."

Axel's smile vanished. "As big as that?" He took a thoughtful swig of beer. "You know, I just might be able to help you out."

"You know who it is?"

"Let's just say I know someone it's likely to be. And if she didn't do it, she'll know who did. She's a slip of a thing, but she's a high-powered witch who can knock you across the room if she doesn't like you."

"Did you find that out the hard way?" Lumi asked from his other side.

Axel burst into laughter. "No, but I was there to see it. Everyone likes *me*."

"You're an imp," Malcolm said dryly. "One step removed from a demon."

Axel shrugged. "There are demons, and there are demons. Even kittens like me."

"Even though your true form would scare the piss out of me," Malcolm noted dryly.

"Beauty is skin deep." Axel grinned again and switched back to the subject. "This witch, just so happens she's having a party tonight. That's not such a coincidence—she has parties every other night because she's rolling in cash and has questionable friends. Why don't you come along and meet her? Bring somebody. Lumi and I will pick you up, and you'll go in with me. It's invite only."

Malcolm assessed the man, who looked back at him

with an ingenuousness that didn't seem feigned. "Why are you so eager to help?" he asked.

Axel shrugged again. "Any friend of Lumi's . . ."

". . . that he brings to this place is probably trouble," Malcolm finished for him. "You don't know me, and you're offering to take me to meet a high-powered witch right off the bat. What aren't you telling me?"

Axel drank in silence then carefully set his bottle on the bar. "I'm helping because you're a dragon. A black dragon, if I have you right, which means you could squash me like a bug if you wanted to. I figure whatever can worry a black dragon can't be good. If something's going down, I want to know about it so I can make sure I'm on the right side."

Malcolm watched him. "How do you know which is the right side?"

"The black dragon's side is always the right side," Axel said with a shrug. "Everyone knows that. Anyone stupid enough to pit themselves against a black dragon is going down hard. I don't want to go down hard."

"You flatter me," Malcolm said dryly.

"Not flattery. Truth. I know what I'm talking about." Axel took a last swallow of beer. "I'll get you in to see this witch, and we'll go from there."

"And what do you want in return?"

The imp blinked carefully as though it had never occurred to him to ask for payment. "Let's just say I like excitement. A good fight, stomp some evil ass, and I'm happy."

"There might be more to it than a simple fight."

Axel's smile vanished, and something ancient and strong flickered in his eyes. "Don't worry about me, black dragon. You wouldn't believe some of the things I've faced, worse than the strongest dragon or witch or most hideous demon. I've survived things that no one but me would be able to survive, not even you. So count me in."

Malcolm sent a few experimental wisps of dragon thought toward him then blenched when he encountered a mind completely alien to anything he'd ever found. The mind was complex and strong, and whether or not it was evil Malcolm could not determine.

Axel grinned suddenly and called out to the bartender to bring them another round, on him this time. He looked completely normal, but then again, he didn't. Malcolm decided to accept Axel's help but to watch him very carefully.

4

Malcolm was waiting for Saba when she exited her building just after five, drained from fighting databases, worrying about the white dragon and the e-mail she'd received, and trying to keep her erotic thoughts of Malcolm at bay. She gave up on the last when she saw Malcolm lounging not far from the front door, talking to a couple of homeless men who sprawled on the sidewalk at his feet.

Malcolm looked up as though he sensed her, his gaze burning her all the way down the street. He was a fine specimen of a man, six and a half feet of raw male sensuality. He'd tamed his dark hair into a tail that hung down his back, but that was the only thing tame about him. Malcolm could seem calm and contained, but when the dragon instinct took over he could be lethal in a frightening and precise way.

Malcolm moved down the sidewalk a little and when she drew near, he took her into the circle of his arms. The feeling of his body against hers enflamed the rampant sexual thoughts she'd harbored all day.

"Saba, this is Wallace and Pete," Malcolm said. The two

men looked very much alike with unwashed, unshaved faces, and tattered coats but they watched her with interest. "Do not be alarmed if you see them behind you—consider them your guardian angels when you are in this part of town. They belong to me now and will guard you when you leave your building and I am not with you."

Wallace and Pete nodded and smiled, and she sensed the dark web of Malcolm's thoughts twining theirs.

"Um, Malcolm," Saba began.

Ignoring her, Malcolm bade the two men good night and tucked Saba's arm in his as he moved with her up the street toward the bus and cable car stops.

"Malcolm." She pulled away from him, both in annoyance and because it was easier to talk when he wasn't touching her. "You can't go around the city putting your mark on everyone you see."

His brows quirked. "Why not? It served me well in the past, and you can be sure that if I do not, the white dragon will." He glanced back at Pete and Wallace who were deep in conversation. "And with my mark on them, they will no longer depend on the alcohol that keeps them from finding work or returning to their previous lives. Pete has a wife and two children, estranged because of his affliction."

"Oh."

"They will keep an eye on you when I can't and report to me." Malcolm eyed the traffic and the crawling buses stopping for loads of people at the end of the block. "It will be faster to take a taxi home. We will be going to a party tonight to meet someone who might be able to tell us the white dragon's plans."

"We are? Whose party?"

"I do not know her. Lumi introduced me to one of his friends, and the friend will take us to see her."

Saba stopped walking. He was doing it again, charging into her life, rearranging things without so much as asking her, not to mention being damn sexy while he did it. "Maybe I already had plans for tonight. Did you think of that?"

His gaze was unreadable. "Do you have plans?"

She flushed. "Well, no, but that's not the point. What if I did?"

"Then you would have to cancel them. This is important."

She bit back frustrated words. Malcolm had a way of turning everything to his purpose, and she knew she wouldn't win, at least not at the moment. Besides, she wanted to find out what was going on with this white dragon herself and find a way to make him stop stalking her.

"He sent me an e-mail," she said. "The white dragon, I mean."

Malcolm looked at her sharply. She told him what it said and watched Malcolm's mouth draw to a grim line.

"Then the white dragon has returned to this world," he said. He took a step closer to her, his male warmth moving over her despite the sharp winter wind. "But you do not need to be frightened, my Saba."

"Because you're here to protect me?"

"Yes."

Completely calm, utterly convinced of his own power. The trouble was, Malcolm really did have that kind of power.

The temptation to slide her arms inside his coat and hold onto him was great, so she started walking again, looking longingly at Sylvia's as she went by. A double latte, two shots of espresso and lots of cream, sounded good about now. "I called Caleb and told him what was going on. He said white dragons were evil."

"Indeed. Cruel and utterly ruthless."

"But that's what I've heard about black dragons," Saba pointed out. She jammed her hands into her raincoat pockets and gave him a sideways look. He walked along, his long leather coat open, the wind lifting the silken threads of his black hair.

"Black dragons may seem that way to others, who do not understand them," he responded. "White dragons have no deeper purpose."

"None at all?"

"No. They exist to eat and fight and mate. They have no other thought processes."

"I see." The conceit level in all dragons was high, never mind what kind they were. She refrained from pointing out his obvious prejudice and turned to their immediate concern. "So, who is this woman we're going to see tonight?"

"Either the witch who brought the white dragon here or one who potentially knows who did. It will be a good thing to speak with her."

Saba couldn't deny that, so she stopped arguing in spite of her annoyance at him arranging her life. Malcolm stepped to the curb and raised a hand to flag down a taxi.

Saba never had luck getting taxis in this part of town, but Malcolm's dragon magic brought two cabs fighting to get to the curb first. Malcolm took the one that zoomed in to cut off the other, waved off the fuming cabby behind the wheel of the second, and ushered Saba into the car.

"By the way," she said as the cab sped into traffic, "you never told me the second reason you'd come back. How long are you going to keep me in suspense?"

Malcolm's eyes went enigmatic again, and she knew he would not tell her the whole reason.

"I want you to do a spell for me," he answered in a low voice.

He was sitting far too close to her. The back seat of the cab was plenty wide, but Malcolm's leg pressed the length of hers, and he laid his arm across the back of the seat, enclosing her in his embrace. He was warm, hard-bodied, and smelled nice, and he had her turned on so much it was almost painful. She pressed her legs together, trying to contain herself. "Could you be more specific?" she babbled at him. "What kind of spell?"

"A locator spell."

She waited, but nothing more came. "Any decent witch can do a locator spell," she said, trying to remain sensible. "You don't need me specifically for that."

"For this, I do."

Now he had her curious. She started to ask him to elaborate, but he indicated the listening driver and shook his head. "We will discuss it later."

Saba had to live with that, because he wouldn't say any more—about anything—for the rest of the drive home. Nor did he kiss her or hold her or do anything to relieve the heat that was melting her from the inside out. She could only fold her arms and be annoyed at herself, and him.

Malcolm readied himself more quickly than Saba and waited for her in the living room of the apartment. As he'd noticed last night, Saba had kept the place mostly the same, not replacing the square, Mission-style furniture he'd purchased for it. But she'd added touches of femininity like brocade pillows on the sofa, a bowl of silk flowers on the mantelpiece, and Japanese scroll paintings of pleasant simplicity.

Two of the paintings contained the snow-covered cone of Mount Fuji, and the third was of a black dragon crouched with a ball between its great paws, a look of ferocious concentration on its face. The background was nothing more than a few suggestive strokes, giving the dragon center space. Malcolm studied the picture for a few moments, amused that she'd chosen a black dragon to adorn the room.

She'd looked at him in vast irritation last night and today made no secret that she was angry he'd come back. He knew she wanted him physically, he'd learned to read the signs during his last visit, but she had not asked him for pleasure, and pretty much had told him she would be glad to see him go again. But then, she'd hung this black dragon painting in her living room, perhaps as a reminder of him. He meant something to her. That was very important.

Saba's voice floated out of the bedroom. "All right, I'm ready. Where did I put my purse?"

She scuttled into the living room, and Malcolm turned from the paintings to appreciate the artwork that was Saba. She'd chosen a minute black dress with an off-the-shoulder neckline that bared the soft half-moons of her breasts. The short skirt emphasized her shapely legs in black lace-patterned stockings. For jewelry, she wore simple silver earrings and a pendant of a Celtic design with a tiny pentacle and an amethyst in its middle.

She was still in stocking-feet, searching the room for her purse and shoes. Malcolm moved to her as she straightened up from looking behind pillows on the sofa and slid his arms around her waist from behind.

"You look good enough to eat," he murmured, liking the just-shampooed scent of her hair.

She jumped, her brown eyes holding a mixture of anger, longing, and even fear. But not fear of him—fear of herself and her reaction to him.

"Why do you say things like that?" she demanded.

"Because they are true."

Her eyes darkened. Under her dress her nipples had become hard little points, and he stroked one with his thumb.

Without moving, she asked, "Why did you come back, Malcolm?"

"I've told you."

"No, you haven't. You've taken over again, and I'm letting you."

"Are you letting me?" It didn't seem to Malcolm that she had welcomed him with open arms. During Malcolm's last visit, Saba had yielded to him almost easily, opening like a flower, letting him bring her powers and her desires to life. This time she held him at arm's length, and for the first time in his dragon life, someone else's reaction to him bothered him.

He'd missed the taste of her, craved it during the long months alone as he prowled the dragon archives. Contemplating knowledge and mathematics should have been enough for him, but it never could be, not when compared to the feeling of Saba under him. He was hardening just thinking about it.

"Obviously," she was saying. "I'm doing whatever you want—again."

She might think herself yielding, but Malcolm knew better. This small, beautiful, defiant woman did things to him he barely understood. Without answering, he took one of her red-tipped fingers and slid it into his mouth, closing his eyes to enjoy her. She tasted good and clean.

He opened his eyes to find her gaze riveted to him, brown eyes flooded with desire mixed with irritation. She swayed against him, her body reacting without her say-so, and he turned her in his arms, her hip bushing against his now-obvious erection.

He cupped the curve of her waist with one hand, the other sliding to her nape to draw her mouth to his. Saba made a small noise in her throat, protest or surrender, he couldn't tell, then her lips opened to his.

It had been far too long since he'd tasted her. He remembered the spice of her, the warmth of her breath, the way her eyes would close, as they did now, in sudden surrender. He eased his hand to her backside, drawing her closer to him, fingers moving on the satin smooth fabric of the dress.

The kiss went on and on, both of them hungry, lips and tongues tangling and parting to tangle again. Her touch feathered down his hard biceps to his hip, her thumb moving between his pelvis and her abdomen, coming to rest on the button of his jeans.

The wanting inside him flared, his groin rock hard. Her body moved in compliance in his arms. Then her fingers began to worm open the buttons of his pants. Malcolm drew a breath, for the first time feeling her fingers on the bare skin beneath his waistband.

When he'd first met and marked her, he'd held back complete consummation of their relationship. He'd given her pleasure but nothing of himself, and he'd never allowed her to pleasure him. As their time together had gone on, he'd found himself wanting to give of himself, and redoubled his efforts to pleasure *her* to keep that urge under control.

Things were different, now. He'd returned to the human

world for a different purpose and no longer needed to hold back, and he hadn't made Saba his slave this time. He'd been glad that she'd learned how to resist a dragon mark, because now when she came to him, it would be her choice.

He did not resist as she worked open his zipper and moved her hand inside his pants. Beneath his underwear, he was hard and ready, and his entire body jolted in astonishment as she closed her hand around him through the cloth.

Sweet gods in heaven. His legs turned to water and he was going to fall down any moment. And drag her down with him so she'd keep rubbing him with that fiery friction the likes of which he'd never felt before.

In his human body during his eight-hundred-year exile, Malcolm had experienced sex, but those encounters had never, ever been like *this*. Saba's touches did things to him he didn't understand, and he was willing to stand there and let her until he figured it out.

When she moved aside the elastic band of his briefs and rested her hand on his bare flange, he thought he'd die. He scraped his hand through her hair, the noise in his throat one of pure wanting. She skimmed her fingers once down his staff, then as they kissed she explored him thoroughly, fingers learning and finding the ridges that made him want to climax in her hand. He crushed her mouth under his, sliding his own fingers beneath her short skirt and finding her thighs bare and warm above the tops of her stockings.

She jerked under him. "No," she whispered fiercely against his lips. "Let me pleasure *you*."

Malcolm couldn't have stopped himself if a freight train had rolled through the room. He nudged her legs apart, and she moved her feet as though she couldn't follow through with her resistance. His thumb dipped into her cleft, her honey flowing hot and liquid.

"Malcolm," she whispered, breath hot on his skin. "Damn you."

He smiled against her mouth. He'd lower her to the carpet and thrust himself inside her, he'd have to, though he'd wanted to go slow, and introduce her to the full pleasure he could give her . . .

The intercom that connected to the door downstairs suddenly buzzed, and a voice said, "Hey, it's Lumi."

They both froze. After a few heartbeats Saba stopped kissing him and slid her hand from his pants. Malcolm withdrew his fingers from between her legs and very slowly let her go, Saba remaining against him as though she couldn't step away. Her hair was fetchingly mussed, her eyes dark and wide.

"I guess we should answer that," she said.

He traced the line of her jaw and drew her lower lip between his teeth.

"I regret . . ." he said. He couldn't continue with what he regretted, but her answering look told him she understood.

Calmly he zipped and buttoned his pants then went to the bathroom to wash while she talked to Lumi through the speaker. When he returned, she was still looking for her purse. He combed his fingers through her short hair to straighten it, found her purse tucked under a coat on a hall chair, and held her steady while she grabbed her high-heeled pumps and lifted each foot to slide them on.

"Lumi's waiting downstairs," she said, out of breath. "He says his friend is here." She straightened up, two inches taller, and raised her gaze to his. "You know you still haven't explained what you want the locator spell for, Malcolm. Who or what do you need to locate?"

Malcolm thought a moment, his own breath still unnaturally fast, unable to put out of his mind how he felt with her hand around him. He mused over how much to tell her, what might frighten her away, and Ming Ue's advice on how to proceed.

He stroked his fingers once more through her hair. "I need you to locate my mate," he said, then turned and walked abruptly out the door.

He heard her follow, high heels clicking on the wooden floor, her exasperated growl as she drew breath to fling questions at him. But she could say nothing, because Lumi stood anxiously below, ready to lead them to the car where Axel awaited them.

Lumi's friend, who introduced himself as Axel, intrigued Saba. She slid into the back with Malcolm, and he cradled her hand in his as the car sped into the night. He held her hand loosely, but she knew she'd not be able to pull away, and she frankly didn't want to. The zipper of his jeans was still bowed outward, his sex not recovered from their encounter in the living room.

Not that she'd recovered herself. She glanced sideways at him, but he looked straight ahead as Lumi drove the car downhill.

He needed a locator spell to find his *mate*? What the hell was he talking about? Did he mean another dragon—a female he was trying to locate in Dragonspace? Or a human woman he'd met when he'd been in exile? Saba knew nothing about his life in the human world before they'd met, and he'd never spoke of it. Maybe he'd been married, wonderful thought.

Did he know his cryptic hints would drive her crazy? Or did he think Saba wouldn't care? *I came here to fight the white dragon and by the way, can you find a woman I've lost track of? Or a dragon whom I want to lay my eggs? But before that I'm going to make you nuts sexually so when I leave it will be even harder for you.*

How did she get into these situations?

She should angrily tell him to find someone else to do his damn locator spell and leave her alone. But she couldn't even unwind her fingers from his, couldn't move her hand from his thigh which was warm and hard beneath his clothes.

The rush of pleasure when she'd stroked him had been impossible to fight. If Lumi hadn't buzzed them, she'd have pulled off Malcolm's pants and shamelessly sunk to her knees in front of him. She'd never considered herself wanton and forward, but with Malcolm all restraints were off.

She wondered if he had put a very subtle mark on her mind that made her throw common sense to the wind once more. But no, a quick assessment showed none of the dark threads that he'd woven over Lumi. She was falling for him again all by her stupid self.

To distract herself, she studied Axel, who rode in the front seat, giving directions to Lumi. He looked Japanese but his comfort with his Western clothes and American speech told her he'd been born in America, perhaps second or third generation.

When he saw her watching him, he looked back between the front seats and smiled. "Saba Watanabe," he'd said, drawing out her name as though it interested him. "*Konbanwa*, Saba-san."

His Japanese was slow and deliberate but delivered with a flawless accent.

"*Konbanwa* to you, too," she answered.

He wasn't human but he didn't have the powerful aura of a dragon or the taint of evil that clung to incubi. He wasn't human, though, her witch senses told her that even if his pointed teeth didn't. If he was a demon, why would Malcolm trust him? Then again Malcolm used people for his own ends no matter who they were, and it was useless trying to decipher what he was doing.

Axel seemed the only one who knew where they were going. He directed Lumi to a house in Pacific Heights not far from Saba's, a tall Queen Anne Victorian mansion that was still a single house and hadn't been converted to posh apartments like the building she lived in.

Whatever magic contrived a parking space close to the house let Lumi pull in next to the curb without fuss. Axel leapt out and opened Saba's door before Malcolm could get around to her.

"Here we are."

Saba took his hand to climb out and looked up at the lighted house hulking over them in the dark. A round tower rose on the right side of the house, windows placed in an upward spiral, probably around a staircase. The mansion was well-preserved, the trim neatly painted, gingerbread curlicues unbroken on the porch. The front door was a mass of walnut and stained glass, left over from an era of gold-rush barons and shipping magnates, when opulence was king.

Someone with money still lived here. They'd have to in order to keep the huge old house from falling to ruin.

"I suddenly feel underdressed," Saba murmured.

"You're fine, Saba-chan," Axel said. "These people are a little weird, so stay close to Malcolm and let me get us in the door."

With that reassuring statement, he sauntered across the lighted porch to the door. Then Saba saw it, hanging out from the back of his jacket—a thin, scaly, lizardlike tail with a barbed and pointed end.

"Axel," Saba called. "Your tail's showing."

Axel glanced over his shoulder, and his eyes widened in mock surprise. "Oops." The tail vanished inside his jacket, snapping against his back. "Thanks. Might have been embarrassing."

"He's an imp." Malcolm's breath warmed Saba's ear as Axel pushed the doorbell, then knocked loudly. "Or so he says."

"Eccentric, anyway," Saba answered. "Where did you meet him, Lumi?"

"At a bar." Lumi blushed. "During my bad times. He helped me out one night. I was hallucinating and half out of my mind, and he got me out of wherever I was and back home. Stayed with me until I felt better. He was one of the reasons I went straight."

"Well, that was kind of him." Saba gazed with better appreciation at the black-garbed man who was now talking to someone through the door.

"But weird," Lumi added. "You aren't wrong about that."

The door swung open to reveal a leggy young woman not wearing much. She smiled at Axel, glanced at the other three, smiled again, and gestured them all inside. Saba followed Axel with Malcolm behind her, his fingers resting lightly on the small of her back.

The opulent house was crammed with people, overlaid with odors of perfume, cologne, cigarette smoke, and scented candles that burned everywhere. The house had been decorated in erotic excess, from artwork depicting naked men and women in various sexual acts to ceilings paneled in smoked-glass mirrors.

The people milling about were dressed in clothing made to go with the décor and reveal as much of the human body as possible. Bustiers with garters predominated among the women and a few of the men. The rest of the men wore skin-tight leather or nothing but Speedos, and unfortunately, not all had bodies flattered by Speedos.

A few of the women wore shining black corsets and high-heeled, thigh-high boots, one reclining on a sofa, stroking a flail like a lover. A few women had collars around their necks. Two collared women clung to a black-leather-clad man and gazed at him adoringly, one of them licking his leather-coated arm.

"Ick," Lumi said.

"Goddess," Saba hissed. "This is a BDSM party."

Axel nodded nonchalantly. "Yes. Didn't I say?"

Malcolm looked around as though the party guests and their costumes didn't faze him in the slightest. "The witch is here?"

"Somewhere. I'll find her, you mingle." Axel lowered his voice. "Watch yourselves. They look ridiculous, but some of these people practice the blackest, darkest magic imaginable. There'll be drugs and some nasty practices in the corners." He glanced at a man and a woman who'd collapsed into each other's arms, eyes glazed.

Saba watched him go, greeting guests like he knew them well. She noticed though, that while Axel was good-looking enough, none of the women, or men, made suggestive advances at him.

"Do you trust him?" Saba whispered to Malcolm.

"I barely know him," Malcolm answered, as though it were no matter. "But if he can find the witch who brought in the white dragon, that will be useful." He moved closer to her, his breath warm in her ear. "Do not worry, I will let no one hurt you."

She believed him. Malcolm was strong, even if his dragon powers were limited in the human world. She didn't think of herself as invulnerable, but she knew Malcolm would be at her defense in a moment's notice.

The person she worried most about was Lumi. Malcolm protected him with the black dragon mark, true, and dark-magic witches would have to work hard to penetrate it. But when Lumi had gone through rehabilitation, he'd had a hard time of it, she'd learned from Ming Ue. Drugs had nearly killed him. If someone here convinced him that taking one hit was fine . . . she knew that as with alcoholics, one hit was one too many.

Silently she invoked a protective spell, mixing it with Malcolm's magic already surrounding Lumi, mentally tracing the shape of a pentagram above Lumi's head. Lumi was a nice guy who didn't deserve to be dragged back into trouble, not to mention that Ming Ue would never forgive them.

As Saba completed the spell, she felt Malcolm's gaze lock on her. He knew what she was doing; he felt their magics entwining. His eyes darkened, and he looked at her as he had when he'd kissed her in the apartment.

Heat stirred low in her belly. She'd never tried using sex to enhance magical energies, but now she realized that with Malcolm the practice would be wildly powerful. Even touching his magic now to do a simple spell excited her.

Her imagination took it further. Malcolm over her in her darkened bedroom, candlelight tracing shadows on his body as he made love to her. Crystals surrounding the bed to catch the massive energy of their climax, the feeling of him deep inside her, his mouth on hers.

She swallowed hard and tried to banish the picture. Malcolm gazed at her as though he shared the vision and was more than willing to put it into practice. If only they weren't at this stupid party looking for a witch and worrying about the white dragon, she could explore her fantasy. All night if necessary. She wet her suddenly dry lips.

Lumi, oblivious to the heat between her and Malcolm, looked around in distaste. Not many people seemed interested in them, but those who did stared openly, trying to sort out what they were doing here. Malcolm certainly didn't look the submissive type, but even so they were all being eyed like fresh meat.

Malcolm led Saba and Lumi through the crowd toward the back of the house, oblivious of the guests' suggestive stares. The three of them stopped in a dim hall that was relatively private, the music and loud conversation in the front rooms providing a blanket of sound to cover their own discussion.

"Something is very wrong, here," Malcolm said. "I feel it."

Saba raised her brows, still not quite recovered from the erotic mixing of their magics. "Really? At a BDSM party with drugs and dark-magic practices? What could possibly be wrong?"

5

Malcolm ignored her humor. "Axel might be helping us, then again, he might not be. He has no reason to be loyal to us. We need to search for this witch ourselves."

Saba tried to sense the witch's presence, but she was nowhere near as attuned to magical strains as Malcolm, and any sensitivity to vibrations was buried under the avalanche of excess and a dark layer of cruelty that blanketed the house. Beneath the calm that Malcolm's magic provided, her skin crawled with the wrongness of the place. She hoped they could find the witch and interrogate her as quickly as possible.

She tasted, as Malcolm obviously did, the taint of darkness in the air, magic perverted. Witches sometimes called upon the dark aspects of the Goddess or asked deities like Kali or Morgan to help them, but those goddesses were not evil and could be very protective. This magic smacked of demons and darkness. And she and Malcolm and Lumi had been led here by an imp.

"Do you think we've walked into a trap?" Saba asked

Malcolm. "I can't feel any dragon magic other than yours. Not that I can sense much."

Malcolm shook his head. "I don't think so. The white dragon is nowhere near here, and none of these people bear his mark. Take Lumi with you and start searching upstairs. I want to find the witch quickly."

"What will you be doing?" she asked him, not liking the idea of roaming the house without him.

"Searching, too. There are cellars under this house, and I don't like what I'm feeling from them. If you run into trouble and need me, simply call for me, and I'll be there."

Saba put her hand on his arm, liking the hard feel of it beneath his jacket. "What if you run into trouble?"

"I'll turn into a dragon."

Lumi gave a nervous laugh. "That should scare them. So if the walls burst apart, we'll know you found trouble."

Malcolm didn't smile. "Meet me here again in twenty minutes whether you find the witch or not. If Axel hasn't brought her back by then, we leave."

He touched a kiss to Saba's lips. The brush of their mouths grew warm, and it was hard to keep it a brief kiss. When he turned away, he gave her a look that promised more to come, then he opened a door that led under the main staircase and disappeared into darkness.

Lumi looked at Saba as the door closed. "So what do we do?"

She sighed. "We go up, I suppose."

As Saba suspected, the main stairs did indeed wrap along the inside of the turreted tower in a spiral, an elegant wooden handrail curving along the wall. Each landing opened off into a dark corridor full of antique furniture grouped around closed doors. Saba didn't stop on the first floor, but kept climbing toward the top, figuring they could start there and work their way down.

They met no one as they ascended, the party staying firmly on the ground floor. It was at least quiet up here, the screams and laughter and music downstairs fading as they climbed.

"It's a little humiliating," Lumi said behind her. "Malcolm sent me with you not so I could protect you, but so *you* could protect *me.*"

"He knows we can protect each other," Saba contradicted. "I against magical attacks, you against physical ones."

"Huh," Lumi said, not reassured.

Saba stepped off the last stair at the very top. The landing here was smaller, with only three doors leading from it, and the stairs went no farther.

"What worries me more is what's in the basement," she said as Lumi caught up to her. "He went down alone, because he knew the danger is greatest there. That's why he sent us upstairs."

Lumi looked startled. "So why aren't we down there helping him?"

"Because he knows we can't."

Lumi chewed on his lip. "I see what you mean. Plus he doesn't have to worry about protecting us while he takes out whatever he finds." He noticed her anxious expression, and tried to look encouraging. "He's a dragon, he'll be all right."

"I keep telling myself that." Saba rubbed her hands over her bare arms. "Maybe if I repeat it enough times, I'll believe it."

"We might as well look around up here, anyway. Where do we start?"

Saba glanced around the square, uncarpeted landing. As she'd climbed, she'd counted eight doors on each floor except here at the apex of the tower. They'd ascended three flights, putting them on the fourth floor, the last flight narrow and ending in the gallery where they stood.

She thought about how she'd studied the tower while they approached the house and frowned. "Wait a minute, there should be another floor. I counted five from the outside if you include the very top room of the tower."

"The staircase ends here," Lumi pointed out.

Saba looked at the low ceiling above her, but the dark boards contained no trap door or any other opening that could lead to an attic.

"The next flight might start in one of these rooms," she suggested. "People liked to build secret staircases and things like that a hundred years ago."

"I found out that my grandmother has a secret room under her restaurant," Lumi said. "It used to be a speakeasy. My cousin Carol wants to turn it into a museum and charge tourists to see it."

"Not a bad idea," Saba answered, cautiously trying the first door.

"Grandmother had a cow," Lumi answered. "She said every family should keep some of its secrets."

"I'd like to see it." Saba peered into the room and found it empty. No furniture, no curtains at the windows, nothing. It was clean, she saw when she snapped on the overhead light, the floor swept, but unused. "Do you think she'd let me?"

"Sure. She likes you. If you bring Malcolm or Caleb or Lisa, she's bound to let you, and probably serve you a ton of food at the same time. She'll do anything for a dragon." He had no jealousy in his tone, just amusement at his grandmother's eccentricities.

There was a door in the room, but it only led to a closet, Saba found when she checked. Saba closed the door and turned to leave. "Nothing here."

She moved to the next room. As Saba started to open the door, it was suddenly wrenched open from the inside, and a white-faced woman stared at them in shock.

Saba stared back. Their witch, maybe? The woman's black hair held a few streaks of gray, but her face was unlined. She wore filmy, floating black that more resembled an evening dress than a witch's robe, and pentacles on necklaces, earrings, and bracelets. Her eyes were red-rimmed as though she'd been weeping, her hands trembling on the doorknob.

"I'm sorry," Saba said. "I didn't mean to scare you."

The woman stared a little longer in obvious fear, then her gaze lit on the pentacle on Saba's necklace. "Are you a witch?" she breathed, clearly relieved. "Good. I need your help."

"With what?" Saba asked warily.

"A spell. I've been trying all day, and it just won't work. I need more energy."

"What kind of spell?"

As Saba spoke she tentatively felt for the woman's aura and that of the room behind her. She found nothing malevolent, despite the party downstairs, no sign of the dark magic, no sign of sex perverted into evil.

"A locator spell," the woman gabbled. "Please."

Her desperation seemed real enough. If this was the witch Axel had brought them to see it might be worth finding out what she was doing. "Go find Malcolm," Saba told Lumi under her breath.

Lumi's coffee-colored eyes widened. "If I leave you up here alone, he'll kill me."

"I'll be all right," Saba whispered. "She's not very strong, and if she knows anything, she's worth talking to. Just hurry."

Lumi stood still, fighting his compulsion to obey the black dragon's command no matter what. He looked at Saba's determined face and the middle-aged witch who stood clutching her hands. "All right," he muttered. "I'll run."

He started down the stairs at top speed, noisy in the relative silence. Saba pasted a reassuring smile on her face and turned back the woman. "I'm Saba. Blessed be."

The woman jumped as though she'd forgotten the Goddess greeting. "I'm Annie. Er . . . blessed be."

Saba kept her smile in place despite her misgivings. "All right, let's do a spell."

Annie bustled back in the room, which was empty like the other except for a large circle of salt in the middle of it. No magic infused the circle; it was only an outline.

"I need to raise the power again," Annie said. "I was doing all right, then everything faded, like it ran into a dampening field."

"Maybe it did." Saba closed the door behind them and pocketed the old-fashioned key without locking the door. She had no intention of letting the other woman shut her in. Annie, gazing worriedly at the circle, didn't seem to notice.

Saba stepped into the salt circle without feeling any prickle of magic. Annie had fashioned an altar from a wooden footstool, upon which she'd placed a candle, incense, bowl of salt, and bowl of water, all surrounding a pentacle made of wood. Fire, air, earth, water, and Akasha—the fifth element or combination of all elements, also called Spirit.

The witch faced her across the altar, her eyes anxious. "Will you close the circle?"

Saba nodded. She felt no malice from the woman, just hope that a stronger witch would be able to infuse the circle with energy. Annie had brought nothing here but representations of the four elements and the spirit of the universe. Nothing evil in that.

Asking the Goddess to guide and protect her, Saba walked the circle, pointing her finger at the outline of salt. After only one pass, a silver blue shimmer rose from the salt to fuse together over their heads, enclosing them in a bubble. Saba felt the other half of the bubble flow through to the floor below, completing a sphere of protection.

She returned to the middle of the circle, her skin tingling with the magic. Annie stared at her, eyes wide.

"You have so much power," she said in an awestruck voice.

"I practice circles a lot," Saba answered neutrally, though the magic had clicked into place more quickly than usual. "Would you like me to invite the Watchtowers?"

The witch looked alarmed. "Not the Watchtowers. I'm afraid of them."

Saba thought of the tough spirits who answered her call

to guard the four points of her circle when she worked
tricky magic. She always saw them as four warriors with
broadswords. She knew the Watchtowers weren't really
four warriors, but they appeared to her in that guise. She
wouldn't mind a cluster of muscle-bound men around her
about now.

"Watchtowers are protectors," she tried.

"Yes, but I can't control them. What if they turned on
me?"

The woman was truly frightened. She had no business
working magic in a strange house filled with negative energy if she couldn't handle a basic circle.

"All right," Saba agreed. "We'll just call the elements
and invoke the Goddess and the God."

"I'm afraid of the God, too."

Saba peered at her curiously. She'd never felt anything
but benevolence and love from the God, who was a father
figure as well as a fertility deity. "Do you belong to a
coven?"

Annie nodded. "I'm new. If they knew I was working a
circle here, they'd punish me. But I have to find her."

"Find who?" Saba asked. "And what do you mean by
punish?"

Uneasiness stirred inside Saba when Annie didn't answer. A coven that punished by fear didn't sound good.

"Who are you trying to find?" Saba asked, holding onto
her patience. "We're safe here, in this circle. You can tell
me."

Annie's throat moved with a swallow. "She's one of the
coven, but she's disappeared. I thought I'd look for her
here tonight, pretend I'd come for the party and then search
the house."

Exactly what Saba, Malcolm, and Lumi had done. She
wondered if the missing witch was same one Malcolm
hoped to find.

"Let's start, then," Saba said. She held her hands out
over the altar, and Annie put her somewhat sweaty hands in
hers. Saba closed her eyes and asked the Goddess to join

them—*Please, I think I desperately need your·guidance here*.

Annie seemed fine summoning the elements. She chanted, "From the east, air, from the north, earth, from the west, water, from the south, fire . . ."

They began the spell. Saba liked to use a pendulum and a map for a locator spell, although to locate the witch within the house a blueprint or at least a rough sketch of the place would be better. Annie hadn't come prepared with anything like that, and looked blank when Saba suggested it.

Saba had to settle for visualizing the layout of the house in her mind, what little she'd gleaned since her arrival. When she asked Annie what she knew about the house, Annie shook her head again.

Sighing to herself, Saba closed her eyes and pictured the house as she'd seen it on the way upstairs, the ground floor with the living rooms and dining room full of questionable guests, then each floor with its landing and doors. From that she visualized the house as though she looked down at the floor plan from above, then pictured a white arrow floating through it.

Keeping her eyes closed, she asked Annie to describe the witch. A tall young woman, Annie answered. Platinum blond hair, very dark eyes. She didn't like to wear much in the way of clothing, Annie added disapprovingly. Saba pictured the young woman the best she could and told the floating arrow to find her.

She braced herself for the magic to not work. She had so little to go on. She felt vulnerable in this house, and Annie was dampening the magic field with her fears instead of lending energy. Saba also worried about Lumi, which didn't help, and she wondered why he and Malcolm were taking forever to get back upstairs.

Something twitched outside the circle, and Saba opened her eyes. She thought she saw a flicker of darkness beyond the circle of power, though the overhead light flooded the room with brightness. But as the spell went on, small fingers of darkness solidified outside the circle, brushing the floor-board like wisps of black smoke.

Saba's heart beat faster. The spell grew within the circle and the darkness drifted closer, as though it sought to feed on something and thought Saba's magic would be a tasty snack. Saba had faith her circle would hold, but as the dark fingers brushed against the nimbus she tasted the bite of something evil, and fear squeezed her throat.

The darkness seemed somehow familiar, like a memory she couldn't place. Some forgotten terror that she'd managed to drive away long ago, rising to taunt her again.

Should she stop the spell? Would the darkness recede or would it hover, waiting for her to take down the circle? Uneasiness gnawed at her. And *where* was Malcolm?

Silently she asked the Watchtowers, if they were listening, to come and help her, never mind Annie's fears. She'd never before simply asked with her mind; she'd always lit candles and made it a respectful request, but she didn't have time for that now.

Please help me.

Annie kept her eyes tightly closed and noticed nothing, but Saba imagined she saw faint shimmering figures grow at the four compass points within the circle. The darkness did not recede before them, but she felt the slightest bit better.

She continued chanting, picturing the arrow hovering in the house, but the dampening effect of Annie's fears, plus the darkness skimming outside the circle, repressed the spell. The arrow in her mind floated and spun and settled on nothing. She was going to have to admit defeat and take down the circle, and she wondered if the darkness would recede when her power flowed away.

Then again, it just might attack. She cracked open her eyes and looked sideways at the black tendrils just as one reared up and attached itself to the glowing bubble of her magic.

A spike of power suddenly shot through her, and something wrenched her arms over her head and pressed her hands hard together. Magic surged from her fingertips in a thin swordlike beam that skewered the ceiling, sending plaster raining down to bounce off the glowing sphere of her magic. The wooden beams beneath the plaster began to smoke.

Annie opened her eyes and gaped. "It worked." She started to move.

"No!" Saba cried.

She dragged her hands down, the magic dispersing, and caught Annie before she could break the circle. Annie saw the fingers of darkness writhing like cords of smoke and screamed.

Just then the door burst open and Lumi rushed inside to be grabbed by Malcolm and Axel and hauled back out.

The three men hovered in the doorway, Malcolm studying the darkness with glinting eyes, Lumi fearful, and Axel looming behind them, grim-faced.

"The witch is in the room above this one," Saba called. "I think. I don't know what's causing *this*." She gestured to the ropes of darkness coiling on the floor like heavy smoke.

"Evil," Axel spat. He pushed past Malcolm and Lumi and faced it. "Get out!" he shouted.

His voice rocketed through the room, and the darkness receded the slightest bit, looking for all the world like a cringing dog. Axel snarled deep in his throat, and the darkness suddenly gathered to one fat point then vanished like a stream of smoke.

Axel turned around and peered through the bubble of magic, cupping his hands around his face as though he looked at them through a window. "You can come out now."

Saba blew out her breath in relief. She held out her hands and withdrew the silver blue light into her, politely thanking the Watchtowers for coming to her aid. Annie watched her in awe.

When Saba stepped out of the outline of salt, she felt Malcolm's power pulsate through the room, driving out and keeping out any remnants of evil. Silver black threads swept into every corner before returning to Saba and wrapping her in a gentle cocoon.

The threads of magic touching her were warm and amazingly tender. All that power damped down for her, lacing protection around her body without force. She met his gaze, finding it fixed on her with silver intensity.

"I think she's upstairs," she said, her voice soft.

Lumi looked around. "I keep saying, there's no way up there."

Axel studied the ceiling and its ruined plaster, then gave Saba a look of respect. "I know this house. Follow me."

Annie cast him a fearful glance, but she left along with the others, sticking close to Saba. Axel strode into the next room without hesitation and to the door on the other side of it. Instead of the closet Saba had found in the first room, the door led to a wooden staircase that bent sharply upward, the rough steps thick with cobwebs.

Axel started to climb, Lumi after him, then Saba and Annie. Malcolm brought up the rear, his protective net still draped over Saba.

The top of the tower was an octagonal room tucked under the roof with windows on four sides. Axel flicked on a wall switch, and a bare bulb glared light into the room. The floor had an intricate wooden inlay that once upon a time must have been beautifully polished, but the boards were scratched and pitted and now soaked in blood.

A woman lay in the exact center of the room in the middle of a perfect circle marked by white rope. She had white hair, peroxide bleached, and was dressed in a teddy trimmed with white faux fur.

Any power that the circle had radiated had long since gone, and the woman was dead. Her hips were twisted at an impossible angle, her face gray with death, her dark eyes wide and staring.

"Goddess." Annie breathed, then she let out a high-pitched scream.

6

"We need to call the police," Lumi said. His face was white, eyes dark pools of horror.

Saba shook her head. "You have a record, Lumi. You don't need to be where drugs are when the police come. We'll call them after you go."

Lumi started to protest, but Malcolm shot him a hard look, and Saba felt him tighten the bonds on Lumi's mind. "She is right. Axel, take Lumi and this woman downstairs and say nothing until I join you."

Axel nodded without argument, seeming to understand and share their protectiveness of Lumi. He spread his arms wide, shooing Lumi and Annie toward the door.

Malcolm had said nothing about Saba, and she didn't count herself among those who needed to be shepherded. She waited until the others had gone, then watched as Malcolm studied the body, one hand cupping his chin.

The witch had outlined her circle with plain white rope, but it was new rope with no feel of magic on it. Saba suspected she'd not had time to finish the circle of power before she was attacked. She'd been twisted in half, her spine and neck broken, and it was clear she'd known it was coming—Saba saw terror reflected in her eyes.

"You shouldn't touch her," Saba said quickly as Malcolm leaned over the body and put his fingertips on her forehead. "You'll leave your DNA all over the place."

"Dragon DNA is different from a human's," he said absently. "They'll think the test is wrong."

"Then you'll contaminate the rest of the DNA evidence. I'd like to get Lumi home—I don't want to explain to Ming Ue what he was doing here."

"I will not take long."

Still speaking in a detached tone, Malcolm walked around the witch's body and touched a ring on her finger. Saba heard Malcolm whisper, saw a thread of his magic drift through the dead woman. A wisp of blackness, inky like tar smoke, rose from the witch and swirled through the window into the night.

Malcolm returned to Saba, his expression unreadable. "I will not contaminate the evidence if another dragon murdered her, which is what I believe happened. She's been dead a day or two. And yesterday evening the white dragon cornered you and tried to force you to work for him. I believe we've determined why."

"He killed the witch who brought him here," Saba said, studying the poor young woman's lifeless eyes. "So he needed another witch. I wish I knew who she was, and why she thought she could handle a dragon."

"Her name was Rhoda." He turned an ironic gaze on her. "Are dragons difficult to handle?"

"Immensely. How do you know what her name was? Did Axel tell you?"

"It was in her mind, still imprinted there. Our name, our true name, is one of the first things we learn and one of the last things we forget."

"I didn't know that."

Malcolm took her hand, the warmth of his touch relaxing her a little. He drew Saba into the stairwell and closed the door so she could no longer see the pathetic young woman.

"When I put my mark on you," he said in a low voice, "I twined my magic around your true name, around the truth of you. Your true name is your essence, and can be used to work great magic."

"And humans have this true name, too? How did you learn mine?"

"I learned it when I marked you last year, and you were too weak to resist. Humans rarely protect their true names, because they know so little about its magic. The white dragon couldn't learn yours, because you now can resist a dragon mark."

"Good thing." She felt cold, wondering what else about name binding she didn't know.

"Anyone with knowledge of your true name holds absolute power over you," Malcolm said softly. "They do not need even to be near you to use it."

"Best not tell anyone what it is, then," Saba said.

"I agree."

She gazed at him in the darkness, at the glitter of his eyes in shadow. In those shadows she saw the imprint of what he truly was, the black dragon, strong and alien, the hint of a long, cruel face and powerful body, vastly magical.

She again wanted to ask what he meant by him wanting her to help him find his mate. Finding one's "true" mate was for fairy tales and romances, but then again, wasn't he a beast from fairy tales? Folk tales often imparted truth most people didn't want to know.

She suddenly wanted to be away from here with him, not standing in an inky stairwell in a house she never wanted to see again, a dead witch in a tower room and dark magic floating around. She wanted to be back in her protected apartment on Octavia Street where Malcolm's magic and hers intertwined in the wards.

Malcolm traced her cheek, blunt fingertips finding the hollows of her face, the tenderness of the caress incongruous with his strength. He pulled his fingers down the cleavage bared by her neckline, his touch like a streak of fire. He remained like that for a moment, touching her lightly and in complete silence.

He stood on the stair below her, and even then she had to raise on tiptoes to kiss him. She took comfort in the kiss, the fear of the dark magic and the shock of discovering Rhoda's body easing under Malcolm's mouth.

She relaxed against him, the fuzziness in her mind telling her he was protecting her again, both from physical and emotional trauma. He knew how to do that.

Of course Malcolm had to protect her from trauma, she thought, because trauma always occurred when he was around. She smiled as the kiss came to an end.

"Now I know you're really back," she said.

He tilted his head to one side, giving her his dragon stare. "I have been here since last night."

She laughed and kissed the tip of his nose. "That isn't what I meant."

He studied her in the darkness—she knew his dragon sight could make out every feature. She'd felt him jump when she gave him the light, playful kiss on his nose. Malcolm was still uneasy with casual intimacy. He might say he wanted to pleasure her, he might have accepted her touching him, but he liked to be in control.

Saba kissed him again, another light touch that people in love might share. "We should go down," she whispered.

Malcolm waited a long moment, breath hot on her face, hand on the curve of her waist. He said nothing, made no reaction, and even with his thought threads touching her, it was impossible to know what he was truly thinking.

Without speaking, Malcolm slid his hand through hers and led her down the stairs.

Lumi waited at his car outside, resting his arm on the open driver's side door and looking over the top. Axel leaned against the opposite door, softly whistling a tune that sounded Asian and ancient.

"Where is Annie?" Saba asked.

"Who?" Lumi started.

"The other witch, the one I did the circle with."

Lumi shrugged. "She took off. Went running down the street. Wouldn't wait."

"Pity," Malcolm said. "She could have told us much. I believe she will be safe for now—she is too weak to be of much use to the white dragon."

Saba thought about the coven Annie had mentioned and knew the woman would only be relatively safe, but Saba would have to deal with that later.

Axel straightened up. "You leave, Lumi. I'll look after these two, make sure they get home all right."

Lumi seemed reluctant to go, but he finally got into the car, cranked the motor and pulled out onto the street. Taillights glowed red as he reached the intersection, then he pulled around the corner and was gone.

Malcolm went back into the house to call the police from a land line, not wanting the call traced from any of their cell phones, then he returned to the two who waited for him, carrying the coat Saba had left in the foyer.

"We're close enough to walk," he said as Saba slid gratefully into the warmth of her coat. The night was clear, but cold.

Malcolm took Saba's hand again, as though he liked the contact with her. Axel shoved his hands into his pockets and trudged along with them in silence. They hadn't gone far when they saw blue and red lights swarm to the house behind them. The police were coming to raid the party and look for a murdered young woman.

The wind blew cold, and Saba shrank close to Malcolm. He slid his arm around her, a gesture both warming and distracting.

"I'm sorry about your friend," Saba said to Axel as the sounds of the police raid faded into the background.

"Hmm?" His brows quirked as though he'd been thinking of something else. "Oh, I didn't know her very well, but she didn't deserve to die like that. Poor thing."

"Her death was conveniently timed," Malcolm observed.

"I show up wanting to interview her, you disappear, and when we find her, she's dead."

Axel stopped walking. A car rushed downhill beside them, bouncing across the intersection. "You think I killed her?"

Saba glanced at Malcolm in surprise. He'd already postulated that the white dragon had killed the witch, but she realized Malcolm was testing Axel, wanting to discover how he'd react to an accusation.

Axel scowled. "Not me, dragon. I'm not a killer—at least, not of humans who don't deserve it. She was murdered by something bigger than me." He looked Malcolm up and down. "Something like you."

Saba moved uneasily. Standing between two powerful beings glowering at each other was unnerving.

Axel went on. "She was killed a few days ago, not tonight. Neither of us did this, but I think you know who did."

Malcolm nodded. "A white dragon."

Axel's dark eyes widened. "Ish. I didn't want to hear that."

"You know about white dragons?" Saba asked.

"White dragons—frost dragons—are mean suckers. Black dragons are bad enough, but you really don't want to mess with the white dragons."

"I already messed with one, not on purpose," Saba said. "I didn't like it."

Axel looked concerned. "You all right?"

"I'll live."

They started walking again, Axel strolling in thoughtful silence. "So Rhoda was working magic for a frost dragon. Trying to control one, maybe, to enhance her own magic?"

"She might have been trying to control him at first," Malcolm rumbled. "But he'd put his mark on her pretty firmly. I found the vestiges of it in her mind still, even after she'd been dead a day or two. He controlled *her*, and then he killed her."

"So where is this white dragon now?" Axel asked.

"I don't know."

Axel glanced up and down the street as though expecting the white dragon to pop out of an alley at them. "Terrific."

"And I don't know why he's here."

"You're a lot of fun to be with, you know that?" Axel observed.

"Do you still think the black dragon's side is the right one?" Malcolm asked.

"Yep."

Saba didn't ask what they meant. She didn't like how worried the strongest beings she knew were about the white dragon—Malcolm, Caleb, and now this imp. She wondered what Lisa thought of the situation, Lisa who had power far greater than the other dragons. But Lisa was in her last month of pregnancy, hardly the time to ask her to go fight a white dragon.

They walked in silence again, Malcolm's arm firmly around Saba. They passed opulent historic homes painted in carefully coordinated shades as they climbed the hill, most of them museums or offices or apartments. "Painted Ladies," the houses were called, and were photographed by tourists the world over. Many were silent and dark, showpieces in which no one lived.

"So what's our next move, boss?" Axel said as they neared Saba's apartment at the top of the hill.

"Find the white dragon," Malcolm said, as though there should be no doubt. "And neutralize him. Are you in?"

Axel thought a moment, then nodded. "Sure. I'm in."

"When you decide you're no longer in, stay far away," Malcolm said. "Do not oppose me. You will regret it."

"No kidding." Axel started to say more, then his head jerked up, eyes alert. "Oops, I'm being summoned. Gotta go."

He lifted his hand in farewell and vanished with a sudden popping sound. Saba blinked at the spot when he'd just been, a rush of displaced air stirring her hair.

"Interesting people you know, Malcolm," she said, letting out her breath. "Let's go in. I'm freezing."

* * *

The apartment was warm enough with a fire blazing in the living room hearth and the central heating on. Malcolm marveled at how warm humans needed to be; his metabolism, even when he wore his human body, allowed him to survive in temperatures far colder or hotter than most people could stand.

Saba had kicked off her shoes as soon as she'd entered the apartment, and flowed down the hall to her bedroom. She hadn't asked if he planned to stay the night, and her annoyed look told him she would think long and hard before inviting him to her bed.

No matter. He built and lit the fire, then rummaged through what he'd brought with him plus the supplies he'd found last night in Saba's cabinet and set everything up on the dining room table. Map, salt, candles—all went in a neat row on the polished wood.

He sensed Saba enter before he saw her, knew the scent of her and her aura like the faint odor of jasmine. She was no less sexy in skinny jeans and a shirt that laced up the front than she had been in the tight dress and black lacy stockings.

She glanced at the table and the accoutrements and frowned. "What is all that for?"

"The locator spell."

"You want me to locate your mate for you *now?*"

He nodded, seeing no reason to delay.

Her dark eyes narrowed. "Why are you in such a hurry? Don't we have enough to worry about with the white dragon? Like where he is and what he's up to?"

Malcolm started to answer, to argue, but he stopped himself. He had no idea what it was about Saba that goaded him to hot words. A dragon did not argue about what he wanted to do, he simply did it and everyone obeyed. He was not obligated to explain his motives.

"Come and sit down," he said, keeping his voice neutral. "I will tell you what you need to know."

Any other person would simply obey. He'd forgotten that Saba, even while under his thrall, had always voiced decided opinions about what he wanted her to do. Now that he had released her, she'd become even more stubborn. She remained standing, staring at him like he'd lost his mind.

"It is a simple thing," he said, pulling out a chair for her.

Saba heaved a sigh, uncrossed her arms and conceded to sit in the chair. She waited while he sat down next to her, her face set in a determined frown.

Malcolm chose his words carefully. "When a black dragon has existed for three thousand years, he is compelled to find a mate," he began. "While others of dragonkind mate whenever they like, black dragons take only one mate, and if the female does not kill him, they remain a pair."

"I've never heard this," Saba said, watching him in suspicion.

"Not much is known about black dragons. We are reticent to impart knowledge of ourselves."

"You don't say." She gazed at him with coffee-dark eyes, digesting his story. "Are you telling mc that as a dragon, you've never mated? Ever?"

He shook his head. "We do not need to until we are ready. Black dragons do not experience the emotion of lust."

"Good Goddess, Malcolm, are you telling me you're a virgin?"

He met her astonished stare. "As a dragon, yes. When I became a human male I discovered lust, and I discovered that humans, particularly males, think of very little besides mating. Perhaps because humans live short lives and bear few young, while dragons may produce as many as thirty to forty offspring with only one coupling."

"And now you're feeling the urge to produce little dragons?"

"Essentially." He kept to himself the other reason for this urge, for now.

"Oh." Saba's eyes flickered, and she looked away. "I never thought when the day started I'd end it with a treatise on dragon-mating."

"Will you do the locator spell?"

She looked up at him, her thoughts beyond his reach. "And if I find this lady dragon for you, you'll return to Dragonspace to raise your dragon kiddies?"

"The female raises the young, but yes, I will return there. First, however, I will make certain that the white dragon cannot harm you."

He watched the swallow that moved her slim throat. He'd not told the whole truth when he said black dragons did not lust—he'd never felt lust as a dragon until he'd met her. But after he'd returned to Dragonspace last year, things had been different. Whenever he sat on the ledge outside the dragon archive, his mathematical brain working calculations at lightning speed, thoughts of her would intrude.

He'd remember her eyes, the taste of her mouth, the beautiful scent of her. The sound of her voice when she came for him, the taste of her honey. He'd caught himself more than once searching for a way to make a door for himself to dive through and have her again.

But dragons needed a witch—or someone like Lisa—to let them through to the human world, and he trusted no witches but Saba. And so he remained in Dragonspace, troubled, distracted and puzzled by his longings.

When Saba called him to this side of the door with the dragon's tears, his human body knew exactly what it craved—her under him, his lips on hers, her hands tracing his hips as he slid into her. Now, alone in this apartment with her next to him he could no longer keep the wanting at bay. He leaned down and licked the shell of her ear.

"Stop that," she said softly, but she didn't pull away.

He was already hard inside his jeans. He recalled her hand closing around him when they'd kissed before leaving tonight, the first time he'd let her touch him. It had been a heady experience that stoked his wanting rather than sated him. He would have her, no matter what it took, even if his only ally was a small Chinese woman with wise eyes.

"Do the spell," he whispered, then sat up again.

The flush on her cheekbones betrayed that she was anything but calm. Saba's fingers shook as she drew the map to her.

"This is Dragonspace?" she asked.

"Yes. I have traveled every corner of it and made the map myself."

"It's so detailed." Saba examined the precise lines and markings depicting the dragon kingdoms of north, south, east and west, the realms of each type of dragon, the mountain ranges, the deserts, and the silver oceans.

"I have some skill at drawing," he said without false modesty.

Saba looked at his hands. "But you'd have dragon claws when you're in Dragonspace. Don't tell me you put the pencil in your teeth. Or held it with your tail."

"I etched it onto a sheet of copper with my mind. This is a print pulled from it. My assistant does that."

"Assistant?"

"His name is Metz. He is irritating, but we get along."

"I'll bet." Her gaze returned to the exquisitely detailed map. "This is amazing."

"If the map gets marred, Metz can pull another one. The etching is stored in the dragon archive. There." He rested his finger in the middle of the map, where a mountain range was honeycombed with caves, the maze of them intricate and vast.

"Dragons keep archives?" she asked.

"Black dragons do. We believe that is why black dragons live so long, to record and protect all the writings we find and catalog."

She looked interested. "And the dragons of other colors, the white dragons and the goldens, don't do this?"

"No. Black dragon intellects are far superior, even among the great dragons."

The lines about her mouth softened. "And you're not conceited about it or anything."

"It is not boasting," Malcolm replied. "It is a statement of fact."

"If you say so." Saba's eyes glinted at the humor she found in his remarks, although, as usual, she refused to explain. "Well, let's get on with it. Let's find your female so you can go have dragon sex with her."

Malcolm touched her hand. "Not just sex. A mate for life."

"If she doesn't kill you first."

"Exactly."

She studied him a moment, eyes unreadable, but he felt her closing off to him. She withdrew her hand. "All right. Let me prepare."

Preparation consisted of Saba setting candles at the four corners of the map, then encircling them with salt and laying quartz crystals at the base of each candle.

This setup was a little different from the one she'd done last year when they'd tried to locate an elusive witch, but he realized she'd progressed in her magical studies, learning different techniques and working with more confidence. Pride warmed his heart as he thought how far she'd come, his witch who'd first looked upon him in fear. He'd told her she would grow, and she had.

Saba dimmed the lights and resumed her seat, candlelight throwing a golden glow over the map and her pointed silver pendulum on its chain. She scattered salt over the map and dangled the pendulum so that it just touched the salt.

"Put your hands over mine," she said.

Malcolm closed his hands around her smaller ones, liking the feel of her fingers under his.

"Here we go," she said tightly.

Saba chanted a rhyme asking the elements to guide her hand and show her the location of Malcolm's mate. Slowly the pendulum moved through the salt, tracing faint patterns, but resting on no one area. The pendulum traveled north, then south, then east, then west, slowly encompassing the entire map that meant Dragonspace.

For half an hour, Saba held up the pendulum until her arms trembled with strain. Malcolm supported her hands with his as the pendulum searched. Then, just as Malcolm was about to tell her to stop, the pendulum swung in a sharp arc and hit Saba on the chin.

She jumped, breaking the spell.

"What was that?" she demanded.

Malcolm hid his smile, keeping to the plan he and Ming Ue had formulated. "Perhaps it could not find her in Dragonspace."

Saba lifted her brows. "Where else would a dragon be? Or do you mean she's here, in human form?"

Malcolm could not help but be satisfied at the glint of jealousy in Saba's eyes. Malcolm as a dragon with another dragon she could tolerate, but Malcolm with another *woman* . . . "Perhaps the pendulum was trying to point to the window, to San Francisco and the human world."

Saba gave a curt nod. "Could be. Let me get another map."

She rose and moved to a cabinet across the room, and Malcolm enjoyed watching her jeans-clad backside as she bent to rummage in it. He also liked watching her hips unconsciously sway as she returned, maps in hand, and unrolled one of San Francisco across the table.

Saba took her seat beside him and recreated the procedure, spreading the film of salt, having him hold the pendulum with her, and saying her chant, this time with a small edge of impatience in her voice. The pendulum ran over the San Francisco map as it had that of Dragonspace, then over a map of California, and then over a map of the United States. Each time, the pendulum ended with its little flip to tap Saba, twice on the chin, once on the nose.

The final time, she threw down the pendulum in disgust. "It's defective. It must be."

"I do not think so." Malcolm's voice warmed as he lifted the pendulum and dangled it against her cheek.

Her mouth tightened. "What are you talking about? It's obvious that either the pendulum needs to be cleansed and reconsecrated, or that I can't find your mate for you."

"You found her." Malcolm laid down the pendulum. "I knew it was so, but I wanted you to do a spell so you would believe it."

She stared in astonishment, making him smile. "It's you, Saba." He touched the soft pad of her parted lips. "My witch."

7

Saba gaped in shock at Malcolm, who sat calmly, satisfaction in his eyes.

"But I'm not a dragon," she croaked.

His expression was warm. "I should have been able to easily forget about you when I returned home, but I could not. No matter how often I told myself you meant nothing to me, still the memories of you cut through everything I did. Black dragons spend much time thinking, years if necessary, but I'd find myself calling an image of you to my mind, wondering what you were doing, and speculating on why I missed you."

"You missed me?"

"I did." He drew his thumb across her lower lip. "My thoughts were ever disturbed by longings for you. It concerned me. But if you are to be my mate, then the longings make sense. Once we are together, no doubt I will be able to return to my mathematics untroubled."

Saba sat still while conflicting emotions raced through her mind. The first was mirth—he couldn't be serious about magic choosing her as a mate, it was like something out of a romance novel. The second was a deep, heartfelt relief that he hadn't forgotten her. The third was amazement, and the fourth was anger.

"Malcolm." She took his hand and deliberately moved it from her. "You're saying you want me to be your mate in order to relieve your tension? So you can go back to Dragonspace, this time without troubling thoughts of me?"

He frowned. "That is not what I meant."

Saba rose, scattering salt, and the pendulum rolled across the table. "Forget it."

Malcolm got to his feet and swiftly blocked her exit from the room, six and a half feet of solid male, his eyes unyielding as ever, his jaw set in a stubborn line. "What should I forget?"

She glared. "Here's an interesting thing, Malcolm. After you left, I did much research on dragons. Nowhere did I come across a reference to black dragons needing to find their true mates. No wonder the pendulum couldn't locate one."

"Then why did it keep pointing to you?"

"Because you had your hands on it and swung it at me. You're making this up."

"I need you, Saba."

The timbre of his voice betrayed faint worry, and she paused. "Why? Other than the obvious."

The teasing, sinful light in Malcolm's eyes faded. He cupped her shoulders, his fingers points of strength, but she sensed deep uneasiness in the threads of thoughts that touched her even if he didn't try to tangle her in them.

"Malcolm?"

He remained silent for a long time while outside several cars went past in a muffled hurry, and the couple who lived downstairs came home, having a playful argument about who would feed their demanding cat. Malcolm stood still, the muscles in his arms stiff and strained, his eyes fixed on her.

"I need your help, Saba," he said after a long time. "I am not lying about that."

The way he spoke troubled her. "My help with what?"

"I'm not quite certain. But I am . . . fading."

Saba ran her hands up his arms, over hard muscles beneath satin skin. "You feel solid to me."

"My magic, my power, my strength. All fading. I have no idea why."

"Illness?" She touched his forehead, which felt warm, but then, Malcolm always felt warmer than a normal human.

"No. Nor is it natural age—black dragons usually live for six thousand years, and I've just reached half that."

"You think you've been spelled?"

"A spell or a curse, I have no idea. I can find nothing. It began a few of your weeks ago, and then you called me to you. I am trying to decide if the incidents are connected."

She let her hands drop. "And you think I can figure it out? I'm still learning the craft. If you don't know what kind of spell is harming you, I doubt I will be able to discover it."

"I have told you many times how powerful you are. I will guide you and you will find the truth." He stepped closer to her, hands coming around to skim her waist.

"This is really why you came to find me?" she asked. "Not this true mate business?"

He shook his head. "When I began to fade, I knew I would need to mate. Dragons must, before they die, it is one of our most basic urges. I thought that was why I couldn't forget you, why I needed to be with you, because of my need to mate soon. I consulted with Ming Ue, and we decided the best way to convince you was to make you believe magic had chosen you for me."

He dipped his head toward her, and she knew he wanted to kiss her. She drew back, exasperated. "You know, Malcolm, you could just *ask*."

He looked puzzled. "Ask for your consent to mate?"

"Ask for my help. Let's get back to this fading for a moment. Why do you think so? That it's not natural aging for a dragon? You are solitary creatures, you don't exactly have a lot of examples around you."

He didn't look convinced. "I read . . . everything. The dragon archive contains many books, composed by dragons and humans, telling of the world when dragons and humans intermingled, before humans stopped believing in legends. I have read every book written by black dragons, and accounts of dragon lives, and none of them mention this."

"You haven't taken into account the arrogance of dragons," she pointed out. "They might not want to admit the slowdown of middle age."

"Dragons are not worried about aging," he contradicted. "Humans believe that once they have lived thirty or so years they should be ashamed of their age. Dragons know that each year makes a dragon that much more learned, that much stronger and more magical. They describe their process of aging quite clearly, which is how I know this is not normal."

"Oh." She inclined her head in acknowledgment of her ignorance. "Ergo, you concluded it is a spell."

"Something magical, yes."

"Why you, though? What is it about you that would make someone want to cast a spell on you, to weaken you?"

He still stood very close to her, although he wasn't touching her at the moment, confident she'd let him into her personal space. And he was right. He was the only one who could stand this close to her without her taking an instinctive step backward. No matter how much she argued with him or expressed irritation at him, there was always this closeness between them. The two of them in a tight space felt comfortable and natural.

"I have narrowed it to three possibilities," he was saying. "First, I lived a long time in the human world and perhaps learned something here that someone wants me not to have learned. Second, I am the keeper of the dragon archive, guardian of a vast cavern of knowledge. I am its protector, although I admit few dragons seem interested in knowledge any longer. Third, I met you."

"Me? What do I have to do with anything?"

"You are a powerful witch. Perhaps whoever is spelling me wants you for himself."

"I am also a powerful database programmer, but no one is spelling my boss so I'll go work for someone else."

The tiny space between them seemed to have lessened even further. "Perhaps whoever it is knows that together, we would be a formidable team," he said. "What they didn't predict was that the spell only urged me to come back to you."

His hands on her shoulders were warm and strong, and she no longer wanted to twist away.

"You mean whoever wants us apart has only succeeded in driving us together? Seems far-fetched."

"Yet, I believe it is true. And I am glad."

She watched him a moment, saw the warmth grow in his eyes. He was worried, yes, but Malcolm would use the situation to his full advantage.

"You could have just told me, you know," she said, voice softening. "You didn't have to go hole-in-corner with Ming Ue and come up with the story about finding your true mate."

A sinful smile flickered across his face. "But my way was more enjoyable. I did not know the meaning of *play* before I met you."

She tried a smile. "That's what those people at the party tonight were trying to do."

"No." He stepped closer, hand cupping her cheek. "They were desperately seeking relief from boredom, release from the tedium of their lives. They reach for the extreme because they cannot be fulfilled by the ordinary."

"And this is ordinary?"

His smiled turned feral. "I would not say that. Those people *could* be fulfilled by simple joys, but they seek them in the wrong places."

"Are you looking in the right place?" she asked lightly.

"I do not know," he admitted. "But whenever you are involved, I always enjoy the search."

He caressed her cheek with his thumb, his body warmth making her own temperature rise. Malcolm never did anything by halves. He wanted her body and he would have it. He wanted her help, and he would have it.

I should resist more, she thought desperately. *I should resist a lot more. Any other man would be on the wrong side of a binding spell by now, and here I stand, letting him touch me, just like I belong to him and have all along.*

He began to unlace her top, fingers sure. "When I was in Dragonspace, I did much research."

She closed her eyes as he drew his fingers over the tops of her breasts, his touch raising goose bumps. "On mathematics and probability?"

"On pleasure," he answered. "As I told you there are myriad texts in my archive describing pleasure. I have read them all."

Saba imagined him sitting in his dragon coldness, absorbing book after book on sexual technique. *The Kama Sutra,* *The Perfumed Garden,* the *Joy of Sex.* Reading with his dragon eyes narrowed, holding the book between the tips of his claws as he perused it.

"So you learned a lot of theory, did you?" she asked, voice strained.

"I learned many things I wish to do to you and with you. I wish to pleasure you, as I did before, to thank you."

She put one hand on his chest, liking the feel of his hard muscle and the slow, steady thump of his heart. "It shouldn't be just for thanks or for payment. If that's what you're offering . . ." She willed herself to say the words. "Then I don't want it."

He tilted his head to one side, his eyes unreadable as he continued to unlace her shirt. "You do not want pleasure?"

"Not if it's for services rendered. That's not what it should be for."

He considered this. "There is much written about pleasure in exchange for other things. When I lived here in exile I observed that exchange often. In the land of your ancestors, Japan, they have geisha who give different kinds of pleasure and came to be much honored. I stayed in Edo for a time; I knew a geisha well and made her one of my own."

Saba's eyes widened. "You went out with a geisha before you met me?"

"Not *go out*, as you say now. She was helpful to me."

Knowing Malcolm, the woman could have been anything from his sexual partner to someone to play Go with on a Saturday night. Geisha didn't necessarily provide sex, but Saba would understand one wanting to make an exception for Malcolm.

"I've learned some of the arts of a geisha," she said. "*Ikebana*, calligraphy, dance. Never could get the hang of the *shamisen*, though."

He shot her a puzzled look. "Why should you play a *shamisen*? You are a database programmer."

"I was joking, Malcolm. But if you start missing the arts of the geisha too much I can always get out my ink brush and scroll."

"I would rather pleasure you instead."

Her heart beat faster. Saba supposed Malcolm had a sense of humor somewhere under all the layers of him. Or maybe his misunderstanding her was his way of teasing, of flirting. He leaned down and brushed his lips to hers, not quite a kiss, but tantalizing.

"How about if I pleasure you instead?" she whispered against the side of his mouth.

He stilled, and she wondered if once more he'd push her offer away. She stared up at him. "Are you going to tell me again that it's best if you don't allow yourself to feel anything for me?"

"That would be best," he said. His voice turned low and dark. "However, I believe it is now much too late for what is best."

Saba's eyes darkened and unlike before, she did not pull away. He expected her to, to tell him in her annoyed voice that he could go sleep by himself in the guest room.

He'd never sleep there, he knew that, because the scent of her magic permeated that room, the blue and silver feel of her imprinted on the walls and carpet and every piece of furniture. If he spent the night in the guest room he'd be hard and needy, his head spinning with erotic visions. Better to be *with* her and relieve the tension.

But she didn't tell him to go away. She looked up at him, her shirt unlaced to show the black edges of her bra, her fingers resting lightly on his chest.

"I want to undress you," she said, her voice soft but with an edge of hesitancy. "Will you let me?"

His pulse raced, but he dipped his head formally. "I would be honored."

"Oh, good." She fingered the edges of his shirt. "Will you sit down, please?"

He seated himself on the dining room chair, wondering what she would do. During his exile in human form, he'd had sex with women, responding to his male body's urges, but never had it been so important to him, never had he anticipated the touch of a woman the way he waited for Saba's.

He knew that after this, there would be no going back. No sitting on mountain ledges pretending to focus on mathematical calculations, no pretending he didn't need her. He'd held back before, knowing that having her would make leaving more difficult. Now it would be impossible, and at the moment he had a hard time caring.

She started with his boots. She tugged each one off, setting them gently next to him before peeling off his socks. She sat on her heels and began to rub his feet, taking her time, fingers kneading and massaging his heels, the balls of his feet, the arches. Her fingers moved in delightful patterns, squeezing and rubbing until his skin warmed and tingled. He'd never thought about foot-rubbing in terms of sex, but now he realized how very good it felt.

She moved next to his T-shirt, skimming it off over his head. She'd seen him naked before, including last evening in the train, but her gaze roved his torso in a flattering way, taking in every plane. She lightly traced the tattoo on his arm, then feathered her hands across his collarbone and around his pectorals, letting his wiry black hair curl around her fingers.

She found his flat nipples and stirred them to life, rendering them hot, hard little points. She skimmed her palms to his abdomen, dipping into his navel, and down his pelvis to stop at his waistband.

Malcolm let her play without touching her, but his heart felt tight, and blood pounded in his veins. Her dark hair shone in the lamplight as she bent her head over his lap, fingers unfastening his belt, then his fly. When she slowly lowered his zipper, he moved her aside and stood up to slide the pants down his legs himself, too impatient to wait. His briefs followed.

He liked how Saba's eyes widened at the sight of his nude body, though he told himself again that she'd seen him before. She'd even slept beside him the time he'd healed her, skin to skin. She placed her hands on his hips, and his hardness rose to her.

"Sit down again," she said.

He obliged, the polished walnut of the chair cool on his backside. She started at his throat and ran her fingers all the way down his body, leaving a trail of fire. She massaged his thighs, and he spread them to accommodate her.

He saw the flush on the curve of her cheek as she contemplated his erection. His hands had become very shaky for some reason.

He bit back a groan when she sank to her knees and grasped the base of him. Her face set in intense concentration, she skimmed her touch over it, exploring the flange, shaft, and tight balls at its base. Malcolm held his breath, hardly wanting to move and break the moment as she stroked and played with him, driving up his body temperature every second.

He lifted his hips as she continued to play, his backside nearly coming off the chair when she leaned over and kissed his tip.

"Saba."

She grinned up at him. "Malcolm."

She wanted him as much as he did her. He scented it on her, the desire of a woman for a man. He knew she'd be wet if he touched her between her legs and that knowledge made him harder and heavier.

Saba swiped her tongue once around his flange in a teasing circle, and he could take it no more. Grabbing her by the arms, he hauled her up and onto his lap.

"Get . . . out . . . of . . . these," he murmured as he pushed at the shirt and bra.

She snapped open the bra's catches and helped him toss it and her shirt off over her head. His fingers shook as he unfastened her jeans, then he peeled the pants and underwear down her legs for her.

There, she was as bare as he was, straddling his lap so he could get to her. He slid his hands between her thighs and discovered that yes, she was as wet as he imagined her to be.

Her opening pressed him and it was time, way past time, to finish this. He grasped her hips and lifted her slightly then slid her straight onto his stem.

And his world changed. Colors he hadn't known existed suddenly slid through his mind along with the heady fragrance of her. And the feel of her clenching him like a fist, sweet and hot and tight. He'd never known it would be this wonderful, or else he never ever could have walked away from her. What was the magic of Dragonspace to *this*?

He gathered her into his arms and saw her watching him, her eyes half-closed, a shy smile on her face. Shy? But yes, she blushed even while she moved her hips, riding him and making him feel this good.

"My witch," he tried to say, but the words were incoherent.

He knew he'd lived three thousand years for the moment of being with her, of holding Saba on his lap, her breasts tight against his chest, and filling her.

Filling her up, hard. His fingers bit into her hips as he

rocked with her, sweat dripping between their bodies sealed so close together. Was this love or lust, or was it best when love and lust were all mixed up?

My mate, my witch, my love. Ride her, stroke her, have her. *Mine.*

She made little noises in her throat, her eyes closing as they made love to each other. He felt her lips on his neck, his shoulder, little nibbles of her teeth in his flesh. He craned his neck to one side so she could bite and lick as much as she pleased. Her nails indented his flesh, and his own hands roamed up and down her back.

"Malcolm," she whispered. She held his face between her hands, still rocking in the rhythm neither of them could stop, and kissed him. She kneaded his bottom lip between her teeth, sucking it into her mouth. All the while she watched him with heavy eyes, feeling deeply what he did to her.

He knew he'd been right not to let her touch him all those months ago, not to take their relationship this far. He'd never have been able to leave her knowing how beautiful she felt. He would have stayed here, in this apartment, having her night after night after night. Returning to Dragonspace had to be the stupidest decision he'd made in his life.

As Malcolm and Saba began to move faster and faster, his thoughts became incoherent, and Malcolm's thoughts never became incoherent. He felt the silver strands he'd woven around her tonight for protection wrap them both, pressing the two even closer together.

Saba's breath came fast, her eyes closed now. She hung onto Malcolm as though she couldn't even think to caress him. "That's it, my Saba," he murmured. "Goddess, you feel so damn good."

Saba gasped and her eyes flew open. "No," she moaned. "Not yet." Her dark eyes held anguish, then her walls pulsed and squeezed around him, slick and hot, her hips grinding her all the way onto him.

Malcolm tried to hold on as long as he could, tightening and tightening, until all thought scattered and his control broke. He came hard up into her, his seed joining with her slick honey. Whatever words came out of his mouth, he had no idea; Malcolm the black dragon, always intellectual and precise, couldn't string two words together. Intellect was gone and emotion took over, emotion that made him want to stay inside her forever.

It seemed like a long time later that his coherence came back, and he found her head on his shoulder, her body damp, her breathing hard.

She raised her head and gave him a tired smile from under mussed hair. "I could almost say that was worth the wait," she murmured. "Except I really hated the wait."

Malcolm smoothed her bangs back from her forehead. "You wanted it that much?" He hardly recognized his own voice, it croaked and rasped like a file on metal.

"I wanted you."

He stared at her in slight surprise. He'd assumed her desire was physical, a need to sate herself, not a hunger for the man that was Malcolm. But she regarded him with her half smile, the one of a woman satisfied with herself. She'd made him fall for her, and she was pleased about that.

Malcolm growled low in his throat. "I won't let you get away with that."

Before she could say, "Get away with what?" he had her off the chair and swept up into his arms. The chair slammed over backwards and skidded across the floor in his ferocity.

He held her tight against him and strode swiftly from the room to her bed—*their* bed—and she cuddled against his chest and smiled her damn smile all the way.

Saba awoke to her alarm beeping an admonition. With a heavy hand she shut it off and rolled over, not eager to face the gray light of a new day. She rammed right into the hard body of Malcolm, who lay face-down like a fallen god next to her, sheets tangled around his waist, the rest of his bronzed body exposed to the early morning sun.

He slept deeply, head pillowed on a bent arm, hair in tangles from the lovemaking they'd finished up with in the bed. Even relaxed, his muscles were honed and taut, skin like bronze poured over a perfect form. His hips nipped in to a tight waist, below which his backside rose in a small mound, the skin the same color as the rest of his body. No tan lines for Malcolm.

A beautiful man who'd sprung back into her life and was now tearing down the walls around her heart. When she was finished helping him this time, would he go again, happy to be released once more? Would he sit in his cave or wherever dragons sat, forgetting about the half-Japanese witch who ate her heart out over him?

Saba sighed. No telling, with Malcolm. She brushed her fingers over the warmth of his skin, then she made herself slide out of bed and hit the shower. The hot water pouring over her body opened her eyes and loosened the stiff muscles that served as another reminder of what she and Malcolm had done last night.

Not only had he made love to her in the dining room, deeper and more satisfying than anything she'd experienced in her life, he'd rushed with her into the bedroom, thrown her to the bed, and sexed her even more furiously, a wild light in his eyes. The more she laughed and caressed him, the wilder he got, until he'd taken her to screaming climax.

She blushed, knowing the neighbors *must* have heard them. She'd tried to stuff a pillow into her mouth to muffle her cries, but she couldn't quite get a hold of one, not with Malcolm growling and sliding in and out of her, pinning her to the bed.

"The people at that party," he'd said to her, his voice grating. "They don't understand what sex truly is."

"I think I'm figuring it out," Saba had replied, or tried to. What she mostly did was scream, and say, "Malcolm, don't stop!"

She blushed again.

The shower door slid smoothly open and Malcolm

stepped in. Without speaking, he pinned her shoulders to the
cool tile and pressed his body over hers, his erection sliding
between her legs. He was already rigid and raw, responding
to the pheromones that must be pouring from her body.

"No," she half-whispered, half-moaned. "I have to go to
work."

"I have need of you, today," he said. "You will come
with me."

I dragon, you minion.

"I need my job. I like my job. And tonight I'm going to
the Japan center for tea ceremony class. I'm going to perform it during the Cherry Blossom Festival, and I definitely need the practice."

The shower spray wet his hair and slid in droplets down
his face. "I called your employer. He is one of mine, as you
know, and he agreed to let me have you for the day."

She drew back, but had nowhere to go but the cold wall
behind her. "Oh, did he?"

"He understands. And we will be finished in time for
you to practice this tea ceremony. I would like to see you
do it."

She heaved an exasperated sigh. She had absolutely no
intention of letting Malcolm take over her life again, but
her body still thrummed with lovemaking, craving his
touch. She leaned into him, closing her eyes as his palms
roved down her arms and across her back to cup her buttocks. He lifted her toward him, covering her mouth in a
long, possessive kiss.

Her back pressed into the tile so hard she knew the pattern would imprint there. Malcolm opened her thighs and
slid her legs around him, at the same time he pressed his
ready arousal up into her. He didn't even need to get her
warm and open for him; he entered her without resistance,
and she could only rock her head back and love the blunt
firmness of his sex pressing her open.

"Malcolm," she murmured. She rocked her hips against
his as much as the tight quarters allowed her to, squeezing
him. The shower pounded on his back, fine spray landing

on her face, which he licked from her skin as he kissed her.

"My witch." His eyes were open, his gaze upon her, no looking away or retreating into ecstasy.

He was so controlled, deciding she'd stay home from work with him, deciding when and where they'd make love with the same mathematical precision he used to navigate the streets of San Francisco or find people to do his bidding. Last night he'd finally let her touch him and consummate what they had, but still he was pleasuring her, calculating every move to have her come apart in his hands.

"Damn you," she whispered, and he smiled faintly, as though knowing her thoughts.

Wave after wave of orgasm rolled over her, and she stopped caring that he controlled every nuance of her life. If he deliberately wanted to make her feel this way, who was she to argue?

At last he showed emotion when he came, the lines around his eyes tightening and a single raw sound emitting from his throat. Then he was kissing her and licking her skin, the scent of the lovemaking overlaying that of the shower and soap.

Malcolm slid her wet body off his and turned her around to deposit her on the rug outside the shower. While he remained under the spray, soaking wet, he grabbed a large white towel and wrapped it around her. Holding the ends, he kept her in place while he deliberately and thoroughly kissed her.

When he finally drew away, she stood a moment taking in his delectable body. He was wet from head to foot, hair slicked back from his face, the black hair on his body plastered to his chest, legs, and forearms. Only the hair at his base stood up in tight curls, his erection thick and dark, still not relaxed from their sexing.

One sinewy hand rested on the shower door, ready to close it, but his gaze roved her own body in a gratifying way. "My witch," he said softly.

Saba flicked a wisp of wet hair from her eyes and smiled at him. "My gorgeous dragon."

He gave her another once-over, then took a step back, as though making himself focus on something else. "Dress yourself, and then we'll go."

"Go where?"

But Malcolm was closing the door, the hiss of the shower door cutting off her words. He cranked up the water, and steam rolled over the room to coat the windows and the mirror with thick condensation.

Suppressing a sigh, Saba left the bathroom on shaky legs and opened her closet's louvered door to rummage for clothes.

"I can't lie," she said out loud to herself. "This is much better than getting ready to go to work."

8

Typical of Malcolm, he wouldn't tell Saba where they were going, only led her to the bus stop then got them on board. The bus headed west toward the Presidio. He rode in silence, eyes flickering as he took in the city in which he'd spent a number of his exile years.

"I remember the great earthquake in 1906," he murmured to her. "It is interesting to observe the changes to the city since then."

"I'll bet," Saba replied.

He did not elaborate in front of all the other passengers, thank the Goddess. When the bus reached Arguelo Boulevard, Malcolm signaled for a stop and led Saba off. As the bus lumbered away, Saba gave him a puzzled look. "We're near Lisa and Caleb's place. Is that where we're going?"

"For now."

Taking her hand, he led her along Arguelo toward California Street, climbing stairs to the door of the Edwardian row house where Lisa had the top-floor apartment, inherited from her Chinese grandmother.

Malcolm drew back uneasily even before they reached

the door, and Saba had to snake her arm around him and push the bell.

"The mark of the golden dragon," he explained, "is deeply embedded here."

"The dragon territory thing?" Saba had learned last summer that two dragons did not like to be anywhere near each other, and territory violations could result in life-and-death battles. A dragon did not lightly tread in another's space.

"As you say, we have a *thing*. I'd not have come here at all if I didn't need to speak again to Lisa."

"You could have invited her out to breakfast."

"I did not want our conversation to be overheard, and I doubt the golden would let her go."

Saba pressed the smooth doorbell again. "In any case, she's much more likely to be able to help you than me."

"I asked her, when she granted me entrance to this world, what the spell was." Malcolm looked impatiently at the door. "She did not know."

Saba's eyes widened. "Good Goddess, if *Lisa* didn't know, how do you expect me to find out?"

Malcolm was saved from answering by Caleb's voice booming through the intercom. "Who visits here?"

Saba leaned to face the speaker. "It's Saba. I hope it's not too early."

"It is never too early for you, Saba." Caleb sounded delighted, then his voice lowered to a growl. "Malcolm is with you, isn't he? I can smell him from here."

"I'd not come were it not important," Malcolm said. "Believe me," he added under his breath.

"And I'd not let you in, did not Lisa tell me to," Caleb retorted. "*Saba* is always welcome."

"Just open the door," Malcolm rumbled.

The door buzzed and the lock clicked. Malcolm pushed it open and preceded Saba into the house. Beyond the foyer an ornate staircase curved around a lift that waited silently on the second floor. Malcolm was too impatient to wait for it, and so he took the stairs two at a time, with Saba following.

As they reached the top of the last flight, Caleb threw

open a door and caught Saba in a crushing hug. "Saba, I am pleased to see you," he announced to the building.

Caleb, a golden dragon when in dragon form, was a warrior whose professed purpose in life was to fight and hoard treasure. Dragons maintained that they sought jewels and precious metals only in order to protect them. Jewels were live things cut out of rock by unscrupulous miners; dragons simply provided the orphaned stones a place that reminded them of their former homes.

As a human Caleb was a tall, strong man, very much like Malcolm in build, with a mane of unruly golden hair and large blue eyes. The irises of his eyes were wider than a human's, filling them with deep azure.

Caleb had an earthy sense of humor, loved television and pizza, and protected and adored Lisa his wife with unrivaled loyalty. He liked to ham up the part of warrior barbarian and was ruthlessly efficient with a sword, but Saba had seen his softer side. He used his magic to bring luck to all he came into contact with, rescued puppies, kittens and frightened children, and treated Lisa with a tenderness that broke Saba's heart.

Right now Caleb's warrior strength squeezed the wind out of Saba in a bear hug, then he released her and ushered her inside. Malcolm just had time to follow them into the apartment before Caleb banged the door closed.

"Lisa is in bed," Caleb said. "Would you like some orange juice?"

Saba flushed. "I told you it was too early. You should have said she was still asleep."

Caleb grinned, eyes sparkling. "I said she was in bed. I did not say asleep."

"Oh." Saba's flush deepened and she moved toward the kitchen. She would have expressed amusement if she hadn't been conscious of the night of intense sex with Malcolm, not to mention this morning in the shower. She had no business teasing him.

"If you want coffee, you will have to wait for Lisa," Caleb called after her. "I can only pour orange juice."

"That's all right. I'll go sit on the balcony." Saba made her way through the kitchen to the balcony door, intending to give Lisa the privacy to emerge from her bedroom without embarrassment. She tried to signal Malcolm to do the same, but the black dragon remained behind, looking around the apartment like a wolf who didn't like that another wolf lingered nearby.

Saba loved Lisa's apartment. Ever since their adventures last summer Saba had been a frequent guest here. Li Na, Lisa's grandmother, had decorated the apartment in shades of red, a lucky color, and punctuated it with antiques brought over from China. There was always a serene hush about the place that was neither dull nor too quiet, more like the peaceful sound of a quiet stream, the air tinkling from the wind chimes in the corner.

Saba stepped alone onto the balcony, drinking in the crisp, clear air and enjoying the view across rooftops to the green trees of the Presidio, the historic army post that was now a park. Saba thought of this balcony as an aerie, a safe place of contemplation both protected and private. Lisa's grandmother and Lisa herself had worked to make the entire apartment a restful haven.

She could also sense the woven strands of Lisa's and Caleb's magic over the entire apartment and even out onto the balcony. She loved feeling their combined magic, but she knew it must be driving Malcolm crazy.

The door opened behind her. She sensed without turning that it was Malcolm even before his strong arms came around her.

"I always feel protected here," Saba said.

His lips warmed her hair. "You do not feel protected in our apartment?"

Our apartment? "Of course I do. I know I'm safe there. But here, I'm at peace."

"At peace. I see."

She couldn't explain that she felt much safety but no restfulness in their—in *her* apartment. Too much of Malcolm was imprinted on it, she supposed. Malcolm meant heady excitement, worry, and exasperation, not peace. Never peace.

"Why are we here?" she asked.

"I need to show you something."

She didn't get the chance to ask what. The wind chimes inside the apartment jingled and a faint music preceded the presence that was Lisa Singleton.

As always, Saba's witch-sight perceived the shimmering magical field that surrounded Lisa, although Lisa herself seemed unaware of it. Her silver dragon aura was multihued, iridescent colors that wove around her body in a loving dance. She was also eight months pregnant, her abdomen distended, her face round, fingers puffy, but her smile was radiant as ever.

Lisa had dark red hair, courtesy of her Scottish father, and dark brown eyes from her Chinese heritage. A white streak she'd inherited from her grandmother wove through the auburn of her hair. She wrapped Saba in her arms, her hug holding strength and joy.

"It is so good to see you, Saba. Everything's all right, isn't it?" She shot Malcolm a look that told him everything had better be all right.

"I have done Saba no harm," Malcolm answered. "That is not my intention."

"When you demanded to come through two nights ago, you were in a big hurry to see her."

Malcolm inclined his head. "Because of the white dragon, who is proving to be as dangerous as I suspected."

Lisa released Saba, but held her in the protective circle of her arm. "Do you know why the white dragon is here? Or what he wants?"

"Not yet."

"It's a white dragon," Caleb said behind his wife. "He wants death and destruction. That's all they ever want."

"I am not so certain," Malcolm mused. "If that were true, he would have acted by now. He's killed one witch and tried to take Saba. He has something in mind, and he obviously needs a witch to help him. The question now is, who?"

"You mean, *which witch*?" Caleb put in.

Malcolm ignored him. "He'll need someone strong, but one who is not strong enough to fight him off. He made a mistake underestimating my Saba."

Malcolm's endearment wove around Saba and warmed her. "I had to scream for help, remember?" she pointed out. "I had to use the dragon's tears."

"But you successfully avoided his mark," Malcolm said. "Only a very strong witch could do that. He will look for one who cannot avoid his mark but who can work powerful magic nonetheless." He turned to Lisa. "I need you to open the way to Dragonspace for me."

"Again?" Caleb frowned. "Say please."

Malcolm shot him an annoyed look. "Please."

"Why?" Lisa asked.

"I need to find out more about this white dragon, and that answer lies in Dragonspace. Besides which, I need to show Saba something."

Saba started. "You want me to go to Dragonspace with you?"

"You are a witch, you may travel to Dragonspace if you please, and you have gone there before."

"In a limited capacity, when I was roped into keeping an eye on Caleb last year."

"Even so." Malcolm turned away, finished with the argument.

He liked to do that, make a statement that sounded supremely logical and then stop talking. If a person wanted to make a point with him, he forced them to run behind and flag him down.

Malcolm had already entered the living room and started stripping off his clothes by the time the other three caught up to him, as though everything had been decided. Folding jeans and shirt carefully on the end of Lisa's sofa he flexed his arms and stretched them over his head, loosening his beautiful body.

Lisa, used to seeing naked dragons come and go, looked

at him without blush or interest. "How long are you likely to be?" she asked.

"Give us twenty-four hours," Malcolm said. "That should be enough time for me to find out about this dragon and what he's likely to do."

Lisa nodded silently, and he walked to the spare bedroom door, behind which lay a gateway to Dragonspace. Most of the time the door simply opened into Lisa's spare bedroom, unless she spread her silver dragon power over it to create a portal.

"Ready?" she asked him.

Malcolm held out his hand for Saba. When she came to him, he gathered her against him, folding both arms around her.

"Ready," he said.

Lisa opened the door. She neither chanted nor gestured or even cut a slit in the air with her finger. The gateway to Dragonspace just *was*, responding to her merest thought. A dry, dust-scented breeze stirred Saba's hair as she looked across a sharp outcropping to a black sky. They stood on a ledge, beyond which lay nothing but shadows and night.

"What do you want me to—" Saba began, then Malcolm propelled himself forward, the momentum taking them both off the edge of the cliff.

Saba screamed as they plummeted downward, then there was a huge draft and *whump* of wings, and Malcolm the dragon carried them skyward. She found herself cradled in a sleek claw against a dragon chest, Malcolm's scales like black silk.

From the ledge behind them she heard Caleb's receding voice. "Knock before you come back. We might be busy . . ."

His words cut off as the ground fell away and Malcolm was lifted on an updraft into the starry night.

* * *

Malcolm glided over Dragonspace, glorying in the wind once more caressing his wings, his body stretched out with the joy of flying. In his palm was a point of warmth, Saba, his witch, who glowed like an ember of power. He couldn't explain how much he needed her, not only to help him find out what was wrong with him but because of a deep longing in his heart to be with her.

She thought he'd teased her when he'd played the game with the pendulum last night, claiming she was his true mate. It hadn't been entirely a joke. A black dragon did need a mate, and Malcolm needed Saba. Taking her last night and this morning had been damn good, but it still hadn't relieved him. He wanted her, his entire body hummed with it, and being in dragon form didn't make the wanting cease.

His dragon memory was sharply honed, and the scent and taste and feel of her was imprinted on his mind for life. She already belonged to him whether she understood that or not.

He angled himself toward his home territory and to the huge basalt cliffs that housed the dragon archive. Most dragons didn't care about records anymore—not even the other great dragons, like goldens or frosts. Black dragons were the archivists, preserving precious history and lore from times long past. When dragons had ruled and could move freely from Dragonspace to the human world whenever they liked, they'd copied and collected all kinds of knowledge—from ancient Chinese libraries, the library in Alexandria, Sumerian archives, and much more through the ages.

After the age of "enlightenment" for humans, when dragons were consigned to legend and lost the magic to open portals by themselves, it became harder for dragons to obtain documents and books, but the black dragons managed it. They recruited human witches and other beings who could travel back and forth, sometimes using even demons, provided they were heavily controlled.

The dragon archive was a place of incredible beauty and ruthless efficiency, appreciated now only by black dragons. Every thousand years, one of their number was recruited to be guardian of the archive, and Malcolm had recently been privileged to be chosen.

Because he'd been exiled in the human world before he became guardian, he'd been able to acquire more documents and books, stockpiling them to send to the archive when he could, even though he could not enter Dragonspace himself during that time. Malcolm had haunted the archives before his exile and knew them well, and he had spent the last months getting reacquainted with them.

The cliffs loomed large, easily dwarfing seventy feet of dragon. Malcolm squeezed through a round opening high in the cliff, spread his wings, and glided down to the smooth cavern floor. He opened his claw and deposited Saba safely on the ground.

Even their difference in size and the fact that he could not mate with her in this form didn't change his wanting her. Malcolm's dragon blood, free from the concerns of humans, beat even hotter, his desire for her almost uncontrollable. The urges puzzled and troubled him, and he did not like to be puzzled.

Saba scrambled to her feet, dusting off her jeans, and peered into the darkness of the cavern. "Why are we here?" she asked. "*Where* are we?"

For answer, Malcolm called up his magic and let it spill from him into the hundreds of globes that were set floor to ceiling in the cavern. Sudden bluish white light flared from the globes and illuminated the cavern, which rose three thousand feet from its floor. Passages honeycombed out from the cavern at all angles, up, down, right, left, and all points in between, easy for creatures who relied on flying to navigate.

In niches placed around the cavern and in the thousand passages that fed into the main room, books and papers and ledgers nested, carefully preserved behind panes of crystal and diamond, sealed away from the ravages of time, dryness, dampness, temperature, and dust.

Saba looked around in wonder, her face bathed in the soft glow of the globes. "What is this place?" Her voice echoed back from the arch of rock high above.

"The dragon archives. You were curious about them."

"Good Goddess." She turned in a slow circle, head tilting to take in the passages, niches, and the lit tunnel openings high above them that glittered like stars. "How big is it?"

Malcolm considered. "It has never been measured, at least not in the terms of humans. A hundred dragons can work together here and not see each other for days. Not that many do anymore. Most of the time it's just me."

"Because you're the keeper of the archives."

"Yes." Malcolm cast his glance into a corridor at his eye level. Something felt not quite right . . .

Saba stared up at him, hands on hips. She might be small, but her aura nearly filled the cavern, the power of a great witch. "If you're the archive's keeper, and you're worried about someone spelling you, why did you leave for two days? Who looks after the place when you're gone?"

"I have an assistant. He knows how to guard the archive when I am not here."

"Really?" She looked around again. "I've never seen anything so huge. I hope you pay him well."

"Metz has been assistant here for a thousand years. He knows the archives better than anyone."

Malcolm raised his head to peer down a passage high above the floor. A thousand manuscripts lay inside, protected by magic, nothing out of place. And yet . . .

"He must be a patient man—I mean, dragon," Saba remarked at his feet.

"Metz is not a dragon," Malcolm said absently.

"What is he then? A knight in shining armor?"

Malcolm rumbled in amusement. "No."

Saba looked around with a witch's appreciation for knowledge and books. "What have you got stored here? It's amazing."

"Every written word from the dawn of dragonkind up to the latest mathematical treatise written yesterday."

"Is everything here like that?" she asked. "Mathematical treatises?"

"No." Malcolm warmed to his subject. "Dragon knowledge encompasses poetry and philosophy, history, mathematics, science. Stories from your world, like your thousand-year-old saga of Beowulf, who defeated a dragon when he was an old man. It could rest side by side with a study of the weight and mass of dark matter. Whatever a dragon writes down or knowledge he finds, a copy goes into the archives."

Saba gestured with one hand, taking in the circuit of the cavern. "Do you have a card catalog for all this?"

"A dragon remembers the exact placement of each record with precision. However, we do have a system for my assistant, who is not as quick of mind."

"The poor guy." Saba's hands were back on her hips. She gave him that look she got when trying to indicate that his words didn't make sense to her. This confused Malcolm, because his words always made sense. "You need a database and a server," she said.

"A database? But we have that."

"Really?" He felt her spark of interest. "Where?"

Malcolm pointed to a lower passage high and wide enough for a dragon's body. Globes of quartz crystal hung on the walls next to those of emerald and ruby and sapphire, light glowing white with spangles of rainbow colors.

Saba walked in wonder down this tunnel, examining the niches filled with hand-copied, illuminated manuscripts. The natural rock of the cavern glittered with quartz and, here and there, with thin seams of gold.

"It's all so beautiful," she said softly, touching a gossamer strand of gold.

"Words are treasures," Malcolm answered. "Why would we not transform their resting place into a palace?"

"I have the feeling I've seen this place before," she said. "And it's not a happy memory. But that can't be right."

"You have never been here," Malcolm said. "If you had, there would be a record of it, and I know one does not exist."

She glanced sideways at him. "You really do read everything."

"What use is all this knowledge if no one reads it?" he rumbled.

Despite the comfort he took in being here and the pleasure of showing Saba the archive, he couldn't shake the sense that something was wrong. The weight of the place seemed different, not profoundly different, but a subtle alteration that changed the quality and weight of the air.

A faint hum came from ahead, and Saba quickened her pace. "Is that it?"

"It is. But not, I think, what you are used to."

The tunnel sloped downward and ended at an opening that dropped about six feet to the room beyond. Malcolm glided in then reached up and carried Saba safely to the floor.

Sheets of crystal spread themselves across the cave, glowing globes of light glittering on its expanse. Lattices of crystal snaked up the walls, twining with gold and silver, colors dancing and alive.

"It's beautiful," Saba breathed. "What is it?"

"The card catalog, as you call it. Our database."

"Holy Goddess." Saba walked across the crystal floor, which pulsed and glowed beneath her. She reached toward a faceted ruby that protruded from a cluster of crystals, each gem humming with energy.

There was a sharp *crack* and a buzzing sound above them, and an annoyed voice shouted, "Don't touch that!"

9

Saba jumped and scrambled away as something boulder-like dropped toward her at high speed. At the last minute she saw that it was human shaped, a small creature suspended from black batlike wings.

"Metz," Malcolm rumbled. "It's all right. She is a database programmer and a witch of extraordinary talent."

Another strange *crack* sounded, and the flying thing halted a foot from Saba. It was a man, or at least a being in man shape, though he was only three feet from head to toe. But this was no beautiful fairy or Tolkienesque elf. His face was the ugliest Saba had ever seen, with a beetling brow, bulbous nose, and craggy mouth, mitigated only by black eyes that shone like pieces of polished onyx. He scowled at her as his wings slapped together, which explained the cracking noise she'd heard.

"This is Metz," Malcolm said. "My assistant."

Metz switched his glare to Malcolm. "You said nowt about bringing a guest, 'specially not a witch," he growled in an accent reminiscent of northern England. "You never know about witches."

"She wanted to see the database."

"Well, now you've seen it," Metz snapped at Saba. "So clear off."

"Lovely to meet you, too," Saba said.

"Is she one of them witches what sent you to exile?" Metz rose a few feet, wings buzzing like a wasp's. "She come to take you again?"

Malcolm lowered his head, his eyes as enigmatic as they were when he was in human form. "On the contrary, she is the witch who helped me while in exile. And she is helping me now."

Metz peered at Saba over his ugly nose. His black eyes were intelligent, and somewhere in them she caught a glimpse of the creature Malcolm trusted, but he wasn't showing his softer side to Saba.

Metz threw Malcolm a look of disgust. "Well, you know your own bloody mind, I suppose."

"Malcolm told me he might be under a curse," Saba said crisply. "I don't suppose you could stop snarling long enough to find out what it is? You must be able to reference thousands of texts here."

"Millions and millions, wench." Metz slapped his wings together, then jerked as what she said struck him. "That true? You said nowt about it to me. Not that you ever confide in me, poor hard-working sprite."

"I am *possibly* under a curse," Malcolm interrupted. "A white dragon has not tried to come here, has he?"

Metz shot five feet into the air, indignation boiling off him. "A white dragon? A frost? Not bloody likely, not in my archive."

"We have a mystery to solve," Malcolm said in his cool tones. "A white dragon sought out a witch to let him into the human world. He then killed the witch for whatever reason and tried to recruit Saba to help him, becoming violent when she refused. Several weeks ago, I began feeling the draining on me, which I dismissed until I found out that a frost dragon has been going back and forth to Dragonspace, up to something. And now something is wrong here."

Metz had hung silently during this speech, his mouth open, but he suddenly hurtled himself around in a circle, coming to rest against Malcolm's head. "There's nowt wrong here. I keep a sharp eye out, I do."

"Even you have to sleep sometimes, Metz."

"Oh, you say. If you think I'm not good enough, then you can bloody well—"

"Peace," Malcolm interrupted, more heat in his growl. "If anything has happened, I do not blame you. The archive is my responsibility. But there is something . . ."

He scanned the air, putting his head to one side as he sometimes did when studying something in the human world. A dragon mannerism, Saba realized. One that didn't disappear when he changed form.

Suddenly Malcolm opened his eyes wide, silver orbs catching the light of the crystals and throwing it back in a sweeping, outraged glow. "A book. He has stolen a book."

Saba gazed at the clusters of crystals, thought about the enormous cavern from which they'd come and the hundreds of tunnels leading off it.

"One book?" she asked. "How can you tell? This place has, Metz said, millions and millions of volumes."

"Six trillion," Malcolm corrected her.

"Even better. How can you know that *one book* has been taken without checking the entire collection? Which I'm betting would take years."

"A niche was opened and the book removed," Malcolm explained in his cool *Trust me until you catch up* voice. "The amount of air the empty niche displaced has changed the pressure in the entire archive a fraction."

Saba felt giddy. "You notice the difference in air pressure from the removal of *one book*?"

"Yes," he answered absently, and she half expected him to continue, *Don't you?*

Metz clearly didn't notice. "You must be mad, master. No one has come in here."

"Go look," Malcolm said. "Twenty-seventh level, fifth corridor. The statistical probability of a book or scroll

missing from that section is ninety-nine-point-nine-nine-
nine-nine percent certain."

"Bloody hell," Metz muttered. He slapped his wings together and hurtled himself through the opening to the main
cavern.

"I have the feeling I know which book it is," Malcolm
said after he'd gone. "This will not be good."

"I'm betting you know the statistical probability of its
being that particular book within ten decimal places."

"I do." Malcolm reached out with his claw and delicately touched a protruding blue crystal. Saba could not
see what he read on it, if anything, but his eyes narrowed to
slits. "And I am right," he said, almost under his breath.

"About what? What is the book that's missing?"

At that moment, Metz came zooming back in, his ugly
face mottled red and white, his eyes sparking black rage.
"He did it. Bloody thief got in past me. Damn his rotten-
hearted . . ." Metz trailed off into barely intelligible words.

"What is the book, Malcolm?" Saba repeated, trying to
keep her voice calm.

"*The Book of All Dragons*," Malcolm answered. "If a
dragon has stolen that . . ."

"Then you're buggered," Metz finished.

"Why?" Saba asked, losing patience.

Malcolm lowered his head to her. "Because anyone who
possesses that book will be able to gain control over dragons. If we do not stop him, he can enslave all dragons, including myself, completely, or kill them, whichever he
thinks is most expedient."

In the tower room of the mansion in Pacific Heights, lit
with witch light, the white dragon caressed the binding of
the book with long, bloodless fingers. *The Book of All
Dragons.*

The witch Saba had thought him foiled when she refused
him. The black dragon, Malcolm, thought him gone. Fools.
Whoever held this book would have mastery over them all.

He opened the book to a golden page that bore an etching of a white dragon, unfurled in all its glory. He read the name engraved on the opposite page, his own true name, revealed to anyone who found this book. Any dragon or witch that discovered his true name would have magical mastery over him, forcing him to obey all their commands, no matter how far physically they might be from him.

The power of the true name was absolute, and now that Malcolm had returned to the human world, there was danger he'd find the book and learn the white dragon's name. And so the white dragon must make certain he never would.

A frost dragon, beast of the north, clever, cunning, and hardy. White dragons did not possess the intellectual coldness of the black dragons or the warrior power of the goldens, but they did have one thing the others lacked. The overwhelming will to survive.

A tray bearing a glass bottle and an eyedropper rested at his side. The white dragon unscrewed the bottle, an acrid odor wafting from it that made his eyes water. He took up the dropper, filled it, then carefully dripped acid onto the gold that bore his name. The lines began to blur, the gold smoking and running together.

He let the page dry and harden, then he closed the book.

Across the room, the drab little witch he'd found lurking near the house held a glass of champagne, but she didn't drink. Her hand shook, her muddy eyes fixed on him in terror. She wasn't much of a witch but she had a few talents, and with his mark on her, she'd be useful.

The white dragon had the book. He had a witch.

All was ready.

He lifted his champagne glass, raised it to toast his new accomplice, and smiled.

"If the book is so dangerous, why isn't it in a vault?" Saba demanded as she hurried after Malcolm toward the main cavern.

"It *was* in a vault," Metz said, buzzing angrily behind her. "Locked behind the best magical security system in Dragonspace. In *any* space."

In the cavern, Malcolm lifted Saba in his claw and flew with Metz to a tunnel that opened high above the cavern floor. They flew upward past honeycombed archives until the passage leveled out enough for her to walk again.

As Saba looked around the relatively narrow tunnel, an eerie feeling swept through her like unbidden, unexplained panic. She stopped, her mouth dry, and Metz nearly ran into her.

"I know this place," Saba rasped.

The tunnel, lit by the magic crystal globes, ended in a blank wall about thirty feet from them. The walls glittered with gems and seams of gold like the cavern and database room below them, and niches that held books and scrolls and wax tablets pockmarked the walls. The end of the hall was empty, no passages leading right or left.

Saba knew she had never been here—logically she knew that—but the image of the passage had imprinted on her mind, and with it, terror.

"You know this place, do you?" Metz demanded, hovering. "Maybe *she* took it."

Malcolm snaked his head down to her, light shimmering on the satin-black scales of his neck. "You have never been to the dragon archives. I told you there was no record of it."

"I know that. I've never gone farther into Dragonspace than outside Lisa's apartment until today. But I've been *here*." She gazed at the walls and along the floor of the passage. "I have a very strong feeling of déjà vu, anyway. When I was here, I was scared out of my mind."

"There's nowt to be afraid of in *this* archive," Metz said in a grumpy tone. "Excepting me."

Saba ignored him. When she put her hand to the wall, she felt the huge pulse of energy of the archive, formidable, but not frightening. "I remember this corridor, and I remember darkness, very much like the darkness in the tower of that house where I did the spell with Annie."

Metz zoomed to the end of the hall, then smacked his wings together, propelling himself straight upward. Saba saw that a vertical passage led upward at a right angle from this one. As Metz disappeared up it, Malcolm eyed her thoughtfully.

"We should explore this memory you have. It might mean something."

"I'm thinking so."

Malcolm lifted her again and flew upward through the tunnel. He could move fast and with precision, despite his size, and wind rushed past Saba's face. They went up and up and up, a thousand feet and more, and emerged into another cavern, this one a little smaller than the one on the main floor.

Saba felt thick and palpable magic in this place like humid heat on her skin. The wards had been carefully laid and then overlaid, probably throughout millennia, Malcolm's magic mixing with that of many other dragons. Anyone but a dragon would find the wards difficult to pierce, and even they would have trouble.

"You see?" Metz said, flitting in front of a wide niche. "The securities are in place, all the protections, but the book is gone."

"Let me see," Saba said.

Malcolm rose until they were parallel to the niche. Only a flying creature could have come here; the walls were smooth and scamless, with no sign of boring or chipping where a human might have inserted climbing equipment.

Saba felt it then, something wrong with the wards around the niche as though a thin spidery line had been drawn through them. She touched the wall beneath the empty hole. "A powerful spell did this."

Metz puffed up. "None can do a spell in here without me knowing. 'Tain't possible, I tell ye."

Saba touched the wall again. The ward had definitely been broken, but she could sense no aura of whoever had done it, not a human witch, not a dragon, no vestiges of lingering magic. This had been broken remotely.

"Malcolm," she said, looking up at him. "I think you've been hacked."

Metz hung at her eye level, his face bright red, eyes sparkling with fury. "Hacked? What the devil does that mean? Bloody witch speaks in riddles."

"Hacked," she repeated. "Invaded by an outside force via computer. If you show me how to get into your database, I'll find out what happened."

Half an hour later, she sat on a chair Metz had grudgingly dug up for her and looked at the bewildering readout on the LED monitor Metz had also found for her. In a back cave he had a collection of human computer parts he'd collected, using them as they helped, discarding them when they didn't. The result was a jumble that could be a collection for a computer museum.

The interface was odd and cumbersome, but Saba soon learned the database's patterns. Programs, at their most basic level, were loops of simple commands, yes-or-no actions based on a series of questions. Databases asked for specific information from the user and decided answers to questions based on that input, or sorted data in increasingly complex ways based on answers to more questions.

That was on the basic level. From there databases could become amazingly complex, but even so programs mostly broke down into two actions, *Do I do this, or don't I?*

The archive computer was lovely, with magic built right into the design, the original programmers taking advantage of the natural vibrations of crystals and the various properties of the amethyst, quartz, gold, obsidian, and basalt already in the cliffs. Saba could linger for hours simply exploring the beauty of the system, but Malcolm and Metz stood behind her, both breathing down the back of her neck, Malcolm's exhalation being a little hotter.

"There it is." Saba pointed to a string of code slightly different from the elegant lines Metz and other keepers of this database had woven. It was a virus meant to do nothing but disrupt a very specific loop in a very specific place.

Metz peered at the screen, his buzzing wings perilously close to Saba's head. "How did that get there? I know nowt about it, I swear to you."

"Of course you don't," Saba said before Malcolm could speak. "It's insidious and was done with extraordinary talent. They hooked up remotely, probably using a combination of dragon and witch magic—witch magic opening a portal to this computer—with one purpose, to steal that book."

"No." Metz sounded heartbroken. He hung onto the rim of the screen as though he could make the code go away by glaring at it.

"Not your fault." Saba tried to be gentle. "Every programmer gets hacked, if only to prove how breakable the code is."

"I disagree," Malcolm rumbled. "It was Metz's responsibility. And mine."

"Malcolm." He wasn't helping.

"His responsibility because he comfortably assumed this place was safe," Malcolm continued. "Mine because I left him here alone."

"Because you thought you were the victim of a draining spell and needed to find out why," Saba argued.

"Because I wanted to make sure you were all right."

Their gazes locked, his exactly the same as when he was human. Saba's heartbeat sped, warmth flowing through her body. Her morning in the shower with him flashed through her head, his body so strong, his face set while he made love to her. She remembered the chill tiles on her back, the slick heat of his body against hers, the amazing feeling of him inside her.

She made herself turn back to the database. "It doesn't matter whose fault it was," she said with effort. "We have to deal with what happened. The virus code is elegant, and what scares me is that I recognize it."

Metz zoomed in a circle, his wings nearly knocking over the monitor. "You recognize it?" He waved a stubby finger. "She did it, she did it!"

Saba's sympathy for him evaporated. "I didn't hack your system, Metz. I told you I didn't even know the dragon archive existed."

"Not true. Up above, you said you'd seen it before."

"In a dream." Thinking back in the haze of her mind, she realized she must have dreamed it. "A long time ago, probably. I can't explain. I certainly didn't sit down and devise a code to hack a system I knew nothing about."

Malcolm interrupted. "What is the code, Saba? From where do you recognize it?"

"From work. This code was devised by someone in my company. We found it in our own system early last fall and had a hell of a time getting it out. Tracing back, we figured out it had been done by someone who used to work there, before I started. Apparently she was a troublemaker, and when she was fired, she left a little time bomb."

"She?" Malcolm asked, voice sharp.

"Yes." Saba remembered the white-haired witch lying dead in the tower room of the mansion. "Her name was Rhoda . . . Rhoda Meyer. I never met her, but I'd be interested to see a picture of her."

"So would I," Malcolm said softly.

"I'll look her up when we get home. Don't want to risk it from here—you have enough problems without me tapping into the Internet."

"The Internet," Metz spat. "A rudimentary network for base-born humans, so crude a two-year-old could destroy it. No, wait, a hatchling—"

His diatribe was cut off by a rumble at the other end of the corridor, followed by a heavy odor of dust.

"And what the bloody hell was that?" He shot away.

Malcolm tested the air, his huge body expanding and contracting with his breath. He suddenly opened his eyes wide, expanding them into orbs of silver rage, the most emotion Saba had ever seen from him. "He *dares*."

"Who dares what?"

Malcolm swiveled his long body with surprising agility and skimmed across the crystalline room, one pump of his wings taking him into the tunnel. Saba's bangs stirred with the draft he created as she scrambled after him, scraping her hands on the rocks as she climbed back to the tunnel.

"Malcolm!"

He'd already disappeared into the cavern. She sped up just as another huge explosion sounded, this one larger than the last, followed by the sound of falling boulders and a cloud of choking dust. She heard Metz shouting, but no answer from Malcolm, not even a flicker of his magic.

Saba sprinted down the hall in panic and emerged into the main cavern. It was dark with dust, the globes barely pinpricks of light in thick gloom. The entrance was gone, some of the ceiling collapsed, boulders and chunks of stalactites still clattering to the floor.

"Malcolm?" she screamed. No answer. "Malcolm, where are you?"

"Help me!" Metz's voice rang, and Saba ran for him, coughing. She found him buzzing madly around a pile of rubble made of slabs of basalt and thick boulders.

"He brought down the cavern," Metz nearly screamed. "He's buried the master."

"Malcolm's under there? What happened?"

Metz hung in midair, wings flapping like crazy. "The entrance came down. Looks like another *time bomb* as you call it. The second explosion dropped half the roof on him. Help him!"

Saba put her hands on one of the huge stone slabs that covered the floor of the vast cavern. The entrance was completely blocked, sealed fast by several tons of rock. If Malcolm was under there, even as a dragon, he was likely crushed, dead.

She'd never move this rock, not by herself, not even magically. Yet, Metz hung next to her, wringing his hands, waiting for her to perform a miracle. Her heart tore. She

couldn't lose Malcolm, not now, and she had no idea how
to save him.

She slapped both hands to the rock, leaving a smear of
blood from her already scraped hands. "Malcolm," she
said, tears in her voice. "What can I do?"

MOVE!

The thought struck her like a whiplash, ricocheting
through the cavern and ringing from the ceiling. Metz re-
coiled and zipped to the topmost tunnel of the cavern and
hung just inside it.

The boulders began to shift. Saba dashed into the nearest corridor just as the mass of stone suddenly erupted in
enraged dragon. Dust and rubble exploded through the
cavern and streamed into the tunnel behind her. Saba fled
deeper, dashing around a corner as the torrent of debris
flooded the passage.

Rocks rattled and dust cloaked the air. Saba turned her
face to the wall and raised a quick power shield to keep the
worst of the dust and flying pebbles from her. Shards of
rock and crystal clicked on the shield and shattered to the
ground.

After a long time, the deluge of rock subsided, the rain
of pebbles dying away into silence. Saba gingerly stepped
into the corridor, pulling a fold of her shirt over her mouth
and nose to keep out the dust. She made her way carefully
back to the main cavern, her eyes stinging, broken rock and
crystals crunching under her feet.

Malcolm reared in the middle of the ruins, eyes and
nose closed against the debris, blood coating his hide in
crimson streaks. But he was whole, alive, upright, and furi-
ous. The globes in the cavern had shattered, but lights from
the tunnels above still functioned, lending an eerie spot-
light effect to the twenty tons of black dragon glimmering
in the middle of the room.

"Malcolm?" Saba said softly.

His eyes opened. Rage made his voice ice-cold, so cold
she was surprised the air didn't freeze around him.

"The entrance to the archive is gone," he said. "We cannot get out. Saba, you must open a door to your world and use the magics to get us through, or we will be sealed in here forever."

10

Saba stared back at him. His witch was so small and vulnerable, but power radiated from her like blue light shot with rainbow streaks.

"As easy as that?" she demanded. "I know you're all right, because you're encouraging me to do the impossible."

Malcolm shook his body, dislodging pebbles and shards of crystal that clattered to the pile of rubble beneath him. "Not impossible for you."

The white dragon had plotted very carefully to get Malcolm here, to seal him into the archive of which Malcolm was so fond. As soon as they entered the place, the white dragon must have triggered the program or spell or whatever it was to bring down the cavern.

The basalt slabs raining on him had hurt, but his dragon hide, as hard as the stones themselves, had allowed him to bear it with only minimal damage. He'd need healing, but he was not in immediate danger.

Malcolm could eventually dig out the tunnel enough to permit them to escape, but that would take time, even with his dragon powers. The white dragon obviously wanted him to stay put. But the white dragon hadn't counted on Malcolm having such a powerful a witch at his side, more fool he.

Saba still had no inkling of the power that lay inside her. It came out when they made love, that beautiful aura of magic that made her so special.

My witch. Mine.

"You have the ability to make a portal," he said to her accusing eyes. "Draw your energy from the magic of this place. And from me. There's plenty to spare."

She glared at him, her anger ten times greater than her size. She couldn't know how absolutely beautiful she was.

"Let me remind you that the last time I tried to make a door for you I nearly killed myself."

"You have become much stronger since then," Malcolm said. "I know this. We must return to your world, quickly."

"What about Metz?"

"Don't you be taking any magic from me," Metz shouted. "I need it."

"I meant, do you want to come with us?" Saba asked, an edge to her voice. "You're trapped here, too."

"No, I am not. I have work to do, cleaning up this mess, and who will guard the archive if I go gallivanting off? Any road, I know secret ways out so small only I can use them."

"He'll stay," Malcolm said. "He is right."

Saba looked around the rubble-strewn cavern. "The white dragon might have put other traps in here."

"I'll risk it," Metz said. "I ain't leaving, and no witch can make me."

"Fine," Saba said tightly.

"Too right," Metz answered.

Saba turned away, deliberately not arguing farther.

She said she thought Malcolm asked the impossible, but he also knew she could do it. Last summer when she'd attempted a door to Dragonspace using Lisa's magic to assist her, the door hadn't worked, Lisa had gotten hurt, and the backlash had nearly killed Saba. She'd survived only because Malcolm had healed her.

But that had been last year. Saba had grown in strength and ability and this time she stood in a place of enormous magic. Malcolm was a powerful dragon, despite his "fading," and Metz, too, radiated magic. Even if he didn't use magic, Metz *was* magic, his aura firm with power. Add to that the magic that had created the archive plus the millions of texts that lay under the vibrant light of the gemstones.

He knew Saba could feel it. Even reaching out to touch the tendrils shot tingling magic through his body.

"All right," she said. "I'll try. Mostly because I want to get out of here, too." She pointed her finger at Malcolm. "But if I die, I'll haunt you forever, I promise you."

"You won't die," Malcolm said. He nuzzled her body. "I won't let you."

Malcolm tasted Saba's worry as she faced the computer chamber, instinctively orienting on the most powerful area of the archive. He wove the threads of his thoughts through her, not enslaving her, but anchoring her and lending her power.

She brought her hands together and closed her eyes, and he sensed her trying to ground herself with the mountain beneath her feet. Saba did her best witchcraft when connecting with the earth, she'd told him, drawing the strength of rocks and stones. She drew a long breath, reaching to the center of herself and fusing that with the basalt below her.

She stayed still for a long time, and Malcolm felt her reach for the steadiness of the mountain. Then she began to raise her circle of power.

Last year Saba had refused to work any magic without drawing a circle in salt and calling on the Goddess and God to protect her, wouldn't spell without consecrated tools and salt and crystals. She had no tools now, and she used the cavern itself as her circle, mentally lifting a nimbus of blue-white light to encompass it.

Once the glowing and pulsing light surrounded them all, Saba opened her eyes. Malcolm felt the energy building around her, infusing her with a field of shimmering blue. She placed her hands, palms together, in front of her, pointing her fingers toward the tunnel.

He sensed the calm that flooded her in earnest, power that brought strength and confidence. The calm filled her with magic, which began to flow from the gemstones in the floor, from the seams of gold that ran warm and hard beneath the mountain, from the globes of crystals struggling to light the cave despite the dust, from Malcolm himself.

Magic seeped from Malcolm in swirls of light, and he gave it willingly, though he knew he'd be spent when he reached the other side. Power even flowed from Metz, who grumbled and growled at being caught in the magical field.

The power built until the very air crackled, tendrils of electricity snaking from the top of the nimbus through the niches, the gems, the globes of crystal, through Malcolm and Metz. Magic swarmed through the tunnel that led to the archive computers, increasing in capacity every second. The power built like a man bringing himself to orgasm, rising and pulsing and tightening, waiting to climax until the very last, unbearable moment.

Saba very slowly raised her hands, still pressed together, and brought them straight down. As she did, she released every bit of energy trapped in her body, focusing that energy on the slit she drew through the air.

The slit took form. It widened, bright light pouring through, a rift between the worlds through which only the most magical beings could pass. Saba braced herself, feet apart, and faced it.

She held the line as the slit widened and the light grew unbearably bright. Behind the light Malcolm could just make out familiar shapes of furniture in his living room, far away in San Francisco. He felt the portal drag at his body, wanting to pull it inward and downward and crush it into the form that could exist in the human world.

She was doing it.

The power jerked at him, and he found himself being sucked toward the slit and flattened as he passed through. This was different from the way the dragon's tears opened the door, or the way Lisa opened the door. Those he'd simply stepped through and became Malcolm the man; this rift dragged him in and commanded him to become human, not giving give him the choice.

He relaxed, letting his dragon limbs become human. The living room drew him into its welcoming arms, a wind wailing through it from Dragonspace. The phone was ringing, an odd, ordinary sound among the drag of the magic, and then the answering machine clicked on with Saba's sensible voice asking the caller to leave a message.

The slit began to close—with Saba still on the Dragonspace side. Her face contorted horribly as she struggled to maintain the opening, but the magic was fading, weakening her. He saw her lips form his name, but he could hear nothing over the roaring of the wind.

"Hi, Saba," said the answering machine. "This is Mamie. Missed you at lunch today and wondered if everything was all right. You know with . . . him. Call me." *Click.*

Malcolm reached back through the slit, grabbed Saba around the waist and jerked her through just as the portal snicked shut. They tumbled together to the carpeted floor, Saba on top of him, where they lay together, panting. The wind died abruptly and the whirl of dust that had followed them in hung for a second in midair, then showered to the floor.

They lay quietly for a long time, Malcolm's skin gritty with sand and streaked with blood, Saba breathing hard, her body shaking. At last Saba lifted her head. Her face was lined with exhaustion, her eyes half-closed.

"Malcolm," she said, her voice barely a whisper. She touched the end of his nose with a shaking finger. "Don't you ever, ever ask me to do that again."

* * *

Saba woke cradled in Malcolm's arms in the Japanese-style tub in Malcolm's cavernous bathroom. The bottom of the tub was gritty with black pebbles from the cave, and Malcolm's skin was covered with bloodred scratches.

"You're hurt," she mumbled.

"Saba." He peered at her, intense eyes showing relief that she was awake.

She touched one of the abrasions on his arm, closed now, but raw. She remembered the ton of rocks that had fallen on him, and her grieving panic when she thought him dead. "Are you all right?"

"It is trivial." He shrugged. "You were more hurt than I."

"I feel all right now." Floating in warm water wrapped in Malcolm's arms was a fine place to be. "I think."

"You were close to death."

Saba swiveled her head to look up at him. "How close?"

"Your heart stopped."

She glanced around the bathroom that looked the same as always. No blood, no defibrillators, no anxious EMTs, no doctors in white coats.

"Why am I not in a hospital?" she asked, alarmed at how weak her voice was. "Or at least an ambulance?"

"I healed you."

She looked into his dragon eyes that were so cool and confident, although she saw something flicker behind his usual maddening calm.

"And that's that? My heart stopped, you healed me, and now I'm all better?"

"Black dragons have great healing magic," he said in his reasonable tone. "You are better than if I'd taken you to one of your hospitals. Healing there is primitive."

"And taking a bath with me was part of the healing?"

"Yes. You needed to be washed."

She was fully aware of his naked body under hers, his thighs cradling her backside, the strength of his torso supporting her. His large hands gently smoothed the wet hair from her temple.

"What about you?" she asked. "Ten tons of rock fell on you."

He gave her a whisper of a smile. "Dragon hide is tough."

"I'm sorry about your archive. Will Metz be all right?"

"Metz will enjoy himself putting everything back together. Don't worry about him."

"And then there was your computer virus." Things came back to her slowly. "I'm positive it was the same one that struck Technobabble last year, set by the same person: Rhoda." She sighed. "If I could think better right now I'd know exactly how she did it and why."

"Later." Malcolm stroked her shoulder. "We'll decide why the white dragon is so interested in witches who work for your database firm. Technobabble's owner bears my mark," he mused. "He should have known a white dragon had coerced one of his employees."

"Not his fault, Malcolm."

"It might have been. I'll question him."

Saba felt faint alarm behind her exhaustion. Malcolm's "questioning" could be terrifying, and her boss, a gentle computer geek, didn't deserve to be bullied.

"Leave the poor guy alone."

He looked down at her. "You feel compassion for him."

"It's just my way."

His lips grazed her hair. "It is a good way."

She sank down, reassured that he wasn't going to manifest into a dragon and chomp down the best employer she'd ever had. Not that he'd truly do that, she knew. Malcolm could possess a gentleness incongruous with his cold dragon eyes and calculating ways. This was the second time he'd saved her, dragging her from the brink of death with his healing power. He hadn't needed to—like the white dragon, he could have discarded Saba and searched for another witch to help him.

And none of that seemed to matter right now. All that mattered was sitting here with Malcolm, his arms around her, his lips in her hair. Real life seemed far away and inconsequential, despite white dragons, witches, imps, sprites, and inky darkness.

She could bask in the heated water, scented with bath salts, relaxing on Malcolm's lap for a long time. No job worries, no database problems, just pleasant heat and Malcolm holding her. Her fingers looked a little pruney, so he must have been sitting with her for a while, which was fine with Saba.

Except . . . she lifted her head. "What time is it?"

"Five thirty-six post meridian," he rumbled. "And twenty-two seconds if it's important."

"Five . . ." She had no clocks in the bathroom. "How do you know that so exactly?"

"I looked at the time when we entered this room and calculated the minutes from there."

"You mean you guessed."

"There is only a point-zero-zero-zero-zero-two-six-percentage margin for error."

It was a most bizarre feeling to have an incredibly sexy man sharing your bathtub and calculating the time to exact seconds with a very low error rate. Even stranger to have certainty that he was not even a nanosecond off.

"I hope you're right because I have a tea ceremony lesson at seven tonight. If, in fact, today is still today."

"It is the same day we left for Dragonspace, yes."

Saba put a reluctant hand on the edge of the tub. "I should start getting ready."

Malcolm hooked his arm around her and pulled her back to his lap. "Given the travel time from here to Nihonmachi plus the time you will need for me to towel you off and help you dress, we have forty-eight minutes in which you may continue to rest."

His touch, plus the mention of him toweling her dry, zapped the last of her strength. Her head sank to his shoulder. "You're better than a day-planner, did you know that?"

His lashes were black and damp, clumped with water against his bronzed skin. "I wish to savor every one of those forty-eight minutes with you."

Her heart warmed and fluttered at the same time. "The bathtub's dirty."

"We can adjourn."

"I don't know. It's so warm in here."

"The bed will be equally as warm."

Definite fluttering, accompanied by heat between her legs. "You said we only had forty-eight minutes."

"Forty-six-point-two-five, now. There are a number of ways in which we may share that allotted time."

She raised her head again, wondering if he'd suddenly grown a sense of humor. "Do you have in your head the precise timing of each and every sexual act two people can do?"

He returned her look without a flicker. "I can if you like."

She started to laugh, shaking the bathwater and sending a few trickles over the edge. "I've never had a boyfriend like you, Malcolm."

His brows drew together. "This word . . . *boyfriend* . . . and its counterpart, *girlfriend*—these are not intimate enough for what we have."

"What would you prefer? I don't know what else to call this, except maybe a weird relationship."

"Lovers." His arms tightened around her. "I like that word. Dragons do not have lovers."

"But you have mates."

"That is different."

"Of course it is." She laid her head on his shoulder again. "How much time do we have now?"

"Forty-four-point-five minutes."

"Then we'd better start figuring out what we're going to do with it."

"I know precisely what we will do with it."

He rose to his feet, catching Saba under the arms and bringing her smoothly up with him. One wet arm went around her from behind at the same time he reached to the pile of towels on the shelf next to the bathtub and pulled one around her.

He proceeded to prove that they did have enough time for certain things. Saba found herself still damp on the towel on the bed while Malcolm licked his way from her breasts to the honey that was flowing hot for him. Then he entered her and took her with an intensity that left her even more exhausted than before.

Malcolm's calculations must have been a little bit off because by the time Saba scuttled into the practice room near the Japan Center, the other students were already there, and Sensei Kameko was regarding Saba's empty place in sorrow.

During the Cherry Blossom Festival in the spring, Saba would hostess a real tea room, which would be traditionally decorated with tatami mats, low tables, and an alcove with a flower arrangement she had prepared. She would dress in kimono, and she and her guests would speak in hushed whispers.

Very different from the church meeting hall Sensei had finagled for practice. Saba let the door bang closed behind her. The other tea hosts and hostesses, in street clothes, already knelt on mats, practicing laying out their accoutrements. Only Saba's mat was empty.

She hurried across the echoey room, out of breath, Malcolm striding behind her. *"Gomen nasai, Sensei-sama,"* she said to Kameko, then folded her hands and made an apologetic bow.

Kameko nodded graciously, but her gentle eyes held annoyance. She believed lateness to be the height of rudeness.

She looked with much more interest at Malcolm. Kameko was a small, delicate lady who had been born in Japan and moved to San Francisco when her Japanese husband was transferred here by his company to work. Kameko professed to love America, despite having to put up with people who were tardy.

She was a flower of Japanese womanhood—petite, graceful, artistic, polite, and soft-spoken. She attended the

Japanese classes she conducted in kimono and possessed an iron will that could make the hardest businessman pale.

Saba bowed to her again. "This is my . . . friend, Malcolm. May he stay and watch the lesson?"

Kameko gave the low, waist-bending bow of someone trying to display humility though she blatantly studied him out of the corner of her eye. Malcolm returned the bow in perfect form, not as low as hers, but low enough to show he considered himself more humble than she gave him credit for.

Then, to Kameko's delight, he launched into a long, flowery speech in Japanese. Saba listened, open-mouthed, as Malcolm thanked her for the privilege of watching the practice, certain she would show him the best instruction he had ever seen in his life. Kameko listened to him go on and on, then Saba's stern teacher actually began to smile and even laugh. She placed her dainty hand over her mouth and giggled shamelessly.

When Malcolm finished his flattering speech, Kameko led him to a folding chair near the mats, indicating it with her hand. "*Hai, dozo.* We will bring you tea, Malcolm-sama."

Malcolm thanked her again in more Japanese before taking his seat. Kameko bowed once more, then scuttled away, her kimono flip-flipping around her feet, to speak to one of her helpers.

Saba dropped her purse to the floor and knelt on her mat, trying to calm herself for the lesson to come. Tea ceremony was a Zen art, where each move was deliberate and slow, partly meditation. She wasn't sure, however, how well she'd be able to meditate with Malcolm sitting three feet away exuding masculinity and reminding her of what they'd been doing not twenty minutes ago.

"You miscalculated the time," she hissed at him.

Malcolm lounged back in the chair, as commanding of his surroundings as always. "I did not. I simply did not wish to stop."

You and me both, Saba thought, then turned her attention to Kameko, who had knelt in her place facing them.

One of Kameko's assistants, also dressed in kimono, approached Malcolm with a wooden tray containing a simple black teapot, porcelain cup and plate of traditional Japanese sweets. Another assistant brought out a folding table, which she set up with delicate movements, and the first assistant gracefully served Malcolm the tea.

Malcolm accepted the teacup from her with murmured thanks. The two young women simpered under his attention, then bowed and moved away, giggling behind fingers in the Japanese way. Malcolm lifted the cup, took a sip, and nodded his appreciation to Kameko, who had been watching him closely.

When Kameko, actually blushing, turned away to begin the lesson, Saba whispered, "You must have been a hit when you lived in Japan."

"On the contrary, I caused much concern. They did not know what to make of me."

Saba would love to hear *that* story, but Kameko had bent her brown eyes on Saba, and she turned her attention to the lesson.

Most of the students were well along in their studies and tonight they would practice those parts of the ceremony that gave them the most trouble. For Saba, it was folding the *fukusa*, the silk cloth used for wiping the tea scoop and the handle of the teapot. It had to be folded precisely, but the silk always slipped in her fingers, and she could never quite get the folds perfect.

Saba admitted that despite her frustration with the *fukusa*, she enjoyed tea ceremony. She laid out her equipment: cup, whisk called a *chasen*, tea kettle, container of tea, dipper for water, and the bamboo tea scoop she'd carved herself. Each piece had its own place on the low table, each had its own history, each would be used with precise movements.

It was much like laying out an altar for a ritual, she always thought, using tea things instead of a cup, a knife, candles, and a pentacle. Rather than invoking the Goddess and raising energy for magic, she put her energy into making and serving the perfect cup of tea. Instead of meditating on her athame, mixing salt, and water in the chalice, she'd meditate on the ladle and mix tea and water in the bowl. The results and purpose were different, but the method was somewhat the same.

She picked up the *fukusa* and started to practice. She felt Malcolm's eyes on her as she raised the cloth and used her thumb to make a perfect fold, or tried to. The cloth slid slightly lopsided and she heard Kameko hiss gently through her teeth.

Saba unfolded it and tried again.

She tried to put all that had happened—the archives and the stolen book; watching Malcolm be buried in falling rock; the draining exhaustion of opening the door; the lovemaking as Malcolm healed her—out of her head so she could sink herself into the simple world of tea. Not easy with Malcolm sitting so near and Kameko's eye on her, not easy when the death of the witch and the black swirls of magic in that house in Pacific Heights still haunted her.

But the mastery of meditation was to focus even when conditions weren't in your favor. She turned her attention to finishing the *fukusa* and then practiced lifting the ladle handle and running it up her thumb before picking it up. She'd almost managed to shut out the turmoil in her head when she noticed Malcolm rise from his chair and move to the far side of the room.

He walked easily, not drawing attention, and everyone ignored him, even Kameko and her assistants. He could do that if he chose, go where he wanted, do what he wanted without anyone noticing, a subtle magic to make people look the other way for a moment. Only Saba, who'd become attuned to every nuance of him, observed him.

The ladle fell with a gentle clatter when she saw the man Malcolm had crossed the room to meet. The man's long white hair stood out in the shadows of the far end of the hall, his intense green gaze moving to absorb Malcolm.

The two men began to talk. Not arguing, not snarling, not

circling each other as Malcolm and Caleb often did. They simply spoke to one another, standing an arm's length apart.

At least that's what it seemed outwardly. Saba's witch's sight saw magic sliding from the white dragon, white threads that snaked around Malcolm and pulled tight. Malcolm's own silver and black threads counteracted them, the two dragons exchanging words too low to hear.

Saba half rose, and Kameko gave her a look of gentle admonition. Saba retrieved her ladle, her heart thumping with dread. She tried to concentrate on dipping the ladle into the water and trickling liquid into the tea kettle, but her gaze zoomed across the room again where the two dragons faced each other.

Suddenly Malcolm jerked, and a pulse of black surged around his throat. Saba sprang to her feet. The other students looked up, and Kameko, who had her back to the drama on the other end of the room, frowned at her. Saba skirted her teacher with a hasty apology and hurried toward the two dragons.

"Malcolm!" she called.

He didn't answer or even turn. The white dragon looked directly at Saba, his green eyes luminous, his face alight with triumph. He pointed at her, and a wave of power sent her stumbling backward.

She struggled to remain upright. "Malcolm!"

Malcolm didn't look at her. The white dragon strode away, and Malcolm followed him without a backward glance. By the time Saba regained her footing and rushed after them, they'd banged through the outer doors and into the night.

Saba wrenched open the door. San Francisco was dark now and cold, a light rain falling. She dashed out of the building and across the lighted street, still full of people shopping and dining in Nihonmachi, the area around the Japan Center.

She saw the two dragons moving quickly through the crowd, people melting out of their way as though an unseen force pressed them aside. Saba abandoned all caution and ran after them.

She caught up to the two men just outside an ornate pagoda in the middle of a tiny green off Post Street, not the Peace Pagoda of the Center, but an artist's structure, given by an organization in Kyoto a few years ago. The Kyoto pagoda was a painted wooden edifice fifteen feet high and large enough around for two or three people to go inside at a time.

The pagoda was closed now, a sign hanging on the door in both English and Kanji to explain the fact. The white dragon, ignoring the signs, wrenched open the door. He disappeared into the pagoda, and Malcolm followed.

Saba put on a burst of speed and caught up to Malcolm on the threshold. She grabbed the sleeve of his coat. "Malcolm! What are you doing?"

Malcolm jerked from her grasp and snarled at her, his eyes harsh. "Stay away. Do not follow."

As Saba wrung her stinging hand he dove inside the pagoda and slammed the door. Saba grabbed the handle, but the door was locked.

Her heart pounded in panic. What she'd seen in Malcolm's eyes was not anger at her, but determination and fury, and behind it vast pain. Pain greater than any man could endure, and she knew with certainty what had happened. Forcing her worried mind to focus, she spelled the lock and wrenched open the door.

The pagoda was empty. The little room inside was ten feet square, large enough to enter and gaze at the workmanship of the wooden building from within. It was beautiful, its carved and polished beams a testament to craftsmanship.

Malcolm and the white dragon were nowhere in sight. A smell like burned wire filled the air, but Malcolm was gone.

11

Malcolm stepped through the magic portal in the pagoda to find himself at a great height, the black waters of San Francisco Bay far beneath him.

"An interesting choice," he said.

Both Malcolm and the white dragon stood steadily against the gale that buffeted them, easily balancing in the narrow platform. Being a dragon, the height didn't bother Malcolm, but of course if he fell, his human body would die.

"I am pleased you find it so." The white dragon rested his hand on the steel girder next to him. "Pass your hold of the witch Saba to me."

"I have no hold over Saba," Malcolm said calmly.

"You live with her, you couple with her." The white dragon gave him a look of vast disgust. "They are just animals, you know. Meat with rudimentary intelligence."

"She resisted my mark," Malcolm replied in a mild tone. "She learned to, which is why she could resist yours."

"Yet she follows you like one of their dogs, she races after you when she believes you in danger."

Malcolm shrugged, remaining placid through the ferocious pain that tore at him. He clenched his teeth at the
fiery threads wrapping his limbs, the music of his true
name binding him as sure as steel.

"Perhaps she likes me," he forced out.

"No one *likes* a dragon. They obey a dragon or flee
from it."

"Then you don't know these animals, as you call them,
very well."

"I don't want to know them well. I have to use them but
I have no intention of becoming *friends* with them, as you
say."

"Then you will run short of allies," Malcolm observed.
"As you will if you kill every human when you're finished
with them, like you did the blond witch."

The white dragon smiled. "The one called Rhoda. She
expressed regret at helping me and threatened to end the
spells she'd set up for me. She had doubts about what I
wished to do—the morals of it, if you please." He showed
his pointed teeth. "You saw the pathetic creature, those parties she used to relieve her strange sexual obsessions. She
had a good mind, almost dragonlike, but Saba's mind is
better."

"You will not touch Saba."

"You cannot prevent me. You belong to me now, black
dragon."

He licked his lips as though he found the taste of Malcolm's name exquisite. The pain of it seared Malcolm's
body and would not disperse until the white dragon chose
to relieve it.

Knowledge of a dragon's true name gave the being who
knew it great power. That power could be gentle benevolence as when a mother called her hatchlings to feed them,
but in other hands it was no less than the rape of the
dragon's self. Malcolm had known the danger when he'd
confronted the white dragon, but he'd needed knowledge
and to learn how to thwart the white dragon's plans. The
risk was worth it.

Malcolm sat slowly down on the steel ledge and dangled his feet over nothingness. Lights of ships passing below were yellow glitters in the darkness, and his dragon sight picked up the white foam on the water in the ships' wakes.

He said conversationally, "You asked the witch Rhoda to program a virus in the archive computers that would build a loop in the alarm system. From what I understand of these things, it would take a few days for the virus to go off, a *time bomb* as Saba called it. You waited until a day I was out of the archive, then you went in under Metz's nose and stole *The Book of All Dragons*. You learned my name and have been using it to drain my powers."

"It worked," the white dragon said dryly.

Malcolm continued, "Whether killing Rhoda was part of the plan or not, I cannot tell. I think it was just pique. You killed her and left her in the tower room of the house, and stalked Saba. You are using the book to . . . I'm not certain, but gaining mastery over dragons is part of it."

"Should there be more?" The white dragon smiled again.

"Since I am the keeper of the archive and you've started on me, I assume there is something there, perhaps the entire archive, that you want."

"Perhaps."

"But you needed a witch to help you go to and from Dragonspace," Malcolm said, keeping his voice steady. "How did you return, if you'd already killed Rhoda?"

The white dragon looked smug. "She was a clever young woman. She could program viruses, as you discovered, to go off at certain times. She could create doors that would also open at certain times. The magic worked even after she was dead. I used the last of those doors to return after you threw me back to Dragonspace. It was the last spell she had laid before I broke her neck."

So proud of her he sounded, and yet, he'd killed her. "Then you'll need another witch if you've used the last of her magic."

"And I've found one. Not as good as yours and not as cute, but I've found one."

"I'm guessing she hasn't succeeded in creating a portal to Dragonspace or you wouldn't still be here."

The white dragon shrugged. "She has other uses. I will have your Saba in the end, though. She is the strongest witch I've ever encountered, and when I finally make her mine I will become the most powerful dragon in Dragonspace."

"I see."

Malcolm could do nothing physically against the white dragon with the music of his true name wrapping every limb, plus the spell of the name kept him from killing the one who wielded it. But while he sat quietly plan after plan streamed with lightning speed through his mind. The white dragon assumed Malcolm helpless, but there were more ways of besting an opponent than brute force.

Malcolm had spent his eight hundred years in exile building layers upon layers of networks of people throughout the world, with loyalties and assets far surpassing any organization a crime lord could dream of. He only had to pull the right strings and dozens of people would come to his aid. The white dragon had no idea how to cultivate relationships if all he could do was kill those who'd disappointed him. Regarding humans as mere animals was a great mistake.

"I'll leave you now," the white dragon said. He picked up a chain that rested on the end of the platform. Manacles dangled from it.

"I have no way of escaping, even if you do not chain me up," Malcolm pointed out.

"You're a black dragon. You'll think of one. Put your hands behind you."

Compelled, Malcolm clasped edges of the girder behind his neck. The white dragon was right, given time, Malcolm's black dragon brain would find a flaw in the white dragon's power and exploit it to escape. He would weigh the risk-to-reward ratio—pain and death being the risk and freedom being the reward—and choose whichever plan fit best.

The white dragon wrapped the chain around the bar and snapped the manacles on Malcolm's wrists. The metal tingled with magic, the spells on them strong.

The white dragon stepped away, and Malcolm felt a surge of power that opened the way from this high perch back to the city.

"I'm off to find your Saba." The white dragon smiled. "You can think about the many things I will force her to do for me—you can wonder how far I will go to bend her to my will."

Malcolm said nothing. The white dragon was obviously trying to goad him to jealousy, rage, anguish, and the rest, and Malcolm stoically refused to give him satisfaction. Not that rage didn't burn deep inside him, glowing embers that would be fanned into full anger when the time was ripe.

Disappointed in Malcolm's lack of response, the white dragon settled for kicking him in the face. Then he turned, stepped through the magic portal, and was gone. Light flashed and the door vanished.

Malcolm moved his jaw delicately and spat out the blood that pooled inside his mouth. He settled himself as comfortably as he could on a narrow steel ledge with his hands chained behind him and a sickening drop below. The wind was cold and sharp, clouds scuttling between him and the moon and starlight.

He busied himself sending out threads of thoughts to people around the city he'd touched during his last exile and counting the ships that passed far below.

Kameko's look of vast disapproval turned to distress as Saba snatched up her things and said she had to leave for an emergency. Kameko seemed to understand it involved Malcolm. "A gentleman," she called him, "who wears the old-fashioned ways. Go find him Saba-san."

Saba fled the auditorium, pulling on her coat and

snatching the cell phone out of her purse. She thanked the Goddess for speed dial because her shaking fingers could never have punched in a full phone number.

"Lumi?" she shouted into the phone when the soft-voiced young man answered. "I need to find your friend—Axel. Where would he be?"

"At a bar in the Tenderloin. Malcolm knows it."

"Malcolm's not here." She outlined what happened, and Lumi made noises of dismay.

"I thought I felt something," he said miserably. "I felt him being pulled, but the bond he has on me didn't break. He's still in the city, I'm sure of it."

"Yes, but where? And the white dragon's on the loose. We need to find him, fast. Where is this bar?" Even as she spoke, she trotted to the bus stop that would take her in the right direction.

"It's called Gary's and it's off Hyde Street. But you're not going in there by yourself. You shouldn't even walk past the place by yourself."

"I'm a witch, Lumi, no one will touch me. If you're so concerned get down there and meet me. I want to talk to Axel, pin him to the wall if I have to. He knows a hell of a lot more than he lets on."

She clicked off the phone over Lumi's protests. As the bus rolled toward her, she punched another number into her phone and waited for Caleb's roaring voice. She needed as many allies as she could get. But neither Caleb nor Lisa answered. She left a message for one of them to contact her as soon as they could.

The bus ride was interminable. Though she reasoned that it would take her longer to return to where she garaged the car, drive downtown, find a place to park, and then find the bar, it didn't help her impatience with the crawling bus. It was full and stopped at every corner, people taking their time getting on and off. Two stops before the one she needed, a large group of ganglike kids piled on and the bus driver refused to budge until they settled down.

Saba leapt to her feet and elbowed her way off, tossing a

tranquilizing spell over her shoulder at the kids. The bus began moving as she jogged away, but she knew she'd move the last two blocks faster on her own feet.

Lumi was nowhere in sight when she reached the bar called Gary's, but she plunged inside, peering into the gloom. She realized instantly why Lumi advised her not to come here alone—only men sat at the bar and tables and none looked like milk-and-cookies types. Half a dozen toughs with scruffy beards filled the back room, straightening up from pool tables as she hurried inside.

"Hi, sweetheart," one called. "Looking for someone?"

Saba ignored him, searching the room for Axel, whom she did not see. Why was everyone suddenly so elusive?

A man came in behind her, but it wasn't Lumi. She didn't recognize the wiry man at first, but he stopped behind her and said, "Don't worry, it's Wallace."

She remembered the two homeless men near her office building that Malcolm recruited to watch over her. Wallace had had a bath and a meal or two since yesterday, but still he didn't look very protective.

The men in the bar didn't seem impressed with Wallace, either. Less so with Lumi, who came bursting in, panting, "You should have waited for me."

"I was in a hurry."

Saba looked over the bar patrons, men with hard eyes that glittered, all assessing her. She had the feeling none wanted to chat about why she liked tea ceremony.

"I'm looking for Axel," she announced. "Is he here?"

One man got to his feet, and she sensed Lumi and Wallace shrink a little behind her. At any other time she'd be amused at the thought of two grown men hiding behind a diminutive half-Japanese girl in a bar of dangerous-looking men, but right now finding Malcolm had foremost importance.

"If he's not here, do you know where he might be?"

"Why do you want to know, girlie?" asked the man who'd first spoken. He had graying hair and the grim look of someone who'd experienced much and cared about little.

Saba drew quick and dirty energy from deep inside herself and mentally traced a circle around her and the two men behind her. A protective nimbus rose, one that would be visible only to another witch but which the men here could not penetrate.

She sketched a pentagram in the air and sent it toward the man who'd addressed her. "Just tell me."

"He should be here any minute." The man looked surprised as the words came out of his mouth. The other patrons seemed disappointed he hadn't played with her a little longer.

"Good. I'll have a beer while I'm waiting."

She stalked to the bar and thunked her purse on a stool, daring the startled barman to say a word. He looked questioningly at the other two men and she shook her head, knowing Malcolm wouldn't be happy she'd brought either of the two recovering addicts into a bar. Wallace and Lumi didn't argue, simply settling in silence on either side of her.

"Saba-chan!" Axel's voice boomed from the pool room. "You should have called, I'd have met you somewhere besides this dump."

She noticed the other men give Axel a respectful berth as he crossed from the back room to the bar. This place might be dangerous, but not for Axel. She had the feeling the imp went where he wanted and did what he wanted with very little stopping him.

In a low voice, she told him about Malcolm going off with the white dragon and disappearing. Axel lost his grin. He took a swig of the beer that waited for him on the bar and wiped his mouth. "We'd better find him then."

"I also want to ask you about the witch you took us to meet," she said, pinning him in place with her gaze. "Did you know before we went to the house that she was dead?"

The bartender shot them a startled look, but she didn't care. She'd lay Axel out with an immobilization spell if she had to.

Axel lifted his hands. "Whoa, stop glaring at me like you'll turn me into a toad. I can't do my job if I'm a toad."

Witches turning people into toads was an annoying stereotype, but at the moment Saba found it an appealing idea. She leaned closer to Axel, holding his brown-black gaze with hers. "Then you'd better tell me all about it."

They moved to a table in the corner so they could have privacy. Lumi remained but Wallace shuffled out the door, his job done. The other clientele, disappointed, went back to their pool games, but they watched out of the corners of their eyes.

"Was the witch's last name Meyer?" Saba asked Axel as soon as they were seated. "Employed at Technobabble?"

Axel nodded, fingering the neck of his beer bottle. "That's her. I didn't know her well, but when Malcolm asked me for a witch strong enough to help a dragon and willing enough to do it, I thought of her first."

Lumi looked puzzled. "If you didn't know her well, why was she the first who sprang to mind?"

"Because when I met her, I read what was in her heart. Ambition, ruthlessness, intelligence, a strong witch self-centered enough to want lots of power. She'd jump at the chance to work with a dragon. Dragons give witches a lot of power."

"And a lot of pain," Saba said darkly. "Poor woman."

"Yes."

"I'd love to find out how you know so much," Saba continued. "But we need to find Malcolm."

"You don't think he went off with the white dragon on his own?" Axel asked her. "To battle him or something? Maybe they both went back to Dragonspace."

"No, they can't enter Dragonspace without a witch or Lisa to open the door. The white dragon might have found another witch to create a portal for him, but I don't think so."

"No," Lumi said decidedly. "They didn't leave San Francisco. I'd know."

Saba believed him. She remembered exactly what it felt

like to be marked by Malcolm, the silver-black threads entwining her mind like steely gossamer. She'd sensed him always, and the brief time he'd returned to Dragonspace without breaking the mark, she'd known how far away he was. And in spite of herself, she'd missed him.

"Malcolm asked if you'd killed Rhoda and you said no." Saba eyed Axel thoughtfully. "But maybe when Malcolm came asking about her the white dragon told you to pretend to help us and then kill her before Malcolm could question her."

Axel in no way seemed offended by the accusation. "That isn't logical. I'd have simply told Malcolm I didn't know anyone when he asked."

"Malcolm can be very compelling. If we could have saved her from the white dragon she would have told us what he was up to. You disappear at the party and suddenly, she turns up dead."

Axel pursed his lips, considering. "She had been dead more than twenty-four hours when we found her. I got that from the coroner's office. So she died even before Malcolm contacted me."

"That doesn't mean you didn't kill her." Saba held his gaze with her own. "It means you knew you had nothing to lose by taking us to her, and by doing so, you might gain our trust."

Axel looked at her a moment longer, something dangerous moving in the depths of his eyes. He was a creature of magic, and this man-shape sitting in front of her was not his true form. The truth of him, good or evil, had not yet been revealed.

Axel placed his hands on either side of his beer bottle, threw back his head and laughed. "You are goading me, Saba-chan. On purpose, just to see what I'll do. I know why Malcolm likes you—you give as good as you get."

Lumi laughed a little nervously. "If you like good debaters, you should meet my grandmother."

Saba kept her gaze on Axel, but he continued to smile. "I did not kill Rhoda, I give you my word on that. The white dragon did it. I could smell him in the room and on the poor girl's body." His laughter faded, but his eyes remained bright. "I am on your side, Saba-chan."

The look he gave her was somehow comforting. She read no desire in him—he regarded her as he would a friend or as a brother would a sister. He gave her a nod as though the argument was settled. "Malcolm must be in trouble, or he'd have informed someone where he was going."

"*Malcolm* would have?" Saba countered. "You don't know him very well."

"He does like to run off on his own," Lumi said glumly. "What about Lisa? She could help find him *and* kick the white dragon's butt."

"I called but she wasn't home. I'll ask her to help, but I don't want to wait."

"Lisa?" Axel asked with interest. "You mean Lisa Singleton who is the mate of Caleb the golden dragon?"

Saba blinked. "Do you know *everyone* in town?"

"Only the important people." He sobered, his look turning remote as though he listened to distant voices. "I think Lisa is busy right now. In fact, I know she is. Very busy."

"How do you—" Saba broke off as her phone began to ring. The readout showed it was Caleb. She answered it. "There you are," she said in relief.

She listened to Caleb's hurried speech, his voice rumbling and growling and worried. Abruptly he clicked off, and Saba turned back to Axel, wide-eyed. "How did you know?"

Axel shrugged, looking unhappy. "I have a knack for these things."

"What?" Lumi demanded.

"Lisa is in the hospital," Saba said numbly. "She just had her babies, four weeks early, and they don't expect either her or the children to live."

12

High above the bay, Malcolm shifted to ease the ache in his shoulders while his mind hummed with thought. The white dragon was out there in the city seeking Saba and wreaking havoc, but he knew Saba would even now be recruiting help. She knew powerful magical people who would surround and protect her—Lisa, Caleb, Ming Ue, Axel, plus the people Malcolm had recruited. She'd find Malcolm or he'd get away—it was just a matter of time.

He wished his heart could wrap itself around the idea as well as his logical brain did. Despite his calm reasoning his very human anger and fear ate at him. Saba was vulnerable, the white dragon hunted her, and here he was trussed up like a duck. He hoped Saba had sought out Lisa immediately, because as strong as Saba was, she was no match on her own for a dragon. He had terrifying visions of her being torn apart by the white dragon, her broken body left in a tangle as the witch Rhoda's had been.

He needed to break the chains and leave this place. Once before in the human world he'd changed to his dragon form, a form which could easily shatter the chains and let him fly away. As soon as the white dragon had vanished, he'd tried to call to mind the exact feel and shape of his dragon-self, to push it up through his human skin to become what he really was.

The pain had been so intense he'd blacked out and come to himself dangling from his wrists seven-hundred feet above the water, the chains straining against his weight. He'd pulled himself back to the ledge, panting and sweating in the cold. He'd have to plan—and wait. The wind buffeted him, his heart gnawed at him, and more plans whirled through his brain.

As he spun out his thoughts he saw, far out over the glittering city, a silver light flash once, then it was gone. He stared at the hole of darkness where it had been, knowing the light had been magical, but not certain what kind.

He continued to watch. A tiny beam of light drew upward over the city, indistinguishable to anyone not looking directly at it. The light sharpened into a point, then it turned and glided smoothly toward Malcolm.

Malcolm's perch lay not far from the city, though he sat high above the fog and in bitter wind. He watched the point of light become iridescent swirls on the wind, drawing closer and closer. It rose above gathering patches of fog and brightened almost unbearably, and Malcolm had to shield his eyes as it came close. The entity reached the tower and began to loop and dive around it, flitting and swirling like it was having *fun*. It flew past Malcolm, its laughter like the singing of wind chimes.

Malcolm wet his parched lips and tried to speak. "Silver dragon."

The words came out a croak, barely decipherable, but the thing seemed to understand him. Soft laughter swirled around him.

"I am she." The voice was female.

"Good. Break these damn chains and get me back to the city."

"I cannot." She swooped around the tower and threaded

herself over his body, nothing but insubstantial silver light. "I am not here, not really."

"Lisa?" he asked.

"Is that her name? No, I am not Lisa, but I *am* she, if you know what I mean, black dragon."

"I haven't the faintest damn idea what you mean. If you can't break the chains, at least go after the white dragon. Keep him away from Saba."

"I cannot," she repeated. "I can travel through time and space but not manipulate anything in my path. You are strong to be able to see me."

Malcolm watched her in surprise. "So you are the true silver dragon—the essence of her."

"I am the original silver dragon, or at least her spirit, from thousands of years ago. I have come to help. She is dying."

"Who is dying?" Malcolm asked in alarm. "Lisa?"

"The white dragon poisoned her, and the children, too. I must help."

Malcolm stared at the silver entity. "How could he have poisoned her? How did he even get close to her?"

"Subterfuge," came her helpful reply. "He slipped poison into her human body, which she might have survived, but there were the babies . . ."

A sudden vision flashed before him of Lisa and Caleb in a dark room full of tables and candlelight—a restaurant. Lisa putting her hand to her stomach and half rising from the table, Caleb springing up beside her, the other diners turning to look. The maitre d' hovering anxiously, someone talking rapidly on a cell phone. Caleb arguing with Lisa, she shaking her head and saying, "No, the babies . . ."

He caught a feeling of shame from someone in the open-view kitchen, a young man with the white dragon's mark around him, and then the vision was gone.

"Son of a bitch," Malcolm whispered.

"I have come to help," the silver dragon said in her musical voice. "But I simply had to discover why a black dragon was perched up *here* of all places. Shall I tell Lisa where you are?"

"If you would," Malcolm said, trying to hold on to his patience. The silver dragon lived a bit removed from all other dragons—all other *beings*—and regarded life as a long string of curiosities. Malcolm supposed she had that luxury because the silver dragon was the most powerful being in the universe.

But the white dragon, with his actions tonight, had just doubled his own problems. If he thought killing Lisa would help him, he was a fool, because now Caleb would hunt him, and Caleb never stopped. Golden dragons were not to be taken lightly, bred for battle in ancient times when dragons could still exist in the human world. Goldens were not thinkers by any means, but when they wanted another dragon dead, they'd hunt that dragon until one or both of them died.

"I must go now," the silver dragon chimed. Her insubstantial form flowed from Malcolm in a string of colored lights. "I feel the golden dragon's grief. They need me."

"Tell Caleb to wait for me and not to do anything stupid. Not that he'll listen."

She laughed and swirled around him once more. "I will convey the message."

She shot away into the darkness, swifter than thought, then disappeared into a pinpoint somewhere above the city. Up on the tower the wind blew cold around Malcolm, and damp patches of fog thickened below him to cover the bay.

Saba actually got a taxi to halt for them by lifting her hand and sending sparks of magic to stop the cab in its tracks. Tires squealed and the smell of rubber bit into the night that was fogging up fast. The taxi driver sullenly waited for Saba, Axel, and Lumi to pile in.

"Remind me not to piss you off," Axel said to her.

The cab raced into traffic. Driving fast in San Francisco was always a hair-raising thrill. Movie producers loved to take advantage of the steep hills and intersections that were mere platforms breaking up the near-vertical streets. The cab strained itself up Nob Hill and around the corner and down to rush toward the hospital Caleb had named.

They reached it, a small private medical center to which Lisa had been going for prenatal care, after a swift and bouncing journey. Axel paid the fare, digging out a wallet loaded with cash. At the front desk Saba inquired frantically for Lisa, got a room number on the third floor and then was told that only Lisa's husband was allowed to see her.

The three of them went upstairs anyway, Saba impatient at the slow elevator and wishing she had the magic to speed it skyward. They finally emerged into a waiting area to find Caleb crammed into a seat made for a much smaller person, his elbows on his knees, head in his hands, his golden mane of hair shielding his face like a curtain.

Saba dropped into the chair next to him. "Caleb."

He looked up. His blue eyes were wet, tears unashamedly leaking onto his cheeks. "She's in surgery."

Saba put her arm around him. Lumi sat down opposite them with Axel at his side.

"She's very strong," Saba told Caleb, trying to sound reassuring. "Remember how magical she is."

"You didn't see her. We were in a restaurant and all of a sudden she turned very white and said she was in pain, then she started to bleed. I wanted to take her to Dragonspace, to my cave where she could heal, but she insisted we come here, because she was worried about the babies. They did a C-section to take the babies out, but Lisa never woke up, and they're trying to find out what's wrong."

He sniffled, face wet, and buried his head in his hands again. They all sat in glum silence a moment, then Axel frowned.

"Wait a minute, did you say *babies*? Babies, plural?"

Caleb nodded. "Twins. A boy and a girl. They're in incubators."

"Oh." Axel sat back. "You had me worried. I was picturing a dozen baby dragons flying around the place."

Caleb shook his head without smiling. "They're beautiful little babies, but so small." He looked at Saba. "They're too small. Malcolm is a healer. He can help them."

"I don't know where Malcolm is," Saba said. "I was trying to find you when you called. The white dragon took him."

"The white dragon," Caleb rumbled, the warrior inside him waking up. "I will find that white dragon and slice him into twenty white dragon pieces."

"You'll have to get in line behind me," Saba said.

"And me," Axel put in, cracking his knuckles.

"Count me in," Lumi finished.

Caleb looked at Saba, grief and fear on his face. "I know you came to me for help, but I'm too worried about Lisa and the babies to think straight right now."

Saba squeezed his hand. She realized with sickening surety that it was up to her. Lisa was down for the count, Caleb's place was with her and his infant children, and Malcolm was in danger, whether he'd gone willingly with the white dragon or not. She thought *not*—she'd seen the magic surround and bind him.

Axel would help, but the look on his face told her he wouldn't take over. This was her fight, she was captain, he was lieutenant.

She drew a decided breath. "We need to find Malcolm. Not only is he powerful, but he's damn smart and likely has twenty-seven plans mapped out with the probability of each one's success calculated to the *nth* decimal space. Then we find the white dragon and have at him." She turned to Caleb. "The white dragon stole a book out of the dragon archive, and Malcolm and Metz seemed very worried about it. *The Book of All Dragons*. Do you know what that is?"

Caleb's blue eyes widened. His irises were larger and bluer than most humans', so it was like gazing into the depths of a lake. "He has *The Book of All Dragons*? Where?"

"I don't know. He stole it from the archive, and then we lost him."

Caleb rose, unfolding to his great height. "You have to find that book. If he's got it, then Malcolm and I don't stand a chance of surviving. Every dragon in Dragonspace is screwed."

Saba got to her feet with him, and Lumi, alarmed, also jumped up. Axel remained seated, leaning elbows on knees.

"I could do a locator spell both for Malcolm and the book," Saba said. "But I'm not sure it will work. Dragons can block locator spells, and I'm sure the white dragon has woven all kinds of blocking spells around the book and himself."

"What about the house?" Lumi asked. "The house where the party was, where the witch lived. We might find some clue as to where Malcolm is or where the white dragon is. Malcolm was worried about something in the basement, remember, and he never told us what."

Axel nodded agreement. "It's worth a try."

"I can't leave Lisa," Caleb said.

Saba patted his shoulder. "I wouldn't expect you to."

Caleb gave her a morose look. She knew he felt bad about not being able to help, but his worry about Lisa and his children consumed him. She patted his shoulder again, herself unhappy that she could do nothing more for him and the woman who had become her close friend.

"We'll be fine," she said, knowing the words sounded feeble.

Caleb started to answer, but just then a doctor in green scrubs entered the waiting area and motioned to Caleb. Caleb squared his shoulders and strode to him.

"She's out of recovery," the doctor said. "She wants to see you. We need to discuss . . ."

What they needed to discuss Saba never learned, because Caleb pushed past the doctor and ran for Lisa's room, the doctor hurrying behind him.

Axel got to his feet. "The house then?"

Saba watched the doors through which Caleb and the doctor disappeared, her heart heavy. She nodded. "The house."

Axel gave her a reassuring smile and laid a strong hand on her shoulder to guide her out.

The mansion in Pacific Heights was dark and looked deserted. Police tape stretched tight around the lawn.

"Breaking and entering is illegal, you know," Lumi said as they slipped into the shadows around the back. The taxi that had dropped them at the end of the block had long since sped away.

"We know," Axel said. "But we're going in anyway."

"The miasma surrounding the house unnerved Saba, which was too bad because the house itself was beautiful. But it had been used shamelessly, and the house had taken on an aura of evil. The next owners would have to call in either a priest or a witch for a house cleansing, maybe both. She itched to run home, fetch a sage smudge and start in.

"This is the basement door." She stopped before a glass and wood door set at the bottom of five stone steps. The taint of evil was strongest here.

"Yick," Axel said, drawing back. "I don't like the smell of this place."

Saba agreed, but Malcolm was trapped by the white dragon and who knew what magic, and she needed to find him.

She put her palm against the lock and breathed a word. A sudden blue of clean magic flared, the lock clicked, and the door opened. Axel deliberately moved Saba out of the way and went first.

Saba followed him down the steps into a dank, unfinished basement that sported cement walls and water pipes. The stench was more than that of evil; a tang of decay sat on the air and made her want to gag.

"It's pitch-black down here," Lumi said, hovering in the doorway.

Saba realized that only Lumi didn't have the benefit of sight touched by magic. She drew a pentagram in the air, her magic making it glow blue, and let it rise to half-illuminate the room. The magic didn't burn as brightly as usual, as though the darkness sucked out its energy. Saba moved a little faster, anxious to finish the search.

"Wish I knew what the smell was," Axel muttered.

Saba couldn't smell much over decay and mildew, but Axel wasn't human and perhaps had a better sense of smell than she did. They moved through debris, bits of drywall, and crumbled cement likely left over from the last earthquake toward the stairs that would lead to the main house.

The air seemed fresher as they climbed, and Saba gladly hurried upward, despite whatever danger might be waiting at the top.

They emerged into the same hall she and Lumi and Malcolm had stood in a few nights ago, but now all was dark and silent. As they explored the first floor, Saba's witch light illuminated the mess of the living and dining rooms, scattered with empty glasses and bottles, plates of crusting food, towels, ashtrays heaped with cigarettes, the smell of stale nicotine, and smoke hanging in the air. No one had bothered to clear up after the party.

"I don't think Malcolm's here," Lumi ventured. "I don't feel him."

Saba had to agree, but the white dragon or his accomplice might be. Saba was angry enough to grab the white dragon by the throat and shake him until he blurted out Malcolm's whereabouts.

"We should look at the tower room again," she suggested.

"I was afraid you'd say that," Lumi answered. "This place is a spook-fest."

"Haunted?" Axel asked. "Not this house. There's a feeling here, a darkness, but not ghosts or ghouls. That's for the movies."

"Some bad magic, though," Saba countered.

"Never said there wasn't. Shall we?"

"Axel," Saba said.

A door had opened on the second floor. A woman

stepped onto the landing and snapped on the overhead lights, chandeliers outshining Saba's floating pentagram.

It was Annie, the colorless witch Saba had met during the party. She was still colorless, dressed in a drab brown skirt and beige blouse, her hair pulled back unattractively from her face.

"He isn't here," she announced over the railing.

Axel put on an innocent face. "Who isn't here?"

"The black dragon. That's what you're looking for, isn't it? But the white dragon has him hidden in a safe place. You won't find him, no matter how long you search."

Saba's mouth tightened. "You work for the white dragon now?"

"I have no choice, do I? He takes care of me, and I do magic for him. I'll never have to go back to my coven again." She sounded smug, a witch who'd found more power than the ones who had shamed her.

"Where is he?" Saba asked the question carefully.

Annie shrugged. "Out. He never tells me where he's going. He'll kill your black dragon, though. He has enslaved him already, and the black dragon would kill himself if Roland wished it."

"Roland?" Axel asked blankly. "Who the hell is Roland?"

"The white dragon," Annie explained. "That is the name he uses among humans."

Axel snorted a laugh. "All that power and the best name he could come up with is *Roland*?"

"There's nothing wrong with Roland," Annie began, her voice petulant.

"Where is he, Annie?" Saba asked again. She made her voice stern, sending her pentagram to hover before Annie's face. "You know the witch's rede, don't you? *Do as you will, an' it harm none.* You are doing much harm being silent about him. I need to find him, and Malcolm."

Annie looked complacent. "That doesn't matter anymore. Roland explained it to me. When I'm under the power of a dragon, the rede no longer applies to me."

Saba sensed the dragon's mark strong over Annie, and she knew from experience that a marked person would defend their dragon unto death. Stealthily she let her pentagram float closer to Annie's face. "Where is Malcolm?"

Annie set her mouth in a sullen line. Saba hadn't really thought she'd answer, even when she used the pentagram to compel her to speak. It was an even bet that Annie didn't know where Malcolm was; the white dragon would likely not confide in her.

Saba had an idea, however. "The white dragon wouldn't have chosen you if he didn't think you had potential," she said. She saw Axel and Lumi glance at her in surprise and hoped they'd catch on.

"Why do you say that?" Annie asked, her tone suspicious.

"A dragon needs a witch to open a door for him. They don't have the magic to do it themselves."

"That is true," Annie agreed. "Why do you think I can open doors for this dragon?"

"Because he seems to be able to move around quite easily, appearing and disappearing whenever he wants to. I followed him tonight, and he vanished into thin air. But I think what happened is he went through a portal that you constructed."

As Saba hoped, Annie looked pleased with herself. "Do you think creating portals is restricted to opening doors to Dragonspace?"

"So you *can* make one?" Saba asked, sounding impressed. "That's not easy magic. Every time I try to create a portal, I nearly kill myself."

"It's not so bad when you're staying within the city," Annie said.

Interesting. "How many have you done? I know you won't tell me where they are, but I'm curious about how many you have been able to do."

"Four. It's not difficult once you know how. The first one was hardest, but they get easier."

"I see."

While Annie boasted of her successes, Saba surreptitiously commanded her glowing pentagram to slide over Annie's head and down her torso, trapping the witch in the middle. Annie gaped, then her face turned dark with anger.

Saba flung up her hand and said in a loud voice, "I bind thee in the name of the Goddess to do my will."

Annie's magic was no match for Saba's. The witch glared at her. "Roland will punish you," she said in a ringing voice.

Saba had no doubt of that, but at the moment she didn't care. She felt Annie struggle with the bond, but the white dragon wasn't here to defend her, and Saba could command her body with the binding spell.

Lumi grinned at Saba in appreciation. "Neat trick."

Saba ignored him. "You and I are going to take a short trip," she said to Annie.

"Where are we going?"

"To the pagoda. The one in Nihonmachi. You are going to show me exactly where you made the door and how to open it again."

13

Annie went complacently with them down the stairs, looking slightly dazed. Saba realized she'd now have to protect Annie and try to get her free from the white dragon, who had already killed one witch and likely would have no qualms about killing another. *I'll put that on my to-do list.*

At the bottom of the stairs Axel declared he wanted to go back out through the basement. Annie did not want to and hung back at the doorway. "He never lets me in there."

"If Axel is going down, I am, too," Saba said.

"Me, too," Lumi said quickly, though he looked as though he shared Annie's opinion.

Saba gave Annie a stern look. "I can't leave you up here by yourself, so you're coming with us."

Annie began to wail, but the binding spell gave her no choice but to go where Saba told her to. She at last followed Axel down the stairs with Saba close behind her.

The basement smelled and looked no different from when they had hurried through it earlier, but this time Axel walked slowly, scanning the floor. Saba's blue witch light cast strange shadows into the corners, reminding her of the inky snakes of darkness that had filled the upstairs room a few nights ago.

Axel stopped suddenly and made a noise like a growl. "Can you shine your light just here?" he asked Saba.

Saba let the pentagram float to stop over Axel's head. He studied the floor at his feet, where cracked slabs of concrete bore scratches around the edges.

"I don't like this," he announced.

Annie held back, her body tense. Lumi, too, looked in no way anxious to see what Axel had found. The two of them hovered just inside the witch light, as though afraid to stray from its circle but not wishing to draw too close to Axel and Saba in the middle.

Axel put his fingers on one edge of a concrete slab and started to pull. Saba hunkered down to help him, and together, they pulled the heavy concrete free.

Saba scrambled back, feeling sick. Axel remained in place, staring down at what he had revealed.

"What is it?" Lumi asked.

Axel pulled up three smaller pieces of stone and threw them aside. In a large, squared out hole in the earth lay a pile of bones. They were picked clean and almost polished, stacked neatly from side to side. They had been carefully sorted—thigh bones and tibias, radii and ulnas, skulls in a pile, each one with the jaw bone removed. They were all human.

Lumi made a gagging sound and swore a few words in Chinese. Annie said nothing. Axel remained staring at the piles, and Saba felt the fury building in him.

"He needs to eat." Annie's voice held strain.

Axel snarled. "He's human when he's here. If he wants meat he can eat at Burger King."

"He can't digest human food," Annie argued. "He told me. He must still eat like a dragon."

"Then he can go the hell back to Dragonspace when he's hungry. This is unforgivable."

Axel looked up, rage shining so hard in his black eyes that Saba took an involuntary step back. His gaze switched to Annie, who stared back at him, open-mouthed. Annie was as guilty as the dragon for this, Saba thought, neither trying to stop him or telling anyone about it, dragon mark or no.

Axel obviously agreed. He rose slowly to his feet, his skin rippling in the shadowy light, whatever dangerous thing he truly was trying to manifest itself.

Saba stepped into his path, her heart beating hard. "No, we need her."

Axel glared at her in mindless rage, and for a moment Saba thought he might shove her aside and kill Annie anyway.

"Please," she said softly but in a tone that indicated she agreed with his anger. "We need her now, we can take restitution after we find Malcolm."

Axel subsided the slightest bit, but his eyes still held black fury. "Later. Oh, yes, there will be a later."

He turned away and replaced the cement slabs almost reverently. They left the house without further adventure and Saba spelled the lock shut behind them.

When they reached the pagoda it was locked again. Saba drew a circle around the lock and spoke a word, and as before, it easily gave way to the spell.

Axel made her let him enter the pagoda first. He studied the carved wood inside as the others peered into the small space. "There's been some fierce magic worked in here," he observed. "It will take a long time for it to wear off."

"Malcolm was here," Lumi said, filled with conviction. "The mark on my mind is pulling me. He's very close."

Saba dragged Annie in front of her. "Is this your work? Your door?"

Annie couldn't keep the complacent look off her face. "Yes."

"Good. Then you can open it for me."

Annie's eyes took on the look of cunning. Saba twined her fingers through the other witch's and held her firmly. "We'll go together."

Annie deflated, but Saba knew better than to relax or to trust her. She brought up their joined hands, fingers pointing in front of them. "Go ahead," she said.

Annie tensed, and Saba's own muscles tightened with rising magic. The energy that came from the woman beside her felt strange, witch magic overlaid with the white dragon's mark and the same thick darkness Saba had seen in the house the night of the party, when she'd worked the locator spell.

In front of them, the air split in two, tingling brightness that seemed to lead nowhere. A cold wind blew through the slit along with dampness and the sharp smell of the sea.

Annie dove through, dragging Saba firmly behind her. Saba heard both Lumi and Axel shout and then the howl of the wind dragged away their words. The slit closed with a loud *pop*, cutting the two women off from Axel and Lumi.

Saba stood on a metal platform only a few feet square attached to a giant metal girder. Wind beat at her and threatened to knock her off the small perch. The darkness around her was absolute, and while she could see nothing below her, she sensed empty air and much of it. San Francisco fog whirled thick about her, water droplets stinging her skin.

She realized where she was, and her heart gave a sickening beat. "Holy Mother Goddess."

In panic she clutched the girder, and just in time. Annie grabbed her with long, hard fingers and tried to throw her off the top of the bridge.

Malcolm, chained to the other end of the Golden Gate's tower, saw the flash of light and the brief surge of magic. The wind blew him a scent he knew, the threads of thought he'd never quite forgotten when he'd released Saba from his mark.

He half stood, arms twisted by the chains, feet so numb they barely supported him. Despite the cold he began to toe off his boots, knowing it would be easier without them.

Again, when he called up the feeling of dragon within him, the pain sent him reeling. White tinged the edges of his vision, and he fell, shoulders wrenching as the chains caught him. He got one knee back on the platform, and he clung to the metal, panting.

A flash of light shot from the other end of the tower, blue witch light that swirled high then disappeared. A darker witch light responded, but was swallowed in the stronger blue.

Saba was holding her own. But the towers of the Golden Gate Bridge were high and precarious and any slip would send her plunging to her death. Malcolm tried to call up his dragon-ness again, and once more knifelike pain speared his body.

Malcolm watched the play of blue light in the darkness as he caught his breath. She would die while he sat chained and helpless, which was exactly what the white dragon wanted.

But she is one of mine. That made him bound to protect her, never mind that he'd severed the mark—a dragon's mark obligated him to protect and watch over those he'd put into his thrall. It was one of the most basic instincts in a dragon. His duty to those he marked outweighed the duty to any who enslaved *him.* The white dragon forgot that, but Malcolm never would.

He got to his hands and knees, gritting his teeth, and reached once more for the dragon inside him.

Saba battled for her life. She knew the other witch was not as strong physically or magically, but Annie fought desperately, as though she didn't worry about toppling from the tower and ending up a battered body in the bay. Saba could see nothing in the blackness and fog but Annie and the red-painted girder. Still, she sensed the empty air beneath the platform and tried to keep her panic under control.

Annie's magic was weak but infused with darkness that cut through it like tar. The darkness was terrifying, but somewhere beneath it, she felt the comforting presence of Malcolm, which gave her heart. He was near, if only she could *see* him.

Annie caught her off guard and Saba slipped and fell. She experienced watery panic when she slid toward the edge, but she thanked the Goddess for maintenance work which left handholds for those painting or repairing the bridge. Saba grabbed the metal loop and clung to it, trying to swing her feet up to gain purchase on the metal ledge.

She mentally drew a circle around her, trying to raise a bubble of power to protect her. Annie launched herself at Saba, physically beating at her with fists. The two rolled precariously on the platform, Saba holding onto the metal grip until she thought her fingers would twist off.

Annie pried at Saba's hand, her nails digging like claws. Saba felt her grip go, and she slid headfirst toward the edge of the platform. She hung there, her foot hooked around the handhold, her head and shoulders over empty space. She could see the underside of the platform and vertigo left her too nauseous to scream.

But what she saw under the platform gave her the strength to scramble back to the ledge. She grabbed the handhold again and kicked Annie's legs out from under her. Annie shrieked and clawed at Saba.

Black fingers of magic snaked from Annie and wrapped around Saba, squeezing her until she thought it would cut her in two. She kicked again and almost by chance caught Annie square in the abdomen. Annie gasped and staggered back, too close to the edge. She flailed, trying to keep her balance, then a sharp gust of wind shoved her and she fell, her scream horrible.

Bile rose in Saba's throat. She lay panting and gasping on her stomach, wind pounding at her, feeling sadness and horror and anger at the stupidity of Annie's death.

Annie's scream abruptly cut off, and a white dragon rose on wings luminous in the darkness. He clutched Annie securely in his claw and bent a green eye filled with fury and hatred on Saba.

He dove once around the tower, then flew straight for Saba, his mouth open. She sensed the magical heat building inside him and knew he was about to encase her in flames.

She drew a breath and shouted in the loudest voice she could, "Aren't you afraid you'll burn it?"

The white dragon's mouth and eyes narrowed as he pinpointed her for a precise arrowlike flame. Saba drew her magic around her as best she could and prayed to the Goddess for help, but she knew she'd never withstand the dragon's fire. She gazed down the dragon's throat as he drew a breath, saw the fire that would end her life.

Then twenty tons of black dragon, chains trailing from his talons, knocked the white dragon aside.

Malcolm's dragon cry rang against the steel pillars of the bridge, his eyes glowing in the fog. But the usual keenness of his gaze was dim and dull, his flight erratic. Saba felt in him vast amounts of pain, felt him struggle to maintain his dragon form.

The white dragon turned to face the new threat. The white dragon—Roland—was rested and at full strength, while Malcolm was already hurt. The fiery music of Malcolm's true name rang in the air, and Malcolm roared in pain.

Black and white dragon fought and twisted around each other like a bizarre parody of yin and yang, rolling and tumbling in the fog. Annie clung to Roland's claws, terrified. Saba could only watch, trying to maintain the circle around her to stave off stray bursts of fire.

The only spells she knew that didn't involve meditation, circles, and crystals were simple glamour or coercion spells and for those she had to look directly into the gaze of her victim. Unlikely with both dragons flying fast and fighting hard, closing eyes for protection against raking claws.

Malcolm was losing. He had to fight his true name as well as the white dragon, and though he battled with all his strength, it wasn't enough. Saba felt the white dragon's glee as he battered Malcolm, singing Malcolm's true name deep in his throat.

You're killing him, stop it.

The white dragon had no intention of stopping. He seized his advantage, kicking and tearing and biting at Malcolm while Malcolm bellowed in pain. Fire gushed from Malcolm's mouth, but Saba knew he struggled to even remain conscious. He had one focus in his mind, and that was to wipe the knowledge of his true name from the white dragon's brain.

But the white dragon was stronger, unhampered by magic and pain. He dodged Malcolm's fire, getting only the edge of it, then turned his entire fury on the black dragon. Saba heard the dragon's gloating laughter, felt the fog heat with the fire from deep within the white dragon's belly.

The white dragon's claws ripped across Malcolm's throat. Saba screamed as bright red blood poured from Malcolm's neck like scarlet rain. Malcolm attacked, but his eyes drooped with exhaustion as he rolled to the side. The white dragon backed up to bathe him in a stream of pin-pointed flame.

The fire engulfed Malcolm's body. His dragon hide was meant to stand it, but the huge gash in his neck caught, flames burning his blood and running inside his throat with a horrible smell of charred flesh.

Malcolm fell in a blaze of fire, his eyes wide with pain. At the last minute, he raked his talons across the other dragon's underbelly, drawing scarlet blood against the white. Then he went down. He spread his wings to slow his descent, but one wing was badly torn, and he fell in a slow tumble.

"Saba." She heard his voice clearly in her mind, all dark velvet and smooth, then it winked out.

14

Saba screamed. She threw every bit of power she could at the white dragon, battering at him with spells and energy. The white dragon flinched when her magic touched his torn underbelly, but for the most part her spells bounced off him, ineffectual. And then he came for her.

She thought of what she'd seen chained beneath the platform. She had no way of knowing whether dumping it might slow him down, but it was worth a try.

She dropped to her belly, trying not to flinch at the incredible emptiness beneath her, held onto the edge of the platform, and looked under it. The book hung just out of reach of any but those who could fly, fastened in place with thick chains. All she had to do was loosen the chains and *The Book of All Dragons* would tumble into the sea.

The white dragon could certainly intercept it before it fell very far, but that would give Saba time to try to open the portal to the pagoda. Axel and Lumi, if they were still there, could get her to safety, where she could regroup and decide what to do.

No, what she'd do was break down and go to pieces

over losing Malcolm. If he'd survived the fall, he'd likely drown in the sea below; she had no way of getting down to the water to help him. He'd only just come back into her life, far too soon to have him wrenched out of it again.

Trying to ignore the heartbreak inside her, she focused her thoughts on the chains around the fat book. A good witch could visualize any possibility and make it happen, under any conditions. She wondered briefly if any other witch had ever tried to dispose of a book while hanging upside down from the top of the Golden Gate Bridge, then she made herself focus. She thought hard about the chains weakening and pulling apart, imagined the book falling, falling into the black water below.

Saba tried to ignore the fast bulk of white dragon zooming at her, tried to calm her mind to everything but loosening the chains. She thought she saw one link move, then she became sure of it. The link stretched and broke, and another began to quiver. The white dragon bellowed in rage.

"Leave me alone," Saba cried. "Or the book goes."

"Stupid witch. If you think I'll let you destroy it . . ."

He turned, preparing to strike a blow with his tail that would sweep Saba from the platform. At the same time, Annie, still secure in the white dragon's fist, screamed, "Look!"

From the dark smudge of shore came a streak of gold, as bright as the city lights and powerful enough to shine through the fog. The gold speck grew until it became discernable, a large glittering golden creature with a wingspan of a hundred feet. Fire spewed from his mouth, heating the fog to boiling steam.

Caleb charged in with the precision of a honed fighter, easily missing the fire and claws the white dragon aimed at him. He swept aside and barrel-rolled, plunging his back talons into the taut skin of the white dragon's wings. The skin ripped like torn silk, and the white dragon slipped, beating injured wings hard to stay aloft.

Golden dragons were larger than frost dragons, born and bred for fighting. A black dragon could outthink any dragon in Dragonspace, but what goldens lacked in thinking capacity, they more than made up for in might and fighting tactics. They knew when to strike and when to dance aside, knew how to taunt and when to move in for the kill.

Annie was shrieking inside the white dragon's fist. He held her fast, but protecting her hampered him, a fact Caleb took full advantage of. He thumped another blow on the white dragon's wings that sent the beast reeling.

"That was for my kids," Caleb snarled. He slammed his tail against the white dragon's back legs, neatly flipping him in midair. "That's for Lisa. You're lucky they all made it, or I'd be *really* pissed."

Beneath her terror and grief, Saba felt a moment's relief that Lisa and the two babies were all right. Then she clung harder to the platform, heart in her throat, as the battle continued.

The white dragon fought hard, but he'd already spent energy on Malcolm, while Caleb was fresh and enraged. The white dragon turned aside to try to grab the book under the bridge, and Caleb used this distraction to renew his attack.

Saba had never seen a true dragon fight before tonight, and she hoped she never would again. Caleb's eyes flared blue, the good-natured hunk who liked to watch television replaced by a savage warrior lusting for a kill. That he would kill the white dragon she had no doubt. Caleb was not trying to scare him off or threaten, he wanted the white dragon's body floating lifelessly in the sea.

Alongside Malcolm's . . .

In desperation, the white dragon turned back to the platform, back feet extended, intent on Saba's death. His blow caught Saba in the side and sent her screaming and tumbling from the platform. At the last minute, she managed to grab the edge, and there she hung, legs flailing, terror pounding through her body.

Saba always wondered how she'd face certain death, whether her life would flash before her eyes or if she'd have a profound thought to pass on to whoever was with her. Now she knew. She didn't bother with dignity or profound thoughts—she screamed like mad and fought to save herself, knowing her numb hands and weakening arms could give at any moment.

Something powerful jerked her off the ledge, and she screamed again, throat raw, but a rumbling voice said. "It's all right, I've got you."

The warmth of Caleb's golden claw closed around her, his strength dissolving her panic. She dragged in shallow breaths and sank against his firm palm beneath her, finding her hands bloody and her face wet with tears.

Caleb hovered, wings pumping, and Saba shoved her hair from her eyes and looked around for the white dragon. She saw nothing but a white speck above the cliffs west of the Golden Gate, heading out to open sea.

"He got away," she gasped.

"For now," Caleb said.

She realized that Caleb had given up the opportunity to make the final kill to rescue her. All she could feel was relief. "Thank you, Caleb."

"The choice wasn't hard," he said, sounding reasonable. "I didn't want you to fall. We'd better find Malcolm's body before someone realizes he's not a whale."

She didn't like his words, but knew he was right. Caleb would have to get Malcolm out of here somehow, to Dragonspace, which meant Saba would have to attempt a door because they'd never get seventy feet of dragon back to Lisa's apartment. And then . . . she didn't know. Did dragons bury their dead? Metz would need to be informed, and another black dragon would have to take over the archive.

Tears slid down her face. "Caleb, wait," she said. "*The Book of All Dragons*. We need it."

Caleb turned, drifting under the platform where she pointed. "I can't believe all this fuss is over a book."

"A very important book." Her voice trembled, and she heard herself babbling. "Very, very important."

"See how dangerous hoarding books can be? Why can't black dragons hoard gems, gold, and silver like the rest of us?"

He grumbled and snarled but at the same time gently positioned himself so Saba could reach up, pull off the chains she'd loosened and take down the book. It was heavy and very thick, bound in supple leather and held closed with an old-fashioned clasp. The cover was inlaid with gemstones and gold that flashed in the darkness. Saba hugged the book to her chest, barely able to lift it.

"Got it?" Caleb asked. "Good. Hold on."

He dropped rapidly, and Saba bit back another scream, but his grip was so true that Saba didn't even have to hang on. Caleb dipped below the fog, the night pitch-black beneath the fog's muffling blanket. An intermittent stream of cars flowed across the bridge, seemingly oblivious to the battles that had gone on far above.

Ships, huge, long, and bound across the Pacific, floated ponderously through the shipping lanes, freighters moving cargo. Caleb flew fast, circling in and out of the fog, keeping to the darkness as he searched.

They found Malcolm well out of the shipping lanes, washed up against the quiet cliffs north and west of the bridge. Malcolm's huge black body lay motionless, wings outstretched in the water, the only thing keeping him afloat.

Caleb dove to him. He dug his back talons into Malcolm's body and half lifted, half dragged him toward the dark, empty cliffs that lined the shore.

"He's alive," Caleb announced.

"What?" Saba's heart thumped faster, adrenaline flaring. "But he fell . . ."

"He managed to survive." Caleb grunted. "Damn, he's heavy."

He let go of the body, which landed on the grass and brush at the cliff top. Malcolm's eyes were half closed and lifeless. Caleb set Saba gently on her feet, then there was a tingle of magic, a rush of displaced air, and Caleb the man faced her.

He was naked, bronzed body a smudge in the dark, golden hair a mess. He removed his fingers from the armband he'd slid on, gold with a dragon etched on it, the armband Saba had made for him long ago. A powerful piece that allowed him to shape-shift between dragon and human form.

Hands on hips, he surveyed the dragon stretched out on the grass and dirt. It was dark here now, and silent, but this was a recreation area that would start to fill with people at dawn. She was about to ask Caleb how they were going to deal with Malcolm in his dragon form, when his huge body shimmered then settled into Malcolm the man.

He was shivering. His body was covered with abrasions and bruises, skin cold and clammy, his eyes half-closed, hair slick with water. Saba dropped to her knees, letting the heavy tome she carried fall to the ground.

"We have to get him warm." She pressed her hands to his chest, barely able to feel it rise and fall. "If I had my crystals with me, or a cell phone . . ."

"You could heal him with a cell phone?" Caleb knelt on Malcolm's other side, darkness lending modesty to his naked form.

"Caleb—"

"I was joking. I can carry you both back to the city— unless he turns into a dragon again. Who knows if he's controlling that or it's something instinctive?"

Saba looked up at him. "Where could you land where you won't be seen?"

"In Golden Gate Park. It's where I left my clothes anyway. I can get help from there."

She nodded tightly. "Let's do it then."

Caleb pulled off his armlet and became fifty feet of golden dragon again. The beauty of him took Saba's breath away, his huge length of gleaming scales and magnificent blue eyes, so different from Malcolm and yet possessing the strength that made dragons so irresistible.

Her tired mind registered little more than that. She had time to lift the heavy book again before Caleb swept up both her and Malcolm, one in each hand, and launched himself skyward.

* * *

By the time they reached Golden Gate Park, a light rain was falling, making the night darker than ever. Caleb pulled on his clothes and started off across the green. "I'll go get the car."

Saba looked up in alarm. "I didn't know you could drive."

Caleb grinned, the mischievous sparkle returning to his eyes. "Don't worry, Lisa's teaching me."

Before Saba could protest he loped off into the darkness, his bare feet padding on the grass.

Saba lifted Malcolm's head to her lap, letting worried tears fall to his skin. The rain drenched them both, the night weeping with them.

"Don't die," Saba whispered. "Do you hear me? I'm not ready to let you go."

Malcolm never moved or stirred. *The Book of All Dragons* rested beside her, now misting with rain, the book for which both Malcolm and the white dragon had been prepared to die. She leaned down and kissed Malcolm's cold lips, wanting to infuse her own warmth into him. He did not respond.

Headlights approached, bathing her in glare. A car rolled to a halt not two feet from her, and Caleb leapt out of it. They were nowhere near the roads that wound through the park nor near a maintenance road—he'd simply brought the car straight across the grass.

"What?" he asked to her stunned look.

"Nothing. Help me lift him."

Caleb bent, hauled Malcolm over his shoulder and took him to the car, where he rested him across the back seat. He brought a blanket from the trunk and wrapped it around Malcolm's naked body, but Malcolm still shivered, eyes moving under closed lids.

Saba rode in the front, her hand resting behind her on Malcolm's body, while Caleb raced the car back across the lawns, narrowly avoiding an ornamental lake. When he reached a road he bumped over the curb, pulling in front of another car that had to scream to a halt. Horns went off, and shouts filled the night. Caleb ignored them.

"Is that it?" Caleb looked at the book in Saba's lap and ran up on a sidewalk.

"Caleb."

"Oh, well. Too dark to look at it now anyway."

He drove in silence, zooming down Fulton Street back toward Japantown and north to Pacific Heights. Saba soon learned not to look out the window. She clasped Malcolm's hand, trying to sense the black and silver threads of his thoughts. Nothing.

The street in front of Saba's apartment was deserted, and Saba had enough strength to magically make sure no one about happened to notice Caleb carrying Malcolm's blanket-wrapped body over his shoulder. She followed behind with the book.

The apartment had never felt so safe and reassuring. The wards were in place, filled with both her magic and Malcolm's, the house dark and quiet. Saba stripped back the sheets on the large bed in her room, and Caleb dumped Malcolm on it, grunting with the effort. Saba covered him in sheets and blankets, knowing that getting him warm was the most important thing. She hastened to gather her amethysts and other healing crystals, candles and salt.

"Want my help?" Caleb offered.

He looked sincere, but she heard the hesitation in his voice. "No, you need to get back to Lisa." She stopped her hurry to give him a quick hug. "Thank you, Caleb. The words seem so feeble, but I don't know what else to say."

Caleb nodded, understanding simple gratitude. "Thank Lisa. She sent my butt out there."

"Is she really all right?"

"She says so. She told me that her silver dragon essence healed her and the twins. Then she told me Malcolm was stuck up on top of the bridge and you were in danger, and to get out there and help. I don't know how she knew, but I guess when you're a silver dragon you find out these things."

Saba squeezed his hand. "Tell her thank you. And con-gratulations." She smiled up at him. "How does it feel?"

Caleb's face melted into a broad grin that made Saba a little wistful. "To be a father? It's the best thing in the world. You have to come and see the twins, Saba. They're so cute, even though they're all tiny and shriveled."

Saba managed a laugh. "Get back there and protect them, then. What I have to do . . . I need to do it myself."

Caleb lost his smile as he looked at Malcolm's inert form on the bed. "Call if you need anything. You know that."

She was grateful he didn't try to stop her or drag Malcolm to the hospital where he would likely die. Here behind the wards Malcolm was more likely to heal.

"There is something you can do for me," Saba began.

"Name it."

She quickly told him about Axel and Lumi being cut off at the pagoda. "Find them and tell them I have Malcolm here. Don't mention the book."

Caleb understood. "Found Malcolm, no book. Got it." He gave Saba a kiss on the forehead. "Take care of yourself."

"You and me both."

He grinned. "Sure." With one last glance at Malcolm he left the apartment.

Saba bolted the doors behind him and returned to the bedroom. She scooped up the amethysts, remembering the healing spell Malcolm had taught her long ago, how the intense power of it had spiraled them both into sexual ecstasy.

The memory drew fresh tears. She thought of how he'd kissed her then and again in the shower this morning and touched her with possessive hands. She bit her lip and approached the bed, and as she did so, her gaze fell on *The Book of All Dragons* shining in its brilliant gold and leather binding and sparkling with gems.

She had to heal him. When she'd done the healing spell with him last year, he'd taught her, held her hands, and lent his own black dragon strength to the spell. Now Malcolm was unconscious, dying, and had no help to give her. She needed powerful, unfailing magic in order to reach him. He wouldn't forgive her what she was about to do, but he'd be alive.

Taking a deep breath, she scattered her amethysts across Malcolm's still chest, unclasped the book, and opened it.

15

Hatred trickled through Malcolm's body, cold and deadly. He knew it came from the white dragon, that somewhere in the world the white dragon still sang Malcolm's true name.

The pain of his name overlaid bone-jarring hurt inside his human body, physical agony groping for attention. Beyond that was a faint tingling in his chest, tiny points of magic too weak to penetrate the wall between himself and the world. And a voice, a soft voice he couldn't place but which set off a profound yearning.

Malcolm.

He tried to remember where he'd heard the voice before—his whole body longed to remember, strained for it.

Malcolm, damn you, I don't know how to do this.

He wished he could help her. In fact, it was important to help her, but the pinning wires of his true name would not let him. He was slave to the name, and to the dragon who wielded it.

I found the book, but I don't know how to use it.

Though he didn't understand the words, he liked the voice, a pinprick of sanity in the fog of his thoughts. He remembered falling, falling such a long way, and the dull rush of hurt. Voices above him, movement, silence. Then the voice of the woman easing into his brain with the sweetness of wind chimes.

Stay with me, he wanted to say.

The voice vanished. Over it he heard a cold chuckle, the cruelty in it sharp.

I will kill you, Malcolm promised.

The soft woman's voice swam back to him. *Don't you dare die on me, do you hear? I'll make you live whether you like it or not.*

The voice conjured pleasant memories. A scent of spice and musk, slick skin under his hands, mouth on his like she couldn't get enough of him. Small hands moving down his chest, fingers ringing his staff in a wildly erotic grip. Hips moving beneath his, soft cries of feminine joy.

He wanted that again. He'd have that again—being inside her, home where he belonged.

He remembered wild black hair, brown eyes he could drown in, small-boned, taut body, lovely, lovely lips . . .

He imagined he saw those lips now, moving in words he could not distinguish. As though he watched from above, he saw her kneeling in a room lit with candles, his naked body on the bed beside her. Glittering salt encircled their two forms and a heap of purple stones whose name he did not remember rested on his chest, a faint violet light pulsing from them.

The black-haired woman had a book open in her lap, a huge thing that nearly dwarfed her crossed legs. Its pages glistened as though made of pure gold. On the right-hand page crouched a black dragon on a background of white, the only color in the picture the blood red of the dragon's tongue. The dragon had wide eyes, a fearsome scowl, and curled claws.

The left-hand page was filled with symbols, swirls, and lines. The lines seemed to move and writhe, dancing in his blurred vision, and the young woman held the book firmly as though trying to tame them. She was reading the words,

chanting and singing them in a strong, clear voice. The
notes strung together into a line of music, breaking through
his pain and the hold the white dragon had on him.

A sudden healing surge roared through his body. He felt
his limbs mend, his wounds close, burning hurt that was
glorious at the same time. *She* was doing it, she was healing him. *My witch.*

A groan escaped his lips. He moved, and amethysts
clattered and slid from his chest to pool on the bed. The
woman looked up at him, brown eyes wide.

The book slid from her lap to the floor as he pushed her
down onto the bed, lips finding hers in bruising, brutal
kisses. She tried to voice a protest, but he ground his hips
against her clothed ones, stopping her words with his
mouth. She gripped his shoulders, as he unbuttoned her
shirt so he could slide his mouth to her breasts.

His staff lifted and pulsed; he wanted her with a craving
so strong he could taste it. He wanted sex—no, his mind
reached for a stronger word—he wanted to fuck her. Nothing less than having her hard and without stopping.

Malcolm pried her skirt upward, marking her soft
thighs with his fingers. He heard her laugh, whisper, "I
guess you feel better."

He wanted to remember her name. Names were important and he didn't know hers. *My witch*, he knew that, but
that was not the whole of it.

He moved the skirt aside and ripped away the thin underwear that covered her. He parted her legs with a hard
hand, the tip of his cock moving readily to her opening. He
pushed inside her, and she made a noise of delight. As he
began to ride her, the hot friction shoving away the last of
the pain, Malcolm's brain at last cleared.

Saba, the white dragon, the violation of the archive, the
pagoda, the bridge. Falling into nothingness and the incredible pain of slapping into the water. Then Saba sitting
cross-legged on the bed, the book in her lap, softly singing
his true name, weaving shining silver and black threads
that closed around him like a steel net.

"No!"

He burst out of her and to his feet, his back connecting hard with the cold wall. Saba looked up at him, brown eyes wide, her legs still parted and the curls between them damp with sex. The air hung with music, the last notes of his true name fading to vanish in the musk-filled night.

As suddenly as he'd pulled out of her, Malcolm was back on the bed, seizing her wrists in a bruising grip. Saba barely felt the pain as he roared at her, "What have you done? What have you *done*?"

"Saved your life." Saba was amazed at the relative steadiness of her voice. "It was the only way."

Malcolm drew back on his knees, eyes bright with rage. "He's still in there." He jammed his finger to the side of his head. "You'll pull me apart. You can't both wield my name. You'll kill me."

Saba's body pounded with their almost sex; the way he'd pushed her down and slid into her had excited her like she'd never been excited before. When he'd pulled out, she'd gasped a groan of disappointment.

But he hadn't been himself, he'd been in the throes of the healing spell, which spilled orgasmic energy over both the healer and the healed. This had happened the last time she'd healed him, and she'd felt the same joyful wanting, the same glorious need to have him.

She reached for him, but he flung her hands from him, kneeling over her with fists clenched. His skin was pallid and covered with bruises and cuts, his hair still wet.

"Why did you do it?" She'd never seen him so angry, not even at the white dragon. "You wanted me as your slave? To obey your every command?"

She stared at him as he knelt upright and naked, anger radiating from him. At that moment, he hated her. But she'd had no choice.

She didn't understand what he meant about two wielders of the name tearing him apart. Last year when she'd

been taught the secret of Caleb's true name, that knowledge had been shared between her and two other witches.
Once Saba had learned what their high priestess meant to
do, she'd sworn off using Caleb's name, and later, Lisa had
erased it from Saba's memory.

This time she shared the name with a being whose motives were different from hers. The white dragon wanted
Malcolm to die—she wanted Malcolm to live. Her healing
spell had closed his more dangerous wounds, but she could
have done nothing without grabbing the very essence of
him and binding it to her. Malcolm didn't realize that the
magic of his name had hurt her, too, that healing energy
had been jerked from her and left her weak and numb.

Malcolm pushed himself off the bed again and yanked
open the closet door, grabbing his clothes. He pulled them
on, wincing as he covered his bruised skin.

She sat up, knowing her skirt was raked high, and she
looked like a wanton. "You need to rest," she said. "The ordeal you suffered . . ."

"I will recover somewhere away from the holder of my
chain."

He snatched up a leather coat and stormed from the
room. Saba sprang up to run after him, hurriedly pushing
her skirt down, in too much of a hurry to replace the underwear he'd torn off her. She caught up to him in the
foyer, where they'd stood two nights ago and kissed so pas-
sionately.

She grabbed his arm. "The white dragon is still out there,
let me remind you. Caleb fought him off but he's still alive."

Malcolm looked down at her with eyes as hard as silver
ball bearings. "Caleb. Fought him off."

She nodded. "Lisa sent him, and he fought the white
dragon after you fell into the bay. You would have died, and
me, too, if he hadn't found us."

A mistake. Males, especially dragon males, didn't like
to hear that another male had done what he couldn't.

"You enslaved him once, too, I remember," Malcolm
said. "You must enjoy enslaving dragons."

"I didn't do it for enjoyment. I *had* to. You would have died."

"You should have let me die. Then I'd be free."

Saba exploded into anger. "And left me alone with the white dragon sniffing around, not to mention that book? Thanks a lot, Malcolm. I notice you think nothing of enslaving *me*. You came back to this world to enslave me again and was surprised when you couldn't."

"It is not the same thing at all."

"Of course not. You're the mighty, mighty dragon and I am the puny human witch—who just saved your life, by the way. I could have left you washed up on the shores of Marin County for the coastal patrol to find."

He swung on her, so much menace in his tone that she backed up a step. "A dragon mark is not the same thing as wielding a name. A dragon mark protects you. *This* is true slavery—you can kill me in an instant if I decide to disobey your slightest command."

"Do you think I would do that?"

"I think that you can."

Saba glared at him. "All right, fine. Rush out there and find the white dragon so he can buy you a beer."

His hand was on the locks. "I will find Lisa, who has the power to release me. The silver dragon understands what this horror is."

"Lisa is in the hospital. She nearly died having her babies—the white dragon again."

Malcolm whirled. "So the vision was true."

"Caleb says she pulled through, and the babies, too. She'll be all right."

She watched thoughts warring in Malcolm's head coupled with renewed worry. He reached for the locks again. "If she's all right, then she'll soon regain her full strength."

He started to open the door. Saba gathered her magic and sang the first few notes of his name.

Malcolm slammed the door. He grabbed her by the shoulders and pressed her into the nearest wall, his body hard against hers. *"Stop."*

Saba's eyes filled. "I'd never hurt you. I'm trying to protect you."

"I know humans, Saba. I lived with them for eight hundred years, trapped here like a rat. They like revenge. It would be very human of you to take your vengeance for what I did to you in the past. It is your way."

"It isn't *my* way. Back then I wanted to help you, too. Maybe not at first, but once I understood what you needed, I wanted to help. You didn't coerce me."

"You thought that because I made you think so. Because of the dragon mark."

"No, you idiot. Because I fell in love with you."

He stopped, lips parting. "You didn't fall . . ."

She pointed her finger at him. "Don't you *dare* tell me what I did or didn't do. When you went back to Dragonspace with no intention of ever seeing me again, that hurt like hell. I loved you—you used me and finished with me. It took me a long time to give up the completely stupid idea that you'd ever come back for me."

He pressed her harder into the wall, his eyes dangerous. "But I did come back."

"Because you needed help again. You'd just love it if I enslaved you, because you wouldn't have to face my true feelings for you. You have no idea what to do with a woman in love with you. But slavery and vengeance, that you understand."

She was crying. He shook his head. "You don't understand what this kind of slavery is."

"Do you want me to command you to make love to me? Would that make you feel better? To pleasure me as much as *I* want, to be my sex slave?" Tears ran down her face. "Maybe I'll get one of those dominatrix outfits with the leather and the heels . . ."

"Stop," he growled. He kissed her, a deep, bruising kiss, halting her words, though he couldn't stop her tears.

* * *

Malcolm forced her mouth open, pinning her firmly against the wall, his broad leg pressed between her thighs. She didn't understand, and he couldn't make her understand. She'd roped him body and soul, and she didn't know that it bound him to her in ways he couldn't escape. She was his mate, and even Lisa wouldn't be able to part the mesh that entwined them. He'd realized that even before she'd stopped him from leaving the house.

He'd felt the threads still tying them together when he'd arrived here three nights ago, even though he'd broken the mark almost a year ago, even though she'd resisted its renewal. But something held them together, and her using his true name tonight would bind them for eternity. Using a dragon's name to hurt him was one thing—that made an enemy. Using it to save him, that made a mate.

Saba broke away from the kiss, her beautiful face wet with tears. "Don't make me fall for you again. I don't want to fall for you again."

"Then stop me." His face hovered an inch from hers, his fists above her head on the wall. "Use my true name, and stop me. Bend me to your will."

"You're trying to make me prove that I'll hurt you."

"Yes."

But it was so much more than that. This was the second time she'd saved him, and he wanted her with intensity. He wanted to celebrate being alive and whole and celebrate it with her. He kissed her again, tasting her lips and delving into her mouth. She always tasted good, like a hint of cinnamon and vanilla. Her blouse was already unbuttoned from his haste in the bedroom, and he dipped his hand inside to find the full globe of her breast.

The nipple pebbled under his thumb as he stroked it to life. Her eyes, half-closed, gleamed with need. He smelled her desire and wanting, and his jeans-clad thigh discovered that she'd not bothered to replace her underwear.

Her brief skirt was no barrier, but how much better

things would be if it were off. He fumbled with the button at her waistband, and her hands helped him open the catch and slide the skirt to the floor. He stripped off his own jeans and shirt again, wanting to be bare with her.

Her stockings pressed his thighs, the lace of them scratching his skin. He lifted her against the wall so her face was at his height, looping his arms under her knees. She made a noise of wanting, her head against the wall, black hair stark against cream white. Her fingers sought his shoulders, tracing muscles, thumbs finding his biceps, his hard forearms, the hands that held her.

He slid his tip inside her, finding her opening as slippery as before, her tight folds relaxing to ease him in. She opened her eyes wide, brown pools to drown him. He moved up inside her, a groan escaping him when her walls squeezed him hard.

Because I fell in love with you, she'd shouted. The words seemed to hang in the air, wrapped around the lingering notes of his name. He did not know what to make of them. The power of a dragon mark could make her think or feel anything he wanted her to, and what she'd decided then might not have been real.

He felt her nails in his back, her tongue trace his lips. Lush, beautiful woman. He was inside her to his full length and still wanting her. Her slick heat gripped him as he ground his hips to hers, breasts firm against his chest.

He'd started out wanting to punish her and segued into enjoying every grip of her fingers, every scent of her body. Soft, warm woman, strong enough to take what he gave her and return it threefold.

I want this for always.
You are bound to me.
My mate.

He made love to her hard, and from her groans of pleasure, she didn't mind a bit. Her body pressed into the wall, her eyes closing as her breathing started to come fast, faster.

At this angle and standing up, with her fitting around him so tight, it was hard for Malcolm to move. He could glide back and forth an inch or two at a time, but he was pushed inside her so far it didn't seem to matter. Her around him, him deep within her, a perfect place to be.

"Goddess, I'm coming," she moaned, sounding annoyed of all things. "Malcolm, why do you always do this to me?"

He could think of many answers: *Pleasuring you is my greatest pleasure. When you come for me, you are truly and completely mine. I need you.*

He said none of them, catching her cries in his mouth, suppressing his own need to come so that her climax could go on and on. Before she wound completely down, he withdrew from her and lifted her into his arms, carrying her down the hall to the bedroom. He laid her on the bed, she still warm from her climax, and stripped off her blouse and loosened bra.

She reached for him, and he entered her again in a single thrust. She smiled and wrapped arms and legs around him.

Part of him said, *Go slow;* but the rest of his body could no longer contain his need. He rode her hard and fast, and after the first few thrusts, he was no longer able to think. The cool mathematical being let his mind go blank to everything but the feel of her around him, her scent, her taste, her cries of delight.

He came in an explosion of emotion, unable to think or see or hear. His entire life spiraled to this one moment, pumping his seed inside Saba, his witch, who had braved death to rescue him one more time. She'd healed him with her magic, determination, and integrity. Without her he would be dead.

All this flashed through him as he sank into her body, his skin wet with sweat, her breath on his face. His groan was heartfelt as he fell onto her, his mouth seeking her.

"I know," she said in her soft voice, trying to soothe him. "Of all the incredible things that have happened the last few days, this is the most incredible."

Malcolm raised his head and found her smiling at

him. Smiling at him for punishing her for using his true name. Smiling at him for losing himself in her. He'd snarled at her, shouted, mistrusted her, and made love to her to regain his power over her—and she smiled.

Her smile was the most beautiful thing he'd ever seen in his long life.

"Saba," he rasped.

"Mmm?" She traced his swollen lips, touch light and loving. "I didn't tell you to do that, you know. You did it all by yourself."

His incoherent brain didn't follow her words, but he loved the sound of her voice. "Ride me," he said.

She sat up lazily, her small breasts moving, smile still in place. "My friend Mamie is right about you, you know. You're no good for me."

He didn't understand her. He tugged her to him, making a noise of relief when she slid her leg over his. "Please."

Her eyes widened in mock surprise. "The great dragon is saying please? You must truly be under my thrall."

Malcolm growled and pulled her down, and she laughed as she slid straight onto him and began the rhythm that brought them both to climax again.

16

When Saba peeled open her eyes in the light of morning, she realized she would miss another day of work. Fresh sunshine poured into the room and slid along the bed, touching Malcolm's bare limbs tangled in sheets. A glance out the window told her the fog and rain had departed on the wind, the sun shining mightily to make up for it.

Malcolm slept hard. His skin bore bruises and raw abrasions, but he was flushed with health, his breathing strong and even. One hand lay clenched on the pillow as though he fought something in his sleep, his dark hair like a satin sheet over his bare back.

Mine to do with as I please, Saba thought.

He'd told her that last night, snarling the words, daring her to give in to the temptation to make him her slave. And the temptation was great. To have this beautiful, strong man under her power, to have him pleasure her and protect her at her whim was giddily seductive. To be able to love him without him stopping her would be heady, too.

And false. He'd hate her for it. Was that what she wanted? To bind him without remorse?

She groaned silently. *Why couldn't I fall in love with a human being? Another computer geek maybe?*

No, that would be impossible while she had Malcolm stretched out next to her like a Greek god. He made all other males insignificant.

One thing was for certain, Saba would not unbind him as long as the white dragon was still around. Her wielding Malcolm's true name would keep the white dragon at bay somewhat, though she worried that Malcolm was right when he said both of them inside him would tear him apart.

She touched his arm, loving the contained strength beneath the skin. He was beautiful as a dragon, all sable and silver, but as a man he took her breath away. She couldn't resist running her hand across his skin, feeling the perfect flare of his rock-hard biceps, tracing the sharp lines of his dragon tattoo.

He opened his eyes, not moving, pinning her with his stare. He let her touch him for a few moments, his gaze following the path of her fingers, then he reached out and scooped her to his side.

The subsequent lovemaking was slow but deep, unlike the frenzy of the night before. She came quickly, profound pleasure hitting her in waves. He tried to keep his climax silent, closing his eyes and making only one muffled groan.

Saba kissed him, a slow, warm, afterglow kiss. If they could just be man and woman, nothing else between them, how beautiful it would be. Not witch and dragon, just Saba and Malcolm, drowsing in the sunshine, letting the day drift by.

The bedroom door banged, and a gravely voice said, "Geez, I thought you'd be done by now."

Malcolm had the sheet over Saba before she could move. Axel stood in the doorway, his hand on the knob, averting his gaze to the ceiling and looking annoyed at the same time.

"How did you get in here?" Saba gasped.

"Through the front door."

"There are wards all over this place. How did you just waltz in?"

Malcolm rolled off the bed and into his pants in one smooth motion. Saba remained under the sheet with it pulled up to her chin.

Axel shrugged. "The wards are for evil things, and I'm not evil. Good to see you're both all right. Of course, I figured that out last night when you were really going for it. I decided to let you get on with it and bring you the message today."

"You came in here last night?" Saba's face heated.

"Don't worry, I didn't watch or anything. Caleb found Lumi and me and told us he'd brought you here. We were worried, so I came up here to see if you were all right. When I heard what was going on in the bedroom, I figured you were healthy."

Malcolm settled a shirt on his shoulders, his face hard with anger. "What message?" he demanded.

Axel looked blank a moment. "What? Oh, yeah. Caleb called me again this morning and asked me to tell you to come to the hospital."

Saba's heart skipped a beat. "Lisa?"

"Sorry, should have said that better. She's fine, and the babies are cute, and she wants to see you. And Malcolm." His gaze fell on *The Book of All Dragons,* sitting square in the middle of the floor. "And that book. I have a taxi waiting—I figured neither of you would be in any shape to drive."

Malcolm felt the presence of the silver dragon the moment he walked through the doors of the hospital. Lisa's magic tingled through his body, touching the bands of his true name as though it explored them curiously.

As they rose in the elevator and walked along the corridor to the patient's rooms, the tingling increased. Malcolm had experienced the magic of the silver dragon before, but it had never invaded him as it did now. She was testing him, probing him, and he didn't know why. He carried *The Book of All Dragons* wrapped in a sheet, hiding its gem-encrusted surface from curious eyes.

Saba knocked on the half-open door, which was opened by a broadly grinning Caleb. He cradled against his chest a tiny bundle, which was nearly dwarfed by his broad forearm. The bundle had a face, small and squished, a dot of a nose and a tiny red mouth. A few strands of dark hair stuck out from under a knitted cap covering its head.

"Hello," Caleb boomed. "This is Li Na Singleton."

Malcolm studied the baby at a distance, looking it over as he would a new specimen of insect. Human babies were a mystery to him. Dragon mothers hid their young in their mouths for the first year and a half, to keep them from predators—mostly other dragons. Human mothers and fathers, in contrast, displayed their children proudly, a practice Malcolm had never become used to. Noticing another dragon's hatchlings always resulted in a fight to the death.

Saba and Axel obviously had no qualms. Saba's face softened as she pressed a small kiss to the sleeping child's forehead. "She's beautiful," she breathed.

Axel rubbed a blunt forefinger over the baby's chin. "Gooble gooble," he said.

Caleb moved slightly toward Malcolm, obviously waiting for his greeting. Malcolm gave Caleb a nod. "Very . . . nice."

"Is that all you can say?" Saba demanded. "This is the most adorable little girl who has ever lived. Where is the other one?" She sailed into the room and soon was at the bed hugging Lisa.

Malcolm gazed with alarm at the shadows under Lisa's eyes and the pinched lines about her mouth. He had thought her immune to all forms of attack, but the white dragon had found a way around that. Lisa was mostly human after all, more human than Malcolm or Caleb or the white dragon would ever be. They took human shape; the silver dragon had taken on human *life*—Lisa's life—and also human death.

Another too-small baby lay in a square crib drawn up to the bed. This baby's face was set in a belligerent scowl, and as Malcolm approached, he opened his eyes and bathed Malcolm in a brilliant blue glare.

Caleb said proudly behind him, "That is Severin. My son."

Malcolm's brows rose. Caleb had lost a son with that very name; he wondered why the golden dragon chose to remind himself by giving the next son the same name.

Caleb returned his look calmly. "To honor him," Caleb said, then he grinned. "He has already turned into a dragon."

"Thank Goddess the nurse had left the room," Lisa said, resting a fond hand on the little boy's belly. "My doctor is astonished at how strong they are for preemies. They've already grown and gained weight since yesterday and were taken off the incubators."

Saba laughed. "The doctors will worry when they start seeing wings and scales." She hugged Lisa again. "They are beautiful, Lisa, honestly."

Malcolm hadn't realized how much Saba loved children. Her brown eyes glowed as she bent over to give the boy a kiss "from Aunt Saba." *She ought to have children*, he thought, *little witchlings to train and raise.*

Lisa looked up at him, something in her eyes making Malcolm pause. Despite her exhaustion and lingering sickness, Lisa looked pleased and even at peace. Her ordeal was over, and she had a daughter through whom she could pass on the legacy of the silver dragon and a son to love.

Her gaze fell on the bundle Malcolm carried. "Is that it?"

Malcolm sensed all eyes, including the babies', turn to him as he removed the sheet from *The Book of all Dragons*. Axel plopped himself into the only chair in the room and stretched his long legs, and Saba curled up on the bed next to Lisa. Caleb seemed content to stand and bounce small Li Na on his arm.

Malcolm gently set the book on Lisa's lap. He'd rather have his skin peeled from his body than show the book to

Caleb, but Lisa was different. She was a silver dragon, magical and powerful and, he sensed, beyond the restrictions of this tome. He hadn't had time to look through it, but he had the feeling the silver dragon wasn't even in it.

Saba unhooked the clasp for Lisa, and Lisa opened the book with a pleasant sound of crackling leather. The pages were made of the thinnest beaten gold, each containing an etching of a dragon on the right-hand leaf. The dragon's name, in swirls and notes, was etched on the left.

"So every dragon in Dragonspace is in that?" Caleb asked, pointing at it. "Even me?"

"Every one," Malcolm answered.

"Who puts them in?" Saba asked. "Wouldn't the person who made the book then know every dragon's true name?"

Malcolm explained. "No one writes in the book. It's a magical object—every time a dragon is born, a new leaf appears, and when one dies, it disappears. Don't ask me how."

"What's the purpose of it?" Saba continued. "Who wants to keep track of every dragon alive, and why? Especially since you keep it locked in your archive so no one can look at it."

"I do not know," Malcolm answered. "*The Book of All Dragons* is a legend that no dragon truly understands. But the book knows us."

Lisa flipped through the pages until she came to a page toward the end. "Including those born yesterday. Look."

Caleb elbowed Malcolm out of the way to bend over his wife. Malcolm saw a page with a small golden dragon on it before Caleb quickly put his hand over the new dragon's name.

"That is Severin," Lisa conceded. "I sang both children's names in my mind as they were born—I didn't make them up—they seemed to come from some part of me."

"Perhaps that is how they get into the book," Saba suggested. "The mother sings their name, and *voila*."

"Is the white dragon in there?" Axel interrupted. "Seems to me we can save a lot of trouble if we find out the white dragon's true name."

"I thought of that," Saba said. "I was going to look, but . . ." She flushed suddenly, no doubt remembering how Malcolm had distracted her with lovemaking. They'd both been too exhausted to look at the book after that.

Axel's smile was knowing. "You thought of it, but you had other things on your mind." He waggled his brows at Malcolm.

Lisa winked at Saba. Caleb absorbed himself in tickling his baby as though he didn't notice, but Malcolm refused to be embarrassed by their teasing. Saba was a beautiful woman, why should he not take her to bed and pleasure her to his content? And hers? They were bound together now, in any case.

"Have you found the white dragon's page?" he asked, annoyed.

Lisa gave him another smile then quietly turned the pages of the book. Malcolm noticed that Caleb didn't object to her seeing the true names of every dragon alive, even though they both knew the silver dragon was siphoning up the knowledge. All dragons trusted the silver—or at least, they knew they could do nothing to stop her.

Lisa's smile vanished as she turned over a page in the middle of the book. Saba bent over to see, then both women looked up.

"It's blank," Saba said, staring at Malcolm. "The white dragon's name has been erased."

Malcolm strode to the bed and looked over Lisa's shoulder. The right-hand page depicted a dragon, his picture pure white against black, green eyes blazing cruelly. Lisa moved her hand across the golden page opposite, which was perfectly smooth, without a line to mar it.

Saba stared at the page in dismay. She'd been so certain that all they needed was to threaten the white dragon with the book, and he'd slink back to Dragonspace with his tail between his legs. But of course he'd have a contingency plan in case the book fell into the wrong hands.

Lisa closed the book with a thump. "Well, that's use-less."

"Perhaps not." Malcolm straightened up, his eyes quiet but holding grim anger. "The white dragon has bound me with my name. Could the silver dragon use the book to un-bind me?"

Was it Saba's imagination, or did Malcolm carefully not look at her? He stood on Lisa's other side, his tall body graceful despite his bulk.

Lisa shook her head. "It doesn't work that way. I need the bind-er, not the bind-ee. I could erase the knowledge of your name from his head if he was standing in this room, but I can't from a distance. I'm sorry, Malcolm."

Malcolm tilted his head to one side as he did when his thoughts moved rapidly behind his quiet expression. He was very dragonlike when he did that, reminding Saba how different they truly were. "Then I will have to find him and bring him to you," he concluded.

"Easy as that, is it?" Saba asked.

Malcolm's mouth set in a grim line. "Yes. And then we return the book to the archive. Finished."

Saba wondered what all he meant to be finished with. The white dragon, this adventure, Saba? She was surprised he hadn't demanded that Lisa remove the knowledge of his name from Saba's mind right then and there.

Caleb's eyes began to gleam in a menacing way. "And what about the white dragon? We let him go?"

"No," Malcolm answered. The word was flat and final. "We hunt him." He gave Caleb a thoughtful look. "A war-rior would be useful in this hunt."

Caleb glanced reluctantly at the little bundle in his arms. The twins were so small, so vulnerable, and so beautiful that they tugged at Saba's heart. She'd always loved children but had little opportunity to be with them—as an only child, she had no nieces and nephews to adore. Being honorary aunt to Lisa's two was the best she could hope for. And perhaps one day, she would have a child of her own.

The child in her imagination suddenly took on Malcolm's

black hair, fearsome scowl, and beautiful eyes. She quickly banished the vision, not wanting to taunt herself with it.

Lisa held out her arms for Li Na. "You go, Caleb. The faster we solve the problem of the white dragon, the easier we all will sleep. I'm fine now, really. I can protect them."

The steely look in her eyes lent strength to her words. A female dragon, from what Saba had learned, defended her hatchlings with a ferocity that would make the most power-mad dictator blanch. Lisa's twins weren't exactly hatchlings, but the protectiveness Saba sensed from Lisa was intense. The children would be safe with her, and Saba also wouldn't stand for anyone trying to harm them.

Caleb handed over the baby and gave Lisa a loving kiss, tugging another string in Saba's heart. "All right." He twined his hands together and stretched his arms, muscles bulging. "Let's go. I'm hankering for another good fight."

Axel rose from where he'd stayed out of the way. "I'll come with you. I'm a good hunter."

Malcolm and Caleb exchanged a glance, then Caleb shrugged. "I'd welcome the help," Malcolm said.

He started to follow Caleb and Axel out the door, then he turned, as though remembering something. He strode straight to the bed, lifted Saba off of it, and gave her a hard kiss.

The kiss went on and on, Malcolm's mouth hot with the remembrance of sex and the promise of more to come. Saba's hands stole around his waist, one sliding toward his backside before she could stop it.

He thumped her back down, stared at her a long moment, then turned on his heel and walked out the door. Saba wiped her bruised lips with a trembling hand and exchanged a smile with Lisa, Saba's shaky, Lisa's knowing.

Lisa opened her mouth to comment, but the door banged open one more time, this time Axel returning.

"I'll keep them out of trouble, ladies, I promise." He poked Li Na in the belly, saying "blurp," then turned and went out the door after Caleb and Malcolm.

"I never know what to make of Axel," Saba said, looking at the closed door.

Lisa fingered the gold clasp of the book. "I'm not certain what he is, but he doesn't feel evil. I think I'd know if he were a danger, especially to the babies. But I sense protectiveness from him." She left off her speculation and bent her gaze on Saba. "All right, what is going on between you and Malcolm?"

Saba wanted to keep her feelings for Malcolm to herself, but it was impossible to lie to Lisa. "I have no idea what is going on between us. Everything and nothing." She leaned her head in her hands. "I'm miserable. The last thing I need is for him to stay, but when he does leave it will tear me in two."

She felt Lisa's sympathetic hand on her shoulder. "I know. Love is the hardest thing in the world." Saba looked up to see Lisa's gaze wander to the babies sleeping together in the crib, her expression so tender it brought tears to Saba's eyes. "But it's worth it, Saba. It's very much worth it."

They both gazed at the babies, so beautiful and vulnerable, emotion preventing them from speaking.

Then they broke into laughter, Lisa snatching up her cup of water as Severin suddenly morphed into a miniature dragon and set the sheets on fire.

The darkness had no name and no thought, but it had awareness. It didn't really understand the concepts of witch *or* dragon *or* demon, *but it knew that it touched them and they touched it.*

It was ancient at the same time it was newborn, and it slithered through the molecules of air until it coalesced enough to become tangible. It had been trapped for such a long time in a place it didn't understand, a place of knowledge, words, thoughts, and records of deeds, knowledge filling and spilling everywhere, shoving out that which became the darkness. And then the one with the thoughts as sharp as steel and mind like white light had come and freed it.

Not on purpose; the being called the white dragon

hadn't been aware of what he'd done. The darkness had ridden on the magic with the dragon to an entirely new world. It was puzzled, interested, and fed on the same magic that the clumsy beings called witches did. The witches tried to shut negativity out of their rituals, which the darkness collected and added to itself. And when the dragon had fed itself, the fear and horror from his victims had only helped the darkness grow.

And then it had touched one it knew. A familiar mind, belonging to a very strong being it had met before, long ago. At that time, part of the darkness had ridden on this strong witch's dreams to the human world—and then vanished. The darkness that had made it to her world had been consumed by something, the remaining darkness did not know what.

This time, it would be more careful. It would study, learn, and find a place where it could gather and build upon itself. The strong witch was the key, it was certain. It slithered away, storing knowledge, waiting for its moment . . .

17

Malcolm, Caleb, and Axel began their search at the pagoda, with the idea that the magic from the white dragon and Annie the witch might start them on the right trail. As the three men made their back way to Japantown, which was not far from the hospital, Axel relayed what he'd discovered buried in the basement of the house in Pacific Heights: the bones of the white dragon's victims. Caleb glowered, and Malcolm's anger stirred.

"He's nothing but an animal," Malcolm said.

"No better than lesser dragons," Caleb agreed. "Mindless beasts."

"But dragons in Dragonspace eat humans," Axel pointed out.

"That's different," Caleb answered. "That happened long ago when the way between the worlds was thinner, and the men caught were trying to poke swords and spears into dragons in order to impress people. But you don't feed on those you choose to walk among, in their guise. That's just—disgusting."

"Mindless," Malcolm echoed. "But white dragons were never known for their brains."

They walked along Post across from the Japan Center, the place now teeming with tourists and locals, and headed for the small park that housed the pagoda. Axel walked next to Malcolm, shoulders hunkered, hands in his jacket pockets. "So, you and Saba. How's that going?"

"What is between Saba and me is none of your business."

"I think it is," Caleb said on his other side. "She's our friend."

"And you two were really steaming up the place last night," Axel put in.

"You should have seen how protective he was of her last year when we were fighting another witch and a pile of demons," Caleb said.

Malcolm scowled. "Because you and Lisa almost got her killed. You should be more grateful to her—she saved your butt more than once, I remember."

"And yours. She's good at saving dragon butts." Caleb gave him a pointed stare. "She saved you last night, too. It was a pain in the ass to drag you to shore—I would have left you to sink if she hadn't insisted I help."

"Sounds like you owe her a lot," Axel remarked.

Malcolm growled. "We are here to track the white dragon, not discuss my personal life, which I emphasize again is none of your business."

"But it's fun to watch you turn red," Axel laughed. "All right, have it your way. You be nice to Saba, though."

Caleb nodded. "I'm right there with him. She's my friend."

Malcolm refrained from rolling his eyes and increased his stride. The last thing he needed was relationship advice from a thick-headed golden dragon and an annoying imp. But then, he sensed a peace in Caleb that hadn't been there before, the same peace that Malcolm had seen in Lisa. The bond the two of them shared was not a burden; it gave them more strength together, and the arrival of the babies had pulled them still closer.

He remembered again how Saba's face had softened when she'd greeted the twins. She wanted that, the closeness of a family. Strange concepts to a dragon who'd spent two millennia alone in contemplation—by choice.

They had to wait for a crowd of tourists who were looking over the pagoda, led by a shrill-voiced tour guide. "This is a small, wooden pagoda, the gift of a Japanese artist from Kyoto. At the Japan Center, we'll find the Peace Pagoda, one hundred and fifty feet high and made of stone, another gift from Japan, given to the city in 1968 . . ." Her voice faded as she led her group away.

Once the tourists had dispersed the three of them ducked inside the wooden pagoda, Malcolm first. The magic that had engulfed him when the white dragon led him in yesterday now smelled stale, and the tingling indicated that the door was nearly gone. The white dragon hadn't come back this way, and likely Annie's magic wasn't strong enough to keep the doorway viable for long.

"We'll have to go back to the bridge," he told Caleb. "Try to pick up his scent from there."

"I last saw him hightailing it west, over the Pacific," Caleb answered, one broad hand on the doorframe. "He might have been able to get back to Dragonspace."

"Only if he found a witch stronger than the one he has now. Saba and Lisa are the only ones I know of at present who can create a door."

"Which doesn't make me like the idea of leaving them alone in the hospital," Caleb said darkly.

Axel barked a laugh. "I'd think twice about taking on the two of them, even if I was a dragon."

"I have to agree," Malcolm answered, although his instincts urged him to rush back to Saba and stand guard over her. "Together they will well be able to withstand him in his human form."

"It's not *your* kiddies waiting there all vulnerable," Caleb muttered.

"Go back, then," Malcolm told him.

Caleb shifted, debating. Golden dragons didn't like debate—Malcolm could see each thought flickering over Caleb's face, the pros and cons of continuing the hunt or returning to watch over Lisa. A black dragon would have calculated ninety-seven different possibilities at lightning speed, a golden dragon had trouble with two.

At last Caleb shook his head. "I want to find the bastard and end this."

End this. To a golden like Caleb that meant killing the white dragon, which suited Malcolm. He nodded. "Back to the bridge, then."

They took a taxi to Fort Point, under the south end of the bridge, the middle-aged female cab driver looking delighted to have three large handsome males in the car with her. Axel parted from them after they piled out, saying that while he could fly, he couldn't keep up with dragons, and he had a few ideas of his own to follow up. Malcolm sent him off with curt thanks—he still didn't know whether to trust the man but if Axel brought results, he'd be grateful.

Caleb and Malcolm strolled along the cliff paths that ran west and south of the bridge looking for a good place to strip off their clothes and become dragons. The day that had begun with sunny warmth had become cold and damp, fickle San Francisco weather, perfect to send all but the most enthusiastic joggers and hikers indoors. They walked into the woods where it was quiet and proceeded to remove their clothing.

"How did the white dragon manage to poison Lisa?" Malcolm asked as he folded his clothes into a bundle so he could carry them.

Caleb, already naked and flexing his muscles, answered. "She already wasn't feeling well but thought going out to our favorite restaurant would cheer her up. It wasn't far, and I didn't see the harm. I blame myself." His expression turned bitter. "I wasn't paying attention. Instead, I was enjoying being with Lisa. He must have gotten into the kitchen and slipped a human poison into her soup."

Malcolm recalled the vision he'd had while perched on top of the bridge, when the silver dragon had swirled around him. "More likely, he got a minion to do it for him," he said, remembering the guilt he'd felt from someone in the kitchen. "He either marked someone who worked there already, knowing you and Lisa went often to that restaurant, or he got one of his minions a job there. That is why neither you nor Lisa sensed a white dragon lurking nearby. I'm betting the poison would have killed a normal human being."

"That's what her doctor said. He was surprised Lisa survived, but he took the babies out to keep them from being affected by the poison, even though there was a risk they'd die being born too soon. The white dragon—*Roland*—will pay for that."

Malcolm fully expected the white dragon to pay. He stretched his own limbs, easing the stiffness from his injuries and the sex he'd had most of the night with Saba. Being with her had refreshed him, and he felt ready to fly.

A branch cracked, and Caleb and Malcolm whirled. A man and woman in jogging clothes came loping into the clearing and stopped dead at seeing two naked men there.

Malcolm eyed them coldly, hands on hips, but Caleb flashed a grin. "Kind of nippy today, isn't it?"

The joggers started to edge away. The man said, "Hey, we're cool with it," then they both looked embarrassed and hurried back to the path.

"I love teasing the natives," Caleb said. "Ready to fly?"

Malcolm studied the sky. "We should wait for more cloud cover."

Caleb spread his arms, and his form elongated into that of a glittering golden dragon, his blue eyes bright with anticipation. "It's close to Chinese New Year. They'll think you're a kite."

He leapt skyward, speeding above the clouds in a heartbeat. Muttering choice words under his breath about golden dragons, Malcolm let his dragonness take over and followed.

* * *

Lisa made Saba lie down. She needed sleep if she would be in any shape to help later, Lisa said. Saba, exhausted from the ordeal on the bridge and overwhelmed by Malcolm, didn't fight the suggestion very hard.

The hospital staff already adored Lisa—everyone adored Lisa—and found Saba a small guest room where she could quietly rest. They would summon her, they promised, if Lisa needed her. So Saba obediently stripped to her underwear, crawled into bed and was asleep almost instantly.

She dreamed of Malcolm, of course. But not of Malcolm making love to her, not of his tall, raw-muscled body glistening with sweat, not his long black hair sliding on his shoulders, his eyes holding back his thoughts.

She dreamed of Malcolm dressed in a formal dark kimono, kneeling and facing her across a low table, his hands on his thighs while she performed tea ceremony for him. They seemed to be in a teahouse, a traditional one, with tatami mats, an alcove with a single flower in a vase, and a door so low you had to crouch to get in, in order to remind you of your humbleness.

Saba had her tools laid out before her, and the water was just starting to boil on the brazier. She'd even formed the ash into pleasing shapes with her charcoal spoon, a tedious process, and felt a beam of pride that they looked so nice.

She was in kimono, too, one of cool silk and bright colors, the rigid sash, the *obi*, tight beneath her breasts. She made sure her sleeves stayed away from the fire as she ladled the water into the stone tea bowl, then she carefully warmed the whisk with the water before she agitated the green tea in the bowl.

Finished, she carefully laid down the whisk, then turned the tea bowl a perfect one hundred and eighty degrees, bowed, and presented it to Malcolm.

Malcolm bowed in return and accepted the bowl. He turned the bowl once, sipped the tea, then gave her a solemn nod as though approving.

She wondered dimly why on earth she dreamed this. The tea ceremony could be a courtship ritual, but she found it odd she'd dream about herself and Malcolm in such constrained formality. Their relationship had been all about wrong timing, danger, and binding magic. This—watching each other over the barrier of the low wooden table—was almost calm.

And yet, not. Something was wrong in this elegant little room, something sinister and ugly. She looked down at the table and found her tools in a jumble. Frowning, she set down the cup Malcolm had returned to her and straightened them again. It was very important that the tools were positioned perfectly in a pleasing pattern, Kameko always said. Pleasing the guest was what tea ceremony was all about.

But no, the *chasen* kept rolling, the tea bowl turned into a glaring green plastic cup, and the fire in the brazier suddenly leapt high. Malcolm was frowning his disapproval, and still he said not one word.

The tea kettle burst, and Saba screamed, ducking under her silk sleeves as boiling water showered around her. Malcolm rose with a grunt of disgust, his large form dwarfing the table and the teahouse.

In silence he turned on his heel and marched to the door, which shot up to his height to accommodate him. Malcolm would never humble himself to hunch through a door.

"Malcolm, wait," Saba called after him. She tried to scramble up but the folds of the kimono tripped her, the obi tightening and cutting off her breath. "Don't leave me alone. I'll do it right."

Her gaze fell on the brazier. The flames died away and she looked at the perfect black shapes of ash she'd so labored over. They were growing, stretching into snakes of darkness to fill the brazier and stifle the fire. Dread formed in the pit of her stomach. She recognized the darkness, the same that she'd seen in the house in Pacific Heights, the same from her dreams long, long ago.

She remembered with clarity running through the maze of the dragon archive, the walls that glittered with gold and gems flashing past as her small legs tried to carry her from the horror. She remembered how the darkness had cornered her at the end of the corridor, above which she now knew had lain *The Book of All Dragons*. How she'd awakened, screaming, in her parents' house in Berkeley, and how the darkness hadn't gone away.

Because it had been real.

She knew it was real now, reaching out from the brazier to surround her and the beautiful wooden table. The fingers of darkness wound about her feet, tearing her robes, and she somehow knew that if it touched her skin, she would die.

She screamed for Malcolm again and tried to run, but the kimono had grown into a huge gown that enveloped every limb. The sleeves flowed well past her fingers and across the floor, and it wouldn't let her move.

Saba gasped and sat straight up in bed, her hands and feet tangled in sheets. The room was quiet, the blind pulled against the afternoon light outside. Her heart beat wildly and her mouth was dry.

Since this was a guest room, there was no call button for the nurse, but there was a phone and Lisa was just down the hall. She reached for the receiver, but forced her hand to stop. Lisa had gone through a terrible ordeal, and she and her babies didn't need to be awakened because Saba had had a bad dream.

Saba withdrew her hand, then froze. She wasn't awake—either that or the fingers of darkness were real. Just as in her childhood dream, the darkness gathered thickly on the floor, tendrils of it oozing up the walls. As she watched in horror it coalesced into a canopy, arching overhead in a parody of one of her witch circles. Then the black bubble began to close.

"Mother Goddess, help me," she prayed with all her strength.

She was no longer four years old and no longer a novice witch and knew something about fighting. She drew a

hasty circle with her finger around the bed, wishing she
had not left every crystal she owned at home today.

Blue light glowed, keeping the blackness somewhat at
bay, but it advanced as though determined to suck her
power into itself. She chanted a spell against negativity and
darkness, and to her dismay the blackness seemed to pull
the banishing spell into itself, growing still larger.

"Goddess, I ask thee for guidance," Saba said desperately. "Holy crap, just help me!"

She felt a shimmer deep inside her as she often did
when the Goddess touched her, and there came the answer,
one that surprised her. The memories of her past sharpened, and she remembered clapping her four-year-old
hands and calling on the Japanese god she had long since
forgotten.

Sitting straight up, she clapped three times and shouted
in Japanese, "Baku, Baku, come to me! Eat this dream!"

She did not really expect anything to happen but then air
displaced with a bang, and there towered the fearsome form
of the Baku, lion's head, tiger's legs and teeth, leathery
wings, and all. Its enormous dark eyes took in the sheets
pulled to her chin, the witch circle that enclosed her, and the
darkness outside of it. The Baku snorted, sounding amused.

And then it ate the darkness, just as it had years ago in
her bedroom while she'd watched in a toddler's terror. The
Baku sucked the darkness into himself and ground it with
sharp white teeth, ruthlessly chasing down every bit. As a
child, Saba had laughed and clapped, now she simply
watched in amazement.

The Baku is real, she thought. *Or else I am still asleep,
or seriously crazy.*

The demon-god devoured every single thread of darkness, then, just as he had when she'd been four, he placed
his hands on his round belly and belched.

He laughed at her gaping stare, then he shimmered and
morphed into the human shape of Axel. He stood with his
hands on his hips, his leather jacket in place, and grinned
at her.

"Hello, Saba-chan. You called?"

It took Saba several minutes to find her voice. "You're the Baku," she choked out.

"*A* Baku," he corrected. "There are many of us. I used to have the entire Berkeley, Oakland, San Francisco area, but now I'm in charge of San Francisco proper and leave the other cities to my assistants. A lot of nightmares out here."

He sank into a chair, crossed his ankles, and patted his now muscular and flat stomach.

Saba decided to file away her amazement of what he was and examine it later. "The darkness was a nightmare then? That's all? Maybe I'm still dreaming, and you didn't really just look like a Baku."

"You're not dreaming," Axel promised. "Yes, the darkness is a nightmare, but something more. A nightmare made manifest. That's not good."

"I saw it in the archives when I was little," she said, "and again in the house where the white dragon killed Rhoda. I was dreaming of it and then it was here. Is the white dragon doing it?"

"I don't know." Axel laced his hands behind his head. "I'm not paid to think, but in this case I've been trying to figure it out. Whatever connection the darkness has to the white dragon, I don't understand, but I bet Malcolm will work it out at lightning speed. He's too damn smart for his own good."

"Where is he?" Saba started to get up, then remembered she wore only her underwear and pulled the sheet higher. "Did I call you away from them?"

Axel shook his head. "The dragons went to check out some leads on the bridge. I decided to go back and search the house in Pacific Heights again in case we missed something. I came up with zip, though. Neither the white dragon nor Annie have been back. I reported the skeletons, by the way. Anonymous tip. Police will be all over that place again by now, and neither Annie nor the dragon will be able to go back without a lot of questions. Maybe now those people can rest in peace."

"You really care about them," Saba said. "I mean more than just human compassion. You grieve for them."

He nodded, his dark eyes filled with anger and sorrow. "You get to know people in this gig. What they fear, who they are deep down inside. You get attached. That's the down side of being a god, you know. You care too much."

"There's an up side, presumably."

He grinned again. "Yeah, I get to do something about it. And I'm ready to kick some ass." He got to his feet. "I'll go make *goo-goo* noises at the babies while you get dressed, and then you, me, and Lisa will talk. Unless you want to sleep some more."

"No." Saba put out her hand as though staving it off. "I'm no longer interested in sleeping."

"Gotcha. See you in a few."

He sauntered out the door like a normal human being.

Saba blew out her breath as the door closed, thinking rapidly about her dream and what had just happened. Casting a fearful glance at the now bare floor, she hopped out of bed, snatched up her clothes, and began to dress.

18

Malcolm and Caleb found the white dragon several hours after sunset, miles up the coast, where cities thinned out and wilder country began. Malcolm felt him before Caleb did, when the yank on the net of his true name nearly tore him out of the sky.

Malcolm landed in woods overlaid with the smell of lake, and heard the thump of the golden dragon settling in beside him. Malcolm smelled something else, too—death, an acrid taint on the wind.

He pulled on the jeans and coat he'd carried with him and trudged deeper into the woods, Caleb following. Caleb had gone into warrior mode, which meant he'd stopped his inane chatter in order to move in near silence. Golden dragons were the best fighters ever created, and Malcolm was glad to have one at his side, although he'd never tell the already conceited Caleb that.

It was Caleb who stopped Malcolm from plunging into the clearing too soon. His hand on Malcolm's shoulder slowed him, then Caleb quietly stepped around Malcolm with the stealth of a predator and led the way out.

The white dragon—human and dressed—sat on his heels in the middle of the clearing, his back to them. He didn't raise his head when Caleb and Malcolm approached. Caleb came to a silent halt behind him, far enough away so that if the white dragon swung a weapon, Caleb could easily spring out of reach.

"Black dragon," the white dragon said without turning around. "What took you so long?"

"I was surviving," Malcolm replied.

"You were with *her.*"

"I prefer Saba's company to yours, yes." Malcolm knew what was going to happen and braced himself for it but managed to keep his voice cool.

The white dragon unfolded to his feet. He seemed in no way astonished to see Caleb standing just behind him. "You belong to me, black dragon."

Malcolm looked past him to what the white dragon had been hunched over on the grass. Stretched out, her clothes a pale smudge in the darkness, was the limp form of the witch called Annie. He sent threads of dragon thought toward her and ran into the golden threads Caleb was also sending. They touched the witch at the same time and exchanged a glance.

"She's dead," Malcolm said. The statement was unnecessary—her thoughts were gone, her mind empty, her body a void.

"You killed her," Caleb said. "You'd finished with her, so now she's dead, too."

"I had to!" the white dragon flared. "She was dying. Was it better that I let her die slowly or end it at once?"

Caleb studied the still form of Annie, her open eyes glistening in the dark. "You don't deserve to count yourself as dragonkind. But then white dragons were always bastards."

"I'm guessing you forced her to attempt a door to Dragonspace so you could escape," Malcolm said. "And she wasn't strong enough."

The white dragon said nothing, but Malcolm knew he'd

hit upon the truth. A sick feeling crept through the vast self-assurance that was Malcolm—he had coerced Saba on more than one occasion to open a way for him, attempts that well could have failed. That could be Saba's lifeless body lying before him, Saba's sightless eyes meeting his own.

The white dragon's rage exploded like fire. "It was your witch bitch's fault," he shouted at Malcolm. "If she hadn't resisted me, I wouldn't have had to kill this one."

"Her name is Annie," Malcolm said, eyes narrowing. "Not *this one.*"

Malcolm sensed Caleb ready to strike, to kill. He wanted to wring a few more answers out of the white dragon, but had to agree that with the dragon's death many problems would be solved. The only trouble was, because the white dragon wielded Malcolm's true name, Malcolm could not bring violence against him. The slave could not harm the master. Caleb would have to do it.

He gave Caleb the barest nod, and suddenly pain ricocheted through him until he found himself on his hands and knees retching into the damp grass. The power of his true name, sung by his enemy, penetrated every molecule of him, bathing him in fine pain.

"Do not worry," he heard Caleb shout. "Once I smash open his head, he won't remember your name. Or even his own." Caleb laughed, happy to get on with mayhem. "Come on, *Roland*, let's rumble."

The white dragon had a weapon, a long knife that gleamed evilly in what little light leaked into the clearing. Malcolm concentrated on climbing to his feet. He might not be able to directly harm the white dragon but he could keep him busy while Caleb went in for the kill.

At first he wondered why Caleb didn't simply turn into a dragon and flame him, but he reasoned that Caleb didn't want the white dragon turning into a dragon as well, thus having the chance to fly off and escape. Caleb wanted to pin and finish the white dragon *now*. Malcolm knew that Caleb probably didn't think this through as Malcolm did—golden dragons didn't reason, they acted.

Caleb acted now. He danced out of reach of the knife, trying to taunt the white dragon into taking a swing so he could get under the man's reach. Malcolm groped in the dark until he found a nice big rock. He couldn't hurt the white dragon, but he could possibly disarm him.

Despite horrible pain that turned his tears to blood, Malcolm threw the rock with deadly accuracy. The white dragon grunted as the stone contacted his hand, and the knife flew from his grip.

Just as Caleb moved in to grapple with him, light flooded the clearing. Above them a helicopter trained a sickeningly bright light on the three men and the dead woman on the grass, and from three sides of the clearing came flashing blue and red lights. Malcolm had dimly heard the helicopter through the roaring in his head but had paid it no heed.

But someone in the human world had definitely gotten edgy enough to call the police. The police had scored a hit finding three men fighting and one woman dead in the clearing.

The white dragon tried to run. A hard, no-nonsense voice shouted, "Freeze," and then came the clicks of pistols at the ready.

Caleb raised his hands. Malcolm kept still; he was in too much agony to do anything else. He sensed the white dragon try to assume his dragon shape and then give up. Dragons had a hard time being dragons in the presence of those who didn't believe.

The police didn't give a damn what they were. They only knew they'd found a possible homicide, and they advanced, black pistols trained on the three of them.

Three policemen and one policewoman surrounded Malcolm, and he felt his hands being pulled behind him, cold metal manacles clasping his wrists.

"This is great." Caleb's voice boomed out over the chopping noise of the helicopter. "I've always wanted to be arrested. Hey, maybe we'll end up on *Cops*."

Malcolm was suddenly glad he'd been handcuffed,

because it kept him from searching for another rock to fling at Caleb.

They were taken to the county jail down a rutted road, Caleb and Malcolm in one car, the white dragon in another. Annie had been strapped to a stretcher and fed into an ambulance, called in as dead on the scene. Malcolm felt sorrow for her passing, so unnecessary and cruel.

They'd been searched for weapons and identification, Malcolm having neither. Caleb carried no weapons, but he had a wallet like the ones humans carried and an actual driver's permit, which must have taken much of Lisa's magic to obtain. The policeman also found in Caleb's pocket a folded photo, printed from a color laser printer at the hospital, of a tired-looking Caleb holding two babies.

"Those are mine," he said proudly. "The one with the yellow hat is Li Na, my daughter, the one in green is Severin, my son. Twins. They were born last night."

One of the policemen made the mistake of saying they were cute. Caleb spent the ride into the county seat telling his captive audience all about his new children. Malcolm closed his eyes, trying to shut out the lingering pain and wishing the police customarily gagged their suspects.

The county jail wasn't large, the block holding only three cells already populated with arrests that night—drunk and disorderly, robbing a convenience store, bar fight, DUI. Caleb frankly told the arresting officer that he would kill the one called Roland if they shared a cell. A fight to the death, he promised.

The officer, trying to hide his alarm, put Caleb and Malcolm in the cell next to the white dragon's. The white dragon was sensible enough to sit on the far side. They wouldn't let Caleb keep the photo of his children, but an officer kindly tacked it up on the wall opposite the cells so he could see it.

Golden dragons, when they weren't fighting, possessed insatiable curiosity and the ability to spread luck and goodwill to those around him. The golden dragon mark began to penetrate this somber place, brightening the eyes of the drunks and the police who would rather be home with families than here tonight. Only Malcolm and the white dragon were unaffected—*thank the gods for small favors,* Malcolm thought.

The arresting officers said each of the three men would have a hearing in the morning, and implied strongly that they'd probably be held over for a murder trial. Malcolm knew that between himself and Caleb they could mark enough people to get free, but so would the white dragon, and the hunt would be on again.

Malcolm got to his feet, ignoring Caleb chatting with his five new friends and walked to the bars that separated their cage from the white dragon's.

"Lisa wants to see you," he said.

He had the satisfaction of watching the green eyes widen in alarm. "I don't want to see her."

"I rather think she doesn't care," Malcolm answered coldly. "It was foolish to try to kill her. A silver dragon is one of the most powerful beings in the universe, and you succeeded in making her angry. They are very protective of their young."

"I didn't realize she had . . . hatchlings."

Malcolm raised his brows in mock surprise. "You mean you didn't hear *him* going on and on about it?" He jerked his thumb at Caleb. "You'd think he was the most virile being alive."

"I don't pay attention to goldens," the white dragon spat.

"Foolish, if you want to control all of dragonkind. You should know a little bit about them or you'll find it difficult going."

"Control all of dragonkind?" The white dragon looked surprised. "Why would I want to do that? I can't stand being *around* dragonkind, especially not you."

Malcolm quieted a moment as he rearranged thoughts in his head. "Then why did you steal the book? You started with me, I assumed you would take Caleb next and go down the line."

The white dragon sneered. "The black dragon who is so intelligent isn't very smart after all. You think too much. I don't want to enslave all dragons. Who would want to stay in Dragonspace all the time to control them? No, I enslaved *you*, the keeper of the archive."

Malcolm sensed Caleb pause in his conversation to listen. Malcolm tilted his head to one side, reassessing the dragon across the smelly cage. "You aren't after dragons. You are after the archive itself."

"Yes." His eyes gleamed with the glint of a fanatic. "How can you live in that archive day after day, how can that bloody sprite live there for centuries and not understand what power is there? It is the key to everything, the secrets of the universe, power beyond imagining. All the writings of the black dragons is there and everything they thought important enough to collect. The key to power, the ability to travel anywhere, in any world, to open any door I wish without having to rely on a witch. Power and knowledge that the black dragons guard and never let anyone near. Knowledge they are too stupid to use."

He ran out of breath and passed his tongue over shaking lips. The other inmates where staring at him, blank looks on their faces.

Caleb stood up. "Wait a minute," he said, outraged. "All this was about the archive? You poisoned my wife and children over *books*?"

"Not just books, you fool," the white dragon said. "Knowledge. You won't need your Lisa if you learn what I plan to learn. You can do anything."

The large man sitting just inside the white dragon's cage understood what Caleb said if nothing else. He rose to his feet and glared at the white dragon. "Hey, man, are you saying you tried to hurt those babies?" He pointed a blunt finger at the picture on the wall.

The other men stirred, restless for a fight, and *this* fight could be justified.

"He did," Malcolm assured them.

The white dragon still didn't understand his danger. "What kind of dragon follows around a female and her clutch?"

Just as the last word left his mouth the four men in the white dragon's cell jumped on him, intent on beating him to a pulp. The white dragon was still very strong and the four-against-one fight was somewhat uneven, favoring the dragon. The men in the other two cells cheered them on until the officers in charge came to break it up. They had to take the white dragon to an isolated room, but Malcolm tasted satisfaction.

When Saba met Malcolm outside the county court-room, he was enigmatic as ever. He held her hand and gave her a brief kiss, as nonchalant as if she and Lisa hadn't worried themselves sick, then driven four hours up here to find them.

Saba knew that the manipulative power of dragon magic had succeeded in getting all charges against Malcolm and Caleb dropped. In fact, everyone in the courtroom seemed to now be Caleb's best friends. Two police officers accompanied him out, congratulating him again on having such beautiful children.

The white dragon was a little more complicated, because he hadn't tried to deny that he'd killed Annie, but Lisa had been adamant that he get released—into *her* custody, although the county sheriff wouldn't exactly know that.

Saba felt a pang when she thought of Annie, the poor witch who had been guilty of nothing but an inferiority complex that had left her vulnerable to the white dragon's mark. Saba thought she should have done something more for her, but it was difficult to know what.

I should have grabbed her and taken her to Lisa when I thought of it, she chastised herself. It hadn't exactly been

Saba's fault, and maybe Lisa couldn't have prevented what eventually happened, but Saba felt she might have tried harder.

"Lisa wants to see the white dragon," she told Caleb, who cheerfully waved good-bye to everyone on the courthouse steps.

Caleb lowered his arm and turned away. "It might be tricky getting him back to San Francisco."

"She's not in San Francisco. She's here." Saba pointed to a newly built motel that stood shining in the sunlight at the end of the block.

"What the hell is she doing here?" Caleb demanded. "She's supposed to be safe in the hospital. Resting. Healing."

"She healed herself." Saba held up her hands. "Don't blame me—I tried to stop her, but I can't fight the silver dragon. She has to have it her way, you know that."

"But the twins. They're too small." His blue eyes filled with worry.

"They're still in the hospital. They've got the whole staff looking after them—and Axel. Axel will protect them with his life, believe me."

Caleb looked skeptical, and Malcolm gazed at Saba in quiet interest. "You know this for certain?" he asked in his cool voice.

"He's a god," Saba said, feeling slight satisfaction when Malcolm's brows twitched in surprise. "He'll protect them. We should go to Lisa now. I convinced her to stay in bed, but if she gets restless she might decide to come looking for us."

That convinced Caleb, who sprang into action. Whatever he did, however he manipulated getting hold of the white dragon, Saba never knew, but ten minutes later a police car stopped outside the hotel, Caleb emerging with the white dragon in his strong grip. Malcolm and Saba had walked, Malcolm still holding Saba's hand, and they all met up at the hotel's entrance.

"How did you convince them to let him go?" Saba asked

as Caleb led the white dragon, still cuffed, along the corridor to the room Saba indicated.

Caleb shrugged. "I can be very convincing."

Malcolm rumbled. "He had everyone in the courthouse eating out of his hand this morning. They'll probably erect a statue."

He spoke with his usual quiet sarcasm, but his voice held something else, a worry that she couldn't place.

Lisa sat propped on pillows in the bed reading a novel, which she dropped when they entered. Caleb went to her, and she held out her arms. He gathered her to him, and they shared a long, intense hug, he holding her tight, she with her head on his shoulder.

Saba sat down in a chair, unable to stand any longer. A profound pain entered her heart and made it beat a little bit faster.

Lisa at last unwound herself from Caleb. He sat on the bed beside her, his arm protectively around her, and Malcolm took up a position in front of the door. The white dragon waited, his hands still manacled behind him, his stance arrogant and upright.

Saba from her vantage point saw the white dragon's fingers twitch in the cuffs, betraying his nervousness. Lisa fixed a brown-eyed stare on him, one that held the penetrating magic of the silver dragon.

"I am very annoyed with you," Lisa said.

It was just like Lisa to make such an understatement. No raging, no bitchy voice, just the quiet tone that said she was unhappy.

The white dragon lifted his chin. "I have no interest in what you think."

"You should," Malcolm said. "She can snuff out your life in an instant. You should be scrambling to find reasons why she shouldn't."

Another twitch of his bound fingers. "She wouldn't dare kill me here."

Again Malcolm answered. "Why not? She can kill you, kick your carcass back to Dragonspace with no one here the wiser. She can easily make everyone who ever saw you forget all about you."

The white dragon took a quick breath. "Do you expect me to beg for my life?"

"No," Lisa told him. "You should beg to make amends. The two witches, Annie and Rhoda, didn't deserve to die. And my children were innocent."

"We are *dragons*," the white dragon said, sounding incredulous. "Witches are nothing to us."

"Thanks a lot," Saba said.

The white dragon cast a glance at Malcolm. "You *bed* her," he said in a voice dripping with disgust. "Why you even let her live is beyond me."

Malcolm made no reaction, not even a flicker.

"Saba is my friend." Lisa's even, calm tone made the white dragon swing back to her. "You are not."

"Then the powerful silver dragon is weak."

He spat the words but Saba could taste his fear. He spoke out of sheer bravado.

Lisa lifted the pillow next to her and pulled *The Book of All Dragons* out and into her lap. Without a word, she unfastened the catch and leafed through the golden pages, their rustling like faint, faraway music. She reached the page with the white dragon and stopped.

"You erased your true name," she said, looking up at him. "Or did you?"

The white dragon started, craning to peer at the book, then he laughed. "I burned it away. You will not learn it there."

"No?" Lisa ran her fingers over the blank gold page. "But this is not an ordinary book. The etching of your true name runs deep. I think I can just feel . . ."

Caleb looked over her shoulder, interested, and the white dragon's face went slightly green. "You feel nothing."

Lisa glanced up. "Saba, would you help me?"

Saba nodded and got to her feet. Only Malcolm hadn't moved during this exchange, remaining immobile by the door. Caleb stood up to make room for Saba, and he went to flank the white dragon on his other side, looking as though he hoped the white dragon would break free of his restraints or otherwise try to escape. Caleb wanted an excuse to spill blood.

Saba sat down next to Lisa, and Lisa spread the book over both their laps. Saba ran her fingers over the page and felt the faintest scratches, but nothing she'd be able to make out.

Lisa smiled at her. "You could do a rubbing," she suggested. "Except with your magic instead of a pencil. Just a thin coating. The letters will shine like fire."

"Do you think so?" Saba asked dubiously.

"I'm pretty sure."

Easy for her to say. Lisa thought anything possible, but then again, Lisa was a silver dragon and could do almost anything.

Saba drew a breath. Magic required a relaxed, healthy, and rested body, none of which described Saba at the moment. She fixed her gaze on the page and forced herself to see it and only it, to forget Lisa radiating encouragement, the white dragon nearly bouncing with fear, Caleb spoiling for a fight, and Malcolm . . .

What was Malcolm doing? Just standing there, his dragon gaze fixed so hard on her she could feel it. Did he expect her to succeed, to fail? Did he care at all, or was he simply bracing himself for the white dragon to command Malcolm with his true name?

Saba wrenched her concentration back to the book. She pretended she could see the very faint indentations that used to be letters, that the blue light that slid from her fingertips could flow over the page and into the tiny crevices that the acid had left behind.

At first nothing happened. The page remained blank gold, and Caleb moved restlessly. Then the blue light began, very faintly, to blacken into fine lines of symbols and script. As Saba continued to focus, the lines deepened, the page absorbing the blackness and causing it to almost glow. She watched, openmouthed, as the gold page hissed, her magic re-etching the name onto its surface.

Saba felt a strange tingle as she looked at the runes and curves and symbols, and Lisa looked delighted. "There it is. Thank you."

19

Caleb strained to look, and the white dragon said in a horrified voice, "Don't let him see."

Ignoring him, Lisa started to read, her voice forming notes of music that jangled and rang and were on the edge of beautiful. The white dragon screamed. He began to writhe, jerking at his bonds as though he'd break his wrists trying to free himself, all the while screaming, his eyes glazing in pain. Despite herself Saba felt a stab of pity for him.

"Lisa, stop," she said.

"Yes." The one word came from Malcolm, his body tense. "That's enough."

Lisa closed her mouth and the music ceased. The white dragon dropped to his knees.

"You belong to me now," Lisa said quietly. "I hate to do this, but it is the only way. You will obey the silver dragon's commands."

"Yes," he panted, his green eyes wide in fear.

"Good." She closed the book with a thump and set it

aside. "This first thing I want you to do is forget Malcolm's true name. Can you do that for me?"

The white dragon looked confused. "I don't know."

"Let me help you."

When Lisa became a dragon, she didn't have the same constraints as did Malcolm and Caleb. No removing her clothes or having to wear an armband or having to be in the presence of those who believed in dragons. She could simply flow into whatever shape she wanted any time she wanted. She chose a string of colored lights that flowed about the room, making a noise like wind chimes and laughter, and wrapped around the body of the white dragon.

"Forget," she commanded in a sweet, gentle voice.

The white dragon closed his eyes. Lisa's form shimmered from lights to pure, radiant silver and back to lights again.

Suddenly she burst away from him and landed on the bed, morphing into her human form, breathing heavily. "I can't."

The white dragon shot her a look of triumph. "Some things even the silver dragon can't do."

"Why can't you?" Malcolm demanded, his voice harsh.

"I don't know." Lisa looked up at him, face strained. "Perhaps because the name came straight from *The Book of All Dragons*? Perhaps it is the *book* that binds, not the dragon's mind."

Caleb paled. "Crap. And you just leave that thing hanging around your archive?"

"No dragon should have wanted to steal it," Malcolm said in a hard voice.

"Oh, that's reassuring," Caleb shot at him.

"I'll find a way." Lisa spoke with conviction, truly believing. She truly did believe she could do anything, and what's more, she was likely right.

Saba kept her skepticism to herself. "So what do we do with him?"

Caleb brightened. "I could crush the knowledge out of his brain. That would work."

The white dragon tensed, and Saba sensed the music of Malcolm's name rising in his mind. In desperation she imagined her own thoughts reaching to the white dragon, trying to damp down the name. To her surprise, she saw black and silver threads, gossamer in the room's half-light, drift from herself to surround the white dragon.

If any of the others saw them, they said nothing although Malcolm stiffened. The name floating in the white dragon's head dissolved.

"We send him back to Dragonspace," Lisa finished. "Bound to obey me and remain in a certain area, nice and chilly, where frost dragons like it."

"You'd let him go?" Malcolm rumbled in disapproval.

"I'm showing him compassion. He needs to pay for his crimes, but he can do that better while he's still alive. He'll serve me now."

The white dragon's hands twitched again and sweat began to trickle down his face. He was fighting Lisa's hold. Lisa smiled and said one word. Instantly, the white dragon was back to screaming, writhing pain. He fell to the floor, begging for mercy.

Lisa leaned down and touched his forehead. He stopped screaming, subsiding to a relieved whimper. "Do we understand each other?" she asked him.

"Yes," he whispered hoarsely.

"Good."

She straightened up, and Saba felt the power growing inside her, the incredible magic of the silver dragon. Caleb shot her a look of concern.

"You need to rest."

"And I will." Lisa got to her feet and regarded him fondly. "As soon as I am finished, I promise."

Caleb growled a little, but subsided. He pointed at the white dragon. "If I see you near my territory or if I think I even *sense* you around someone I love, you are dead meat."

"He will be confined," Lisa said.

She spoke with confidence, but Saba saw the cunning in the white dragon's green eyes. Roland was foolish if he thought he could best Lisa, but then again, he might have some contingency worked out.

She glanced at Malcolm, who was watching the white dragon just as carefully. If she knew Malcolm, he would have at least *forty* contingencies in his head—what the white dragon might do and how to counteract each plan. That was Malcolm's way.

Lisa sat down on the bed again. She focused on a point just beyond the white dragon, pressed her hands together, and drew a straight line down with her fingertips. Her body flashed into incandescent lights, then back into Lisa sitting cross-legged on the bed.

There was a tearing sound, and then a bright light, a rush of freezing wind, a swirl of snow. The white dragon staggered to his feet with a look of intense panic. The light grew, slicing into the room to clutch at the white dragon and pull him back toward the slit.

His body began to change from human to dragon, his torso thickening and lengthening, his hair becoming pure white spines on his head and neck, his green eyes enlarging and moving backward on his head. His clothes tore from him as he changed, a painful process if Malcolm told the truth. The manacles burst from the dragon's wrists and clanged to the floor of the motel room. With a sudden flash of white leathery wings, the dragon was gone.

Lisa drew her hands upward again and the slit closed. The wind died, the cold vanished, and silence took its place.

Saba felt a momentary pang of envy. Lisa could create a door to Dragonspace, just like that, without even getting out of bed. She regretted her envy instantly as Lisa sagged, and Caleb caught her against him.

"Caleb's right about resting," Saba said. "You shouldn't have even come up here."

"I had to." Lisa looked up from the circle of Caleb's arm, her voice weak. "Something needed to be done about that damned dragon. He's now confined to a small area of Dragonspace. He can hunt, but that's about it."

"He wanted to use the dragon archive," Malcolm said. He explained what the white dragon had revealed in jail, that he'd planned to use the archive itself to gain knowledge, gather power, and wreak havoc. "He seemed very familiar with the archive and all it could do. Suspiciously so."

Saba met his gaze. "You don't think Metz let him explore the place, do you?"

"It is possible. Perhaps the white dragon offered him a share of knowledge and power he hoped to gain. Metz has worked in that archive a thousand years. He would know the important books from the unimportant."

Saba considered. "I don't know him as well as you, but he seemed very devoted to the archive. Wouldn't even leave when the cavern caved in."

"I do not know whether to suspect him or not. I am pointing out possibilities. When I return *The Book of All Dragons* to the archive, I will question him." He advanced to the bed and held out his hands as though ready to receive the book and leave right then.

Lisa gave him a wan smile. "Not yet. That drained me more than I thought it would."

Malcolm dropped his arms, eyes flickering. Saba got to her feet. "Even silver dragons need their eight hours. Let the poor woman rest, Malcolm. You look like you could use a little sleep yourself."

He looked down at her, puzzled. "Very well."

Lisa laughed. "Give me some time to sleep, and I'll send you back to the archive. The white dragon is confined, and your sprite is probably still puttering around, but you can confront him later. The book will be safe with me."

Caleb said nothing, but the belligerent stare he turned on them spoke louder than words.

"I get the hint," Saba said. She reached for Malcolm's hand, suppressing a shiver of warmth as she touched him. "Come on, Malcolm, time to go to our rooms."

His frown increased, but he followed her to the door. Before she opened it, Saba turned back. "Oh, Lisa, I almost forgot. I also learned Malcolm's—"

Her words cut off as Malcolm shoved Saba out into the chilly morning and banged the door behind them.

"You said she needed to sleep," he growled. "Let her sleep."

Saba drew a breath to protest, but Malcolm fixed her with a silver stare, and she gave up.

She pulled two plastic key cards from her pocket and shoved one into Malcolm's hand. "I got you the room next door."

He gazed down at the small rectangle of plastic, then at her. "You do not stay in this room with me?"

She swallowed. "Mine's the one beyond."

Malcolm slid his keycard into his jacket pocket, took her elbow, and pushed her to the next room down. "Then we will use yours."

Saba started to argue, then subsided. She hadn't thought Malcolm would want her with him after his anger at her for learning his true name. Not three minutes ago he'd been ready to dive back into Dragonspace without a thought for her. Once Lisa had rested he'd no doubt badger her to make another door and then he'd be gone.

For good this time. Once Malcolm was back in his archive, his book restored, he'd have no reason to leave it.

"All right," Saba said. Hands shaking, she slid her keycard into the slot and pushed open the door into the stuffy motel room.

Malcolm took a shower. Saba sat on the bed watching inane morning television and listened to water beating on tile in the next room. She tried not to imagine droplets streaking down his well-muscled body, tried not to think of water slicking his hair and beading on his eyelashes and the hollow of his lips.

She tried not to think about anything at all as she stared

blankly at the images on the screen. Ideas drummed through her head nonetheless, things falling into place—the white dragon's quest for the archive, Metz the grouchy sprite who refused to leave, the flowing music of Malcolm's name, the dark ropes of magic that had tried to kill her.

The water shut off with a squeal of pipes. After a few minutes, the door swung open, letting out a swirl of steam and Malcolm with a towel around his shoulders.

He'd tied back his hair, which was black with water and hung in a long, dripping tail down his spine. His body was damp, the black hair on his chest and legs and between his thighs pressed into flat rivulets. The mirror showed the pale tightness of his bare buttocks, a droplet from his hair sliding between the cheeks. He hadn't shaved in two days, and a black brush of whiskers covered his face.

Saba stared at the delectability of him, her finger hard on the off button of the television remote.

"Most men wrap the towels around their waists," she said, surprised at the steadiness in her voice.

"Why?"

"I don't know. To cover up, I suppose."

His wet brows drew down. "If I trust a woman to sit in the outer room while I shower, I must trust her enough not to cover myself with a towel."

"Yes, well, I suppose there's logic in there somewhere."

He studied her with a measured gaze. "Why are you not sleeping? You had as wakeful a night as I, and you are tired."

"I was waiting for you."

His eyes darkened. He moved to the curtained windows and moved one drape over another shutting out the last crack of light. Then he walked to the bed, his very uncovered erection rising in the gloom. He stretched himself out on the bed next to her, letting the damp towel fall, and ran his tongue across the hollow of her throat. The remote fell from Saba's nerveless fingers.

"Why didn't you let me tell Lisa I knew your true name?" she murmured.

"She could not remove the knowledge from the white

dragon," he answered, busying himself with her neck. "So I want you to keep the knowledge, too."

"You told me that I and the white dragon could pull you apart."

"You can. But as long as he knows the name, I want you to keep it as well. It is important."

"I don't understand any of this."

"That doesn't matter."

"Exactly the kind of cryptic thing I expect you to say."

His breath touched hers in the dark. "If you know I will be cryptic, why do you ask me questions?"

She shrugged. "On the off chance I might get a straight answer?"

He looked like he actually might smile or at least think about it. He nuzzled her neck again. "Would you like to pleasure me?"

Her voice quavered. "I wouldn't mind."

He drew warm fingers along her jaw and kissed the side of her mouth. "What will you do this time?"

Saba's mind whirled with possibilities. "Well, since you're already unclothed, why don't you lie down on your back?"

He took his time, giving her a long, slow kiss. Then he rolled over flat and laced his hands behind his head, waiting expectantly. Saba rose to straddle him, her knees on either side of his body. She watched his arousal, high and hard, lifting between them.

It wasn't long before she decided to slide her fingers along the heavy length of him. His shaft was warm, her entire hand barely able to fit around it.

"You are trusting me with your name," she said, lightly tracing the flange and the skin beneath it. He moved in pleasure. "Just like you trust me enough not to wear the towel around your waist?"

"I have no choice but to trust you."

"You do have a choice," she said softly. "I wish you would believe that I'd never harm you, no matter how much power I had over you."

Malcolm spread out his arms across the bed, opening himself to her. "You have it over me now." His voice was a velvet rumble in the darkness. "Do what you will."

Saba remembered the same velvet of his voice when he said *Saba* as he plunged toward the bay, convinced he was going to his death. The last word he'd thought had been her name.

Tonight he lay here still tired from the fight and from spending the night in jail, and he was telling her to do her worst. He was at her mercy.

She looked him over, the beautiful, strong man, muscles firm, flesh stretched tight. Bruises still dotted his torso, but the incredible strength and healing power of the black dragon had erased most of his wounds already. His wet hair left droplets along his neck and shoulders, and the first thing she did was lean down and lick them off.

Malcolm clenched his fists, making a warm noise in his throat. She loved doing this, watching his eyes grow heavy with passion, feeling him jump under her touch, hearing the soft sound that he couldn't hold back.

She'd always wanted to do one thing to him, had dreamed of it. He'd be standing, sometimes in a bathtub just ready to get out, wet like he was tonight. She'd smile at him and make him stay where he was while she slid to her knees. Then she'd open her mouth and take his long luscious staff inside, all hard and waiting for her.

She'd imagined the taste of him—her dreams for the last eight months had driven her crazy, taunting her with it. After she'd done the locator spell for him, when they'd made love on the chair in her dining room, she'd been able to touch his tip with her tongue before he'd dragged her up to him to make love fully. She wanted more, wanted to taste all of him.

Saba was still dressed, and she pulled off her clothes so she could be bare against him. Running her hands down his thighs, she positioned herself between his legs and bent over to slide her lips around him.

His groan vibrated the bed. Daringly she put her hands

on his wrists, pinning him down, though he wasn't fighting her. She used her tongue to tease his flange, and then opened her mouth to slide her tongue all the way around him.

"Goddess, help me," he whispered. His hands were in her hair, restless.

He tasted heavenly. A warm dark taste, velvety good. She busied herself with him, licking from the faint saltiness of his tip all the way to the base, his hair coarse against her tongue.

Saba liked the way he moved under her as though he couldn't get enough. She liked the way his head tossed from side to side, his hips involuntarily rising. The way his fingers tangled in her hair, the way his hands trembled as he held back from pressing her as hard onto him as he could.

She felt, beneath her strokes, the buildup to his climax, the slight jerking motion that began below his balls and rose through his stem. Suddenly he seized her arms in an iron grip and hauled her up to kiss her.

"I wasn't finished," she said with a pout.

"I want to be inside you." His words were hoarse, eyes gleaming slits of silver.

She gave him a little smile. "I suppose I'll have to be contented with that."

He glared at her. *"Now."*

She laughed, loving her power. She slid her leg over his hips and stroked her hands down his torso, fingers finding ridges of scars. "Are you sure you're all right?"

"Perfectly." He spoke in a grating whisper, jaw tight. "You healed me."

"I wish I felt more healed. I'm not a dragon or a god of some kind. Just a human who feels every bruise."

Malcolm slid large hands over her wrists. "I will heal you."

She let sin enter her smile. "How were you planning to do that?"

For answer he seized her hips and pulled her hard down

on him, lifting himself all the way inside. Saba's skin rippled with gooseflesh, hot and cold at the same time. She couldn't help her groan of delight, and her head went back, the ends of her hair tickling her neck like warm silk.

They made love in the half light, Malcolm holding her, Saba riding him. His fingers bit into her thighs as he drove deep inside her. *The last time,* she thought. *This might be for the last time.*

Malcolm would return to his archive and become absorbed in cataloging and protecting his collection. A century might pass before he thought of Saba again, and then . . . there would be faint regret that of course the witch was long dead and in his past.

Tears formed in her eyes and slid down her cheeks. Malcolm brushed one away with a gentle finger.

To punish him for being so tender, Saba squeezed every muscle she had, and he clenched his jaw as he felt it. He bumped his hips harder and higher and held her fast as his seed shot into her.

With Malcolm, she'd learned, there was no collapse and basking in afterglow. He slid her from him and onto the bed, then he rolled onto her and showed her how much he knew what pleasured *her*—in this case hard and fast, rough and erotic sex.

When she was screaming with climax, he withdrew, eased her onto her stomach, and covered her again with his body. He slid himself into her once more and began to pump, slowly and gently at first, then building to where she'd been and beyond. Her knees and hands ached from the rough blankets, her throat hoarse from screaming, and Malcolm took the pleasure still higher.

After a long time, he softly grunted his own release, and stilled. They lay together for a long time, his limbs twined with hers, his body slicked with a mixture of sweat and dampness from his shower. He kissed her bruised lips, and she felt the heat of his mouth on her temple.

"I will never forget you," he said. "Never."

Saba closed her eyes quickly before he could see her

tears. She stayed like that, not looking at him, while he stroked her skin and kissed her.

He was leaving, no doubt of it. She tried to stay awake and argue with him, but Saba's exhausted body, after a long day and a full night and the frenzy of lovemaking, slid her toward sleep.

He did that on purpose, was her last thought, then nothing.

Malcolm dressed noiselessly, trying not to look at Saba tangled in the sheets. If he looked at her, he'd want to stay, and he had too many tasks to perform to linger.

She was safer here in any case. She had Lisa and Caleb to look after her, Lumi to befriend her, Axel to protect her, Ming Ue to guide her. Malcolm felt a momentary twinge of guilt when he remembered his promise to Ming Ue that he'd participate in the Chinese New Year's celebration, but Caleb could go in his place. The golden dragon loved to show off.

Saba would be protected and loved and go on with her life. Malcolm would do what he needed to do to destroy the white dragon, rebuild the archive, and discover the extent of the damage. He thought of Metz with cold anger—if his trusted assistant had anything to do with this mess, he would pay dearly.

Malcolm quietly pulled on his coat. It would be easy to leave now, while Saba slept. He should go quickly in case she woke, but something made him stand at the end of the bed for a long time watching her sleep.

Her short black hair stuck up every which way, her head was pillowed on her white arm, dark lashes against her cheek. The swell of her bosom peeked above the sheets, one hip bared by the folds. She was so painfully lovely, and she always had been. From the moment he'd found her in that rundown apartment in SoMa, he'd known Saba belonged to him.

He'd seen her face when she beheld Lisa's babies, the

longing in her eyes. Caleb and Lisa could have children together because Lisa was so very magical, but Malcolm was
a dragon and Saba was definitely human, and very likely
their efforts would produce nothing.

She deserved so much more than nothing.

Before Malcolm finally left the room, he reached to the
side of the bed and took Saba's cell phone with him.

20

At the end of the balcony that overlooked the parking lot, Malcolm flipped open the cell phone and dialed Axel's number.

The imp answered cheerfully. "So they sprang you," he said. "What's up?"

Malcolm and Axel had a very long conversation and discussed many things. When Malcolm hung up, he thought he understood very well what was going on.

It was late afternoon, and thankfully, he heard no sexual noises from the bedroom that housed Lisa and Caleb. He rapped gently, and the door was opened by Caleb in jeans and nothing else.

Lisa wasn't asleep; she sat at the rickety table in the room eating a take-out Chinese meal Caleb had fetched for her. She looked up as Malcolm walked in and Caleb closed the door behind him, her face relaxed, the exhaustion gone. The silver dragon had amazing powers of recovery.

Malcolm was direct. "I need you to send me back to the archive, if you're ready." He laid the cell phone next to a white cardboard take-out container. "And give this back to Saba when she wakes up."

Lisa pinched a bit of chicken and rice between her chopsticks. "You don't want to wake her up now?"

"No."

Lisa watched him, and Caleb came to stand behind her, strong arms folded over a bare chest. Lisa ate and laid down her chopsticks. "I'm very fond of Saba."

"I have already heard this from Caleb and Axel." Why Saba's friends supposed he would simply desert her was beyond him. He was bound to her in ways no one could fathom.

Lisa's eyes softened. "I don't mean to lecture, Malcolm. I simply don't want to see her hurt. She's suffered enough."

"She will suffer no longer." He lifted the book from the table next to her and held it against his chest. "I need to return the book and put things right. There is much to do."

"I agree the book must be secured in the archive again," she said. "It is quite dangerous."

Caleb rumbled. "Bloody books. You could protect it, Lisa, better than he can, obviously."

"I have so many things to protect now." Her eyes softened even more and a longing entered them, and Malcolm knew she thought of her children waiting back in San Francisco. Well, once he was off to the archive, she could return to them, taking Saba with her. "This is Malcolm's responsibility," she went on. "And he will execute it."

Caleb frowned at him, but Malcolm understood. The silver dragon expected him to fix everything and make the world safe again, and if he didn't she'd be cross.

"Why didn't you kill him?" he asked. "The white dragon?"

Lisa smiled, eyes glinting. "Because I'm cruel. I'd rather have him suffer for nearly costing my children their lives. If he escapes his confinement, he knows what I will do to him. Death would be too easy."

Malcolm raised his brows as he shed his coat and shirt. "You and my Saba, you make a formidable pair."

"We certainly do. Are you ready?"

Malcolm stripped off the rest of his clothes without embarrassment and lifted *The Book of All Dragons* in his arms. "Look after her for me."

Lisa gave him a gentle smile as she rose to her feet. "I will."

Saying nothing more, she created the door, and Malcolm stepped into the bright light and became a black dragon.

"Good riddance," he heard Caleb rumble and then the slit closed.

Malcolm cradled the book in his front talon and launched himself into the sky to fly the short distance to the archive.

Not much later, Saba stared numbly at the cell phone Lisa handed her. Containers that had once held Chinese food were scattered all over Lisa's room, two pairs of used wooden chopsticks placed in a careful pile.

Lisa laid her hand over Saba's. "I'm sorry. He was right; he needed to go."

And he knew that Saba would argue with him, insisting on going with him. He'd wanted to avoid a prolonged discussion, and worse, agonized good-byes. At least, agonized on Saba's part.

"Not your fault." Saba swallowed on her dry throat. "The black dragon does what he pleases. I'm the one stupid enough to fall in love with him."

For once Caleb refrained from sarcastic comments about Malcolm. He patted her shoulder, looking sympathetic. "I saved the veggie noodles for you. I know you like those best."

Saba dissolved into tears and had to sit down hard on the bed. Through blurred eyes she saw Caleb and Lisa exchange a glance of worried friends who didn't quite know what to do.

"I'll be fine," she lied, wiping her eyes.

Caleb started to say something, likely to offer her more

Chinese food, when someone thumped on the door. Saba craned to see who it was through the sheer curtains and couldn't. The thumping came again, the sound of someone kicking a door instead of knocking on it. Caleb lifted the sword Lisa had insisted on bringing up here and wrenched open the door.

Axel stood in the doorway, in the act of kicking it again. He had a wriggling, wrapped bundle in each arm and thrust them both at Caleb.

"Here," he said. "I think these are yours."

The archive was dark, no light glowing in the dragon-sized tunnels. Malcolm sent tendrils of magic to the gems and crystals in the walls, and they flickered but did not spring to life.

He tilted his head and listened, dragon senses much better than his human ones. What he heard he did not like. Not the faint, glittering music of an archive full of knowledge and the quiet weight of learning, but the heavy silence of magic not quite right.

"Metz," he growled softly.

After another long silence he heard a slap and a buzz and Metz darted out of a hole in the ceiling. "Oh, he's bothered to return, has he?" the sprite snarled. "With not a word to me about where he's been?"

Malcolm stopped Metz's tirade by swatting him down and pinning him to the floor between his claws. "Why is it so dark?"

"The lights don't work right," Metz answered, voice muffled.

"The lights never *work*, Metz. They live. What has happened?"

"Something bad, master."

"Elaborate, please."

Metz sighed, very calm for someone pinned under a dragon's talons.

"I can't say for certain, master. But losing that book has

loosened some bad magic. The archive has always had it—the books are powerful but some of them have dark power, negative power, you know? If the books are all together in their right places, then it's fine, but if one gets stolen . . ." He made a whistling noise like a falling bomb. "That's why they each get their special niche, to keep it all in balance. It's tricky, it is. Sometimes the balance is a bit off, but I manage to fix it, to keep on top of it, like. That is until that damned white dragon took the most powerful book in the archive."

Malcolm dropped *The Book of All Dragons* out of his other claw. "Why did you never tell me about this?"

"Didn't want to you worry you, did I? It never happens while you are here. Your power keeps everything nice and sweet."

"And yet the white dragon managed to break in." Malcolm touched the book. "Here is *The Book of All Dragons* back again. Is that enough to restore the balance?"

"Weeell," Metz hesitated. "To tell the truth, everything's a gone a bit pear-shaped around here. The database is mostly destroyed, or at least I think it is. It will take some expert work to repair it."

Malcolm's claw started to flatten. "And how did it all go *pear-shaped* to begin with? How did a white dragon—who has a brain capacity very little above that of animals—manage to learn so much about this book of power and *my* archive?"

"I don't know." Metz stopped. "Wait a tick. Are you accusing *me*? Me what's been loyal to this archive for a millennium and more? You are saying I flung open the door to a clod like the white dragon and let him waltz on in?" He fumed and swore in the language of a dozen different species. "I might forgive you that someday—if you're lucky."

"The only explanation for the ease with which the white dragon was able to bypass our security is inside help."

"Well, it weren't me!"

"Then who? We have you, and we have me."

"I don't know, master. This darkness, it has a mind all its own. Kind of eating things as it goes."

"Like the lights?"

"You've got it. It seems to be pretty clever. It could have used the white dragon's ambition to grow bigger and bigger, like a mushroom feeds on rot."

Malcolm slowly eased his claw from Metz. The sprite stood up, planting his fists on his hips, bat wings flapping in anger and worry, but looking not at all anxious that Malcolm wouldn't believe him.

"What happens when the darkness eats everything in the archive?" Malcolm asked, partly to himself. "What does it do then?"

"Goes out looking for snacks," Metz answered. "I imagine you and me would be carcasses."

Malcolm sat up on his back haunches, spreading his wings for balance. "You've been in here battling it alone?"

"Yep. Ain't been easy, but I learned a few tricks."

"You'll have to teach me," he said.

Malcolm thought of Saba lying in the sheets, her lovely body doing wild things to his heart. Even as a dragon, even this far from her, he still yearned for her. She'd touched him deeply, they were bonded. Whether she liked it or not.

He was glad, however, that he'd left her behind. If the darkness wanted to gnaw on *his* bones, so be it. But he'd be damned if he let it come near Saba. He had to find a way to stop it before more of it leaked into the human world and found the woman he loved.

"San Francisco is nowhere near safe for the little critters." Axel threw himself into a chair in his favorite position, legs outstretched, ankles crossed. "What happens is, I'm in the nursery playing babysitter, and up comes those snakes of darkness right at little Li Na's bed. I had to chase them away and kill them where the nurses couldn't see me. I don't know if there's more, but the darkness seemed determined to go for your babies. It knows power where it smells it, I guess. Hey, are these veggie noodles? Anyone mind? I'm starving."

Saba waved her assent, worry tapping her. They'd already told Axel that Malcolm had returned to Dragonspace, an event Axel viewed with annoyance. "Sure, just when things get bad," he muttered, then fell to eating.

"Oh, by the way," Axel said around a mouthful of noodles. "There might be a kidnapping charge against me. The hospital didn't want to let the babies go, so I smuggled them out when I got the chance. I tucked them into the back of your car, Lisa, and drove nice and careful all the way up here. I couldn't stop Severin turning into a dragon every now and then, so the back seat is a little singed."

"He's going to be a handful," Saba warned.

Caleb beamed with pride and cuddled his son close.

"I had a long talk with Malcolm on the phone," Axel went on. "He called me and wanted to know all about the darkness and Saba's dreams, and what I had to do with it. I don't know what the darkness is, but I know evil when I taste it. And I think it's coming from Dragonspace. The white dragon brought it with him, and probably you, Saba, when you and Malcolm came back from the archive."

Saba thought about that. "But what about when I was little? You can't tell me I opened a door to Dragonspace when I was four years old. I wasn't even a witch then, and it almost kills me to do one now."

"You were dreaming," Axel explained. "Floating around the—as you call it—astral plane. You weren't really *in* Dragonspace, only your dreaming mind was, because you had strong enough powers to enter Dragonspace astrally without knowing it. It gave the blackness enough of an entrance to the world when you came back to your body. And you can see me as a Baku, which tells me a lot about you and your powers. Not everyone can."

Saba sat back, remembering. "When I told my father and mother you had come to my summoning, my father said I'd grow up to be a wise woman." She smiled fondly. "My mother thought I was making it up, of course."

Axel plopped the empty noodle container back on the table. "I am thinking that Malcolm is going to have a few problems back in Dragonspace. Plus I can't guarantee that the darkness didn't follow me here. It hones in on power, and right now there's more than plenty in this room."

Saba exchanged a glance with Lisa and Caleb. Severin chose that moment to morph into a dragon, and Caleb busied himself keeping hold of the tiny winged creature before the baby settled back into human form once more.

Saba fixed Lisa with an urgent gaze. "We have to help Malcolm."

"I agree with her," Axel said. "If he can destroy this darkness on the Dragonspace side, well and good. If he can't, then these kiddies aren't safe. None of us are."

Lisa bit her lip. "We'd have to take the babies."

"Straight into danger?" Caleb said. "I don't think so."

"But possibly there'd be more danger in leaving them behind," Lisa argued. "We can't protect our children if we're in Dragonspace."

"I'll go, you stay," Caleb said, steel in his voice. "You, Axel, and Saba can deal with the darkness here while I give Malcolm a hand."

Saba stood up. "Both bad ideas. I will go. Malcolm will figure out how to fight it—that brain of his is worth *something*. I've seen the stuff before, maybe my experience will help." Lisa started to speak again, but Saba held up her hand. "No, I'm right. You have to protect your children, Lisa, especially little Li Na. You have to protect the heritage of the silver dragon—that is the most important thing of all."

Axel nodded. "You and Caleb can squish out the leavings here, while Saba and I help Malcolm." He grinned at Saba. "What, you thought I'd let you have all the fun? Besides, what better person to have at your side than a god who eats what scares other people to death?"

Malcolm explored the archive, which was dismal and gloomy without the glowing crystals. As a dragon, he could see well in the dark, but not well enough. Trying to coax the lights to glow again didn't work; it was as though they'd absorbed the darkness and had no heart left.

He decided not to return *The Book of All Dragons* to its usual place, because that particular niche lay in the worst of the gloom. Instead he put it for safekeeping in a corridor Metz had managed to free of darkness, secure behind a cover of glowing diamonds.

The entire archive needed to be cleansed. As Malcolm made his way to the database room where Metz tinkered, he thought about how Saba cleansed things in her witchy way, with salt, water, and smoldering sage. She knew how to make everything sharp, clean, and free of evil.

He needed her for other reasons as well. He wondered whether Saba had confessed to Lisa she knew his true name after finding him gone, but he knew with certainty Lisa hadn't erased the name from Saba's mind. Though he and Saba were now in different worlds, he still sensed his tie to her, and it was intense.

"It's one big mess, that's what it is," Metz said from behind the banks of the database. "Whatever egg that witch laid, it hatched and spread problems."

"The virus," Malcolm said.

"A virus what divided itself and had babies. It's going to destroy the place, master, and nowt we can do to stop it." He brightened. "That witch you know, that Saba, maybe she can help. She knows all about databases, I could tell when she sifted through it."

"She likely could, but I don't want her here. It's dangerous, as you have observed."

"True," Metz conceded. "She can hold her own, though, I warrant."

"I want her alive, well, and unhurt."

Metz looked thoughtful, his wings moving slowly back and forth. "It don't work that way, master. You can't keep her all cushioned and locked away like a golden egg or *The Book of All Dragons*. We thought *that* was all nice and safe, and look what happened."

"I have to keep her safe, Metz. If something happened to her, if she died . . ." He trailed off, unable to express his feelings.

Metz gave him a sharp look. "It's like that, is it? The big bad black dragon has gone and fallen in love?"

"Love." The black dragon that was Malcolm examined the emotion and put it through several mathematical calculations. The man that Malcolm had become knew for certain. "Yes, I believe that is what I've done."

Metz cackled with laughter. "Poor old sod."

"I am more to be envied, I think."

The statement sent Metz into further gales of laughter. He wiped his streaming eyes. "It's caught you flat, and that's a fact, master."

From somewhere down the corridor came a distinct *boom*. After a moment, dust floated into the database room, dimming the lights. Metz sighed more in annoyance than fear. "Now what?"

Malcolm's nostrils flared. He smelled the stink before he felt the pain in his mind, the fiery tether that made him turn and go before Metz could splutter out questions.

The white dragon waited in the ruin that used to be the cavern. As large as Malcolm, the dragon radiated white light and his eyes burned green. Darkness swirled around his white haunches, snaking up and down his body.

"Slave," he hissed. "This is all mine now."

Malcolm gave him a cool stare despite the burning in his brain. "The place is in ruins. Have you come to help clean up?"

"I am free now," the white dragon said, ignoring him. "The dark magic freed me, because I freed it. It sent me here."

"I wouldn't exactly say free," Malcolm observed, watching the tendrils wrapping the white dragon's haunches.

The white dragon sneered. "You have no understanding. The silver dragon bound me, yet I escaped. It proves her power is limited, that even she can fail."

Metz, who'd followed, now zoomed upward, flitting next to Malcolm's head. "Is he daft, or what?"

"Daft," Malcolm agreed. "Insane."

"No," the white dragon said. "You are simply blind. You fear the silver dragon, but if I can escape her how much more should you fear *me*?"

White-hot pain streaked Malcolm's body, and he felt blood begin to ooze from under his scales, but he felt no fear. Instead, rage strong enough to tear down the cave lashed through him. To be bound to such a stupid and evil *thing* infuriated him. Black dragons had pride and arrogance that could bring down moons, and to be a slave to one such as this enraged him beyond thought.

"Perhaps I should let Caleb bash in your brain, as he keeps crudely offering to do," he said.

"I would make you stop him. In fact, I could have made you slaughter them all, and I believe I will, once I bend the silver dragon to my will."

"I don't think so," said a female voice at their feet.

Malcolm's heart skipped a beat. He lowered his head to study Saba standing in front of him, hands on hips, her magic glowing around her. Next to her was Axel, the imp who was a Japanese god, hefting a sword he recognized as Caleb's, and grinning.

"Saba get out of here," Malcolm growled. "I will kill you, Axel, for bringing her here."

"Hey, she brought me. Lisa sent us both, actually. We thought you could use a little backup."

"Not at the price of Saba's life."

"This is charming," the white dragon purred. "Malcolm, my slave, I order you to kill her. It will be easy, she is so small and vulnerable."

Malcolm bent his head to put it level with Saba's. Her delightful scent filled him, femaleness, soap, and faintly beneath that, the scent of their lovemaking. She studied him with her brown gaze, which could be so serious one moment, so light and full of laughter the next.

She was delicate and graceful, as when she performed the dancelike movements of the Japanese tea ceremony, and then wild and wicked in bed. His black dragon brain calculated the probability of finding such a woman again in his life—and came up with ninety-nine-thousand-nine-hundred-and-ninety-nine-to-one odds.

Odds which any other being would call *luck*.

"No," he said in response to the command.

The white dragon hammered magic through him, and Malcolm felt his veins catch fire. "You must kill her or your true name will kill you," the white dragon said in triumph. "That is your choice."

Idiot.

"The witch also holds my true name. I cannot destroy one who wields it."

The white dragon paused, blinking at this new information.

Saba glared up at him. "I can read *The Book of All Dragons,* too, you know. Especially if you leave it lying around chained to bridges."

"That doesn't matter," the dragon said, recovering. "*I* have no restrictions against killing her. It might be even more satisfying to force you to watch."

Malcolm lowered his talons over Saba, enclosing her in a protective cage. "No."

"I order you to get out of the way and give her to me."

"No."

"You are asking for it, black dragon."

Malcolm regarded him calmly, despite the agony burning in every limb. "You have no understanding of the true name. You believe that you read it from the book and have me your slave forever, but you bound me in hatred and ignorance. Saba bound me in love, to save my life. Love wins, and I will protect her against you."

The white dragon raged. The name sang through Malcolm, eating away at his brain until blood began to drip from his skin. Dimly, beneath his talon, he felt Saba's magic like a spot of coolness in a lake of fire.

"Malcolm," she shouted. "What is the darkness? What is its magic?"

Malcolm could not answer. He tasted blood in his mouth and squeezed his eyes shut.

"I know that one," Metz said, buzzing high around Malcolm's head. "It's negative magic, negative power from the archive. It's trying to get out of the archive and spread—the white dragon let out a burst of it when he stole the book. We're trying to contain it, but he keeps interfering." Metz shot himself at the white dragon, then danced out of the way as the dragon snapped teeth at him irritably.

Saba's calm voice broke through the haze in Malcolm's brain. "Are you up to this, Axel?"

"It's a tall order. But I don't mind tall orders."

Malcolm had no idea what she was talking about. Her next words froze his heart. "Metz," she said in a voice like golden chimes, "shut down the database."

"What?" Metz screamed. "You're crazy, you are. That will destroy all what's left of balance and stability in this place. Do you know what would happen? Negative magic all over the place, battling anything in its path, destroying everything, including us."

"I know," Saba said. "Shut it down."

Metz folded his arms, his bat wings moving in a blur like a hummingbird's. "I don't take orders from anyone but my master, and he's not as daft as you. Black dragons are *smart*. He'll know what to do to get us all through this without harm, you hark at him, he'll . . ."

"Shut it down, Metz," Malcolm rumbled.

"What?" Metz screamed. "Not on your life. You're as daft as she is!"

"Do it." Malcolm's words died into a whisper. Even through his agony, he understood what Saba meant to do. It was dangerous and even foolish and the odds of succeeding were . . . Malcolm stopped himself calculating the odds, because he knew they were terrible and if he saw them in his brain he'd never agree.

He drew a ragged breath, his body sagging to the floor. "Shut it down. That is my command."

The white dragon reared back, ready to flame Metz out of the air. A bright blue nimbus shot around the sprite, aimed from Saba's outstretched fingers. Malcolm batted Metz, enclosed in the blue sphere, down the tunnel toward the database room.

Metz screamed and cursed. "I'm not a bleeding billiard ball!"

The white dragon's flame missed him. Saba, on the other hand, was vulnerable, and the white dragon swung around to aim at her. Malcolm flung his body between them, absorbing the flames that were hardly more agonizing than what went on inside him. The white dragon sang his name, but Malcolm belonged to Saba, and he'd defend her to the death.

21

Saba screamed as the flames engulfed Malcolm's body. She had no time for circles and chants; she simply threw whatever magic came into her head at the white dragon and prayed for the Goddess's help.

A puff of air exploded beside her, and Axel became the Baku, complete with wings like Metz's, on which he rose. Axel's magic was made for devouring nightmares, not battling huge enemies, but he darted around the white dragon, taunting him, drawing his fire.

Suddenly the cavern went dark. Not just the cavern, every tunnel that opened like stars in the roof dimmed and went out. The two dragons, Saba, and Axel were plunged into darkness. Metz had shut down the database.

Here we go, Saba thought, her heart thumping hard. *Here's where we find out, the hard way, whether I'm right.*

Saba scuttled behind Malcolm. The white dragon flamed once, thankfully not hitting any of them, then his flame disappeared.

She had no idea where Axel had gone. The darkness was so heavy that she could not see her fingers in front of

her face. Next to her Malcolm bulked, the warm smooth-
ness of his scales comforting. She touched him with the
music of his name, flowing in past the pain the white
dragon had caused, trying to soothe him.

I am here, she whispered on the music. *I am yours.* She
paused. *Even if you did skip out without telling me. But
we'll talk about that later.*

He responded without words, black and silver threads
of his thoughts winding around her, and this time, she did
not resist his mark. Being bound to him again was nearly
as heady as when they climaxed together. Saba sighed and
leaned her forehead against him, letting herself be one
with him.

This is love, she thought. *And magic. This is the truth
of it.*

She felt a shift in the darkness, something tangible sliding past her legs. She flattened herself against Malcolm,
clinging to the thought threads, feeling his love.

The fingers of darkness retreated and went to look for
easier prey.

"Come on," Axel said from on high, an edge to his
voice. "I'm hungry."

The white dragon screamed. He flamed once, and in the
light of the flames, Saba saw the darkness crawling over
him, seeking something to devour. She shuddered as he
screamed and fought, but the darkness, at last released to
do as it pleased, was going for the most vulnerable creature
in the place.

"Axel," she shouted. "Help him!"

"I'm going in," he yelled back. The Baku was small
against the nightmare darkness, but he swept through it like
a streak, laughing all the way. "Release Malcolm," he said
to the white dragon. "Don't be an idiot, he can help you."

"No," the white dragon shrieked. "He will kill me."

"You'd rather be eaten by this stuff?"

The white dragon raged and fought, and Saba felt his
hold slip the slightest bit from Malcolm's mind. Malcolm
felt it, too. He raised his head, his strength returning.

"Release me," he said, voice rumbling to the far end of the cavern.

"You will die with me," the white dragon ranted. "You and your witch-bitch."

The darkness fell over him in a clump, damping his flames. The hold on Malcolm's mind loosened as the negative energy began to devour the white dragon's sanity. Malcolm rose on his haunches, black wings beating for balance. Saba's pull to him grew even stronger, and for a moment she saw through his eyes.

The world looked different to a dragon. They saw more colors, more shapes, and more textures than a human could. Malcolm watched, by the light of his own flames, the white dragon be pulled down into the dust, his bright green eyes eaten through with black. The horror he'd produced now devoured him, while Axel flew back and forth in it, trying to keep it at bay.

The white dragon suddenly rose and focused on Saba. A dragon didn't need to see; it could smell with pinpoint accuracy. The white dragon drew a breath to focus his flame on her, intent on her death.

Malcolm, finally freed, reared up, knocking the white dragon aside, and the two dragons began to fight.

Saba sprinted up a side tunnel, huddling away from the great beasts that screamed, clawed, and bit at one another. No movie special effect could be as frightening as two dragons battling each other. Every swipe of a barbed tail, every stray flame could send a bystander to his death.

The rising dust choked her, and flames heated the air until sweat poured down her face. The fires incinerated the thick dust in the air, creating small explosions that added to the smoke and confusion.

Still linked with Malcolm, Saba felt him taste blood and triumph as he lifted the white dragon by the neck and slammed him down again. The white dragon tried to wrap a wing around Malcolm's neck, then there was a loud *snap*, and finally stillness.

Saba scrubbed dust and soot from her eyes and ran in a

half crouch to the end of the passage. The cavern was still pitch-black, lit only by dying sparks from burning dust. Saba saw, in the last second of light, Malcolm falling onto the white dragon and the darkness closing in on him.

"Malcolm," she whispered, then she turned around and shouted, "Metz! Start the database. Fire it up!"

She heard Metz yelling a response and trailing off into swearing. "Hurry," she urged.

Snatches of Metz's words came to her. "Easy for you . . . completely dead . . . virus wiped . . . sequence . . ."

"Damn it," Saba muttered. She calculated the distance to the tunnel that led to the database, took a deep breath, and dashed out into the cavern.

The darkness turned and rushed at her, looking for a new victim. Her connection with Malcolm's dying mind was weak, and darkness already blanketed him. She struck out with her blue magic light, for whatever good it would do. The darkness receded a little then pressed to her again as though liking the energy that flowed around her.

She felt herself snatched up by the shoulders, then Axel grunted as he propelled her into the correct tunnel. "Help him," he shouted. "Go!"

"You can't possibly fight it all. It's killing Malcolm."

"No kidding. Which is why you and Metz need to get that thing going." Without another word, Axel turned and flew back into the cavern.

In the database room, lit by a single mundane candle, Metz had resorted to kicking the crystalline columns that held the database.

"That won't help," she said, although she wanted to do the same thing.

"No, but it makes me feel better."

Saba ran her fingers over the dark crystals, wishing she understood how they worked. Metz had left the monitor and keyboard he'd hooked up for her before, but without knowing how to power up the database, the keys would click on nothing.

"We're screwed," she said, her voice strangely quiet.

"That we are, lass. Good idea, though." His tone held grudging respect.

"I have a better one." She stood up.

Saba had grown up surrounded by love, and even when she'd eked out a living working freelance from a cheap apartment, she'd known she had friends and family to help her at the other end of a phone call.

Then Malcolm had scooped her up and taught her about the magic she had inside her, not to mention the incredible pull of desire, and she'd met Lisa and Caleb, who had showed her plainer than anything the power of love. She'd met Ming Ue and Lumi and learned about friendship that crossed racial barriers.

She'd learned much from the people she cared for, and she also learned all about sacrifice. Making sacrifices to protect the one you cared for was the most powerful love of all.

Only one being was strong enough to finish off the darkness and save Malcolm, Metz, Axel, and the dragon archive—and perhaps all of Dragonspace and the human world, too—and there was only one way to call her.

Saba pressed a shaking hand to the nearest block of crystals and cleared her throat. "Get out of the way, Metz. I'm going to create a door."

Metz said, "But . . ." even as he scuttled aside.

"I know. The last time I did this it almost killed me." In fact her heart had stopped, and only Malcolm had brought her back to life. Now Malcolm lay weak and dying in the cavern and couldn't help her. She didn't even have his powerful magic from which to draw energy to create the door, and the archive was effectively dead, so no help there either. The magic had to come from her.

"I can open it enough for you to call Lisa," she said. "After that it doesn't matter what happens to me."

Metz gave her a narrow look. "You mean it doesn't matter if you die?"

She ignored his statement. "Once Lisa gets in, she'll destroy the darkness and help Malcolm. Whether I make it or not is a secondary concern."

Silence. Saba couldn't see Metz clearly in the light of the one candle, but she felt the weight of his stare. "His nibs will kill me if I let something happen to you."

"I could knock you out first, if it will help," she suggested. "You can tell him I overpowered you."

"Cheers all the same. What do you want me to do?"

Saba drew a breath. "Fetch me some crystals and then get out of the way. If this spell backfires, I am not certain what it will do to you."

Dimly through pain and darkness, Malcolm saw a glow in the tunnel leading to the database. Not the normal glow of the cave's lights, but the feeble flicker of candlelight bouncing from quartz crystals heaped in preparation for witch magic.

Strong witch magic that would drag every ounce of strength out of the being that attempted it. He heard her begin to chant and knew.

Saba was going to open a door.

No! his mind screamed. *Too dangerous. Stop her!*

The blackness pinned him down, worming its way into his mind where the tendrils of his true name had linked him to the white dragon. He still felt the bond between himself and Saba, and the blackness attempted to access it as well, to get at her and the power she raised in the other room.

"Saba." The word came out a croak.

She sensed his pull, he felt that, but she ignored him. She centered herself, closing her eyes, trying to shut out the world and focus on opening a way out of Dragonspace.

"Axel," he called. "Make her stop."

Axel flitted in front of Malcolm's face. "I'm the only one who can do this dark stuff any damage. I need to stay out here."

Malcolm growled, a faint echo of black dragon rage. "She'll die. Take her out of here, to safety."

Axel stared at him, his black eyes and very sharp teeth

gleaming in the darkness. "What about you? And the archive?"

"Saba first. Archive later."

Axel stared some more, then closed his mouth. "Huh," he said. "All right."

He dove to the floor, landing on his feet and morphing into his human self as he sprinted up the tunnel. From the end of the passage came a burst of light, and Malcolm knew that Axel would be too late.

The crystals Saba had laid around her cast harsh white and blue light into the gloom. She'd drawn the circle and charged it, and now the dome of magic rose over her head, the other half of the sphere sinking into the rocks beneath her feet. The magic touched the crystals of the database, but it didn't answer.

Metz cowered behind a rock, peeking around it. She heard running footsteps and Axel skidded to a halt in the cave, breathing hard. "Saba," he began.

"Ain't no use talking to her," Metz said. "She's already drawing the energy."

"Take some from me," she heard Axel through the rushing in her ears. "There's not enough power in this cave for you to do it alone . . ."

She could no longer hear him as throbbing filled her ears, a small amount of energy in the archive that the darkness had missed touched by her magic. Triumphant, the white energy poured into her, filling her from bottom to top until her skin felt stretched and her head ached. The positive energy of the archive was trying to escape, trying to help her banish the darkness.

Saba, she heard Malcolm's voice in her head, the smooth velvet of it comforting.

The power was splitting her in two. Desperately she grabbed the black and silver tendril Malcolm held out to her, the last of his strength. She felt him falter, then flicker out and her heartbreak nearly killed her.

No.

Through her grief, she pulled herself together. She had to do this, if only to avenge him.

She brought her hands together and sliced open the air, crying, "By Isis and Hecate, by Horus and Inanna, open to me."

Nothing. Saba drew a breath, willing herself to focus the magic that filled her to bursting. She'd never handled magic like this before, had never truly known what it was to wield power. It was like trying to keep all the moving parts of a faulty engine going at the same time, by hand. Or juggling twenty balls, all of which were on fire.

She pointed again. "By Isis and Hecate, by Horus and Inanna, by Diana and Aradia, I command that this door be opened."

Sudden power spiked within her, more than she'd ever felt in her life, drawing a reserve of strength she didn't know she had. Malcolm had known—he'd told her he sensed something inside her, but she'd never known it would be like *this*.

The air in front of her grew incandescent. A blast of hot wind struck her, sending her hair dancing, and there was a sharp, tearing sound.

Saba fell to her knees, power ripping out of her, its fibers unmaking her body. Dimly she heard Axel swearing something in Japanese, Metz screaming things she didn't understand. And over all that, the sound of Caleb shouting at Lisa to get back.

Beyond the circle, the darkness pounced.

Saba felt it smothering her, gleefully eating power it had craved and wanted to devour. She couldn't breathe any more, and blackness covered her eyes. She desperately reached for the comfort of the goddesses, but the darkness blotted them out.

It pressed the air out of her, and she knew she was dying. She felt regret that she'd never explain to Malcolm, staring him down and making him listen, exactly what she felt for him. That no, she hadn't done all those things for him last year because he'd compelled her to obey. She'd done it for *him*, for the dark man with sinful eyes who made her feel like lightning in his arms.

She would never have the chance to hold his child and feel a love flow from deep inside her. She wanted to hug that child and then look up to see Malcolm watching her, warmth in his eyes. To wake up in the night with Malcolm stretched beside her in bed, hers for always.

The darkness closed in on her, until the joy of even those thoughts slid away.

Then came the music of the silver dragon as Lisa slid through the crack Saba had opened, her laughter like the soft ringing of wind chimes. "Saba," she whispered sadly in passing, then Saba sensed her plunge into the floor of crystals that made up the archive's database.

Suddenly the crystals burst into life, light skittering into the cave as Saba dropped, exhausted and numb. Through half-closed eyes, she saw the light grow into unbearable magnitude, and heard the crystals in the outer cavern and all over the archive answer.

She heard Metz shouting in glee, Axel's laughter, Lisa's answering voice. The darkness hissed, and then Lisa said clearly, "I am very put out with you."

Saba heard nothing from Malcolm. She tried to reach him through their thought threads and found emptiness. Her aching heart was the last thing she felt.

Malcolm opened one eye as Lisa flitted by in the form of air and colors. The cavern radiated light, every tunnel lit and glowing. The darkness was dispersing fast, sparking and dying, Lisa's magic destroying it like fire destroying paper.

"I see you are still with us," Lisa said. She morphed into her silver dragon form, her scales too bright in the brilliance of the cavern. "I worried I was too late."

Malcolm lay utterly drained. The darkness had weakened his body already half-destroyed by the white dragon,

and giving his magic to Saba had completed the process.
Lisa, as usual, was smiling at him, irritatingly cheerful.

The silver dragon touched his nose with hers, and immediately a spark of strength flowed through him. Black
dragons were healers, but their healing powers were nothing compared to those of the silver dragon.

He lay still a moment, basking in the strength that
flowed like water through his empty limbs. His heart beat
stronger, his wings lifted, and life and energy seeped into
him.

He remembered the last flicker of Saba's thoughts on
the other end of the silver and black tether, the love and
need, then nothing. He lifted his head. "Is Saba all right?"

He saw a somber light enter Lisa's eye and he froze. "I
said, is she all right? Why didn't you help her first?"

"Because she needs you," Lisa said. "Go to her, Malcolm. Not as a dragon, as a man."

He stared at her. "We are in Dragonspace. I have no
choice but to be a dragon here."

"That is true," Lisa said thoughtfully. "In that case, I
will give you a gift."

She sent out a small silver and white tendril that ex-
panded to become a flame. Malcolm flinched as it touched
him, but it did not burn. Instead, transparent silver fire engulfed him from head to tail, tingling instead of scorching,
wafting the odor of cinnamon and spice over him.

He felt a familiar pull on his skin and suddenly he was
Malcolm the man, standing on the floor. He looked up at
the ceiling of the cavern he'd never realized was so vast,
seeing the sparkle and glow of gemstones from very far
away.

"From now on you'll be able to change at will within the
archive," Lisa explained. "Go to her now. She needs you."

Without analyzing the situation or questioning further,
Malcolm turned and ran down the hall to the database
room.

He found the cave dancing with light, the crystals
singing, humming, and chiming. Metz flitted from one

bank to the other, his wings buzzing. "It works! It works! She did it!"

Axel, now man-shaped, knelt on the floor, lifting the limp form of Saba against him. When he saw Malcolm he shifted over, allowing Malcolm to hold Saba against his own bare and scarred chest. Saba lay unmoving, face white and drained, her breath shallow and faint.

As Malcolm bent to press a kiss to Saba's forehead, he realized the extent of Lisa's gift. Not only did her magic allow Malcolm to use his human shape in Dragonspace, she'd let him retain his full powers as a black dragon.

He sent his healing magic through Saba, finding the music of his name still inside her, weaving them together. His healing filled her, and color rushed through her skin, her chest straining for a long breath.

Her eyelids fluttered. Malcolm waited, tense, until Saba opened her lovely brown eyes and looked directly at him.

Axel creaked to his feet and clapped Malcolm on the shoulder. "Good work, black dragon."

He winked at Saba, then strolled away and left them discreetly alone. Malcolm heard him strike up conversation with Lisa in the outer room, who was singing to herself as she continued to heal the archive.

Malcolm smoothed the hair from Saba's forehead. "My witch," he said. "You did it."

"Only because you helped me." Her voice was barely a whisper. "Is everything all right?"

"The white dragon is dead, the darkness is gone. Lisa got here in time."

Saba collapsed against him, blowing out her breath in relief. "Thank the Goddesses." She looked around at the humming, buzzing brightness and Metz swooping happily from crystal bank to crystal bank. "You see?" she said, smiling weakly. "I knew all it needed was a good re-boot."

22

Saba had to rebuild the database. Once she could stand, Metz herded her to the monitor and keyboard he'd once more attached—by magic, seemingly. The archive database had no conventional cables or ports.

"It's a mess, a complete, bloody mess," Metz moaned, hovering behind her. "Can you fix it, lass?"

His respect for Saba had gone up markedly now that she'd summoned the silver dragon and blown away the darkness from the archive. Instead of snapping and snarling and giving her accusatory looks, he rubbed his hands and looked at her hopefully. *I.T. geek to the rescue,* she thought silently. *I should get a cape.*

"I don't know." Saba took a deep breath. "I'll have a look."

Her body relaxed against the chair as she scrolled through the odd patterns of the database. It had been erased to the basics, but perhaps somewhere in here the original catalog was preserved. Metz had given her a blank look when she'd said, "Backup copy."

The silver dragon drifted to her side and became Lisa

again, looking fresh and rested, dressed in one of the light dresses she favored. Saba still felt as though she'd crawled out of bed three hours early after no sleep to discover she'd run out of coffee. Her eyes felt sandy, and her limbs ached.

"This is going to take a while," she said. She glanced sideways at Lisa who looked too cheerful to be real. "Know anything about databases?"

"No." Lisa peered uncomprehendingly at the squiggles of code. "I trained to be a chef."

"Well, that's helpful." Saba turned back to the screen. "You've just reminded me how hungry I am."

Metz buzzed behind them. "There's bound to be something I can scrounge up here. We get mice and bats. Tasty, fried on a skewer."

Both Lisa and Saba said, "Eewww."

"Metz," Malcolm rumbled from the doorway.

He'd retained his human form, which was extremely distracting, because he hadn't brought any clothes with him to Dragonspace. Saba felt his warmth behind her, then saw his tight biceps as he leaned over and rested his fists on the crystalline surface next to the keyboard. Dragonlike, he didn't even notice his own nudity, and dragonlike, Lisa seemed not to care. No one was fully human in this place but Saba.

"I can possibly help," Malcolm said. "I have never programmed computers, but programs are mathematical formulae, very simple ones if I understand correctly."

"More or less," Saba agreed. "The trouble here is not rebuilding the shell of the database but restoring the records. How many books did you say were here? Six trillion?"

"About that, yes."

"How long to input all that again, I wonder?" She looked up at him. "I suppose a task that takes a thousand years sounds fun to a dragon."

His lips twitched into an almost smile. "I can think of more entertaining things to do, believe it or not."

The warmth in his voice made her hope that those entertaining things involved her.

"Then we need to find out if the computer made an auto-backup of the records," she said crisply. "Many databases build that in, in case of a crash, although most people rely on off-site storage." She met Malcolm's silver gaze. "I suppose you don't have off-site storage, either."

"I might."

She studied him in surprise. "Thank the Goddess for small favors. Or anal-retentive black dragons. Where is this off-site storage?"

The slight smile increased. "Would you like me to show you?"

Saba glanced at Lisa, who'd suddenly found great interest in the computer screen. Malcolm held out his hand, his scarred, bruised hand covered with dust. The battle had been hard on him, and like Saba, he needed a long rest and time to recover.

"Yes," Saba said, keeping her voice calm. "I'd like that very much."

"Lisa," Malcolm said, bending an eye on her.

Lisa looked up, her expression innocent. "Don't worry, I've taken care of everything."

"Everything what?" Saba asked in suspicion.

Lisa beamed a smile at her. "Never mind."

Through the thought threads in Saba's mind, she felt something pass between Lisa and Malcolm, but she had no idea what. Thought threads weren't the same thing as telepathy—it was more an empathic bond and a feeling of being wrapped in a cocoon than mind-reading.

"I hate it when dragons conspire," she muttered.

Lisa only laughed and turned her attention back to the computer. "Not too long," she said to Malcolm. "I need to get back."

"We won't be," Malcolm said. He looked at Saba again, his hand still extended. "Shall we?"

Saba got to her feet and closed her fingers around his. "I'm game. Let's go find your off-site storage—wherever that may be."

* * *

They had to fly, of course. Malcolm felt his dragon-ness take over his body as soon as they walked out of the archive through a man-sized hole Metz had cleared in his absence. On the ledge outside the cavern, Malcolm's form changed to dragon, and he swept Saba up as he plunged from the cliff.

He could feel Saba's magical presence under his claws, soothing hurts he didn't realize he had. He remembered the conspiratorial smile Lisa had sent him when he'd glanced at her in the database room, willing her to understand what he wanted. Lisa had done everything short of giving him an obvious wink.

Damned chipper, gloating, silver dragon, he thought, growling out of habit. No wonder she and Caleb got along—both of them were shiny objects.

They flew through the lands of the black dragons, on the western side of the world. Here lush forests covered craggy mountains, impossibly high waterfalls drained into deep folds of valleys. Wild deer and antelope climbed up and down these valleys, running in terror as the black shape of the dragon loomed overhead.

Once, in the distance, Malcolm caught a glimpse of another dragon, but when Saba bellowed a question, Malcolm shrugged off the occurrence. "Just a blue dragon. A dumb beast."

"But he flies so gracefully. Look at him dive."

"He is a fool to hunt in the territories of the black dragons. He is lucky I have better things to do."

Saba didn't reply, but when Malcolm drifted to a halt far up a cliff next to a thundering waterfall and released her, she stared up at him with that look—the one that said he'd done something annoying.

"I didn't want to say anything when you could drop me," she began.

Malcolm swiveled his gaze to her. "Yes?"

"But black dragons are insufferably arrogant," she finished, then she looked around and gasped. "Goddess, what a view."

The waterfall tumbled several thousand feet into the river below, mist boiling upward and swirling in its own wind. Trees here grew straight out from the cliffs, twisted, fragrant juniper and trees like the piñon pines in Saba's world.

A large cave mouth led from the basalt cliff into Malcolm's home. Saba walked inside without waiting for him, curiosity in her eyes.

"Where are we? It's not a bit like the dragon archive."

"No," Malcolm answered. "It's only a dragon's cave."

Black dragons didn't hoard as much as goldens, but they agreed that gemstones and precious metals were happiest when in the seams of their home mountains. The floor of this cave was paved with onyx, the walls coated in diamonds and quartz.

"This is your cave," Saba said, catching on. "I thought you lived at the archive."

"I spend much time there, yes. But this is my home."

The word rang against the cavern walls, echoing back. *Home-ome-ome-ome*.

Saba drifted across the cave, touching the walls in wonder. The cave was not very large—although large enough to hold Malcolm and give him room to move. Black dragons didn't keep to one cave, however, they had vast territories with many caves and clearings in deep woods they called their own.

"*This* is your off-site storage?" Saba asked. "Which you leave totally unguarded?"

Humor touched Malcolm. "No. And it is not truly unguarded. No other dragon would dare to venture here."

"No one but a white dragon bent on stealing the secrets of the universe."

"The database backup is not here," Malcolm said. He concentrated on the new power Lisa had given him and felt himself compress into his man-shape.

Saba watched, her mouth a round "O." "Then why did you bring me here?" she asked.

"To show you my home." Again the word echoed, lending it a significant note. "I also brought you here for healing."

She looked nervously around at the stones, both precious and semiprecious. "Onyx and obsidian are good for that."

"So are black dragons."

He came to her and placed his hands on her shoulders. He read exhaustion in her eyes, bone-tiredness in her body, her mind still in a daze. Metz had had no business insisting she plop herself down in front of his database right away and restore it.

He was tired as well, but the magic of the silver dragon had done its work. The hurts he'd suffered fighting the white dragon and the terrible drain from the fingers of darkness had already faded. Saba, on the other hand, was still wounded deep inside.

Saba tried a laugh. "I remember how you *healed* me last time. The floor in here looks a little hard for that."

Malcolm remembered as well, how he'd ridden her on the bed in their apartment until his brain went blank with climax. A black dragon's mind never went blank, but Saba drove him over the edge every time.

"I did not mean by having sex," he said.

"Oh." Did she sound disappointed?

"We will—*fuse*. The silver dragon's magic kept me from death today, and I will share that magic with you, as well as my own healing powers. This is something dragons rarely do, except in times of dire need."

Saba gazed at him uncomprehendingly. "Should I be honored? Or terrified?"

"I will try not to hurt you."

Her look turned ironic. "That's what I love about you, Malcolm. You're always so reassuring."

"I tell the truth."

"That's what I mean."

His brows drew down. "You mean I should lie to you?"

"Sometimes." She withdrew from his touch and took a step back. He didn't like not touching her, it was like having an itch he couldn't reach. "Sometimes lies are comforting," she said. "Will we do this fusing in here?"

"In the woods nearby. There is a place that is calming and magical."

"I see. I hope I don't get altitude sickness."

Malcolm took a step toward her, concerned. "Are you unwell?"

"A little, but it's not a big deal."

"We will fix that." He held out his hand. "Come with me?" he asked softly.

"Stuck up here in a cliff-top cave, I don't have much choice, but it's nice of you to ask." She took his hand, and then laughed suddenly. "That was a joke, black dragon. We need to work on your sense of humor."

He became a dragon again to fly Saba not a mile away to a velvety meadow on the cliff tops. Up here the mountains flattened into huge bluffs covered with woods and grassy glades. Looking across the terrain, Saba never would have guessed the bluffs were high except for the occasional crease that dropped sickeningly to the lush valley thousands of feet below.

Malcolm touched down, released Saba, and became human again, bronzed skin over honed muscles none the worse for wear.

"How can you be a human?" she asked. "I know Lisa let you be one in the archive, but we're not in the archive."

"It is what I asked of her before we left. To let me be human here in my own territory. At least temporarily."

"And she agreed?"

"She is very agreeable at present."

Saba put her hands on her hips to disguise the fact that her fingers shook. "She's excited about the babies. We should go back soon and let her go home. She needs to be with them."

"We won't keep her long. Caleb can care for them at present. He is a fighter—he'll defend them to the death."

"Yes, but he also has to change their diapers and feed them." She began to laugh as she thought of Caleb the hunky warrior dashing from twin to twin trying to soothe first one, then the other. "Poor Caleb."

"He will manage," Malcolm said. "He wanted the babies."

"What if it were you? Would you want them?" Saba closed her mouth quickly, wondering what had prompted the question.

Malcolm regarded her with an enigmatic expression. "I would. I told you, remember, that a black dragon has need to mate at least once in his life, to produce offspring."

"You sound like a narrator on the nature channel."

"It is easier to speak of it that way."

Saba thought about what he'd said. If he was having the mating urge, he would need to find a female dragon and go for it. "So you do want children. Or little dragons, anyway."

Caleb had described to her, ad nauseam one day, how dragons carried on in a mating frenzy that lasted for days, then the female turned around and tried to kill the male. Caleb had survived two such matings, he boasted, before he met Lisa. From the gleam in his eye, he much preferred mating with Lisa.

"Is that why you brought me out to this beautiful place?" Saba asked. "To let me know you're flying off to find a mate?"

He gave her his *I have no idea what you're talking about* look. "I brought you here to complete the healing, as I told you." He hesitated. "And . . ."

Saba braced herself for more she wouldn't understand about black dragons. "And what?"

"I asked Lisa for something more."

"Seriously taking advantage of her good mood, are you?"

"I am, yes, but I would not if it weren't important."

Saba waited. Malcolm stopped, and for the first time since she'd met him, he looked uncertain. Malcolm uncertain was

an incongruity interesting to behold. Usually the man had
an arrogance that no mere human could match. But now he
looked at her with a pucker between his brows, his eyes
holding caution.

"I asked her to give me another power," he said. "I
asked that if I took you as my mate, I could give you my
seed. I asked that the child be viable, though I am dragon,
and you are human."

His words were so unexpected that for a moment Saba
could only gape at him.

"Are you . . . ?" she broke off, wet her lips, and tried
again. "Are you saying you want me to have your baby?"

"Yes." He looked relieved that she understood. "That is
what I mean."

She blurted the first thing that came into her head, "But
we're not married."

Malcolm shrugged with a ripple of muscle fine to see.
"We can perform such a ceremony in your world. We have
none like it in Dragonspace."

"Because female dragons always try to kill the male."
Saba laughed shakily. "I can see where there'd be a short-
age of bridal showers and rehearsal dinners."

He gave her the odd look again and remained silent.

"Why?" she demanded. "Why do you want to have a
child with me?"

His dark brows drew together. "Is this not what you
want? Children and a family? Whenever you look at Lisa's
young I see it in your eyes. The longing."

She passed over the phrase *Lisa's young* and got into the
heart of the matter. "Of course that's what I want. But why
do *you* want it? Because of your black dragon mating urge?"

"I do not know." He came close to her, his six-foot-six
perfect body looming over her. "I only know I cannot
imagine mating with anyone but you, siring children with
anyone other than you."

Saba stood still, feeling the cool breeze ruffle her hair.
The sharp odor of cedar and resin came to her and the silence of the day, broken by the hum of insects and the

calling of birds that sounded alien to her. A different world—different birds, trees, insects. And dragons.

She couldn't quite take it all in. "I am not sure if this is the most romantic moment of my life," she said softly. "Or the least. But perhaps we can discuss it later. What is this *fusing* you were talking about?"

"Healing," he responded, his eyes never losing their watchfulness. "It is like a healing spell."

"And we both know what *those* make us want to do."

"A risk I am prepared to take."

Saba peered at him. "Was that an actual joke? Never mind, what do you want me to do?"

He backed away a step, his eyes going dark. "Remove your clothing. Clothing would hamper us, and I want to see you bare to the sunlight."

Saba swallowed as excitement began to trickle through her. "All right." She raised shaking hands and began to unbutton her blouse.

Malcolm watched her clothes come off, Saba stripping for his delight. She stood up, her young body honed by the exercises she did at her gym as well as her natural slight build. He knew she worried about her height, but to Malcolm, she was just right.

Her breasts were round and plump, not too small, not too large, and the quim that showed between her slim legs sweet and tight. Even her knees were sexy.

She spread her arms, looking shy. Sunlight dappled her body and burnished highlights in her hair. "Well?"

He went to her. As he brushed his hand through her hair, she lost her smile and whatever quip she meant to make died on her lips.

"Join with me," he whispered.

Her eyes held puzzlement and wonder. Before she could answer, he kissed her.

He loved kissing her. He loved how her eyes drifted closed, not before he saw the glimmer of desire in them.

He loved how her arms stole around his neck, how her fingers twined in his long hair.

He loved the taste of her, the scent of her, a mixture of salt and magic from her spell-casting and female musk. He especially liked her scent just after they made love.

The silver dragon had shot him through with magic, which he felt tingling in his blood. A generous thing for the silver dragon to do, considering the trouble Malcolm had caused her in the past. But Lisa cared about Saba, her friend, which was the reason for her outpouring.

Malcolm closed his eyes. Saba's bare body was warm against his, his arousal rising in anticipation. He slid his hands down her shoulders, fingers picking out her collarbone, her breasts, the tight pucker of her nipples. He cupped her buttocks in his hands and let the kiss deepen as he started to infuse her with the magic.

Saba gasped when she felt the first bite of it, but Malcolm held her still and deepened the kiss. Silver magic trickled through his body like scalding water, then entered Saba, drawing her into its net.

He was painfully erect and wanted nothing more than to enter her hard and fast. He held himself back, needing to give the magic time to heal her. He could feel the tiredness of her muscles, the buzzing weakness in her mind, the exhaustion from expending magic on top of little sleep. The silver magic coupled with his own healed that. Muscles knitted, synapses relaxed, and she started to smile.

"Mmm, this feels good."

He rested his forehead against hers. "It makes me want you."

"I'm pretty randy myself."

Without realizing he did it, Malcolm lowered her gently to the grass. The magic whirled and burned inside him and flowed into her. It made him want her *now*, not that he wasn't crazy with need already.

She scrabbled at him with anxious hands. "Come on, Malcolm, don't hold back."

The look he gave her was raw. He briefly glimpsed

himself from inside her—the magic again—and saw a grim face and feral eyes. He was man-shaped but still a beast.

He pressed her into the grass, one hand parting her legs, the other lifting her buttocks to raise her hips. She let out a long moan as he entered her. Saba already moved feverishly, this was more than pleasure, it was brutal, hard need.

As Malcolm drove into her the magic flowed thick and hot between them. Bright silver flashed, and they were one. Then it flashed again to make them Saba and Malcolm, man and woman.

He wasn't getting enough of her. He rode until she screamed, feeling her closing around him. He climaxed swiftly, his seed flowing deep inside her, but still it wasn't enough.

She didn't think so either. When he pulled out, she clutched at him. "Not yet."

Malcolm was already hard again, not close to being sated. "Get on your hands and knees," he said.

Saba beamed a smile at him and turned over, raising her beautiful hips so he could catch them in his hands. Then he was driving inside her from behind, hips thrusting swift and hard, fingers pressed into her flesh.

He'd never felt sex like this. It wiped everything from his brain but the mindless need to rut her. It had everything to do with nature and seeding her and nothing to do with seduction.

"Goddess, Malcolm," Saba moaned under him, driving her hips back into his.

He came soon, but the magic wouldn't let them stop. They took each other in frenzy again and again in that meadow, she riding him, he taking her from behind, he on top of her.

They made love until, with a sound like wind chimes and laughter, the silver magic left them.

Malcolm dropped to the ground beside Saba, panting. She fell limply next to him, and he felt a pang of worry.

"Did I hurt you?" he asked.

To his surprise, she laughed. True, mirthful laughter, no hysteria. "No, that was . . . Goddess, I don't know what that was. Amazing."

"It was the magic."

She rolled onto her side and snuggled her head into the curve of his neck. "I don't care what you call it. Is this what we have to do every time we want children?"

"I have no idea." He truly didn't know; the magic of the silver dragon was inexplicable.

"Or maybe Lisa spiked it, so we could have a little fun."

"Spiked?"

"You know, gave it a little extra edge. You don't *have* to enjoy making babies, it's just better when you do."

"I see."

She laughed again. "No, you don't, but it's all right." She paused. "I'm damn hungry. Starving, in fact."

Malcolm sat up. "We should be getting back." But he couldn't do anything but sit there and look down at her, enjoying the beautiful picture she made stretched out on the grass.

"Maybe we should wait until we can walk first," she suggested.

He let his gaze drift over her body, from her mussed black hair stuck over with bits of green grass, the Celtic tattoo that skimmed around her upper arm, her curved body, the relaxed way she bent her knee, her hand cradling her head, her warm eyes.

"I want to make love to you again," he said.

Her eyes widened. "You've got to be kidding me."

"Not because of the magic, or for healing." He touched her hair. "Me, making love to you."

"Why?" she asked. Her voice held a hint of challenge. She wanted him to say something, and he wasn't sure what it was.

He told the truth. "Because I want to."

Saba studied his eyes. What she saw there must have satisfied her, because her smile widened. "All right," she said, and held out her arms for him.

23

By the time Saba and Malcolm returned to the archive, Lisa and Metz had nearly finished patching up the database. Axel lounged nearby, "Supervising," he said, though he made it clear he didn't know the inside of a computer from its outside.

Saba parked herself on a flat crystal slab to check what they'd done. Metz knew how to program, she saw that. Lisa's contribution had been magical; she'd slid her silver dragon form inside the database, as she had when she'd started it up again, and given it enough energy to almost rebuild itself. The only thing missing was the data, which did not make Metz happy.

"Erased," he fretted. "That damned virus erased every record that ever existed. *Humans.*"

He spat the last word, and Saba felt her brows climbing. "Malcolm claims to have a backup, not that I've seen it yet."

Lisa gave her a shrewd look, knowing exactly why Malcolm had dragged Saba off to his cave. Her wink told her she'd say nothing, but Saba blushed.

"I do have one," Malcolm said. "It is safe enough for now. Is the archive repaired?"

"Repaired," Lisa said. "And warded, even stronger than before."

"I still don't understand what the darkness was," Saba said. "Negative magic, you said? Like what I try to keep out of my circles when I cast them? But then, it seemed to like the energy of my circle."

"It is what lies between good and evil," Lisa said. "When there is an excess of evil, it leaks out. Normally it's very small, and you, Saba, easily banish it with a chant or a black candle. The atmosphere of this place is so magical that the negative magic collects. What followed you in your dream when you were a child was only a tiny fraction of it. But when *The Book of All Dragons* was stolen, the balance tipped badly, and the darkness grew and spread."

"It followed the white dragon because he had the book?" Saba asked.

Lisa sobered. "It followed the white dragon because he did evil deeds. The white dragon killed, out of malice and for his own gain, and he used people and cast them aside. He murdered for no other reason than others were weaker than he, and the darkness liked that."

"It fed on the imbalance he caused," Saba said, understanding. "Until at last it fed on him."

"Very smart of you to shut down the database so that it would go after the font of negativity, as it were," Lisa said approvingly. "And then call on me to restart it."

Metz buzzed in front of them. "Aye, it were smart," he said, flicking a grudging glance at Saba. "But the database is empty."

"Better that than completely dead." Lisa stood up and brushed black gravel off her skirt. "I must go back now. The twins need me."

"Good," Metz muttered. "A bit of peace, a bit of quiet. I could do with it."

Saba looked at him. "Don't you get lonely here with nothing but the books?"

"Not a bit of it. I'm busy, busy, busy, and books know how to keep a body company. Besides," he added as he buzzed back to the tunnel on his way to the cavern, "the books don't talk too much."

Saba, Malcolm, and Axel followed Lisa through the door she opened to the motel room in California where Caleb waited. They arrived to see Caleb sprawled in an armchair, a baby cradled on each arm. Caleb's head was thrown back on the chair and a long, hard snore issued from his mouth. Severin and Li Na stared at them with the mild interest of newborns, but Caleb didn't wake.

Malcolm quietly gathered the clothes he'd left there and dressed, then opened the door to lead Saba out. Caleb still didn't move until Lisa leaned over him and kissed his forehead.

Blue eyes fluttered open, and a warm smile spread across Caleb's face. "Hello, love."

Very soon, Lisa was in his lap, holding little Severin, and Axel closed the door on them, following Malcolm and Saba out.

"Best leave them to it," he grinned. "We can take my car back to San Francisco." He darted a glance from Saba to Malcolm. "Or should I leave *you* to it?"

Malcolm did not bother to smile. "It is time for us to return to the city. We will take up the offer of your car."

Good thing, Saba thought silently. She wasn't sure she could take any more sex today, not without a long rest first.

Axel drove. Malcolm sat in the back seat with Saba, his strong arms cradling her. They rode out of town to a main highway and then to the interstate. Woods gave way to vineyards and then suburbia, the sun shining hard and warm.

Malcolm's black leather jacket creaked as he leaned across Saba in the back seat. He began kissing her, the slow, warm kisses of a man happy he'd made love to a woman and wanting to do it again. Saba relaxed into the cracked vinyl seat while his tongue swirled and dipped inside her mouth. She held onto the lapels of his leather coat and enjoyed every second of it.

He raised his head. "I can't get enough of you."

Axel was changing the radio stations in the front seat, humming and singing along with whatever he came across, seemingly oblivious to what was going on in the back.

"I love you," Saba whispered.

Malcolm watched her a long moment, his intense eyes framed by black lashes. She thought for a moment he'd respond, but he kissed her again instead.

Saba swallowed her disappointment. Malcolm was a black dragon after all, a being of cold, calculating mind. She couldn't expect him to experience the same human emotions she did, as nice as that would be.

When Malcolm sat up again, leather creaking once more, she caught Axel watching her in the rear-view mirror. He gave her a knowing look and a smile, as though he knew everything would work out all right. *I'm a god,* his look seemed to say. *I understand these things. Trust me.*

Chinese New Year in Chinatown was an event not to be missed. Saba joined Ming Ue and family on Kearny Street to watch the parade, one of the largest Chinese New Year parades in the world, out under the stars. The February weather behaved, and the night was almost warm. Saba needed only a windbreaker against what little chill came in off the bay.

Lumi arrived with Grizelda, the red-haired witch he'd met during their adventures last year. Both Saba's age, the two threw poppers to hear them bang with as much enthusiasm as Lumi's four-year-old cousins.

Carol Juan, part owner and technically CEO of Ming Ue's restaurant, came in her sleek blue business suit, her hair and makeup perfectly in place. She frowned hard at Lumi as he dashed a popper under her feet.

"It drives evil spirits away," Lumi said, grinning.

Saba threw one under Lumi's feet to prove his point, and he shouted as he jumped in surprise. Ming Ue leaned on her cane next to her quietly smiling nephew, Shaiming, and laughed at them all.

Caleb and Lisa had debated coming because the twins were so young. Saba craned to look for them in the crowd, but the press of people had grown dense. Ming Ue, an important businesswoman in the Chinese community, had a little area corded off for herself and her family, but beyond that was a mass of people who'd journeyed from all over the country to watch the parade.

Axel had arrived, dressed in a festive red Chinese jacket, arms full of souvenirs, including dragon flags and a hat with dragon wings. He had a handful of poppers which he tossed around as enthusiastically as Lumi. *"Gung hei fat choi,"* he greeted others in the crowd.

"You're not Chinese," Saba said to him.

Axel shrugged. "I embrace all cultures. You should see me in a serape."

Saba's friend Mamie arrived to hear his last remark. "I'd like to see him in *nothing but* a serape," she murmured to Saba.

Saba introduced the two, looking for a flicker of interest from Axel, but she detected none. *Ah, well.* Mamie gave him sideways looks, but Axel had his eyes on the parade. Maybe one day the flicker of interest for Mamie would manifest, either that or for . . . Saba stole a look behind her to the neat-as-a-pin Carol Juan, who was thirty and took life much too seriously. *Could work,* she thought.

Saba wondered why she'd become a matchmaker all of a sudden. Her erstwhile boyfriend—lover, whatever he wanted to call it—had become enigmatic of late. Two weeks ago, when Axel had dropped them off at the apartment on Octavia Street Malcolm had rummaged in a drawer in the study and pulled out a cubical crystal about one inch each side.

"What is that?" Saba had asked.

Malcolm held it up between his thumb and forefinger.

"The database backup. This cube contains every record of every item entered in the archive. Diamond crystals have an amazing matrix."

"It's a *diamond*? And you just threw it into a drawer?" Saba felt faint. "I could have lost it any time or thrown it away not knowing what it was, or used it in my magical ceremonies."

Malcolm walked to her and placed the crystal on her palm. "Try to throw it away."

Saba stared at the square for a moment, then she found herself walking straight to the desk and replacing it in its little niche in the drawer. She closed the drawer and looked at him.

"Why did I just do that?"

"You were compelled to," he answered. "If you had tried to throw it away, your hand would have stopped. If you had tried to use it in a ceremony, you would have decided not to and put it back where you found it."

Saba shook her hand as though it tingled. "Nice spell."

"A simple one."

"So you left the backup of the archive lying in a drawer. *This* is your off-site storage?"

"Yes." The word was maddeningly calm.

"But what if I moved? Sold the apartment, went back to live in Berkeley with my parents?"

Malcolm regarded her with quiet eyes. "You would not have."

She lost her temper. "I see, this was off-site storage for me, too."

"If you like."

"You know, Malcolm, sometimes I'm not sure whether I'm in love with you or want to bounce you down the stairs."

He looked puzzled. "I am far too large . . ."

"Oh, stop being so literal-minded. You know what I mean." She raged a few more minutes then a thought struck her. "You always meant to come back."

"Yes."

"Why?"

His voice went quiet, even somber. "How could I help it? In my head, I made no such plan. I thought I should never return to the place of my bitter exile. But my deeper self, my subconscious—my heart, as you like to say—told me differently. I needed to come back."

"Can I fish and ask, because of me?"

Malcolm actually smiled. He opened the drawer and extracted the diamond cube again and tossed it in his palm. "Of course, because of you. That is why I gave you the dragon's tears, I wanted you to call me back."

Saba could only stand on her side of the room and stare at him. Now was when he should rush to her, take her in his arms, and carry her off the bedroom. But no, that was *Gone with the Wind*, and this was Malcolm. He slid the cube into his pocket.

"I must ask Lisa to send me back to the archive so I can give this to Metz." He came to her and pressed a brief kiss to her lips. "Then I must go to Ming Ue. I promised I would help with the dragon she is sponsoring for the Chinese New Year's parade, and she will want me to practice."

Saba caught his arm as he turned away, giving him a suggestive look.

He shook his head. "If I do not go now, I will not go," he said, his voice low. He smoothed a lock of hair on her forehead. "Au revoir, my witch."

He turned away, snatched up his jacket, and let himself out. That left Saba alone and frustrated for the rest of the afternoon.

She hadn't seen him much since then, because he always had something to do either with Ming Ue, back in Dragonspace helping Metz, or reuniting with the elusive contacts he'd made back when he'd been in exile. He spent nights away, and Saba spent all her days at work, and was never certain when she'd see him.

Now she waited in the February night with her friends as the parade flowed past, groups of brightly-clothed children dancing in formations and waving silk streamers, lion dancers in glowing yellow satin-silk, tumbling acrobats, this year's Miss Chinatown USA waving regally to the crowd, and of course, dragons.

Men in costume carried long rippling dragon bodies behind huge dragon heads, dragons whirled from poles, dragon flags waved in the mid-February breeze. One dragon float rolled by, and rolled by and rolled by, two hundred feet of golden, glittering scales, fire and smoke belching from its nose and mouth.

"The best in the parade," Caleb's voice rumbled behind Saba. She looked up to see his form towering over her. Lisa, babies in arms, stood by Ming Ue, who feasted her eyes on the children.

"It is the longest dragon in the parade," Caleb went on over the crowd. "And the best and has won the prize for floats. A golden dragon, of course." He smiled hugely.

"And the one with the biggest head?" Saba shouted up at him.

Caleb nodded in all seriousness. "Indeed. Where is Malcolm?"

Saba decided to cease teasing him. "Somewhere in the parade, if he made it back from Dragonspace today. Ming Ue's float hasn't come by yet."

"He will be here." Caleb gazed at the golden dragon retreating down the street, then at the acrobats running and tumbling after it. From time to time he glanced worriedly at where Lisa and Ming Ue cooed over the babies. Shaiming smiled at them, his teeth gleaming.

"They'll be all right," Saba assured him. "I think they are the strongest children in the world with Lisa's magic in them, not to mention yours. The cold won't bother them."

"It isn't that," Caleb said. "Severin is too young to understand not to turn into a dragon in front of people. I don't think I could explain why my son suddenly sprouted wings and tried to flap around his father."

Saba laughed. "He can't change around people who no longer believe in dragons."

"But so many people here tonight do. Dragons are lucky, especially this night, and he feels that power."

Saba felt it, too, the collective seeking of luck and good fortune for the coming year. These people *wanted* dragons. And here was Saba next to a real golden dragon with a silver dragon in the background and a black dragon who wanted to marry her and have children with her. "I must be the luckiest girl in the world," she said ironically.

Caleb clapped her on the shoulder with staggering strength. "You are indeed. Look."

Lumi and his cousins started to cheer. Carol and Ming Ue craned to look, and Shaiming silently watched, eyes shining.

A huge piece of black silk trimmed with silver wound up and down the street, snaking behind a large dragon's head. The dragon had silver eyes and snarling teeth, and beneath the massive head were the unmistakably long, strong legs of Malcolm.

Dancers in red and cymbal players ran along beside the carriers who toted the black cloth along on poles. Ming Ue clapped, pleased, and the small crowd inside her roped-off area shouted and waved.

The black dragon swiveled and ran right for them. Grizelda screamed in delight, but the black dragon made straight for Saba. At the last minute it turned aside, but Malcolm's hand snaked out and dragged Saba under the canopy with him.

She heard Caleb roaring encouragement, and Ming Ue saying in her chortling voice, "Black dragons are very lucky."

"Malcolm," Saba gasped.

He was stronger than she was and enclosed her in his arms that held the dragon's head. She had to run with him to keep from falling and being trampled by the enthusiastic dragon carriers.

His voice rumbled in her ear. "You wanted to be with a dragon."

"This isn't exactly what I meant."

"But you do want to be with a black dragon, do you not? For the rest of your life?"

"We discussed marriage, yes." The giddy conversation they'd had in his cave in Dragonspace seemed long ago and far away.

"I have arranged it," Malcolm said. "For tomorrow at the courthouse. We must sign the license then."

Saba struggled to maintain her footing, panting at the frenzied pace. "You need to learn a thing or two about proposals, Malcolm."

He enclosed her in one arm, his other keeping the dragon going, showing her once more how incredibly strong he was. "I love you," he breathed in her ear. "Marry me, my witch."

"Well," Saba said, giddy. "If you put it that way . . ."

He put it that way again later that night after the New Year's celebration at Ming Ue's restaurant when they all stuffed themselves with dim sum and champagne, a combination Saba had never tried before. Malcolm, as solemn as the others were rowdy, stood up and announced the engagement, the marriage, and his hope that Saba carried his child.

After a stunned silence, the room filled with shouted congratulations, more champagne corks popping, Saba surrounded and hugged by Lisa, Grizelda, Mamie, Carol, Ming Ue, Lumi, Axel, and a crushing embrace from Caleb.

In the small hours of the morning, they were home again, Saba wanting very much to call her parents in Berkeley, but reasoning that they'd want to be woken with the news *after* the sun was up. She didn't have much chance to use the phone, in any case, because as soon as they entered the apartment and locked the door, Malcolm lifted her and carried her to the bedroom as she'd wanted him to days before.

He carefully stripped off her clothes, laid her down on the bed, kicked out of his own clothes, and made love to her in pure dragon frenzy. When they lay exhausted several hours later, Malcolm kissed her tired lips.

"You will not change your mind?" he asked.

"I don't think so."

He raised up on an elbow, his strong hand trailing across her body. His eyes were intense, gleaming with dragon power. "How can you be certain?"

Saba touched his face. "Simple. Because you told me you loved me. While we were under the dragon float."

"I did." He tried a smile, which died, his eyes still questioning.

"I was kind of hoping you meant it."

He rolled over onto her, obviously not yet tired. "How can I help but love you, my Saba? You are damned beautiful, stubborn, magical, and you make me forget all about mathematics."

Her eyes widened in mock surprise. "Oh my, you must be serious."

"I am." He held her close, and whispered savagely in her ear. "Don't ever make me almost lose you again."

"I don't think I'll be doing any more hard magic for a while. I might light a candle and do a chant to the moon, but that's it." She traced his cheek, then kissed him, and they made love again, this time slowly, both of them tired and languid.

Saba drifted into sleep after that and began to dream. She was in the teahouse again, dressed in a yellow and red silk kimono, facing Malcolm over the table, the water in the kettle just starting to boil. Malcolm, in a dark kimono with silver embroidery, watched her expectantly.

Saba folded her *fukusa* with nary a slip, then lifted the ladle in a perfect motion and poured water into the bowl. She wet the whisk at the same time so the bamboo wouldn't crack, and whisked water and tea together.

Malcolm watched intently, his gaze on the patterned ash in the brazier. This time it stayed ash, no morphing into snakes of darkness to devour her. She laid down the *chasen*, bowed politely, turned the bowl in two perfect turns, then lifted it and offered it to him. *"Hai, dozo,"* she murmured.

Malcolm took the bowl. Their hands made contact for a moment and something flared in his eyes, love and wanting all mixed up. *"Domo arigato gozaimashita,"* he said, using the most formal version of thanks, then he drank the tea.

She waited, slightly worried she hadn't made it right, then he lifted his gaze over the bowl and broke into a sunny smile.

The sight of the smile, showing white teeth in a handsome face, startled her. Then she smiled back, her heart warming.

He laid down the tea bowl, bowed formally, then stood and hauled Saba up and over the table. Violating every rule of tea ceremony and teahouses, he lay her on the tatami and rolled himself on top of her. As her kimono miraculously disappeared, she gave in to the dream and let it happen. If she was going to have an erotic tea ceremony dream, why not enjoy it?

Unseen by either of them, a god called a Baku shimmered into existence near the alcove with the single iris in a vase. It morphed briefly into Axel, stared at the two on the floor, chuckled, and became the lion-headed, winged Baku again.

"Hmm," he said. "I love a happy ending."

He reached to the table and grabbed the tea bowl, drained it, and wiped his mouth. "And a good cup of tea," he said, then he popped out and left them to it.

EPILOGUE

Five years later

Malcolm awoke suddenly in the night. He knew what had awakened him, a muffled cry from the bedroom down the hall that had been converted into the room every little girl wanted. Every little girl who was half-witch, half-dragon that is. Instead of ruffled canopies and dollhouses, she had stuffed dragons and Chinese lions and a strange little fold in time and space, created by Aunt Lisa, where small Adara could learn to fly.

The cry came only once, so tiny that Malcolm's dragon hearing barely caught it. Saba half-heard, as every mother sensed her child calling out in the night, and stirred.

"*Shh*, rest," Malcolm breathed, wafting his dragon magic over her.

Saba murmured something in her sleep, then sank down. She had been tired lately between her new job as supervising manager at Technobabble and taking care of two spirited children.

Malcolm slid out of bed and pulled on a black silk robe. He padded down the hall, stopping to first look into the baby's room, where his son, two years old, snored happily.

Malcolm drifted to him and touched his hair, feeling the odd pull on his heart that he knew meant love. His son, *his*, that he would watch grow up and teach what it meant to be a black dragon.

His son slept on without dreams, and Malcolm moved to the next room, which housed his daughter. He heard her faint laughter from inside, and then she clapped her hands. "Do it again!"

Malcolm eased open the door in time to see the lion-headed Baku do a backflip and blink out of sight. Adara clapped again, her round cheeks pink with smiling, her brown eyes, so like Saba's, shining in delight.

Malcolm crossed the room and sat down on the bed. Adara launched herself into her father's arms, holding him in a hard hug he never got tired of.

"Papa-chan," she said proudly. "I called the Baku, and he came to eat my nightmare. Just like mama-san said he would."

Malcolm smoothed his daughter's black hair. "You had a nightmare?"

"Yes, but it's all gone now. The Baku ate it."

Malcolm held her close again, kissing her cheek. He loved her, this sweet daughter that he and Saba had conceived in the high mountain meadow in Dragonspace, the gift Lisa had given to them. Malcolm hadn't been certain they would have more than one child until Saba had announced to him with a smile two years and nine months ago that she was pregnant again.

There were four of them now, and Saba had a gleam in her eye these days as though she had a secret she was saving up to tell him. Malcolm had the feeling they'd soon have to expand their living space.

He lifted his daughter and balanced her on his knees.

"The Baku?" he said, his voice admiring. "It isn't everyone who can see the Baku, Adara-chan. You will grow up to be a very wise woman, a very wise woman, indeed. Just like your mother."

Don't miss the first book in the series

DRAGON HEAT

Available from Berkley Sensation!